PERILOUS ATTRACTION

Justin pulled her into the circle of his arms.

"Justin, we shouldn't," she whispered even as she wound her arms inside his coat and clung to his waist.

He moved his mouth over hers and devoured its softness . . . it became a slow, drugging kiss.

When Davina felt his arousal press against her thigh, she was electrified and tried to move away.

"Don't pull back, Davina. Let it happen."

His husky whisper was a command, and she obeyed. She returned his kiss with reckless abandon, and her hungry response threatened to send Justin's world out of control.

Justin gave a deep sigh and stepped back from her. "Something is happening between us. You feel it, too, don't you?"

Davina ached at his touch, but knew their attraction was doomed to failure. "Yes, I do. It's only sex, though, pure and simple."

Justin reached out for a lock of her hair and rubbed it between his fingers. Slowly, inexorably he drew her to meet his mouth in a surprisingly gentle kiss. They both drank from its sweetness as if they knew it could be their last.

BOOK YOUR PLACE ON OUR WEBSITE AND MAKE THE ARABESQUE ROMANCE CONNECTION!

We've created a customized website just for our very special Arabesque readers, where you can get the inside scoop on everything that's going on with Arabesque romance novels.

When you come online, you'll have the exciting opportunity to:

- View covers of upcoming books

- Learn about our future publishing schedule (listed by publication month and author)

- Find out when your favorite authors will be visiting a city near you.

- Search for and order backlist books from our line catalog

- Check out author bios and background information

- Send e-mail to your favorite authors

- Join us in weekly chats with authors, readers and other guests

- Get writing guidelines

- AND MUCH MORE!

Visit our website at
http://www.arabesquebooks.com

PICTURE PERFECT

SHIRLEY HARRISON

BET Publications, LLC
www.msbet.com
www.arabesquebooks.com

ARABESQUE BOOKS are published by

BET Publications, LLC
c/o BET BOOKS
One BET Plaza
1900 W Place NE
Washington, D.C. 20018-1211

First Printing: February, 1999
10 9 8 7 6 5 4 3 2 1

Printed in the United States of America

*This book is dedicated to
my mother, Minnie Reeves and my husband, Wilber*

Acknowledgments to:
Nancy Knight—she held the door open for so long;
My sons, Rodney and Reggie, and My sisters, Sharon, Brenda,
Harriet, Carol, and Dianne—they encouraged me to go through,
And Adrianne, Jan, Marcia, and Monica—they wouldn't
let me leave.

PROLOGUE

Winter, North Miami Beach, Florida

My Father's Keeper

The hospital bed was flanked by modern, state-of-the-art machinery that interrupted the deathly silence of the room with measured hisses and beeps. The IV suspended from the mobile pole continually dispensed life-saving fluids into the white-shrouded figure on the bed. It was useless, however. James Spenser was dying. His thin arm had found its way from beneath the starched sheets and now beckoned to the sad, young woman huddled nearby.

Davina Spenser sat on a narrow, gray metal chair, her head bowed from weariness. She had alternately sat and paced all day in this room of familiar, antiseptic odors, where she patiently watched the strains of light from a new day turn to the dark remains of yet another pain-filled night.

"Come here." His whisper was a rasp in the quiet room.

At her father's words, she straightened in a jerk and moved swiftly to the sterile bedside. The only illumination in the small room came from the painted metal lamp attached above the hospital bed; its stark glare increased her father's deathly pallor. He lay on his back, his sunken eyes half closed.

"Daddy?" She was unaware that she reverted to the childhood name she hadn't used since her early teens. She gently picked up his hand and placed it in hers. Veins showed a delicate blue through his thin, fragile skin. His fingers closed around hers.

"Come here, Davina, so I can talk to you." The words struggled to find release in his labored breathing. An oxygen mask lay nearby, unused.

"Daddy, I'm right here." Grateful that he recognized her, she gave him a brave smile. For the last two days, he hadn't always known who she was. He had even called her Estrella, her mother's name. She looked into his brown, weathered face and smoothed his brow and sparse wooly hair, peppered with gray. With an effort, she willed her tears not to flow.

"I got to tell you something."

The hospital door opened with a squeak, and an ever-widening triangle of light fell into the room. It was her older brother, David, returning from his pace in the hallway.

"How is he?" David's voice was hushed. With soft steps, he moved his long body quietly to the other side of the bed.

"He wants to talk."

"Is he delirious again?"

"He called my name." She looked hopefully at her brother and saw her own concern reflected in his eyes.

"Are you still here?" Their father's quiet whisper broke into the studied silence.

"We're both here," David assured him. "You're to rest, remember?"

"That's all I've been doing," he whispered, then paused to catch his breath. His left hand still lay in Davina's. With his other, he feebly reached out for David's hand.

"I know things should have been better," he began. "You raised yourselves, and took care of me. When your mother died twenty years ago, a part of me died, too. Davina, you kept the family together." When she shook her head in denial, he continued with, "It's true. I wasn't around when I should've been and I'll soon have my judgment day." He drew a ragged breath. "Children's memories should be about good times with their parents. I didn't give you that."

"You gave us love, and you did the best you could." His guilt pained Davina, but she was grateful that he was lucid.

"God help me, I'm so sorry." His voice cracked. "It's not fair that all I've left is misery for both of you." And then, tears rolled down the corners of his eyes and onto the pillow while he stared at the ceiling. Davina glanced away, and she allowed her own tears to course down her cheeks.

David gently wiped his father's face. "The past is done, Dad, and very little is fair. What matters is we love you."

"The past does matter. That's what I have to tell you." He paused as he took in careful breaths. "I have an old friend, Jacob Hardy. He's been holding something for me. I tried all these years to forget Jacob and everything that happened, but I know this is a way for me to leave something for the grandbabies I'll never know. You can tell them their granddaddy wasn't all bad."

Davina looked at David. She didn't recognize the name her father said and wondered if he was delusional again.

"Why don't you rest," she coaxed.

"No, listen to me." James Spenser's words rode on waves of fragmented breaths. "Find Jacob. He'll know what to do. He's a good man."

Davina felt an acute sense of despair as she watched him struggle to talk.

"You see, I've put off telling you about Jacob because I knew I'd have to tell you about my devils . . . the ones that followed me most of my life." He stopped to catch his breath.

And then, as tears continued to roll from his eyes onto the pillow, he began again. But this time, he talked slowly, as if each word was a gift of gold. "I was involved in some trouble a long time ago, before either of you were born, and I've been paying for it, one way or the other, ever since."

For Davina and David, it was the start of a tale that would become, at once, both fantastical and believable.

Outside, the late winter weather had brought a fierce rain storm to the gloomy night. The coconut palms arced in a crazy dance that Davina could see from the chair where she still sat, her father's hand in hers. Her blank expression hid an inner turmoil that threatened both her sanity and all she had come to believe.

"Promise me you'll watch out for her, son. She's stubborn as a mule and lets on that she can handle everything."

"I promise." David walked around the bed to Davina and draped an arm around her shoulder.

She looked up at her brother, more shaken than she would admit by her father's confession. "David . . ."

He nodded his head. "I know," was his own unsettled response.

James Spenser spoke in a slow, airy voice. "Estrella and her flowers. Always picking them, even from the side of the road." His eyes moved to the window. "That was my special one, you know. I saw her from the window when the light was just right." He closed his eyes.

"Dad, you need to rest." David poured iced water from the plastic pitcher onto a tissue and moistened his father's lips.

The water seemed to revive him, and he opened his eyes. "I can be at peace if I know you have something pure and clean that was a part of me, and will be there for your future. It'll make up for everything I wasn't. Promise me you'll find Jacob."

Davina moved to her father's side. She put an arm around David's waist as she held on to her father's hand.

"Daddy, I promise. We both will. You have to rest," she urged.

"It'll be my legacy to both of you," he continued. The beginnings of a smile showed on his cracked lips and he closed his eyes. He settled back into the pillow. his bout of strength fading again. The white covers across his chest rose steadily as his breathing became shallow. Davina swallowed hard and silently gave the signal to David.

"I'll get the doctor." He left the room.

Davina looked around the chilly, inhospitable room. A colorful bouquet of gerbera daisies on the counter caught her eye and she allowed herself a regretful smile. It had been her mother's favorite flower, so her father said, and that had made it her father's favorite as well. Thinking he was asleep, she started to release his hand, but he held on with a surprisingly strong grip.

"Don't leave."

"I'm right here." The tears, so much a part of her life recently, flowed again.

His grip tightened on her hand. "I love you, Davina."

She choked back the sob before it left her throat. "I love you, Daddy."

His eyes fluttered open briefly, then closed. "Tell David, too," he whispered.

Davina fought to control her sorrow and didn't allow her hand to lose contact with his.

Almost two hours later, an emergency alert was sounded on the floor. Davina kept her promise and held on to his hand until the full medical team arrived. Paralyzed by grief, she stood with David against the wall, and silently vowed to keep her promise. She would see to her father's legacy.

CHAPTER ONE

Eighteen Months Later, Atlanta, Georgia

Davina's Folly

The walls of the dark conference room began to close in on Davina. Her heart thumped loudly in her chest as she crouched in the shadows for what seemed an eternity. Just moments ago, she had heard voices and had almost been discovered in the hallway. To escape, she had retreated to the first unlocked door in her path. Now, alone in this claustrophobic dark, and in possession of stolen property, she wondered about her foolproof plan.

The oversized canvas bag pressed against her leg and reminded her of what she had done. She ran shaky fingers through her hair and smoothed the ever present headband that controlled her dark, thick curls. There would be hell to pay when David learned she had pulled the robbery off, but the plan didn't call for her to get caught. Davina massaged her neck, stiff from tension, and considered her predicament. With no idea of how she would explain away her presence, she knew she had to get out of here.

The voices in the hall were louder and Davina gulped her fear. She scooted across the carpeted floor toward a large conference table, the canvas bag dragging after her. She pushed the bag under the table and prayed it was out of view.

Without a break in motion, she scampered back to the wall behind the door and flattened against it just as the handle turned.

A click near the door introduced a flood of light into the room.

Davina squeezed her eyes tight. With teeth and fists clenched, her heart pounding, she waited to be discovered.

"I don't see anybody," a deep voice whispered. The door threatened to crush Davina as it was pushed wider to offer a panoramic view of the room.

Another voice also whispered, "I didn't say I *saw* someone. I just thought I heard a door opening down here. No one should be on the gallery floor."

Click. The light was extinguished. Davina remained frozen behind the door that closed in a slow, pneumatic manner.

Davina listened as the first voice continued to growl. "You're supposed to keep on top of these things."

The second voice complained, "Don't blame me. I can't be everywhere.'

"No need to panic. Just keep your eyes open."

The door finally closed with a soft thud.

Davina opened her eyes to the darkness and exhaled. She raised a clammy hand to her face while the other clutched the strap of her purse. A few moments passed as she waited to ensure that the voices had moved farther down the hall.

On weakened knees, Davina crept to the table and hefted the canvas bag with its valuable cargo onto her free shoulder. Opening the door, she peeked out into the solemn, pale gloom of the low lit office. The hall was clear. She took a deep breath, stepped from the conference room, and headed for the reception area that would lead her to the corridor . . . and freedom.

The limo eased into the early evening traffic at Hartsfield Airport and swiftly merged onto Interstate 85 for its downtown destination. Justin Hardy sat in the rear seat with his eyes closed. The cold breeze from the air vent was a welcome comfort from Atlanta's choking summer heat. He needed a clear mind for the upcoming meeting. All he seemed to do since he became head of Hardy Enterprises was meet. He preferred action.

Justin had just come from a meeting in New York where he first spent time with a prospective investor. Then he met with the agent who represented a new artist his company wanted to acquire. Artists were a quirky lot, and different from his writers. He preferred to talk with artists directly and offer personal assurances that their work would not be abused, artistically or financially. Unfortunately, the agents, attorneys—everyone but the creative talent—staked their claims first, a necessary evil in this business.

Newly installed as the president since his father's untimely death three months earlier, Justin knew Hardy Enterprises had a lot on the line right now. Its very existence as a family-owned fine arts business that had diversified into publishing and artist management was in jeopardy. The investors' cash and the art show bid held equal importance right now. Justin desperately needed both in order to generate capital to help Hardy's stock position and squelch the rumors of a takeover attempt.

Small, successful, independent businesses were ripe for the business sharks, another evil he had faced these past months. It was still hard to believe his father had let the company get into the financial bind it was now in. It would be ironic, Justin thought, if the decision to go public with Hardy's stock came from him, the investment analyst son who never intended to work in the family business.

The limo driver's voice came through the speakers and interrupted Justin's thoughts. "Mr. Hardy, we should arrive shortly."

"Thank you."

He stretched his long legs and rested his head against the soft, leather cushion. He'd be wound tight for the next few hours, so he allowed himself a few more minutes to enjoy the quiet and solitude the limo afforded. The problems he faced, though, seeped into his consciousness and denied him the tranquility he sought. Wearily, he opened his eyes to deal with the business at hand.

Justin reached into his leather valise and withdrew a sealed portfolio. It contained the company's latest business and stock reports. He was searching the side pouch of the bag for a pen when his fingers encountered something. Curious, he clicked on the overhead light and fished the object out. No longer restrained by the pouch, soft, black material unfolded from the bag. He recognized the feel of silk and raised it to the light. It was a lacy garter belt. He smiled as the feminine piece of fluff brought a vision of Linda Daniel's lush body to mind. He felt a familiar, pleasurable tightening and knew that was the reaction she wanted. Only, she would have preferred his discomfort in the middle of a meeting.

Justin sighed as he replaced the lingerie in the pouch and retrieved his pen. Business now, and he'd deal with her later. He looked at his watch before he broke the seal to the portfolio and, with resignation, read the reports.

Davina made a cautious journey down the hall; her head turned in a constant vigil. She maneuvered through the obscure light to the reception area that loomed ahead. Then, the awkward bag brushed across a desk and toppled a metal cup of pencils. The resulting clang reverberated through the quiet pall of the office.

"Hey, what are you doing in here?"

The heavy, raspy voice made Davina's hackles rise. She was caught. Not willing to give up, she didn't look back as she rushed through the empty aisle toward the door. She could still hear the murmur of the gravelly voice behind her.

The hall door was now just a few yards away. Davina knew that if she reached it, she would be in the relative safety of the corridor and convenient stair exits. She had left the door jimmied for an expected quick departure. What if the door had been discovered open, and was now locked? She couldn't think about that now.

Her heart pumped with fear and Davina allowed the rush to carry her to the door. She leaned into it and pushed down on the handle, but it moved only slightly. She peered through the dimmed light. The momentum of her purse's swing from her shoulder had caused the strap to catch on the door handle. Losing precious seconds, she untangled the purse and pushed the handle again to gain access to the other side.

Davina stole a backward glance to see if whoever had called out had continued pursuit. She strode through the long corridor and came upon a water fountain alcove. She flattened herself into the opening and listened.

The groan of wood against metal perked Davina's ears. The door she had just left through opened.

"The hall is clear." The low voice was barely audible.

"Let's look around again." It was the deep-voiced man.

She didn't dare breathe as she willed the men not to come down the corridor.

"And this time," he continued, "lock the door." The door groaned closed.

Davina allowed herself to breathe while she listened.

Silence. She peeked first, then ventured out into the empty hallway, past the glass doors of another suite, and toward the bay of elevators.

Davina could see the coveted stair doors located on the other side of the elevators even as she kept a watchful eye on the hallway. She sensed that freedom was near and slowed her pace. She stared back over her shoulder as she crossed in front of the elevators, and crashed directly into a broad chest.

She felt hands grasp her shoulders in a protective hug, then drop to encircle her waist. She was held tight to prevent further stumbling. Davina experienced a moment of panic until she saw that her pursuers were not around.

"Hey . . . slow down," a husky baritone voice declared.

Davina knew a man held her before she heard his words. She was pressed against a big and powerful body. Her own hands still gripped her purse and bag when she looked up at the stranger. His clean, tantalizing smell was a mixture of maleness and aftershave, and was seductively disconcerting.

"Oh, I'm sorry . . ." Davina stopped in midsentence, caught off guard by the striking, handsome face that stared down at her. He had exceptional looks, with black, short cropped hair, heavy brows, and eyelashes that seemed to go on forever. Clean shaven, he had a squared chin that supported well-shaped lips. As each stared at the other, his lips parted in a smile that revealed strong, white teeth against an even, brown complexion. He was at least a full head taller than her own five-seven.

Davina required a few seconds to compose herself. As she tried to back away from his hands, she swallowed hard and launched into the apology again. "I'm sorry for walking into you, but, if you'll excuse me, I have to go."

His hands lingered a brief moment, then fell from the curves of her waist. She backed away and, again, headed for the exit door.

He followed her. "Don't go yet. Can you at least tell me your name?"

Intent on escape, Davina replied, "No, and I don't have time for yours."

Experience told her to expect a reply, and she paused to look back at him. Her expression dared him to give one. He stopped, then simply smiled and shook his head. Davina now saw him as a tall, dangerously handsome stranger. Immaculate in an olive green two-button suit, his powerful, well-muscled body moved with easy grace as he turned to retrieve his leather bag from the floor where it had dropped. Davina thought he looked like he had stepped from a magazine, and her heart did a somersault.

"I can already tell that you're a handful." He smiled and walked toward her. "And let's get something straight. You ran into me and stepped on my foot. I should be the one to be upset." The huskiness lingered in his voice. He stopped in front of her, his brows arched in humor.

Davina did not mean to smile at his wit and charm but, caught off guard, she did anyway. At once, and as always, her smile transformed her usually stern demeanor into a thoroughly engaging one. It had its usual effect on the stranger as well. He no longer smiled, but simply stared at her.

"You're a beautiful woman. You should always smile." He took another step forward as Davina stepped back. His eyes lowered and took in her entire form, ostensibly camouflaged by her long-sleeved, calf-length dress. But the soft, dark material that curved against her bosom and legs, and contrasted with the honeyed glow of her exposed skin, revealed much more than Davina imagined it would. His face showed he was pleased with the revelation.

Both his comment and perusal annoyed Davina. Her smile faded, her eyebrows knitted, and her teeth clenched. She was back in reality. Men, she thought, and turned away from him to continue her walk to the stair exit door.

"Don't you want to use the elevator?"

She ignored him and clumsily made her way through the doorway with her bulky canvas bag.

Justin Hardy enjoyed the graceful sway of her hips and the sleek curve of her calves and ankles revealed by the ebb and flow of her long dress. He didn't know how long he stood there before a familiar voice spoke.

"Welcome back, Justin. Why are you standing out here?"

Justin recognized his friend and business partner, Marcus Randall. He replied without turning his head from the direction of Davina's now departed figure. "I just had a run-in, literally, with a very lovely creature." He turned and walked with Marc down the corridor. "I wonder if she works for us, or in this building?"

"You didn't ask?"

"She wouldn't say." A smile played on Justin's lips as he glanced at his friend. "In fact, she ran away from me."

Marc returned the glance with a grin. "That's a first for you." He chuckled at this turn of events. "But, if she did, obviously your reputation still precedes you."

Justin scowled at Marc's joke, all business now. "I don't need that kind of distraction, anyway. Is everyone here?"

"Everyone except Linda."

"That figures. Come on, let's get this meeting started."

Davina inserted the key into her apartment door. She took one last nervous look behind her, then made a quick entry before she reset the lock.

The two-bedroom apartment had become an extension of Davina and she felt some of the tension of the evening ease as she rapidly moved through the softly lit living room and into the kitchen.

She absently dropped her keys and purse on the counter, then purposely placed the precious baggage in the center of the table. She backed away, both bewildered and astonished by what she had done. When the counter's edge jabbed her back to stop her progress, she reached behind and flicked the wall switch. The flood of light in the tiny room emphasized the prominence of the bulging canvas bag. It beckoned her, daring her to open it and satisfy her curiosity.

It won. Davina's fingers worked fast and furious to pull apart the large snaps at the top of the bag. She reached inside, grasped the wood edges, and took a deep breath while she slowly pulled the canvases to freedom in the light of the kitchen.

The first canvas, and the largest at eighteen by twenty-four, was done in brilliant, unmixed oil colors, and showed a group of black children at play near a seaport. The next measured sixteen by twenty and was a colorful study of five black men engaged in a raucous game of checkers. The last painting was the smallest. It was a delicate oil done in a luminous mix of gentle colors, and was almost ethereal in its depiction of a young woman picking flowers from a garden. The twelve by fifteen stretched canvas was attached to a beautifully carved frame.

The signatures on the canvases were the same illegible mark, but Davina wasn't concerned about the signature.

She knew the artist. He was her father.

CHAPTER TWO

The Calm in a Building Storm

Davina recognized her brother's insistent ring and hurried to the door. "I'm coming, David. Hold on."

When she opened the door, he rushed in like a great wind. Dressed in trousers, buttoned-down shirt and tie, his hair still pulled back in a makeshift ponytail, she knew he had come straight from the small law firm where he worked as a corporate attorney. Their warm, cinnamon brown coloring and tightly curled hair hinted that they were siblings, but where Davina was tall and slender, David was six feet of solid, well-developed muscle.

He looked at his sister and shook his head. "Please tell me you didn't break and enter, Davina, and then commit grand theft tonight."

She closed the door with one hand, and pointed in the direction of the kitchen with the other. "In there," she whispered.

Davina watched his expression grow hard with disbelief before he headed for the kitchen in long, purposeful strides. It wasn't a good sign that he'd used her given name, not the nickname he'd favored since they were kids. That meant he was angrier than she'd expected. She wrapped her arms about her waist like armor, and listened for his reaction. It came quickly.

"Davina! You took three?" His roar caused her to cringe.

She quietly entered the little kitchen. Like Davina, he slowly circled the table where the paintings rested under the bright kitchen light. He said nothing while he eyed them in a studious inspection, one after the other.

"That's the one of Mother with the flowers," Davina helpfully pointed out.

To her disappointment, he only mumbled, "I know."

His struggle to hold his temper showed clearly. In careful, studied words, he said, "Why did you have to take them? I mean, didn't we agree it wouldn't come to this?" He continued around the table, his eyes never leaving the paintings.

"We agreed to do things legally," he added. "Now, you've gone off on this crusade and pretty much closed that door. Even when you considered finding out if they had the paintings, you never said you'd steal them. Nothing we say now will mean much next to a grand theft charge." His last words were emphatic.

David seldom lost his temper with his younger, headstrong sister. He knew and appreciated the sacrifices she had made for him and their father while growing up without a mother. She was determined to make good on the promise to their father, no matter the consequence.

Tears began to pool in Davina's eyes. "I'm sorry," she apologized in a small voice. "I know I said I wouldn't do anything drastic, but they ignored us and nothing was happening. I knew they had the paintings, and when I got inside and actually saw them, I had to take some . . . as evidence."

At David's silence, she continued. "Can't you see we needed this evidence because they'll say they don't have them?" She silently begged forgiveness for stealing, but it was the only way to get past the lawyers at Hardy Enterprises. "I saw other ones, too." David remained quiet and a dread started to build within her that all was lost with her brother. Her tears burned for release.

David turned his gaze from the paintings to his sister and, in the next moment, drew her into his wide embrace. "I made a promise to Dad that I'd always be here for you, even if I wanted to kick your butt." Her arms wrapped tightly around his middle. "We'll figure something out," he said. "You're too reckless for your own good."

Davina let out a loud sob of relief against her brother's chest as the enormity of her act took hold. The tears broke away. She hadn't realized how much David's support meant until she realized he might not offer it. He was her only family, and she had to believe his love was unconditional.

They returned to the living room where Davina curled into the corner of the sofa. Under David's watchful eye, she dabbed at her tears with her sleeve. "I won't let what I've done affect your position at the law firm, David. I promise."

"That's not my concern," he said, and walked over to the window. "I don't want you to mess up your chances to get your own career started."

David glanced around the small apartment decorated in a functional style that reflected his sister's good taste and limited funds. The soft shades of mauve and green, mixed with whites, imbued the room with a sedate charm. Samples of her hard work as an artist were everywhere. Her more recent works of nudes in different mediums, and painted in various shapes and forms, covered the walls. A few sculptures sat on tables. He saw the faraway look on her tear-stained face.

"David, the things Dad told us . . . do you think it was all true?"

"You mean you planned this and didn't believe Dad?" Amusement was evident in his voice as he sat on the other end of the sofa.

"The paintings I saw at that private exhibit in Miami had to be fakes, if what Dad told us was true."

"He was delirious part of the time when he talked to us. I don't know. What we have are a lot of maybes." He handed her a box of tissues from the end table.

Davina hiccuped and wiped her eyes with a tissue. "I have to keep my word to him, David. The answers are out there, I know they are."

Before he replied, the doorbell sounded, but the ring was a playful melody.

"That has to be Natalie." David's voice dripped sarcasm as he rose from the sofa. "You called her, too?"

Davina nodded. "I left a message on her machine. Be nice, and that means no arguing. You sure are touchy since you broke off with Sheree," she teased.

"It doesn't take much to start an argument with Natalie." He opened the front door as the bells sounded again.

Natalie Goodman had struck a pose in the doorway. "What took you so long?" Extending herself on her toes, she pecked David on the cheek, then sailed past him toward Davina. In her wake, David rolled his eyes heavenward.

"Come in Natalie. It's good to see you, too." He closed the door before joining the women.

From the sofa, Davina observed her friend's entrance and her brother's reaction. Natalie loved life and did her best to find pleasure and humor at every turn. When Davina was angry or hurt, Natalie could be counted on to make her smile. David couldn't figure out their enduring friendship when they appeared to be such opposites, but Davina was glad he had come to terms with Natalie's constant presence.

And Natalie did require some coming to terms with. She had an unabashed fondness for black, and had confided that it reduced the appearance of her ample curves. Davina thought her friend's figure was exceptional. In order to survive the rigors of Natalie's wardrobe, it had to be. Now, wearing a black pants suit, a tight black silk shell, with her short, black hair slick against her head, Natalie resembled a very shapely fifties beatnik. Few would guess that she was a CPA with a large firm.

"I got your message and came as soon as I could." Natalie bent to receive Davina's hug and then sat next to her on the sofa. "So, everything went okay?"

Davina nodded her head and tried to convey caution through her eyes.

"You've been crying," Natalie said, and looked closely into Davina's strained face. She turned and gave David a daggered look. "David . . ."

"He didn't do anything, Natalie. I'm fine."

David gave Natalie a tight smile. "You owe me an apology."

"Well, David, sometimes you can be so uptight about things," she explained with a wave of her hand.

"You're not getting to me tonight." He sighed as he sat forward. "What you want to see is in the kitchen. It's pretty amazing, too."

Natalie cocked her eyebrows at the invitation and, with a wide smile, scrambled from the sofa and rushed to the kitchen.

"Wait a sec." Davina hopped from the sofa to go after her.

Natalie's lilting voice soared back into the living room. "Oh, my God, Davina, you were only going to take one. They're magnificent."

Davina stopped at Natalie's words. She squared her shoulders and gave David a guilty glance before she returned to the sofa. The hurt look in his eyes caused her to flush with shame again.

"So, you did plan to take one all along?" he asked quietly.

"I didn't tell you because I knew you'd worry and talk me out of it. I feel badly that I kept this from you, but I couldn't let you stop me." Both of them possessed that family stubbornness that was destined to cause trouble, but Davina carried it with more poise and polish. Once her mind was set, it became a fortress.

David pulled himself from the chair and thrust his hands into his pockets. His wrinkled brow reflected his confusion with his sister's actions. He spit angry words in her direction. "Why do you have to be so reckless? You used to think things through."

Before she could catch it, the wound to her pride surfaced. "I used to think, until I met Lawrence. Is that what you're saying?" The hurt poured from her. She dropped her head onto the back of the sofa and squeezed her eyes shut.

"You know that's not what I meant. I've never thought that way. You're the one who continues to punish yourself by reliving that nightmare."

As quickly as the wound opened, it closed. "I'm sorry." She raised her head and looked at him. "I guess I've said that a lot tonight, but I know what I'm doing. Trust me to see this through, okay?"

Natalie walked in from the kitchen. "They're absolutely exquisite and in great shape." She looked from Davina to David. "All right, both of you stop it. The deed is done and there's nothing we can do about it now. I want to know how you did it."

David shrugged resignedly and gave his sister a small smile. "So do I." He returned to his chair. Davina's exhausted eyes smiled back at him.

"When I heard your message, I knew you'd gotten out," Natalie said.

"You called me before you went in, so all I could do was wait," added David. "After your second message said to meet you here, I didn't know whether to be happy that you got away or mad that you tried it. Suppose you had been caught and carted off to jail?"

"Yeah," chimed in Natalie. "Strip search is no fun with the wrong person. I know." David and Davina looked at her. "What?" was her innocent query.

Davina sat up on the sofa. "All right, what do you want to know?"

"Start at the beginning," David said, and eased back against the cushion. "And, Natalie, nothing out of you, please."

"Maybe I shouldn't give details," Davina started. "That way, no one can accuse either of you of withholding evidence of a crime."

"Davina!" David and Natalie protested in unison.

"Okay, okay," she said, and recalled her plan for them. "I used a visitor's pass to reach the third-floor gallery. It took two visits to find out where they show and store art. So, when I got in today, I mixed with the visitors and employees, hid, and never came out. The gallery level is keyed for entrance with a card, but you can exit without it. A lot of canvases were stored there, but I found three I easily recognized, including the one of Mother that Dad talked so much about. Then I left by the door I had jimmied earlier, and took the stairs back to the ground floor."

"And no one saw you, or stopped you?" Natalie asked, her eyes wide.

In a split second, Davina decided not to tell them about the voices or the stranger at the elevator. Why worry them unnecessarily? "It was a piece of cake."

"You handled it like a regular cat burglar, huh?" David's voice was rough with anxiety. "I don't think you realize how serious a crime this is. And since you don't know their internal security system, the missing paintings could be discovered a lot sooner than you expect."

"Maybe not," Natalie piped in. "Galleries loan from their private collections all the time. It could take a while for them to track missing paintings."

"Stop encouraging her with that talk."

"I'm just giving her a little peace of mind, David."

"I'm a lawyer, for heaven's sake," he shouted. "I know the consequence of what she did tonight, and it was not smart. Don't tell me about peace of mind."

"Well, you're not helping with the gloom and doom," she sniped.

"Would you two stop it? You talk like I'm not here." Davina avoided her brother's eyes as she said, "Natalie is right. They probably aren't concerned about some old stored paintings." Her thoughts unwillingly returned to the man at the elevator and the voice that demanded her to stop.

"We don't know what their concerns are," David said. "That's why I didn't agree to force their hand. Of course, if they find out what you did and decide to prosecute, we could always return the paintings in a plea bargain that allows you to claim temporary insanity." His caustic comment drew Davina's narrowed eyes.

"There's nothing temporary about her insanity when she has a cause," Natalie said, her smile widening. "Remember when she was arrested for leading the college's art department in a boycott when they wanted to ditch that program?"

Davina flushed. "I didn't know they'd keep the program and fire the instructors."

"No, no, no," David interrupted, and rested his forehead against his hand in defeat. "I can't take memory lane right now."

"Anyway, Hardy Enterprises is well known in the southeast. What would they gain by prosecuting me?" asked Davina.

"We don't know their agenda. Unfortunately, Jacob Hardy was our only contact and he's dead. We have to deal with his son now." David frowned. "Justin Hardy is the one who wants us to go away."

"Do you know anything about him, David?" Natalie asked.

"Only what I've read since his father's death. He had a reputation for living in the fast lane while he was in New York. He showed up pretty regularly in the gossip columns."

"I can handle some rich playboy who's out of touch and soft from his daddy's money. They usually don't have any backbone when they're born with a silver spoon." Even as she spoke them, Davina doubted her brave words. She knew that with wealth and position came power. Depending on how Hardy wielded his, this could be an uphill battle.

"Don't sell him short," David said. "When he took over Hardy, the newspapers said he was already a pretty savvy businessman in his own right. He made his own wealth and reputation on Wall Street, as a stocks and bonds trader."

"The business was still handed to him," Davina said stubbornly.

"Those paintings mean a lot to us, but they represent money and who knows what else to Hardy Enterprises," argued David. He leaned forward. "Did you check out the signature on the paintings?"

"Yes. Just like Dad said."

"Everything's adding up," agreed Natalie.

Davina got up from the sofa and went into the kitchen where the paintings rested. David and Natalie came up silently behind her.

"We can't keep these a secret forever," David said. He put his arm around her shoulders.

"We have to use them to prove our point against Hardy." Davina looked at the dazzling pieces of art that had once belonged to her father. "We've got them, and I'm going to prove they're ours. Hardy will never possess them again."

Justin Hardy pushed away from the conference table and walked toward the floor-to-ceiling glass windows. Outside, Atlanta's midtown city lights twinkled through the dusky twilight of the early summer evening. From the third-floor conference room, he could see the northern perimeter of trees that marked the vast expanse of Piedmont Park. With arms folded, Justin leaned against the window's support column and faced the four people at the conference table who made up part of Hardy Enterprises' management team.

"Why wasn't this brought to my attention sooner?" He spoke with a quiet that belied his steadily building anger.

Under Justin's scrutiny, they looked at each other. Marc, vice president of Operations, stood and joined Justin at the window.

"Legal felt they could handle the problem much the same way they handle any other claim inquiry."

"And . . ." cut in Justin, a sharp look directed at his friend.

"She didn't even have her attorney contact us. In one of her letters, she let on that her brother is a lawyer. We did a cursory check, of course, and found out that he's an associate attorney in a small firm. From what we can gather, the woman is the instigator of this." Marc dropped his hands into his pockets.

"What do we know about her?"

"We checked the basics. She's single, employed as a layout artist in an ad agency out on the perimeter. When she upped the ante this week, I thought it best to fax the details to you in New York. As you read," Marc continued, "Legal still concluded there was no reason to react any differently. We had already dismissed her as a crackpot, possibly after a monetary settlement. We told her we didn't know what she was talking about and no meeting was offered. We figured she'd fade away if she was ignored."

"Unfortunately, you figured wrong." Justin's dry comment was met by nods of agreement from the table. He looked over at the head of his legal department.

Raymond Miller leaned back, his portly figure threatening the sturdy chair's tenuous hold on gravity. He had come highly recommended to Hardy Enterprises four years before. "The problem is that her last letter threatened press coverage if we don't investigate her claim. She doesn't appear to have anything except that threat and wants us to help her," he explained. "Do we take the chance?"

Justin noticed Nora Watts, his very capable executive assistant, tapping her watch, a signal to remind him that he had to attend a reception later.

The huge executive conference room, which could easily seat thirty for a leisurely luncheon meeting, had become stifling to Justin. He had experienced a lot of frustrations over the years in his turbulent relationship with his father, and definitely during his stint on Wall

Street, but the problems within this company that he had been obligated to take over as CEO and president seemed to have multiplied in the last months. Had his father seen them coming? Were they the cause of the heart attack he had suffered?

He had only been head of his father's company for three months. Interesting, he still thought of the company as his father's. Did he really know the people that made up Jacob Hardy's management team? His team now.

Nora was an efficient firebrand in a tiny package who kept things running smoothly while she jealously guarded his time and schedule. Ray had the least seniority of the group and was sharp; not much got past him. Although he was white in a predominantly black organization, he meshed well with the staff.

Douglas Bradley was the business manager and the most proven of the group. He had been with Hardy since the beginning and was admired in the professional community. The oldest of the team, Douglas had been Jacob Hardy's close friend and a frequent visitor at his home, and now he was a surprising mentor to Justin.

The only one of the four Justin knew well was Marc Randall, a friend since college. It was ironic that Justin shrugged off his father's offer to come into the business and chose, instead, to cut his own successful path in the investment field. Marc, however, had interned at Hardy Enterprises and accepted the offered help. Last year, when father and son bitterly split over yet another of Justin's refusals to come into the business, Marc was there to smooth things out. Now, due to circumstances beyond Justin's control, he was Marc's boss. It had come as a total surprise to Justin that his father had named him as the interim successor. Justin and Marc worked well together, and in these trying times, he was relieved to have someone he could trust with the company's best interest.

"It's just that the woman's claim comes at the worst time, and she's tenacious." Justin realized Marc had started to talk again. "With her recent threats to go to the press, you needed to know we refused to let her meet the full board on Monday." Marc returned to his chair near the head of the table.

Douglas flattened his hands on the table top and let out a deep breath. "Well, I believe that to be a tactical error on our part. Ray is aware of my feelings on this. The negative publicity she could generate in the press with her David versus Goliath tale could do a lot of harm. Don't forget that our stock base is suffering and the employees have been disrupted by the takeover rumors.

"Jacob's death, an untried new president . . ." Douglas looked over at Justin, nodding toward him as he said, "No disrespect, son."

Justin smiled and acknowledged the nod. "None taken."

"All of these things," Douglas continued, "have already hurt our first-quarter net income. How do we get the necessary capital when the potential investors are scared off by declining earnings? I say, let the woman have her say before the full board and let them decide about her claim. At this point, it won't hurt."

With arms folded across his chest, Justin started to pace, deep in thought. He glanced over at the team members who looked to him for direction.

"I agree with Douglas," he said.

"But, Justin—" Ray started.

Justin held up his hand and brooked no arguments on his decision. "Nora, I want a letter delivered tomorrow morning to . . ." He couldn't remember the name.

"Davina Spenser," offered Nora.

"Yes. Davina Spenser. An interesting name. Allow her fifteen minutes in a closed session at the end of the agenda, and require a twenty-four-hour RSVP. Now, is anything else going on that I should know?" Justin asked. The lightness in his voice alleviated the tension, and a collective sigh echoed in the room.

"Did you learn anything while you were in New York that'll give us the inside track on acquiring that new artist?" Douglas asked.

"I met with the agent," Justin replied. "He got solid promises from us, but wouldn't commit or arrange a meeting with the artist until a decision was made. So, we'll have to follow up. This is Linda's acquisition, and she's not here. I think you know how important it is that we get the rights to this show as well as secure new investors. They'll give us much needed positive publicity as well as inject quick life into our capital position. The next four months are crucial to our survival. You'll get a memo from Nora."

"Which reminds me," Marc said from the table. "Accounting is going to inventory the property for a revised P & L statement. The storage lockers haven't been cataloged in years. The inventory will include all artistic properties, including family-owned pieces. Those assets are still under corporate control. We need to look very good on paper. Linda will coordinate the details with Accounting, and should be finished next week.''

"Did someone mention my name?'' Linda Daniels had quietly sauntered into the room, late as usual, but impeccably put together . . . . as usual. As Legal liaison, her main responsibilities centered on contractual obligations and new acquisitions. She was dressed for an evening engagement, from her low cut, cocktail-length satin black dress down to the matching sequined shoes and bag. Her lips and nails were a blood red, all of which set off her pale, light-skinned coloring to perfection. The eyes of the others in the room were drawn to her as she approached the table. Justin's irritation at the interruption was obvious in the set of his mouth.

"Where have you been?'' Ray complained. "The meeting started an hour ago. We were just talking about the art show and the inventory update.''

Linda strolled the distance to the conference table as if it were a runway. She headed for the vacant seat nearest the head chair that Justin recently occupied. With all eyes still on her, she placed her evening purse on the table with a flourish, and turned to address the group.

"I'm not going to apologize for missing this meeting. You see, I stopped by the reception that Broadside's is giving for Winston Barkley. Well, I learned he only signed a one-book deal and is open for other considerations. So, I've been pushing his agent to consider us for his next book.''

This news was greeted with compliments to Linda for acting on such good instincts. She sat in the chair and crossed her legs with an audacity only she could pull off. "I decided to come back here and make sure Justin attends the reception.''

While small talk broke out among the others at the table, Linda gave Justin a longing look as he made his way back to the conference table.

He greeted Linda with a raised brow. "Reduce your contact to writing and we'll see what kind of inroads you really made. I'll expect it tomorrow.''

"Anything you say." She held Justin's gaze long enough to convey her sultry thoughts.

Justin cleared his throat and proceeded to conclude the meeting.

As the small group disbanded, Douglas pulled Justin aside and spoke to him earnestly. "You're doing a fine job as president." He grasped Justin's shoulder. "It's a shame that Jacob can't see how well you're handling these problems. We know what's happening is not your fault. I believe he'd be proud of you, son."

In a warm show of affection, Justin turned and took Douglas's hand into his. "I appreciate and welcome your support."

Justin walked with Douglas to the conference room door just vacated by Marc, Ray, and Nora. Closing the door behind Douglas, he walked back to the table now solely occupied by Linda and gathered his papers.

"Miss me, lover?" she purred.

"I didn't have time to. I found your garter in my briefcase."

"Oh, you got my little surprise." She let out a throaty laugh. "It was just a reminder of our good times." Her smile revealed tiny, perfectly even teeth.

As if he were reprimanding a brazen child, Justin scolded Linda. "I've asked you not to do that. You can take a joke too far." He slid the papers into his leather valise and snapped it close.

"I thought you liked my sexy surprises," she said knowingly. "Remember when I wore the raincoat to the restaurant, and the fun we had with the maître d' that night." Her throaty laugh pierced the air.

Justin propped himself on the edge of the conference table near Linda and smiled from the memory. "That's definitely in the past. There's a lot going on around here. We both knew things would change when I took over as CEO. We enjoyed each other, but I've got to give my full attention to the business and these problems. Things aren't like they were before, when my time was my own. Besides, I'm your boss, now. It doesn't look right for us to be together."

Linda pushed her chair away from the table, uncrossed her legs, and moved to stand in front of Justin. A former model, her high heels made her nearly as tall as Justin. "Well, lover, tomorrow is soon enough to worry about business. Let's go to your office and get you changed into your tux for the rest of the reception. Since you used the limo, I'll take you home . . . later." Putting her arms around Justin's neck, she pressed against his length and playfully attempted to secure a kiss.

It was Justin's experience that anything Linda didn't want to hear, she ignored. He was serious about ending their relationship, though, and refused to allow desire to overtake him. Catching her in his arms, he held her away while she looked at him. "I mean what I said."

She removed her arms from his neck, and he released her. Reaching for her purse, she walked to the door. Once there, she turned with an inviting smile and said, "We'll see."

Justin shook his head, annoyance in his eyes. He picked up the valise from the table and joined her at the door. As they walked past the elevator to his office, he was reminded of the attractive woman with the beautiful smile he had bumped into earlier. He reluctantly found himself comparing the sophisticated Linda to that awkward sprite. There was really not much comparison, so why was he intrigued by a woman who was rude, arrogant, and, yes, not the least bit interested in him? And what was she doing in his building, and on this floor, anyway?

David and Natalie had left over an hour ago. Thoroughly exhausted by tears, explanations, and recriminations, Davina rested her head against the edge of the wide garden tub and allowed the swirls of warm, fragrant water to wash up against her neck. She marveled at the fact of how therapeutic this was. Having Natalie as a friend didn't hurt, either. She smiled.

They had known each other since high school in south Florida. When David left for college in the northeast, Natalie filled a lonely void in Davina's life, and their friendship flourished. But soon after, Natalie also left to attend Spelman College in Atlanta. Davina was left to care for her increasingly ill father and take college courses when she could spare the time and money. After law school, David settled in Atlanta with his new job, and Davina joined him later. At about the same time, and quite by accident, she and Natalie discovered each other in Atlanta. Now, they both resided at the same apartment complex.

Poor David. She felt awful about the worry she caused him, but she liked having control of her life. It hadn't always been this way. It felt good to spread her wings, discover herself, and do what she wanted to do, not what was expected.

Her thoughts turned to what was ahead. She had already wrapped the paintings for storage, and intended to secret all three in a safe place tomorrow. What were the words, "hide in plain sight"? Well, that's just what she meant to do. She'd go to work as usual and continue to press Hardy Enterprises to investigate her claim. In the end, she'd get justice for her father, with or without their help.

Davina stepped from the cooled water of the emptying bathtub and wrapped her sleek body in the terry bath sheet. Walking into her bedroom, she dropped the towel on the footstool near her vanity and mirror and dispassionately observed her familiar image. She reached for her scented lotion.

Her oval-shaped face was framed by unruly, shoulder-length curls, tightened even more by the steam from the bathroom. The soft light from the vanity flattered her cinnamon coloring; the silky skin that surrounded the dark peaks of her full breasts glowed. She lowered her eyes and regarded her slim waist and hips. Considering her love for food, she could only count the slimness as a blessing.

Davina sat on the footstool and squirted the mango-scented lotion into her hands. As she gently massaged the fragrance into her skin, her eyes closed, and a vision of the stranger at the elevator appeared. Her eyes flew open.

She remembered the encounter with crystal clarity and felt her face grow warm from the thought of him. Then she grimaced as she considered the antics men go through to pick up women. She was sure he was used to women falling for him, because he was surprised when she didn't. Her experience taught her to avoid his type at all costs. They were usually arrogant and full of themselves. She had to admit, though, he was one handsome devil. Too much so.

She vowed she'd bow to experience. Life had been a pretty good teacher, thanks to Lawrence Parker. It had been almost two years since she d fancied herself in love with him. The thought didn't hurt so much anymore. Natalie teased that she had become a practicing nun and kept setting her up with dates, and David kept protecting her from them. Meanwhile, she had learned to take care of herself.

Davina finished the lotion ritual and drew a man's large white T-shirt from the cherry highboy drawer. She pulled it over her head, then walked through the small apartment, checking to make sure she was safely locked in for the night.

As was her custom before bed, Davina said her prayers, and at their conclusion, asked only for the strength and courage to get through whatever was in store. She couldn't remember when she'd stopped asking for specific things in her prayers. Maybe it was as a child that she realized wishes were just that.

Yawning, Davina crawled under the comforter. She had a lot to do tomorrow and she had to plan her next moves. And, she allowed herself one last delicious thought of the handsome stranger at the elevator.

CHAPTER THREE

The Muck and Mire That Lies Make

The letter from Hardy Enterprises shook in Davina's hand as she read it again. Earlier, when she'd arrived home from work, it had been waiting in the apartment manager's office. As she'd returned to her apartment with the sealed envelope that carried Hardy's logo, curiosity prevailed and she had torn it open.

Davina sat on the edge of the lounger at poolside where the afternoon heat glazed her bare arms. She was oblivious to her neighbors who enjoyed the hot sun and cool water because a mild panic whirled through her body. What if they knew she had been in their gallery and intended to expose her as a thief before their board? What if the meeting was a ruse to embarrass her into dropping her demands? *Stop it*. She tried, but she couldn't shake the idea that something was wrong about the invitation.

Stealing had been distasteful, but Davina had resigned herself to do whatever was necessary to regain possession of the paintings and keep the promise she had made to her father. She allowed herself a tight smile as she wallowed in the irony: She only took the paintings because the company wouldn't listen to her; now, after she'd put everything at risk, they invited her to speak to the board.

A hot breeze whipped across the thick hedge of azaleas and slapped at Davina's face, disturbing her thoughts. With the letter clutched in her hand, she stood and stepped out of her pumps. It had been a long day, and it wasn't over yet. She picked up her shoes and, sighing, slowly padded across the smooth, warm pavement. She had to be careful about what she said at the meeting, very careful. First, though, she had to break this news to David and Natalie.

Justin parked his car with the others already settled in the graveled parking area next to the front gardens of the spacious Hardy family home in Southern Woods Estates. One of the vehicles belonged to Douglas Bradley, whom he was expecting for dinner. Another, he didn't recognize. He stepped through the front door and into the wide, two-story foyer just as Elizabeth Hardy entered from the dining room. Justin blinked from the contrast of the dusky light outside and the sparkling rays of the huge chandelier suspended from the second-story ceiling.

"Son, you're home," she said. "I was beginning to wonder if you'd make it to dinner at all." She was dressed in a fashionable business suit that fit her new lifestyle of committee woman and volunteer for half a dozen organizations. Her black hair was liberally sprinkled with gray—at fifty-eight, she was quite comfortable with it—and was worn in a boyish short cut that complimented her small build.

"Hi, Mom." Justin closed the heavy oak door and walked across the foyer to greet her with a kiss on the cheek.

"You look tired," she said in a concerned voice. "Everyone is waiting, including Edward." Edward Nelson was both the family's attorney and a member of the legal staff at Hardy.

"Oh?" Justin was surprised.

"I asked him to stay for dinner. I didn't think you'd mind."

"No, I don't. Although, sometimes I think you're too gracious for your own good." He winked at his mother, then looked at his watch. "Thanks for getting everyone here. Give me a few minutes to freshen up, and I'll be back down, ready to eat anything Mrs. Taylor puts in front of me." Mrs. Taylor was the cook and housekeeper, a valuable helper at the house.

"It's your favorite . . . salmon," Mrs. Hardy called out to his departing figure.

Justin had already loosened his tie when he entered the drawing room.

His youngest sister, Alexandra, better known as Alli, stood just inside the door; her petite, doll-like figure was dressed in studded green leather and huge, dangling earrings. Her short black hair curled tightly against her head. She stuck her arm out and slowed him down as he passed through the room.

"Justin, Mom wouldn't let me have Chazz over tonight. What gives?"

He continued across the room as he answered, "Family business, that's all. You can circulate later." Just graduated from college, Alli worked as an intern at Hardy. He hoped that wasn't what she had worn into the office today. Too tired to spar with Alli right now, he kept his thoughts to himself.

Justin exited the drawing room and turned the corner for the back staircase. There, standing on the bottom stair facing Edward, was his middle sister, Carolyn. It was well known that Edward had a soft spot for the elegant and serene Carolyn, and it was just as well known that the feelings were not returned. It looked like she was cornered. Justin decided he'd rescue her.

"Hi, Carolyn. Good to see you, Edward." Justin saw the relief in her eyes when he leaned over and gave her a kiss. Edward nodded his greeting.

"I was on my way upstairs when I ran into Edward. I'm sure you two have things to discuss." With that, Carolyn turned and quickly maneuvered the steps up to the second floor, her shoulder-length dark brown hair bobbing as she moved. Both men watched as she slipped from sight.

"I dropped by to have you look over some papers," explained Edward. "Are you going to tell them about the new speaker on the agenda?" He took a sip from the drink he held in his hand.

"That's right." Justin reached for the banister. "Listen, I've got to get upstairs and clean up for dinner. I'll see you shortly."

"I'll just wait here for Carolyn to come back down."

Justin smiled and bounded up the stairs, two at a time.

Carolyn was waiting for him in the upstairs corridor. "You have great timing." She took his briefcase and hooked her arm through his.

Justin pulled off his loosened tie as they walked down the hall to his suite. "Why don't you put him out of his misery? He's disgusting when you're around."

"You know I've tried. I think he does it out of habit."

Justin glanced at Carolyn with a bewildered smile and raised eyebrows. Like himself, she was tall, an obvious contrast to the other petite women of the family. A few years his junior, she was a beautiful woman who should have had lots of beaux, but she chose to throw herself into her career. They were the only two Hardy siblings who had carved their own way into the business world. It had been a point of contention with their father.

Justin entered his sitting room and tossed his coat, along with the discarded tie, across the sofa. The masculine room was paneled in rich oak, and dressed with burgundy leather furniture. A relief of alabaster rosettes worked their way down the side of the fireplace, adding a touch of warmth. He walked through to the bedroom and headed for the adjoining bathroom.

Carolyn set the briefcase on the floor near the desk and curled into the plush chair near the window, ignoring the silk of her pants suit. She called out to Justin, "Why did you want us here tonight when there's a board meeting coming up?"

"You remember the woman who wrote those letters claiming part of the business stock and ownership of some paintings?" When Carolyn answered affirmatively, he continued. "I've invited her to speak to the board."

"We're going to meet her?" Carolyn asked in disbelief. She left the chair for the bedroom and leaned against the wall near the bathroom. "Why?"

Justin's voice came through the door. "To head off the damage she could cause us in the newspaper."

"Have you met her?" Carolyn asked.

"No, but she sounds tenacious."

Carolyn crossed her arms. "I know things are shaky at the office. Can she really cause serious damage?"

"We'd go into a tailspin if we lost assets and half of our stock. And, with all the takeover rumors, we'd have to go public with the company."

"Are you sure handling this mess was worth leaving your investment business, leasing your New York apartment, and moving back here?" When he didn't respond, she said, "You aren't still trying to prove a point, are you? That you could succeed without Dad's help? You've done that already, Justin, and Dad realized it before he died. Why do you think he chose you to run things?"

Justin came through the bathroom door, his muscular chest bare. "Don't worry about me. When I accepted the presidency, I accepted the problems, too. And, it's not so bad at home with Mom and Alli. This house is big enough to get lost in." He stepped into the walk-in closet. "Enough about me and business. How's the family engineer doing these days? Your hours are worse than mine."

"I know," Carolyn lamented. She folded her arms and walked back into the sitting room. "How does Stephanie manage a new magazine at the office, a husband, and two kids?" Stephanie Hardy Rogers was the oldest of the Hardy siblings. "It helps that I don't have a personal life."

"You're not alone," he called out. "I'm hanging loose, too, or at least until I gain control of things at the office."

"So, you and Linda had a falling out?"

Justin walked back into the sitting room, buttoning his clean shirt, and noticed Carolyn's raised brows. He knew his sister and gave a cautious answer. "Let's just say we've agreed to see each other only for business."

"We? I think not."

"Carolyn, don't start," he warned.

She ignored him. "First, she won't agree because that kills her chances to get you to marry her, and you obviously aren't thinking that way, not unless you want to give Mom a heart attack. Second—"

"Who said anything about marriage? You're getting to be as bad as the rest of the family," Justin complained while he tucked in his shirt.

"Second," an unruffled Carolyn continued, "sex is what you two are about. She exudes it." She raised gleeful eyes to Justin. "Tell me, can she do anything besides swing those hips when she walks?"

Justin was about to comment, but Carolyn's words brought forth the delightful image and feel of the alluring hips he had held, then watched sway away from him at the elevator last night. *Where did that vision come from?*

"Find me a woman who all of you approve of, and who I want in my bed, and I'll show you the woman I won't let get away." Satisfied with his response, he returned to the bedroom to brush his hair.

She laughed and followed him. "Don't be so cynical. The problem is, you avoid the right women, and since you're not involved, I want you to meet Marilyn—"

Justin laid his finger to Carolyn's lips. "I don't want to hear any more about Linda, blind dates, or marriage, okay?" He set the brush on the dresser. "Let's go eat." With his arm around her shoulders, the two walked from the room.

"I think Edward is waiting downstairs." He managed to keep a straight face.

As it turned out, Edward was still there, to Carolyn's chagrin and Justin's revengeful delight.

Davina woke up with a start. Her dream of being arrested at the board meeting and thrown into jail had been decidedly realistic—

right down to the strip search done by the stranger at the elevator. She sat up with her head in her hands.

"Come on, get a grip," she said out loud.

Davina padded across the dark room to her bathroom and splashed cold water on her face. The nightmare had already begun to ebb away. She draped a hand towel over her face and returned to bed.

A glance at the dial on her clock showed it was almost five in the morning. Disgusted, she fell backward onto the bed. She was definitely a night person, which meant mornings could be straight out of hell. Her passion had always been art—painting and sculpting. Her favorite medium was oil-based paint, and her current fascination was the human nude form. So, when sleep eluded her, she'd retreat to her crowded workshop filled with art paraphernalia, located in what used to be the second bedroom.

Fully awake now, she gave up on sleep, particularly since the board meeting later today played heavy on her mind. David was out of town on business for at least a week, so Natalie had agreed to lend herself as support.

Davina left the hopelessly twisted covers of the bed and walked down the short hallway to her workshop. Old paint shirts dangled from hooks just inside its doorway. She slipped one over her T-shirt before she treaded lightly into the small, conveniently cluttered room and switched on lights. Canvases in varying stages of completion, along with frames and sculpting forms, were stacked along the walls.

She moved in front of the standing easel where a work in progress rested on its ledge. Next to it stood a table filled with tubes of paint, stands of brushes, a palette with residue of past projects, and several jars of mineral spirits. She climbed onto the stool and contemplated the canvas—the beginnings of a portrait of her father as a young man. Underpainted in a monochrome, it was a composite of a few photographs she had unearthed. Davina methodically squeezed slivers of paint from four tubes onto the palette.

Davina and her brother had recently found the photos. She had even fewer pictures of her mother, but vaguely remembered the beautiful lady with the equally beautiful voice. Davina frowned and forbade her thoughts to drift to the dark, easy places.

She picked up a paint rag in one hand, swirled the sable fan brush into the umber paint with the other, and began to work the shadows into the painting. She fought the current of memories, but knew the lure would be strong; and as before, she was charmed into their misty trap. Davina allowed the waves of bittersweet memories to wash over her as the paint-laden brush glided across the canvas.

"Stop chewing your lip and relax," warned Natalie. "You're making me nervous." She sat across from Davina in the reception area of Hardy Enterprises.

Davina waved Natalie off. "Why don't they hurry up? I'm ready to get this over with." She sat on the edge of the stiff chair and felt she was about to be thrown to the proverbial lions. Only divine intervention could save her now. She had been here for almost an hour; Natalie had only just arrived, and they still had thirty minutes before she would address the board.

The receptionist, a rather staid woman with a formal manner, made her way over to them. She had waited patiently for Natalie's appearance.

"These are your visitor badges. I've let Mr. Hardy's assistant know you're here." She handed each of them a small clip badge with the Hardy logo affixed on one side and a magnetic strip on the other. The word VISITOR was in bold red lettering across the logo.

Davina avoided recognition by averting her face. She studied the woman's sensible heels while she listened to her speech on badge etiquette. So intent was the woman's recitation, she failed to see Natalie's eyes roll in merriment.

She droned on. "The board meeting is held in the executive conference room on the gallery level located on the third floor. If you'd like, you can now go up. Mr. Hardy's assistant will be waiting." Her duty completed, she returned to her desk while Davina and Natalie clipped on the badges.

Natalie nudged Davina and whispered, "I see why it was a piece of cake."

Davina smiled back. "Let's go."

They entered an empty elevator in the lobby. The inside of the doors were mirrored and Natalie adjusted the colorful scarf slanted across her black suit.

"Maybe I should have worn a dark suit," Davina said in a worried voice. She looked at her navy ribbed sweater under the white, oversized linen jacket. Her long and lean midcalf skirt was completed by simple pumps and natural hose. She wore very little makeup on any occasion, and today was no different. "I should have gone for a power look, you think?" Davina's mirror image was classic, not what she wanted when she met the devil known as Hardy Enterprises.

"What you're wearing is fine. Stop worrying."

"You're right." She ran her fingers through her tangled curls, held in place by a silken headband. "I've never been to a board meeting. What do I know about what to wear? For once, I want to make those attorneys squirm in their seats."

"That's the attitude. Stick to the plan, appeal to the family members and then, like David said, get out of their building."

The elevator bell announced their arrival on the third floor.

"We're here." Davina squared her shoulders and stepped off the elevator into the lobby. There was a surreal familiarity to the place. She fought the dread that built in her bones and walked in the direction when she knew the office was located. The corridor boasted additional illumination from a skylight and now seemed much larger. Had she imagined the fear that had crawled into her spine that night? Was the stranger as remarkable as she remembered, or had that been imagined as well?

"Davina, do you hear me? The woman on the other end is signaling us."

The words pulled Davina from her cold reverie and she looked at her friend's quizzical expression before she turned to the direction indicated. Indeed, an older woman was motioning them to come to the other end of the hall. Exchanging glances, they went to her.

The woman gave them a piercing gaze. "Which of you is Miss Spenser?" Her tone was imperious. Although no more than five-three in her high heels, her authority was a palpable presence.

"Not me. You want her." Natalie pointed to Davina.

"I'm Davina Spenser."

The woman's heavy stare rested on Davina. Perplexed, Davina

quickly dropped her proffered hand when the woman turned abruptly and opened a door that led into a business office.

"My name is Nora Watts," she finally said. "I'm Mr. Hardy's assistant. You won't be allowed in the boardroom until the closed session starts. Follow me to the anteroom where you can be comfortable while you wait."

"I'll bet," whispered Natalie as they followed the assistant. With a look Davina warned her to behave.

After a momentary pause in front of a set of massive mahogany doors, the small woman threw them open and proceeded inside.

Davina's first impression was that she had entered a large, comfortable living room. The well-appointed room boasted sofas, chairs, love seats, and appropriate tables and lamps where necessary. The walls were hung with paintings, and sculptures were set about the room. A large tapestry covered a part of the far wall. The live flower arrangements on the tables emitted a pleasant fragrance. A tall, scrolled mahogany bookcase displayed a collection of books, some of the volumes beautifully bound. Davina could only describe her surroundings as exquisite.

At the opposite end of the room stood another set of wood doors, with the words BOARDROOM etched in gold and prominently displayed on them. On either side of the doors, a slim column of glass allowed a view into the room.

"The bar contains refreshments." The woman's voice cut into their perusal. "I'll return shortly and escort you into the meeting." She turned to leave the room, but made an abrupt stop, then faced them again. "Oh, I should tell you only the invited speaker is allowed inside unless, of course, you're legal counsel, Miss . . ." she looked at Natalie.

"Natalie Goodman, ma'am," Natalie quickly spoke up. "And, no, I'm not."

"In that case, Miss Goodman, you'll wait in here until Miss Spenser returns. She backed out of the room and pulled the double doors closed.

"When did you become Miss Manners?" Davina inquired sarcastically. She walked around the impressive room.

"What can I say? She reminds me of my fourth-grade teacher." Natalie performed a slow pirouette. "Is this place fabulous, or what?"

Davina wandered over to the doors that led to the boardroom. She peeked through the glass and into a big room with a huge, elongated, oval-shaped table in the center. Tall-backed black leather chairs were pulled up to it. She could see that some of the chairs were occupied, and the table's short end faced a slightly raised podium with a speaker's mount. Because others in the room milled about, she presumed they were at a break in the proceedings. *Waiting for me.*

"I'm going to have a soda. Do you want something before you go in?" Davina heard Natalie ask. "I'll get it."

"Sure, mineral water, club soda, or something like that, please," she replied.

The podium was now occupied by two people who stood with their heads bent as they read from something. Davina recognized the woman as Miss Watts. The other was a man, and incredibly, something about his stance reminded her of . . .

"Here's a club soda with a twist of lime." Natalie handed the drink to Davina. "Part-time employment in this room might not be too bad," she laughed.

"Only you could find humor at a time like this."

Davina took a swallow of the soda and looked out to the podium again. Miss Watts was gone and the man faced Davina as he buttoned the coat of his dark business suit, his head still down. Her heart quickened. The cup stopped near her mouth as she stared at the man. Something about him was disturbingly familiar. He made a motion to someone across the room, and raised his head. That's when Davina saw a full view of his face, his smile wickedly broad.

He was the stranger at the elevator!

The cup slipped from her nerveless fingers and softly thudded across the floor; its contents splashed chaotically across her skirt and legs, and the Aubusson rug.

"Davina, are you okay? You look like you've seen a ghost." Natalie's fist was filled with paper towels retrieved from the bar.

"I'm fine, really." She hazarded another look to make sure she was not mistaken. No mistake, it was him—but what was he doing here? Was he somehow associated with Hardy Enterprises? Good Lord, she had practically handed him the paintings that night. Her head began to spin with possibilities. She took some of the paper towels from Natalie and helped to clean up the spill.

"Good grief, your skirt is wet."

"It'll be okay." Davina tried to hold in her panic. In her best nonchalant voice, she said, "Look through the window and tell me if you've ever seen the guy on the podium before."

Curious, Natalie lay the towels down and peered into the boardroom. "You mean the fine brother in the dark suit?"

"Yes. Have you seen him before?" It was becoming harder to hold in her panic. She anxiously blotted the soda from her hosiery.

At that moment, the doors behind them opened and Miss Watts came in. "The board is ready for you. We can enter through the doors near you." She walked toward them as Natalie snatched paper towels from the floor.

"Excuse me, ma'am," Natalie blurted, "but, who is that man on the podium?"

Davina cringed at the question, yet was thankful that it had been asked.

Miss Watts opened the door to the boardroom with one hand and motioned for Davina to follow her with the other. "That's Justin Hardy, of course, president of Hardy Enterprises." She raised an eyebrow as though affronted by their ignorance, then left them rooted in their spots. The door closed behind her.

Davina watched Natalie fall back onto a sofa in a fit of laughter.

"This is royal, Davina. You avoid good-looking men like a plague and this one turns out to be your Justin Hardy."

That was the least of her concerns. As she gave in to her panic, Davina's ears rang and her feet wouldn't move her forward. At once, it became clear to her why one should always be careful of what one wishes for.

Justin was seated at the table and ready for the closed session. The woman guest was a puzzle he wanted solved as soon as possible. As expected, her brother didn't show, and she didn't bring a lawyer. He decided he would require her to speak from the podium rather than allow her the comfort of a seat at the table. That way, she wouldn't have a chance to relax and consider her words. Always use whatever advantage is handed you. That's the way of business.

He saw Nora come in and move to the visitor seats near the far wall, away from the conference table. It was customary to seat guests in that area until they were formally introduced to the board. He turned to get a glimpse of the speaker, only to have his shoulder tapped by Marc Randall.

"Justin, I'm going to table discussions of department reports. With the revisions expected on the P & L's, the reports will change," he explained.

"That's fine. When the closed session is over, make the motion before the board with my approval." He leaned back in the chair, his mood relaxed.

Marc left and Justin, again, directed his gaze to the visitor seats. The person he sought turned, then raised her head.

Justin's eyes met Davina's.

He immediately remembered her.

"What in the world . . . ?" he exclaimed, and slowly slid forward in his chair. What was she doing at this meeting? Surely, she was an employee who attended the earlier information session. At least now he knew she worked for his company. He relaxed again. This time he wouldn't let her run away. He had admired her spunk the other night, and she had definitely peaked his interest with her disinterest. And yes, she was still the beauty that he remembered, but what was different? Her expression said she was scared to death.

Something was wrong. The closed meeting would start in a few minutes, and everyone should have been cleared out by now. He quickly scanned the room. The board members were returning to their seats. He looked at the woman again. This time, she didn't meet his stare head on, but turned away.

Nora took her customary seat near Justin. "All right, boss," she said. "Everything is ready." Justin disliked being called that, but she did it occasionally because she could get away with it.

He was puzzled. "If the meeting is about to start, why is that woman still over there?"

"I tell you, no one knows a thing around here. That's our next speaker,'' she announced with ill-disguised impatience, ''the infamous Davina Spenser.''

CHAPTER FOUR

When Boy Meets Girl

Davina looked warily toward the table where Justin Hardy's big body leaned forward. He stared at her and she defiantly lifted her chin as she met his gaze. It wasn't difficult to figure out his curiosity—he remembered her from the other night.

She broke off the stare to look around the spacious room where people milled about. One tall, attractive woman separated from a group and crossed the room to an antique sideboard where she joined an older woman.

The walls supported art pieces backlit for optimum presentation; some were by artists Davina quickly recognized. There were no windows. The recessed ceiling lamps allowed soft lighting to fall on the opulent leather chairs that surrounded the oval-shaped table. Each corner of the room held a stone pedestal adorned with a huge flower spray. It all suggested a deliberately sedate atmosphere. As Davina scanned the room, she received both curious and cursory glances. Her eyes lit upon the two women again, and she openly returned their inspection.

''We meet again.''

The deep-timbred voice was unexpected and Davina turned toward it. Justin's figure towered over her, and she strained her neck to look up at him. Her eyes roamed his lean face. Yes, he was just as she remembered.

''It's you.'' The moment the awkward words were out, Davina regretted them.

"So, you do remember? I seem to disappoint you each time we meet." He absently stroked his chin while his eyes pierced through her composure.

Davina noticed his hand and his well-kept nails. A gold wrist chain fell against his starched white cuff and sparkled under a stream of pale light from overhead.

"You didn't tell me your name the other night." He offered his hand to her in a greeting. "Davina Spenser, right?"

She didn't realize she held her breath, and it expelled in a rush as she rose to her feet to give him her hand.

"Yes. Thank you for the invitation." His smooth, cool hand grasped hers firmly. His thumb slid gently down the slopes of her fingers, and across her mother's engagement ring, as he slowly released her. She was uncomfortably warm and fought the urge to move away.

"Don't thank me yet. You're only here so we can find out what it is you want from us and why." He spoke with cool authority.

His challenging remark reminded Davina of the reason she was here and what she had to protect. "I believe I made that perfectly clear in my letters. You did read them, didn't you?" His gaze didn't waver, and disturbed her in every way. Again, she warmed under the intense scrutiny of his eyes—eyes so dark they appeared black.

"Do you want to tell me what you were doing in my building the other night?" He quirked his eyebrow questioningly. "Maybe I should guess. Which is it?" When Davina didn't respond, he thrust his hands into the trouser pockets of his dark blue suit, his legs apart in a masculine show of intimidation.

Asked the very question she had no intention of ever answering caused a surge of apprehension to gnaw at her confidence. She'd change the subject. "It's obvious that neither of us is what the other expected."

"Oh? Were you gaining some advantage playing coy at the elevator?"

Davina bristled at the idea. "I didn't know who you were any more than you knew me, or so you say. Anyway, you were the one flirting."

This time, he was indignant, and his tone wasn't apologetic. "I was only being courteous to a woman I had every reason to believe worked in my office."

"Do you normally grab women that work for you?"

He sighed. "Next time, I'll let you fall. Of course, I don't expect our paths to cross again, unless you're going to make a habit of visiting here after hours."

She had to hand it to him, he was quick; but Davina would not be coerced to reveal more than she meant to. "Yours isn't the only business located here."

"A good seventy-five percent of the building is ours."

Frustrated by his persistence, she moistened her dry lips and, shocked, watched his eyes boldly follow her motion. Her awareness of him only intensified and was accompanied by a tingling in the pit of her stomach. She pursed her lips.

"Let's see," he continued. "I believe the flower shop was closed, and besides Hardy's old paintings, are you interested in restored books?"

At the mention of old paintings, her eyes guiltily jerked to his. "Restored books?" she repeated.

"The other business on this floor. If you weren't there, my original question stands. What were you doing on my floor?"

Davina was used to speaking frankly, which did not translate well to avoiding his questions; but, neither did she like being put on the defensive. "I didn't expect to be cross-examined so soon, Mr. Hardy."

"Oh, but you should have." He folded his arms across his chest and slowly studied her face. "You've made accusations and claims against us. You're only here because you threatened not to go away quietly." He paused. "And, you're right. You're not what I expected."

Davina barely heard his last comment. She was too busy looking past his shoulder to another dark-suited man who made his way over to them. Justin turned in the direction she looked and acknowledged Marc's presence with an introduction.

"It's good to meet you." Marc smiled and reached to shake her hand.

Davina responded with a polite nod.

"She's not at all what we thought, huh?" he suggested to Justin, as he squeezed her hand. "What you say ought to be interesting, Miss Spenser."

She saw the eagerness in his eyes, and without realizing it, compared the two men. He was not quite as tall as Justin, and his soft, light brown eyes gave him an open, friendly appearance, unlike Justin's more edgy persona. For the first time since arriving here, she felt at ease, and smiled broadly. She was unaware of the captivating picture she made when she smiled.

A brief silence followed before Justin cleared his throat and Marc, belatedly, released Davina's hand. Embarrassed, Davina turned to retrieve her purse from the adjacent chair.

"We're on schedule," Marc said. "Are you ready to start?" His eyes followed Davina's bent figure.

Marc's interest was not lost on Justin, who frowned. "We'll be along shortly. Give me a minute, okay?"

"Sure." Marc gave Davina, who now stood with her purse, a parting smile.

"I see you're still the charmer," Justin said as Marc walked away.

Davina had grown tired of his sarcasm, and recalled Marc's earlier comments. "What did you expect me to be, Mr. Hardy? I don't believe you know a thing about me, least of all my charms."

"I only hope you brought evidence to back up your claims." His mouth twisted wryly. "Honoring Marc with your smile won't get you very far."

Her eyebrows shot up in surprise. What was his problem? "I was pleasant to a friendly person. Unlike you, Mr. Randall hasn't attacked me with questions at every turn."

"You're still not going to answer me about the other night, are you?"

"That has nothing to do with why I'm here today," she said defiantly.

They sized each other up as both recognized the other's obstinacy.

"Your board members are staring," she announced pleasantly.

Justin turned and looked across the quiet room. The board members all silently watched. His eyes narrowed at Davina's tight smile.

"Fine. We can agree to disagree." He turned on his heels and started for the podium.

Not sure whether to follow him or wait to be called, Davina remained near her chair, thoroughly ticked off at his insufferable attitude.

When Justin reached the podium, he stopped and turned back to

Davina, as though surprised she was not behind him. He motioned with his hand for her to follow. "Well, come on."

That he made her appear inept brought Davina's indignation to full bloom. She salvaged her confidence and made her way purposefully across the room, convinced more than ever of both his arrogance and the fact that he wielded it like a broadsword. How long could she put off the truth about her presence in the building? Justin Hardy was a formidable challenge, and she hated to think David was right about him after all.

Justin watched as Davina shifted uncomfortably. She had started with a statement about her letters and now answered questions from the board. He knew the proceedings required his full attention. But instead, he absently scribbled on the pad before him, irritated by her earlier behavior and the fact that his thoughts, and eyes, were drawn to her. Her crisp voice carried throughout the room, but he also noted how easily she resorted to frowning. What was she hiding?

She wanted something from Hardy in return for her silence with the media. Money? What other reason did she have for the accusations? She should have been grateful for the chance to speak today. Yet, she had acted as if it were her right. Hell, she wouldn't even answer his questions about the other night.

Justin continued his leisurely observation. She kept her curly hair under control with a silken band. The thick, dark brown corkscrews played touch with her shoulders as she moved her head. A single lock had escaped the band and fell to the side of her face, and he idly wondered what it felt like. She stepped to the side of the lectern and he could see the sweater beneath her open jacket hug her breasts, flattering their fullness. It took a moment for Justin to drag his eyes away, but they were quickly drawn to her legs, long and lithe like a dancer's. His eyes followed slim ankles and calves that disappeared beyond her long hem. She had managed to cover every lovely curve he knew was there.

What was wrong with him? He dropped the gold-ribbed pen onto the pad and turned his head to break the spell.

Carolyn Hardy was asking a question as she leaned forward. "Wouldn't there be some record of this agreement?"

Elizabeth Hardy added, "If there was a record, we'd have found it a long time ago. Surely you have something from your father?" A murmur of agreement swept the table.

Davina had been introduced to the board's members at the start of the meeting, and she remembered the Hardy family. She looked, first, at the woman with the soft eyes who so much resembled her brother, and then their mother, a small woman with a confident presence. "I'm not sure it wasn't an oral agreement. It was years ago and may have been sealed by a simple handshake—"

"You expect us to give up half of the company's control on your ridiculous notion of a conversation that occurred over three decades ago?" Justin asked.

"I don't expect anything that's not rightfully my father's. And, if you'd let me finish," she caught her breath over her pounding heart, "I would ask your board to help me search for the truth. That's all I want." She spat the words at Justin.

"What about the property we're supposed to have?" Marc asked. "We've diversified since then: publishing, fine arts, and presentation. Art shows are part of our activity, but our collections are accounted for."

"Given the time span that's covered, there could be works that have been forgotten. If there's no immediate recollection, I'm hoping my father's property will show up in your storage records.

"I'm sorry, but it's preposterous to think we don't have documentation," Ray said as he shifted in his chair.

Justin had not heard anything new and began to tire of her speculations. He decided to conclude this. "We're not in the fifties, Miss Spenser, and this is a business. We honor tangible contracts and agreements, not daughters with hopeful stories."

Davina stiffened at his condescension. "This is no story." She gripped the edges of the lectern and looked hard at Justin. "I would think you'd want to know if you"—she tried to think of a nice word—"inadvertently kept property that didn't belong to you, or held property in trust for someone else."

Alli Hardy had been a quiet observer up to this point. "What you're saying is we have paintings that belong to your father? And not only that, my father cheated yours out of a partnership interest? That's pretty heavy stuff," she said bluntly.

Justin sighed as he looked down the table at Alli, dressed more conservatively than usual, but in purple all the same.

Carolyn took up the argument. "Alli is right. You make a strong accusation. Do you realize what we have at stake if we agree with your take on things, or allow you to dictate to us with threats?"

Jamal King, the state legislator, spoke up. "This company serves the Atlanta community well. Their reputation is spotless." The others agreed.

Davina looked at the stern faces, one by one, but scrupulously avoided Justin's dark look. "I don't want your business. I just want to regain my father's legacy. You have the power to help me do that if you open your archived records so I can research his past connection with the company and your late president."

"Legacy?" Justin's voice thundered. "We have never done business with James Spenser, your father. And, there is no knowledge of a partnership forged with him, oral or recorded. That's our bottom line."

"Are you afraid to consider the possibility?" Davina's voice baited him. "Do you think I'll unearth something that could prove it?"

Justin folded his arms across his chest as he leaned back in the chair. "Oh, no, nothing like that. I'm afraid you're on a fishing expedition with a hidden agenda. For the life of me, I can't remember when I heard a more harebrained reason to get into private records and inventory."

Many of the members chuckled. Even stonefaced Douglas Bradley gave a resigned grin. Only Elizabeth Hardy's face reflected concern over the effect the laughter would have on their speaker. Justin saw the imperceptible shake of his mother's head when she looked at him, and read her look of caution; but he ignored it, compelled to see this through.

The blood pounded in Davina's temples, and her face clearly showed her embarrassment at being the reason for their laughter. She gritted her teeth in humiliation. "It's not a joke. My father may have been a lot of things, but he was an honorable man."

Justin enjoyed putting her on the defensive. "Well then, why don't you tell us about his honor. Maybe he's more deserving of our respect than you are."

"That's it. Enough with your insults." Davina was livid. "My father also said Jacob Hardy was an honorable man. In your case, it skipped a generation."

The board quietly listened to the exchange between their president and the woman. It was not often that Justin got as good as he gave, and in such a public fashion. He was well known for his unique brand of charisma, especially with the opposite sex, but things were different today.

"What you need to do," Justin said as he stood up, "is put forward your best argument right now because your fifteen minutes are up. You haven't given one good reason to extend your time any further."

"I didn't want to tell you about this before I found hard evidence of my father's ownership in Hardy, but . . ." Davina moved from behind the podium. She had little choice left but to share details with them. David would understand her predicament.

"Well?" Justin urged her on.

Davina glared at him before she moved her focus to his mother, and her concerned expression. "The paintings that belonged to my father and used to seal his partnership with Jacob Hardy are the pieces you have by Maceo James."

"What are you talking about?" Justin's voice was filled with disbelief. "His work is strictly collectible status. They're not on the open market and in a gallery. What makes you think we have any of Maceo James's work?"

"Because Maceo James told us."

For a moment, the only sound was the rush of white noise from the intercom. Then, the room filled with the low hum of voices. Justin slowly made his way to Davina. He glanced at Marc and saw his surprise, too.

Elizabeth's voice cut through the room. "Child, are you saying *the* Maceo James knew your father, that you've met him?"

Davina hesitated only a moment. "Yes, we . . . my father . . . knew him."

Confusion lit Marc's eyes, and he said what was on most of their minds. "How can that be? Maceo, the painter, disappeared and was presumed dead long before you were even born. The police tried finding him for years."

"He dropped out of sight over, what, thirty years ago?" Douglas suggested.

"That's right," Justin added. He was at the podium, eye-level with Davina, and stared pointedly at her. "And no one has heard from him. Except, of course, you and your father."

"It's true," Davina said earnestly. She looked from Justin to the audience. "Maceo and my father knew Jacob Hardy well. I just learned the truth myself."

"Then why are you only now coming forward?" Carolyn asked.

"This information started to reveal itself close to two years ago, and then your father died; that's why I've been so persistent. All I'm asking is your help to confirm what I know. I need access to your archives for that."

Justin shook his head. "The fact that your family knew Maceo doesn't prove a connection with Hardy Enterprises. In fact, the police may be more interested in questioning you than us."

Edward Nelson from the legal staff quickly rose from his chair. "Miss, I'm legal counsel for the Hardy family. If necessary, we can keep these claims of yours in the courts for a long time. Unless, of course, what you really want is to be paid to go away."

Davina's eyes narrowed as she remembered the letter from the legal department. Her nose flared wide as she stared at Edward. "You think I want your money, that I would resort to blackmail?"

"You should know I've already advised the family shareholders as well as the rest of the board to ignore your claim if no direct evidence is presented."

He had known her less than twenty-four hours, but Justin knew, instinctively, that Davina was put off by Edward's pompous response. She would be leaving with a loss, and he wondered if they had pushed their win too far. When possible, he had learned, you always leave a graceful out for the opponent.

"You're not interested in the truth. You're afraid you'll lose your money. Well, I believe my father has a clear connection with your company. You see, I'm going to prove Jacob Hardy knew Maceo and my father. I'll also prove that my father's collection of Maceo paintings were left in Jacob Hardy's custody to secure their partnership."

She took in a deep breath. "If I have knowledge of Maceo and where his signed works are, why is it so implausible that I would know about a business deal? So, prove me wrong, Mr. Hardy and Mr. Nelson. Prove you don't have any Maceo collectibles, that Jacob Hardy had no connection to Maceo and my father." She paused before she added, "I don't believe you can."

Davina looked into the angry scowl that was Justin's face. The muscle at his jaw pulsated in a rhythmic throb. She felt a small triumph in the fact that she might have actually gotten under his skin. She raised her brow in a petulant gesture, and said, "You know how to reach me when you're serious about talking."

Davina grabbed up her purse. "Maybe you'll reconsider after you read the details in the newspaper." She quickly stepped down from the podium and briskly headed for the anteroom and Natalie.

No one moved until Alli, fully attentive now, gleefully commented, "This has been one interesting meeting."

Justin strode after Davina's fast departing figure as the room came alive again with the din of conversation.

Marc's eyes followed the twosome in their race to reach the door first. Davina won. In total agreement with Alli, he murmured, "Well, ain't this something."

CHAPTER FIVE

A Clash of Wills and Wants

When Davina burst into the anteroom, Natalie sensed an urgency and threw aside her magazine. "What's wrong?" she asked and scrambled from the couch.

"Let's get out of here," Davina said as she continued across the room.

On the heels of her comments, Justin swept through the door. He caught up with Davina and blocked her exit at the other door.

"Wait a minute . . . what are you doing?" She attempted to move around him.

"We need to clear the air right now. You don't just come here, make these incredible statements, then leave because we won't play your game."

"Hey, what's going on?" Natalie watched as they glared at each other.

Suddenly aware of another presence in the room, Justin turned and looked at Natalie as if she'd grown another head. "Who are you?"

"Natalie Goodman." Her hands were posed on her hips, ready to do battle. "And she can leave if she wants to."

"She's with me," Davina said. "I'm okay, Natalie. I'll explain this later."

"You're not going anywhere until we have a few private words." Justin laid his hand on Davina's upper arm when she tried to shrug away.

"Hey, get your hands off her," Natalie piped in. "Is he trying to force you to stay here?" she queried. "What happened in there?"

Justin stood behind Davina and grasped both of her arms as he gave Natalie a tight smile. "This is business, and no one's being forced. We're just going to talk. Isn't that right, Miss Spenser?" He pressed her to walk with him.

"I'll humor him, Natalie, but only for a minute."

Justin guided her to an unmarked door in the anteroom, and Natalie followed. "I'm right here if you need me."

Davina sparred with Justin as he pushed her into a small office. "You had your chance. I don't want to talk now, and especially not to you."

"Oh, yes, you will, and make no mistake, you'll talk to me."

He stopped suddenly and released her arms. She lost her balance. With a yelp, she fell onto a love seat and sprawled, head first, into its softness. She was left to extricate herself as Justin strode back to the open door.

Nora appeared, with Natalie on her heels, when Justin stopped them.

"I don't want to be disturbed—by anyone," he told Nora, and closed the door. He returned to a sputtering Davina who straightened from the unflattering position

"You need a few lessons on how to treat women." She smoothed her skirt.

Justin stopped in front of her. "I know how to treat a woman. You're just stubborn."

Davina looked up at him, flushed from anger and exertion. "I'm stubborn? You dragged me in here."

"Maybe willful is better. We both know you wouldn't have stayed if I just asked." He watched her brush her hair off her face, the simple gesture both graceful and seductive.

Davina pushed herself off the sofa. "In my opinion, your attitude during the meeting doesn't merit any consideration on my part."

"Your opinion isn't the only one that matters." Justin moved to the desk and sat on its edge. With legs apart and arms folded across his chest, he watched her. More of the dark, silky corkscrews had escaped their band. He frowned at the direction his thoughts kept taking. "Your attitude can put people off."

"You're quick to find fault. So, why did you corner me in here if I'm so bloody unpleasant to be around?"

"What am I going to do with you?" Justin slowly shook his head as he contemplated this bad-tempered, but not wholly unpleasant, woman. "You realize the board will never agree to your demands with this self-righteous attitude. The question is, are you really going to go to the papers and talk against us?"

Davina rested her hands on her hips and began to pace the small room. The guilt over the treachery she had already committed hammered in her head. "All I want to do is look at your records. For heaven's sake, I'll be supervised. What harm can that do?" she reasoned.

"A lot." Justin thought about the takeover rumors and the information leaks that had already scared off investors, and wondered if her sudden appearance had anything to do with those events. "We intend to keep our business records private."

"Aren't you even curious about the truth? it's obvious your attorneys aren't. They accused me of blackmail."

Justin's exasperation soared in his voice. "Edward is thorough. But what did you expect? You accused us of stealing, Davina."

Her heart skipped when she heard him use her name. She darted a glance at him, then matched his tone. "I'm the one telling the truth."

"Let's back up. If you know something about Maceo—"

"And I do."

"If you have information about him, don't you realize going to the press will cause just as much havoc in your life as in ours? They'll have a field day digging into our privacy. And, we'll both lose."

"Then, I guess it'll come down to who has more to lose." Davina inclined her head as she came to a stop in front of him.

"All right, Miss Hardball, we can strike our own deal."

"I told you. I don't want your precious money."

Justin sighed deeply. "You do if you want my paintings and stock. And you're naive if you thought that little speech you gave on honor would do the trick."

"You haven't listened to a word I've said."

"Yes, I have, but every time I think the story is straight, you come up with a new twist and expect me to accept it. We're back to square one."

Davina shook her head in frustration. "I know this sounds strange, but I can't explain it now. I thought I'd be talking with your father. By the time my brother and I figured out who had the paintings and where they were, Jacob Hardy had died. My father told the truth, and if your father were alive, he'd have believed us."

"What is it you can't explain?" Justin's question was met by silence. "I knew my father, too. He never said any of this." He was puzzled by her firm stance. "Okay, tell me about Maceo."

"It didn't matter in the boardroom. Why now?"

"The man was notorious if you believe all the stories circulating about him when he disappeared. Was your father a painter, too? Is that how he knew Maceo? Were our fathers close?"

Davina sighed. "I'll share everything I know if you help me."

Only inches away, he breathed in her fragrance, a dusky, floral scent that assailed his senses. He jerked his head away, not liking the way she affected him. And, he wasn't here to help her. He would play her hand and find out how badly she wanted his help. "Did you ever think there are better ways to bargain?" His eyes drifted from her face to caress her graceful neck, down to the tight bodice that cupped her breasts. "Maybe you're using the wrong thing." He sought her eyes for a reaction.

Davina's shock was registered in the grim line of her mouth and the slant of her eyes. She swiftly raised her hand, and he easily caught it within his before it made contact. She tried to snatch free, but he held her in his grip.

"You'd better grow thicker skin if you plan on making these kinds of demands. You say money isn't your goal, but you're holding out for something." He dropped her hand and walked around the desk. It shouldn't matter, but he was relieved by her outrage at his bogus suggestion. She was still a problem, though.

Davina's anger had left her speechless. The fact that he dared to proposition her spoke volumes, and she was ticked off. Without a glance at him, she reached for her purse and headed for the door. The afternoon was now an official fiasco.

She opened the door to a hovering Natalie. "Let's go," Davina said tersely, and the two retraced their way to the elevator.

Justin, meanwhile, stared at the open door a full minute before he realized what his impromptu test could do. Any hope to control the damage he may have caused would soon be gone, and he dashed into the hallway.

He overtook them at the elevators, and blocked Davina from entering behind Natalie.

"I'm sorry for what happened. I guess I should apologize."

"You guess?" Davina asked, astonished. "Why, you arrogant bastard."

Natalie watched their exchange in silence, looking from one to the other:

"Be that as it may," he continued, "we need to work things out."

Davina gave him an incredulous look. Her teeth set, she yanked the visitor badge from her chest as she ducked around Justin and joined Natalie in the buzzing elevator. She reached over and snatched Natalie's badge, as well.

"Go to hell," she said, and thrust the badges into his broad chest.

It was a given that she received a measure of satisfaction from his look of surprise as he watched her disappear behind the closing doors.

Later that evening, Davina was in her workshop. She worked on various pieces of art propped against the wall of the crowded, brightly lit room. She was comfortably barefoot in a paint splattered smock worn over similarly splattered blue jeans. Natalie had also changed and sipped on a cola as she occupied a worn armchair, the only other available seat in the room.

They had enjoyed dinner after the meeting, with Natalie requiring that she relive the meeting's embarrassment in minute detail. David, still in Chicago on business, had called and was apprised of events, with the notable exception being the offensive suggestion received from Justin. Not expecting to return home for a few more days, he could only impart through the phone his concern over her revelations to Hardy about their link to Maceo.

"It's hard to believe that gorgeous hunk is your Justin Hardy," joked Natalie.

Davina frowned at her. "Stop calling him mine. You saw how arrogant he was. Self-centered, too." She grunted in disdain. "I could've killed him."

"I think you each got under the other's skin." Natalie smiled. "Only you could get a specimen like him to cross your path and find he's your worst enemy."

"He doesn't bother me. Can you believe he thought I'd settle with my body?"

"I don't know. Maybe a test ride wouldn't be so bad." Natalie grinned at Davina's glare. "You may not be in the market, but you're not dead either."

She knew Natalie teased, but she had been uncomfortable with Justin's brusque sexuality. "Help me out here. You're on my side, not his."

"You know I'm kidding. Lighten up." Natalie shifted in the chair. "David is another matter altogether. He wants me to call him tonight."

Davina sighed. "He's going to ask about your take on things. Tell him the truth, but don't tell him what happened later. He'll want to punch Justin out. Men, including my brother, can be so overbearing."

"If you tried, you could have Justin Hardy doing somersaults for you."

"You know I'm not into games. I don't have time for them."

"I know . . . you're too busy wearing your nun's habit. When will you stop thinking every man is like that jackass, Lawrence Parker?"

"And why not. None have proven themselves to be otherwise."

"You won't try to find out. Two years is two years too long to let that louse control your life."

"Don't start on me, girl," she warned Natalie. "I've had enough for one day."

"This has to end. For God's sake, you still have those paintings, or did you forget? If the man gets ticked off with the small stuff, how do you think he'll react if he finds out you took his paintings?"

"I don't intend for him to find out until I get the evidence I need to make him eat his words. And don't worry about the paintings. They're safe."

"In that case, you'd better string him along and stay on his good side."

Their conversation was interrupted by the phone's ring. Natalie answered it. After a moment, she whispered, "It's that agent friend of David's in New York. He says it's urgent."

"What now?" Davina muttered. She wiped her hands and took the phone.

He walked from the outside gloom of the late evening into the bright artificial light of the Marquis Hotel in downtown Atlanta. Bypassing the front desk in the cavernous, open lobby, he made his way directly to the escalator, then the elevator and the agreed upon suite. His knock gained him entry to the low lit, smoky room.

"Glad you could make it at such short notice." The mellifluous accent floated from the shadows near the window. The elegant gentleman there inhaled deeply from his cigarette. "We're concerned with these latest developments." His hand fluttered in the general direction of an empty chair. "Have a seat."

The newest arrival sat down and willed himself to relax with the small group scattered around the room. He thought it best to begin with good news. "You'll be glad to hear everything is on schedule."

"The buyers are getting nervous," the gentleman suggested.

"That's to be expected. There's nothing to worry about, but we're being careful in light of these new events."

"And the girl. Tell me about her. What kind of threat is she?"

He wet his lips and answered with dwindling confidence. "None. She doesn't have anything after all."

"I understand she appeared at the meeting and is quite self-assured." With a flick of his hand, a red arc of cigarette ashes glowed to the floor.

"She won't give us any problems." He wet his lips again and looked to the other silent occupants, expecting to be contradicted at any moment.

"You'd better be right. The syndicate I've lined up doesn't like bad news."

"There's nothing to worry about." He hoped. "I'll keep our regular contact date for the next delivery. Is that okay?"

The gentleman in the shadows nodded. "You keep your end of the bargain and we'll do the rest."

"I intend to."

When the gentleman at the window didn't respond, it was the signal to leave. He quickly stood and exited the room; no pleasantries, no goodbyes. In the safety of the hotel corridor, he wiped his brow with his coat sleeve and, looking over his shoulder, made a hasty retreat to the waiting elevator.

CHAPTER SIX

Suspicious Minds

The silk sheet that covered Justin's nakedness was thrown back as he swung his legs to the side of the king-size bed. He hit the nearby alarm before it sounded its six o'clock wake up for his morning jog. He had endured another restless night, and he knew where to lay the blame. Davina Spenser. He walked to the bathroom, splashed his face, and ten minutes later he was out of the house.

Justin reserved his jogs to map out problems. This morning, he had concentrated only on the run and now braced for the final hill beyond the bend. The sun remained hidden, but his tank top was saturated from exertion, the trickles of sweat cool across his skin.

The run worked him hard, but Davina seeped into his thoughts again. They should meet and work things out. For the first time, he didn't know quite how to approach the problem—she was like no other woman he had met. She tried his patience with her tenacious ideals, yet she intrigued him for the same reason.

She was definitely a contradiction of how he viewed women. Not only did she enjoy provoking him, she disliked his company. Justin had known, since he had moved beyond the gawkiness of puberty, that he was attractive to the opposite sex, but she was impervious to anything he tried. One minute he wanted to wring her neck, the next to stroke it. This conflict threatened his sanity. There was something else that gnawed at the back of his mind. Perched on the edge of his memory, it eluded his grasp.

In the distance, he could see the iron gates of the house, and crossed the street. A number of meetings had been scheduled today. The inventory reports had been delayed, but were expected when he met with Marc. His sister, Stephanie Rogers, had missed the board meeting due to the new company magazine, and would stop by for a briefing. And, he had to discuss the serious information leaks with the department heads.

Like it or not, he had to make the first move to patch things up with Miss Spenser . . . for the company's sake. He loved a challenge, and not given to excuses, it was how he attacked life. She was shaping up to be one hell of a challenge. He wondered if her brother thought differently from her. So far, David Spenser had kept a low profile. Justin pulled air deep into his lungs as he tackled the last stretch before he arrived at the house.

It was during the final hundred yards through the house gates that the previously elusive thought emerged and took shape. Finally, it dawned on him what was so troubling about Davina Spenser. Energized by the revelation, he pushed toward the house. As he rounded the front gardens, the circular driveway came into view, and Linda leaned against her car, waiting for his return. The comfort of a hot shower and solitary thought would not be his reward for rising early.

Davina sat at the worktable in her small, overcrowded cubicle and applied glue to the fabric. The miniature model she worked on for the sales staff was needed by three o'clock, and it was already after eleven. Her shoulders slumped as her thoughts returned to the call she'd received from her agent. Actually, he wasn't her agent. He was David's friend, Martin Yancey, an entertainment lawyer. Martin agreed to review the offers to back her first solo art show, then reduce them to the best ones. She had to make a decision from that short list soon.

There were other decisions to make, too. It had been three days since she'd told Justin Hardy to go to hell. It had also been three days of expecting him to keep his word and show up when she least expected him.

The phone rang and drew her attention. She wedged it between her shoulder and ear and continued to work as she talked.

"Davina Spenser," she said into the mouthpiece.

"Hi." Her brother's voice brimmed with humor. "What kind of sling have you gotten your butt in since we last talked?"

"David," she said delightedly. "When are you coming home?"

"Not for a few more days. We're in the middle of depositions for this case. Anything new from Justin Hardy and his company?"

"Not a thing." She had to concentrate on what she said to her brother, and pushed aside the model as she moved from her chair to the high swivel stool. "I can wait it out and let him contact me first. He'll want to talk."

"How much time before you have to choose from Martin's short list?"

Davina hesitated before answering. "A week or so at the most."

"You aren't scared, are you?"

"No, never." She answered too quickly. "I mean, it's a solo art show, what I've worked for."

"Think of Martin's news as an opportunity dropped in your lap. We can use it now to get what we want. Don't play the ace card just yet."

"Hardy will make a move soon." She hoped, if her bluff worked with Justin.

"What's your impression of Justin Hardy? Don't you think it strange nothing's happened since the board meeting?"

Davina didn't want to answer those questions. "David, I've got to go. I'm in the middle of building a model. Call tomorrow and I'll let you know anything new."

"Vinny . . ."

"I know, stay out of trouble." They said goodbye and she replaced the phone. She squeezed her eyes tight for a moment and leaned against her slant table. This waiting for the other shoe to drop was driving her crazy.

She returned to the glue and model, and knew she'd have to work through lunch. Her coworkers thought her talents were ill-used and wasted by the ad agency. That sentiment hardly mattered when the rent was due; but a real art show could change all that. She felt a moment of exhilaration and just as quickly, butterflies filled her stomach.

When would Justin swagger into her life again? It would mos

likely be only when he wanted to and she least expected him. The possibility of that happening became a warm trail that streaked through her body. Actually, sparring with him hadn't been altogether bad; in fact, it had been invigorating. She frowned. Where had that come from?

Justin leaned back against the soft leather of the wide chair that had belonged to his father for so many years. He had occupied the spacious office for a few months, and little had been done to make it specific to him. Earlier, he had shed his coat and now he talked with Marc from behind the numerous reports that lay stacked on his desk.

"You're serious, aren't you?" Marc asked while he shook his head. He sat in the wing chair across from the desk as he listened to Justin.

"It makes sense in a crazy way, but it would've made one heck of a coincidence. I spoke to Linda about the incomplete talent report she submitted. She was waiting in the drive when I returned from jogging."

"I told you she wouldn't go for the breakup quietly, man. She won't give up."

"I warned her what would happen, and it did. We had a disagreement on business, and she brought it to a personal level."

"So what happened?"

"What do you think? When I told her I wanted to review her entire file on Vinny Richards, she pouted and left in a huff. But she's still the professional and the file was on my desk this morning, including a better quality head shot." Justin pushed away from the desk. "When I saw the photo, I knew I'd guessed right. Vinny Richards and Davina Spenser are one and the same."

"How did that get past Linda?" Marc asked. "You saw the reviews in her report. Vinny Richards is being touted as a 'sensualist,' an up-and-comer."

"That's what they said. You'd never figure it from our meeting." Justin rubbed his chin as he remembered her. "She came off . . . umm, a little on the conservative side."

Marc picked up the folder that contained Linda's report and thumbed through it. "Linda's prospectus for the new show is basically sound, except for the bare bones bio and no photo. The shots of Vinny Richards's work, the expected revenues, and the reviews clinched it for us, remember? They were dynamite. No matter what you think about Miss Spenser, or Richards, or whatever she goes by, she has a fresh eye, especially for the human form.''

''You don't have to defend Linda. I didn't say her talent instincts were dulled, but her habit of telling us only what she wants us to know backfired this time.''

''Jacob did give her a lot of leeway, and things slacked up over the last year.''

''I know, Marc, but we can still regain our footing. Our little painter of sensual nudes is full of surprises and secrets. I rechecked the background report our PI did on Davina Spenser, and there's nothing much there. It's no surprise we got pretty much what we expected. Besides, who suspected she used two names.'' Justin absently drummed his hand on the table as a plan formed in his mind.

''What next?'' Marc asked. He slid the folder back across Justin's desk.

''The woman that's been writing us is a mystery. She's an artist, a very good one, actually, but her claims to the business make no sense.''

''Don't forget she says she has firsthand knowledge of all this from an artist everyone else believes is dead.''

''That adds to the confusion. And why didn't she use her art show as leverage against us to get what she wanted?'' Justin pounded his fist on the desk. ''We're going to find out who she is. I've already put Connie to work on it.'' Conrad Preston was a friend as well as a local PI the company used on an ''as needed'' basis. ''We'll play her game while we figure out what she's up to.''

''Do you want me to handle Connie's investigation?'' Marc offered.

''Thanks, but I want the reports. I'll keep you informed.''

''You're figuring if we back her show, she won't bite the hand that feeds her?''

''I wouldn't be too sure about her bite.'' Justin came around the desk and joined Marc. ''Keep this between us until I get more details from Connie.''

''Sure,'' Marc answered. ''Does Linda know?''

"Only that I'm interested in her entire artist file; and since she wasn't at the board meeting, she doesn't know what Davina Spenser looks like."

"Linda won't like this. I can feel it in my bones." Marc smiled at his friend. "Another thing, do we really need to use our manpower on an inventory check?"

Justin sighed. "Linda is not a concern, and Accounting promised to handle the inventory quickly. It's been years since a complete audit occurred, and it's long overdue. For now, I think I should pay our little thorn in the side a visit."

"She's already told you to go to hell once. Why don't I talk to her."

"No." Justin's response was abrupt. "You have enough to do. I'll do it."

"She's not shy about speaking her mind. She could refuse you again."

"That's because I let her. If I have to wring her pretty little neck, she'll talk to me again and she'll do it over dinner."

"Can I place a bet on that, gentlemen?"

Both men looked up as Stephanie Rogers walked through the door and came up to her brother's chair. A hand rested on her hip while the other held the latest marketing reports for *ethniCulture,* the magazine she ran. Short and petite like her mother and Alli, she was the epitome of business—from her no-nonsense haircut to the cut of her blue suit and pumps. Her eyes, however, carried a gleeful spark.

"If there's a woman involved, I'm betting on Justin." She looked at him. "Lord, brother, when are you going to run into a woman that can tell you 'no'?"

Justin smiled as she bent to give him a sisterly peck on the cheek. She then moved to the other side of his desk and made herself comfortable in his chair.

"Don't despair. I think he's found one." Marc laughed.

"You mean the woman Alli told me about from the board meeting?"

"That's her," Marc said with a broad smile.

"I've got to meet her." She laughed at her brother's expense.

"What's the big deal?" Justin asked innocently. "Everybody ticked her off."

"Stephanie, you should've seen them at the meeting, like oil and water."

"So I heard," she agreed.

"If I didn't know better," Marc said, "I'd think there was already some history between them."

Justin gave his sister a look that she easily interpreted.

"Okay, okay," she said. "I'm not going there this time, but I like the woman's attitude. Demand satisfaction."

At that moment, Nora knocked on the open door and brought in another file folder. "These are the last of the reports Accounting dropped off."

"Finally," Marc said.

Justin accepted the file and immediately began to look over the documents inside as Nora left the room.

"I brought the projections you asked for on *ethniCulture*'s debut. Good specs are coming through," Stephanie said from behind his desk.

Justin, still engrossed in the file, glanced up. "Fine."

"I'm here a little earlier than you planned. Since it's almost lunch, I can come back if you and Marc aren't finished. She got up from his chair.

"No, no." Justin responded absently before looking up from the documents.

"Reading anything interesting you want to share with us?" Marc asked.

Justin closed the file and placed it on his desk next to the other stacks. "I'm sorry. I have to sort through all this before the afternoon staff meeting. Why don't you and Stephanie go on to lunch. You can join me when you get back."

"You aren't going to eat anything?" Stephanie asked.

"Nora will order something from the deli." He returned to his chair behind the desk and tiredly dropped into it.

Marc rose from his seat. "All right. Stephanie, you choose today."

She smiled. "And you can pay since Justin isn't coming."

No sooner had they vacated the office than Nora appeared, as if by magic. "You're not going with them? Do you want me to order in?"

"Ah, Nora, you're a bright spot in my hellish day. Yes, order me something; but before you do, I want you to find Peterson in Accounting and tell him to get in my office fast. I need to talk with him before I see anyone else."

"I'm on it, boss." She quickly left and closed the door after her.

Justin looked at the newest file that lay on his desk. He now understood why it had taken so long for the inventory study to be presented. He leaned back in the big chair and picked up the file. He skimmed the summary notes and came upon the damning words. And again, one name came to mind: Davina Spenser.

Davina was breaking down the display model in the meeting room when she received a page that she had a visitor. After all the hard work and diligence, not only had she ruined her skirt with glue, but she was hungry after missing lunch. Natalie was meeting her for dinner, and an exhausted Davina summoned her good spirits to greet her friend.

She turned into the corridor to her cubicle and stopped short. Her brown eyes widened in surprise when she saw Justin's tall figure at her entrance. He glanced at his watch, and didn't see Davina; but, she saw the covert looks offered him by her coworkers. Ungraciously, she figured the attention would add to his already inflated sense of self. She took an unsteady breath and went to him.

If he was the subject of curiosity, he didn't show it as he stood casually against the wall. He stood there, in a dark business suit with his arms folded, as if it were the most natural thing in the world to wait for her. Davina stubbornly decided he was used to the attention. In her mind, that was probably the greater shame.

She walked up to him. "Are you here for a consult on a project?" Her attempt at nonchalance was made with a straight face.

He unfolded his arms when she approached, and openly studied her. "No." His deep voice resonated as he ignored her sarcasm. "I came to see you."

"Oh." He was really laying it on thick, Davina thought, and fought it for all she was worth. "I hope it's not to offer another one of your sad excuses for an apology," she replied caustically.

"Point, set, and match," he began formally. "I apologize for my, shall we say, inappropriate words the last time we met. They were unwarranted and unnecessary, but said at a time when we were both driven by emotion. Am I forgiven?"

She didn't think it quite had the ring of an apology, and watched him warily.

"We're making a spectacle of ourselves in the hallway," he said in a low voice. "Do you want to continue this inside?" He held his hand toward the door.

"It would have been nice, even considerate, if you had called before showing up." She was not ready to concede her anger from their last meeting.

His face brightened with faint amusement before he launched into an explanation. "I left a message earlier when you were unavailable. I was told you'd be tied up most of the afternoon until now." His voice lowered even more. "So, here I am."

Davina gave up. She was extremely conscious of his virile appeal, and didn't look forward to a talk with him. He seemed to bring out the worst in her, a knee-jerk reaction.

"My office is small, and I've got project materials everywhere, including on my skirt." She looked down at the wide glue stain across her long, wrapped skirt.

"I'm game if you are. I won't take up much of your time, I promise."

She gave him a resigned look before she nodded her agreement.

He stood at the doorway and made a sweeping motion. "You first."

To Davina's chagrin, he didn't remove himself entirely out of the way. She tried to slip by and avoid his touch, but she stumbled over his shoe and fell against him. She grabbed his waist. With little effort, he agilely caught her to his chest. Again, she was in the circle of his arms, and uncomfortably jolted by the contact.

"Haven't we done this before?" She heard the humor in his deep voice. Theirs was an odd dance as they stepped into the cubicle entwined just so.

They looked at each other as they came apart. She pushed her hair back from her flushed face and gave him her back while she regained her composure.

Davina gave the tight space an objective look. It was a work area in the strictest sense of the term: an elevated slant table, boxes of pens in every color, rolls of colored paper and fabric, T squares, and assorted rulers.

"As you can see, seating is at a premium."

She pulled a straight-backed chair, stacked with sample books, away from the worktable. Justin was quiet, but she felt his eyes when she placed the books on an uncluttered corner of the floor. She dusted the chair. "You can sit here."

"It'll do." He cautiously sat down and bent his long legs to conserve space.

Although the small room was cluttered, other things marked it as her personal space. Four bonsai plants were ingeniously fastened to the cubicle wall, a framed photo of Davina and a good-looking, muscular man was set on the table, and a soapstone sculpture of a contorted female figure rested on top of a cabinet. An unusual ink drawing of an ascetic male torso commanded attention on the other side of the cabinet.

While he surveyed the room, Davina pulled herself up and onto her high swivel stool. She carefully crossed her legs and asked, "Now, why are you here?"

Justin returned his attention to Davina. Upon settling in their respective chairs, they realized the seating arrangement was wrong. Justin's chair was lower and allowed his line of vision to traverse directly across Davina's legs. When she saw his eyes stop there, she fidgeted uncomfortably and uncrossed her legs—another mistake, since the motion caused the wraparound skirt's flap to slide down and the entire lengths of her legs were exposed to his attentive eyes.

Mortified, Davina clamped her knees and quickly pulled the flap back across her lap and held it. She imagined Justin's train of thought and felt her face burn.

"Well?" she said, impatient to get past this embarrassment.

"Oh . . . where were we?" He stumbled with the words and reluctantly dragged his eyes from her legs.

"I asked, why are you here?"

"Maybe this isn't a good place to talk after all." He sat forward in the chair and rested his hands on his spread knees. "We need to

work some things out and there's a definite lack of privacy here"—
he darted a look at her legs—"and not a lot of space. Why don't we
talk over dinner?"

"No dinner. That's out of the question." Davina's outward calm
belied her mushrooming inner turmoil.

"This is business."

"I don't care. No." Davina was emphatic. Something happened to
her when he came around. Afraid to name it, she'd definitely avoid
it. "I have plans tonight."

"I'm sure he can do without you for a few hours." He frowned
and gave the framed photo a quick glimpse.

Davina considered correcting his assumption about David's picture,
but decided not to. "Excuse me, but you don't know my plans."

"Right, but I thought you'd want to discuss our mutual business,
and as soon as possible. You're not married to the guy, are you?"

She ignored his question. "I'm surprised your evening isn't taken,
Mr. Hardy. Are you married?" The question was more an afterthought
than to mock his words.

"Only to the business." He sat back in the chair and regarded her
from beneath narrowed brows. "Do you know you have this odd
ability to change a subject while sidestepping the question?"

"I tell her that all the time," Natalie said, entering the doorway.

Justin and Davina abruptly stood from their chairs, as though they'd
been caught guiltily indulging in some secret sin.

"Well, what do we have here?" Natalie had the look of the cat
that ate the canary as she looked between the two, crowded together
in the small space.

"Natalie," a flustered Davina warned. Her friend wore a black
micro-skirt and body-hugging jacket. Today, she eschewed the gel in
her short hair and wore it as a mass of curls.

Natalie took a few steps forward and imperiously offered the back
of her hand to Justin. Not sure if he should kiss it or shake it, he
opted for the latter.

She flagrantly batted her lashes. "What a pleasure to meet you
again; that is, if you remember me from that wild day at your office."

Justin returned a dazzling smile to her and said, "I remember you
quite well. You were one of the few highlights."

"I understand you did a pretty good turn as a highlight yourself," she replied.

Davina rolled her eyes at their outrageous flirting.

Before she could intervene, Natalie turned to her and said, "If you aren't ready to leave for dinner, I can keep myself busy while you talk with Mr. Hardy."

She groaned at his self-satisfied smile as Natalie prattled about their plans.

"Miss Spenser mentioned dinner," Justin said. "I was trying to coerce her into having it with me instead, so we could talk through some things. Business, you know." He arched a brow and looked earnestly at Natalie.

"I told him tonight was out of the question."

"No, you two go ahead," she said to Justin before turning her gaze to Davina. "Girl, we can have dinner anytime, but business is business. I'll call or drop by the apartment later, okay?" Not waiting for an answer, she winked for Davina's benefit before retreating to the doorway. "See ya." And she was gone.

Justin turned to a frowning Davina and said, "Is she always like that . . . a whirlwind?"

"You manipulated her shamelessly."

"I'm not sure who did the manipulating," he said. "But, she obviously didn't mind. Now, about dinner. It's after five already. Do you want to go now or meet later? You can decide the time and place." He stood with his hands in his pockets.

Davina sighed, intent on regaining the upper hand, and gave the name of a small restaurant outside of the business district. "Benny's, at seven thirty."

"Good choice." He started to leave.

"Wait. You know that restaurant?" she asked in surprise.

"Sure. Ben serves some of the best ribs and margaritas in the six-county area. I'll see you there."

Davina watched him step through the doorway, then turn to her. He had a mischievous look on his face as he said, "You weren't trying to manipulate me just then, were you?" He darted out before she could give an acid-tinged retort.

CHAPTER SEVEN

An Uneasy Truce

The once sparkling club soda was flat and sat untouched on the long bar that faced the door. Justin nursed the drink in Benny's, impatient for Davina's arrival. He considered what he'd say during the next hour. He smiled as he remembered telling her, on the night they bumped into each other, that she was something else. She had definitely lived up to that first impression. In the few times they had crossed paths, she had put him through a different hell on each occasion. The questions had multiplied and she seemed a part of every answer.

Nothing about her added up, and everything he knew warned him to stay away. He felt compelled, though, to satisfy his curiosity. She had made her own disinterest in him obvious with her cool demeanor, but something warm was just below the surface. No one could create her art and not have a font of passion to draw from. An image of her long legs, spilled before him, came to mind. The certainty that her body was that cinnamon color all over was met by an exquisite tightening in his loins.

"Is everything okay, Justin?"

Justin looked up from his brooding and saw his apron-clad friend, Ben Parris, the proprietor of Benny's.

Justin stood and met his outstretched hand with a hearty clasp and hug. "It's great seeing you, Ben. You haven't aged a bit." He smiled at the graying beard of this old family friend.

Ben laughed. "Lisa told me you were in here." Lisa was Ben's only child. She and Justin had met through their parents' friendship a number of years before, and dated for a short time. Ben's hopes of having Justin as a son-in-law were dashed when the young people amicably split; but neither family allowed it to change their friendship.

In a more somber voice, Ben added, "I know your dad's death was hard for you, but I hear you've taken over the business. How's your mother doing?"

Justin acknowledged the sympathy with a nod of his head. "Mom is fine." They exchanged family greetings and promised to see each other more often now that Justin was back home.

"What brings you out my way tonight?" Ben asked.

Justin watched as Lisa walked toward them. She was just as lovely as the last time he'd seen her, with dusky skin smooth against high cheekbones. She had always managed the restaurant with her father, and tonight, she acted as hostess. "I have a business dinner, and it was suggested we come here. I agreed."

"The least I can do is offer a bottle of wine on the house. Advertising is great, especially if it's cheap." He laughed before turning to his daughter. "Lisa can take care of it."

"Sure, Dad," Lisa said as she smiled at Justin.

"I've got to get back to the kitchen." Ben offered a fatherly slap across Justin's shoulder. "It's great seeing you, man."

They watched Ben leave. "You don't look any worse for wear," Lisa said.

"If possible, you're even more beautiful than the last time I saw you." He sat down at the bar and regarded her smiling face. "I understand you're married?"

"You weren't asking, so what's a girl to do?" Her symmetrically cut page boy flowed with the casual tilt of her head.

"She waits for the right man to come along. He apparently did."

"Aaron is great. I'd like you to meet him. And what about yourself? You still haven't done anything, huh?"

"Nope," he agreed with a grin.

At that moment, Justin noticed a bright movement beyond Lisa and saw Davina standing in the shadowed foyer, patiently waiting at the hostess station.

Justin's head inclined in Davina's direction. "My dinner guest has arrived."

Lisa followed his nod, then turned back to him. "Business?"

Justin took a sip of the flat drink and grimaced as he set it back down. "Strictly business." He stood and straightened his coat while Lisa walked to Davina.

Lisa led her back to Justin's side. "This way to your table, sir." Lisa's offered smile was not lost on Davina.

"Glad you made it," Justin whispered near Davina's ear.

"I'm surprised you noticed," she whispered back.

They followed Lisa through a maze of intimate tables, some already occupied by diners. She led them to a quiet corner near a large window, then left. Justin was at Davina's side, his hand brushing her back as he held her chair. Her pulse quickened at the unexpected touch, but she managed a quiet "Thank you."

"Do I need to apologize again for something?" he asked as he sat down.

She ignored his question. "So, how do you know about Benny's?"

He leaned back in the comfortable chair. "His business is a landmark in this area. Why wouldn't I know of it?"

"I thought maybe it was a little . . . common for what you're used to." Davina wanted to say he was too cosmopolitan to dine at a neighborhood-based eatery, but she decided to hold her tongue.

His eyes sparked with humor. "Taking a page from your comments, you don't know me well, so don't draw conclusions about my tastes."

Davina flushed when he turned her words on her, and chastised herself. "I deserved that."

"You changed clothes." He clasped his hands on the table, and allowed his eyes to sweep over her. "I like your style."

"This isn't a date, so don't feel compelled to compliment me." Davina found a perverse pleasure in challenging his charm and watched him sit back in his chair, a scowl replacing his smile. In deference to the warm summer evening, she wore a peach-colored silk tunic over matching trousers. Nestled between her breasts was a large gold locket suspended on a heavy, gold link chain. A pair of low, open-toed sandals completed the outfit. Her hair flowed behind a black satin headband.

Neither of them spoke, and they each wondered if anything could be said that wouldn't somehow offend the other. Their perceived differences became a miniature wall across the table. The centerpiece candle on the white linen tablecloth flickered slightly and allowed a dancing shadow to play on the sharp planes of Justin's face and soft curves on Davina's.

Justin sat up in his chair, about to speak, when their attention was drawn to Lisa's return with a bottle of wine and two glasses. While she quietly proceeded through the ceremony of opening the bottle, Davina raised her eyebrows at Justin and silently delivered her message. *What is all this for?* She quickly saw the reply in his eyes: *Don't make a scene.*

Justin approved the wine, and Lisa poured a bit of the claret-colored liquid into each glass as she informed Justin that it was compliments of the house. She placed the cloth-draped bottle in the ice bucket and smiled. "Enjoy." She left them and the bottle chilling.

Davina couldn't contain her impatience any longer. "Wine? On the house? You must have made some impression on her."

Justin laughed. "Are you always this suspicious? Her name is Lisa and her father, Ben Parris, owns the place. They're both family friends."

"So, that's how you knew about Benny's. I should have guessed you'd figure a way to get the upper hand and see his daughter, too."

"There's no chance of that. Lisa is very much a married lady."

"Oh, I doubt that would stop you. You don't believe in marriage, do you?"

"I believe in it very much." His smile reached his eyes. "That's why I'm not married."

He reached for the glass of wine and took a sip. "Come on, try it, okay?"

She did. Why had she agreed to this meeting when he infuriated her so?

"The silence is getting us nowhere," Justin said. "There's no reason we can't be civil. In fact, it's in both our best interests to be reasonable."

"Of course," Davina said, warily. "What do you call reasonable?" She took another small sip of the wine.

Justin watched with interest while she licked the residue from her lips. "Let's start over."

"From when?" She met his eyes across the table.

Justin watched her raise her glass again. "How about the first night we met."

His words caused her to start, and the red liquid gently sloshed in the glass, a small amount finding its way over the side and onto the tablecloth. "Look what I've done," she muttered. She replaced the glass and reached for the napkin.

"Does it bother you that I mentioned that night at the elevator?"

Davina looked up, her guilt razor sharp. "No, and if you're going to badger me the way you did at the meeting . . ."

"Hold on now, we called a truce, remember?" He gave her a smile.

She liked his smile. It softened his angular features, and there was that little thing he did with his brow . . . Wait, what was she doing? She cleared her throat and straightened in her chair. "You're right, Mr. Hardy. A truce."

"Please, call me Justin."

"You can call me Davina."

"That's better . . . Davina. No nickname, just Davina?" he asked. She nodded.

"Things escalated at our meeting," he said. "We were both angry and shocked to learn we had met each other before, I was protecting my company, and you wanted much more than I was able to give at the time. Does that sum it up?"

"Pretty much. But until you seriously consider my claim, any truce will be short-lived." She boldly met Justin's gaze.

"And there's nothing else you want to tell me, no brand new twists to anything you've already said?"

"No."

"I've been thinking about this and I have a tentative proposal for you." He leaned on the small table, his arms resting across the expanse, almost touching Davina's hands. "Promise me there'll be no news stories initiated by you or your brother and I'll approve, at least initially, your research into materials relative to your father's name associated with our business. All this is predicated on a few details being worked out, including your claim about knowledge of Maceo and his involvement with your family."

Davina could hardly believe it. A part of her wanted to know why this complete turnaround had occurred. The other part felt intense relief that she wouldn't have to continue a battle against this man. Her main objective, to establish her father's history with the paintings she took, preferably before they were discovered missing, was still a reality. As a measure of relief flowed through her, her mouth unconsciously curved into a smile.

"I can live with that," she said.

"And I believe this is the first smile you have ever purposely sent my way." He held his wine glass up in a toast. "To more smiles and proposals. Why don't we eat and enjoy dinner? We both have some things to think over. No more business talk, though, until dessert."

She raised her glass to his before taking another sip. "There won't be much to say."

"Sure there is; we'll take turns picking topics."

"All right." She looked at the single-sheet menu in front of her. "Let's start with food. I love salmon. Have you tried his blackened salmon cilantro?"

He grinned, enjoying her enthusiasm. "No, but suddenly I'm hungry. Very hungry."

Justin watched the whipped cream from the chocolate mousse disappear into Davina's mouth. He had already decided her full lips formed a mouth that was just as luscious and provocative as her legs.

"I love whipped cream," she said between swallows.

"I see," Justin observed lazily.

"Aren't you going to try yours?" She eyed the creamy concoction that sat untouched in front of him.

"I'm fine." He reached for the wine bottle to replenish his glass. When he reached to refill hers, she covered it with her hand.

"That's it for me. We have to drive," she said in a mock stern voice.

Justin knew it was time to broach the subject that could destroy their tenuously built trust.

"Davina, we have to talk about you in my building that night."

She paused a moment before she carefully laid the empty spoon beside the dessert plate and looked at Justin with questioning eyes.

He leaned forward in the chair and rested tented fingers on the table. "I received an audit report that inventoried Hardy's assets. Things are going on that prompted its preparation."

His eyes caught and held hers. "Our auditors can't seem to locate certain valuable pieces of art. What makes it interesting is that some of the missing pieces are by Maceo." Justin watched as her eyes blinked.

"Maceo's paintings?" Her quiet question seemed almost a statement.

Justin nodded. "You're the only person that's been interested in his work recently." He watched her chest rise with her deep breaths. "Davina, did your presence that night have anything to do with the missing paintings?"

Her brows rose in shock before she glanced away. Justin wouldn't let up.

"I think it did." He spoke with cool authority.

Davina fiddled with the silverware. "We both know Maceo's paintings are valuable since they're no longer on the market and he disappeared in a cloud of mystery. A lot of people want them. You only said they can't be located." She made a weak smile. "They'll probably show up somewhere on their own."

"You had a large bag that night. It could've held five paintings. Is that what you were holding so tight?" he pressed.

Davina darted a haunted look at him. "I . . . I didn't take your five paintings."

"Then tell me what you were doing there?" His eyes pleaded with hers. "It's too much of a coincidence, and anyone with the facts would say the same thing."

She sat up stiffly in her chair and sputtered, "Was this dinner meeting a ruse to catch me off guard and then accuse me of theft?"

"No. It's to give you a chance to come clean if you're over your head. Talk to me about that night," Justin demanded. "I want to believe you."

Davina stared across the table and shook her head. "I can't talk to you. I almost forgot that we have different goals and you judge easily, even though you reminded me of that error a while ago." She pushed her chair back. "I'm leaving."

He looked at his watch. "It's still early. We have to resolve this."

Davina ignored him and looked around the room. "Where's the waiter when you need one." She reached for her purse on the table's edge.

"Don't do this."

She avoided his eyes. "I have to go."

Justin tossed his napkin onto the table. "Then, we'll both leave." He signaled the waiter who quickly presented the check. From his wallet, Justin unfolded a large bill and placed it on the tray.

When Davina saw the money, she opened her mouth to speak. Justin knew she was about to refuse his payment of her share of the tab.

"Leave it alone, Davina," he warned.

As he walked with her to their parked cars, neither broke the silence that surrounded them. The moonlit night was still clear, but the earlier warm air had become humid and smelled of rain. They came upon her blue Honda.

She stood next to it and fished through her purse for the keys. Justin rested his arm on top of the car and watched her.

"I haven't shared the report with the board. I'll put it off for a few days. After that, I'm honor bound to tell them about the missing paintings, and that includes your unexplained visit in the building. If you return the paintings before then, there won't be a need to divulge anything about you."

Davina remained stubbornly silent in the dim light and tried to insert the door key in the lock. Frustrated, she gave it a shove that missed the slot, and the entire key ring clattered to the asphalt.

"I'll get them," Justin said.

"No, I can do it."

They stooped to the ground simultaneously, and in the close, moonlit space between the parked cars, their knees collided and heads bumped.

"Oh, I'm sorry," Davina apologized and touched her forehead.

"I found them," Justin announced. He rose from the ground with Davina.

Her face tilted to his, the moonlight accentuated in a creamy glow on her face. Davina pushed the loose curls back and held her hand out for her keys. Rather than hand them to her, Justin lightly touched her shoulders and pulled her to him. The unexpected movement caused her to brace her hands against his chest.

"Justin?"

She was drawn closer and panicked. She couldn't stop what was happening.

"No."

He ignored her entreaty and strong arms brought her flush with his body; his hand dropped to her back and massaged away any thought of retreat.

"I've wanted this all day, and so have you," he whispered, and lowered his mouth onto hers.

Warm lips met Davina's in a kiss that assaulted her senses; she was consumed by his mouth and body. His hand glided to the nape of her neck and caressed the sensitive skin there as the other slowly pressed into the small of her back. He conquered her lips, first with small nibbles, then in an erotic foray with his tongue. Davina welcomed him as her arms curled around his neck.

What started off for Justin as a simple kiss to assuage his curiosity had quickly turned into a storm of emotions. The intoxicating weight of her breasts pressed against his chest, the delicate taper of her back, and the delicious taste of her mouth, whipped cream and wine, worked his own senses to a frenzy. But the sweetest discovery of all was that she returned his kiss, and she could never take that back.

A car door slammed in the distance. Davina reacted first and pulled away, but Justin held on to her hand. She laid the other across her mouth, still warm and moist from his kiss. "What was that?" she asked.

Justin's smile teased her. "Has it been that long since you've been kissed? Want to try it again?" He reached for her.

"No, no . . . I'd better be going."

"Are you sure you don't want to stay? We could go back in."

She pulled her hand from his. "It's better that I leave now."

Justin unlocked the car door for her and watched as she got in. "Think about what I said."

Davina nodded before he closed the door.

The car's engine roared to life, and Justin stepped back as Davina pulled out of the parking lot. He walked to his own car and decided he'd call her later to make sure she arrived home safely. Justin couldn't quite understand his emotional pull to Davina. She could hurt his company, had most probably stolen their paintings, yet he felt an empathy for her. It was obvious that things were going on she didn't want to share. And he was going to find out what they were.

Davina swayed against the inside of her apartment door, weak from the tension. Her world was in the process of being turned inside out—what was she going to do? Her head swirled. She had to rethink her plans, maybe her life.

To add to her problems, she had kissed Justin Hardy. Why didn't she pull away? Instead, she had enjoyed it—and worse, he knew it. He didn't know how close to the truth he was when he questioned how long it had been since she'd been kissed. She squeezed her eyes closed and the smell and touch of him crept into her thoughts. She wanted to scream out at her stupidity. But, that was not the answer. Davina opened her eyes to the darkness and swallowed her self-pity. First things first. Put on a pot of water for tea, and then calmly think things through.

Reluctantly, she separated from the door and walked through the dark hallway to the kitchen. She cut the light on and filled the teapot with tap water. After it was placed on the electric stove's eye, she leaned against the doorway and contemplated her next move.

Davina didn't see the moving shadow that lengthened across the floor behind her until it was too late. She turned, and a dark object swung down. Her head exploded with a violent white pain as everything turned black. . . .

CHAPTER EIGHT

A Brush with Fear

Justin entered the foyer at home and met Alli on her way out. Her jewelry jingled as she fished through her purse. He raised his brows at the short dress.

"You owe me, so don't even think about saying anything." Her words were low and rapid-fire as she jerked her thumb toward the interior doorway. "You-know-who has been waiting in the library all evening, and she came close to being put out. I have a life, but Mom had me play hostess." She found her keys and reached for the door handle. "What's with you these days? You can't handle your women." Alli smiled and winked before darting behind the door.

Justin closed his eyes for a moment and rubbed the bridge of his nose before he dealt with Linda. It had never bothered him that his family showed no genuine interest in her, nor she in them. Lately though, that seemed rather pathetic.

He tugged at his tie knot and released the top button on his shirt. He walked through the main salon toward the library. Rubbing his neck, he felt the tension gathered there and thought of Davina's earlier caress. A smile played across his lips. No matter how it ended, the evening had not been a total loss.

Before he could reach the library, Linda appeared at the door. Her red lips, contorted in anger, rivaled her red linen suit.

"Where have you been?" she demanded.

He quietly strode to the doorway, his own anger held in check. Resting his arm against the door frame, he looked down into her face. "Wrong question, Linda. What are you doing here unannounced?"

She abruptly changed her facial expression to one that was more conciliatory, and slowly paraded into the library. "I haven't had a chance to talk with you since you got back from New York." She whirled around dramatically to face him again. "And, you haven't returned my calls."

Justin pushed away from the doorframe and joined her in the library. He made his way to the studded leather sofa in front of the fireplace.

"I believe you know why." He sat on the edge of the sofa and watched her walk over to him. "We've already talked about this, and more than once."

"Just because we talked doesn't mean I agree. Anyway, I'm sure you'll get over it. You're only here as temporary president. I know you. You can't wait to leave and return to the New York life. In the meantime, we can see each other . . . away from prying eyes, if necessary." She sat on the sofa and turned to him. "We can make it work," she suggested.

"No, Linda, it won't."

"Our past means nothing to you? You can just toss me aside without a thought because of business? I don't mean any more to you than that?"

"Stop being melodramatic." Justin stood and walked to the fireplace. He rested his foot on the raised hearth and leaned against the mantel. "Look at me Linda," he commanded. "And be honest. Have I ever implied there was more to our relationship than one that served both our purposes? We enjoyed each other, we had fun together, and we never complicated it with a lot of promises."

"Well, I want more now."

"I don't." He walked toward the door.

"Where are you going?" Linda complained as he left.

"To let you out. After that, I'm going to bed—alone. I'm tired and I have a lot to do tomorrow. I believe you have a report to finalize by then, as well."

She followed him to the door, protesting her treatment all the way. Amid her protests, he managed to avoid her lips, but she did sneak a peck on the side of his twitching jaw.

"Good night, Justin. We aren't over yet. I know you too well."

He watched her get in her car on the far side of the driveway, the reason he didn't see it when he arrived at home. Satisfied she was gone, he closed the door.

In the past, their tiffs resulted in a few days of forced solitude, the obligatory gift from him, and finally, her eager forgiveness. Things would then continue as usual. This time was different, and Justin knew Linda could tell.

Troubled, Justin raked his fingers across his hair and bounded up the foyer staircase, two steps at a time, to the second level corridor that led to the family living suites. He knocked on his mother's sitting room door that stood ajar.

"Mom, do you mind a visitor?"

"Of course not, come in." Elizabeth Hardy was relaxed in a recliner as she read from Terry McMillan's latest book. She was cocooned in a long robe, and a cup of tea rested on a table within her reach.

Justin dropped to the damask-covered sofa and let out a sigh before looking at his mother. "When did things get so complicated?"

Elizabeth closed the book. "Did Alli give you a hard time?"

"Nothing I didn't deserve. I'm sorry Linda showed up and caused problems."

"If Alli and Linda aren't the problem, what is?"

"It's not a what, it's a who. Davina Spenser."

"The young woman at the meeting? Has something else happened? She does speak her mind, and you two sure got the best of each other."

Justin shared the recent reports with his mother. Always supportive, it had been easy to share his thoughts with her through the years.

"Paintings are missing?"

"Five are Maceo originals." He stood up and pressed his hands deep into his pockets. "Something else happened tonight. I had dinner with Davina, and then accused her of taking them." He offered a wry smile to his mother's raised eyebrows.

She watched as he crossed the room. "Is there evidence of that?"

"No, just a hunch. At best, the accusation will keep her from the media and we get the paintings back. At worst, she'll still make good on her threat and talk to them."

"And she would have been hurt uselessly. You think she'll admit to this?"

"I gave her two days to convince me otherwise. Afterward, I share what I know with the board."

"How is she supposed to do that?"

Justin rubbed his chin in thought. "I don't think she can."

"Don't you think you should have gathered more facts before you accused her and gave her an ultimatum?"

"Mom, she has so many question marks associated with her, I don't know where to begin for answers. So, I've started a new investigation into her past. First, I want to know about this connection she supposedly had to Maceo. In fact, you can help with that." He shrugged from his coat.

"How?" Elizabeth asked.

"I want to talk with her brother." He tossed the coat onto the nearby chair, followed by the tie. "Invite them to dinner—tell them you want to share your early memories of Maceo with them."

"If I invite them, it won't be on a pretense. I want to talk with them, too."

"Do you remember Maceo, and what happened?"

Elizabeth relaxed against the chair and sighed. "I know he had a wonderful eye for color and texture, and it showed in his work." She let out a laugh. "Your father told me Maceo was some salesman. He always figured a way to barter because he never had any money. That changed when he was discovered."

"What did the critics say about him?"

"Jacob also said Maceo liked to think his art subjects were born of his soul, so he never used popular ones." She looked at Justin. "I didn't know Maceo as well as your father did, but Jacob knew he was excited about breaking into the big time of galleries, patrons, and money. Any artist wants that for their work."

"Is that when Maceo ran into problems with the police—after he began to receive recognition?"

She nodded. "Yes, he got into trouble all right, but then one day he was gone." She snapped her fingers. "His disappearance made him a legend in the community. No one ever suspected, least of all his friends, that his paintings would become so wildly popular."

"Of all the originals we have at the house, none are Maceos.

They've always been kept in storage at the gallery. Do you know why?''

''I don't know specifics. I do remember your father refusing to let me have one hung at the house. He didn't give a reason, only that he preferred they stay together at the gallery. I figured it was because of some investment strategy.''

''How did Dad get our originals—off the street or from another dealer?''

''I imagine the ones in the storage vaults were acquired either during the time Maceo bartered everything away, or when he disappeared and everything available on the street was bought up,'' Elizabeth answered. Then she paused, before she spoke again. ''Except for that big one.''

''The portrait of Dad?''

''Yes,'' she said. ''I remember that was done by Maceo as a gift for Jacob. I don't know the occasion or reason behind it, but you know as well as I do that it's always been kept in his office.''

''Is it possible Dad got some of his paintings from Davina Spenser's father after all?''

''Anything is possible. But it still remains that none of us ever heard of James Spenser before she brought it up.''

Justin walked to the window and noticed that the promise of rain had been fulfilled. Through the raindrop-dotted glass, he looked down onto the floodlighted garden and pond. Even from the distance of the second floor, he could see the large, colorful koi dart aimlessly in the illuminated shallow water amid the lily pads. He unfastened the buttons at his neck, unconsciously seeking a similar freedom.

''What are you thinking, Justin?'' Elizabeth asked.

''That we need to seriously consider what we plan to do if any of Miss Spenser's claims prove true.''

The first thing Davina saw when she squinted into the bright light was Natalie's African death mask brooch. After the initial shock, she merely closed her eyes against the pounding in her head.

''Davina, thank God you're all right.'' Natalie kneeled on the kitchen floor while her friend's head rested in her lap. ''What happened?''

"Oh, my head . . ." She opened her eyes once more.

"Let's get you up." She helped Davina sit up on the floor.

"I was making tea and . . . I heard or saw something. When I turned, this pain exploded . . ." Davina reached up and gingerly touched her head.

"You were probably hit over the head."

"The person could still be here." She struggled against Natalie to stand.

"Calm down. Whoever it was probably left through the back door. It was open when I came in. How long were you out?"

Davina blinked at her watch. "It's been almost an hour since I got home."

"You need to see a doctor, then we'll call the police." Natalie propped a woozy Davina up with the help of her shoulder.

"No, no. I don't need a doctor; I'll be okay. Just help me get to a chair."

The two maneuvered through the kitchen door and headed for the living room and the sofa. Natalie flicked on the hall light as she came alongside it.

The sight of her ransacked apartment took Davina's breath away. Everything had been moved or knocked over; even the draperies dangled from their rod.

"Oh, my goodness, look at the mess," Davina exclaimed.

"I know, honey, but thank goodness you weren't hurt any worse than a knock on the head. I don't have to tell you things could have been much worse."

Suddenly, Davina's eyes grew wide. "Natalie, the paintings," she wailed.

Despite her throbbing head, she whirled from Natalie's shoulder and loped down the hall to the workshop.

"Oh hell, you kept them here?" Natalie rushed after her.

Davina could smell the familiar waft of paint medium when she reached the workshop. A jug of the noxious liquid had been turned over on the worktable.

Her head continued to pulse as she moved to the far corner of the room, dragging the high stool with her. She quickly climbed onto it and, reaching up, pushed aside an already crooked ceiling panel.

"Be careful, girl." Natalie grasped Davina's legs to give her support.

Davina's hand probed the ceiling, then she pulled herself up enough to peer into the opening. What she didn't see was like a sledgehammer blow to her chest.

"They're gone, Natalie."

"Oh, no," was all Natalie could manage.

"Quick, help me down," Davina demanded.

Using Natalie's shoulder as leverage, she pounced from the stool into the rubble on the floor and headed for her bedroom.

"Now what?" Natalie called to her, right on her heels.

Davina stopped abruptly at the sight before her, and sagged against the doorway as Natalie came in. Drawers were pulled out and clothing dumped onto the floor. Even potted plants lay on their sides with dirt spilling out. She closed off her pain and dashed to the bed where the covers had been stripped away and the mattress was askew, separated from the boxspring.

Davina barked orders to Natalie. "Help me move the mattress."

First, they lugged the mattress across the room, then struggled to turn the boxspring over so that it now rested, upside down, on top of the mattress. But Davina wasn't finished. She ripped open the linen lining stapled to the wood.

"What in the world are you doing?" Natalie asked, as she watched her friend's manic moves.

Davina didn't respond. She reached inside the gauzy lining and, using both hands, pushed the metal fasteners aside that held the springs in place. She felt the sturdy package before she saw it, and sent up a joyous prayer. With one hard pull, she released the last painting from its hiding place, and held it to her chest. Then, she sat amid the clutter and let tears of frustration wash down her face.

The drone of the shower was a faint echo in the living room where Natalie pushed and pulled displaced furniture. Davina was taking a shower while they waited for David to return their phone call. She intended to stay the night since Davina insisted that no authorities be notified. The reality was that two of the paintings were gone. The one left, of Davina's mother, had been returned to its hiding place since chances were slim the assailant would strike twice that night.

The phone rang. "That's David," she said out loud. She scrambled to find the phone, and by the fourth ring, located it under a cushion in the corner.

Breathless, she spoke quickly. "Hello . . . David?"

"No, Justin Hardy. I'd like to speak with Davina Spenser."

She took a deep, rushed breath and stumbled over her words. "She's, um, not available right now."

"Natalie, is that you? Is something wrong?"

"Yes, I mean, no. Oh, man," she mumbled.

"Where's Davina?" he asked, his voice deceptively calm.

"You'll find out anyway," Natalie said. "She was attacked in the apartment."

"What?" His voice boomed through the phone. "Where is she now?"

"She's resting. I'll have her call you later when—" Natalie heard a click on the other end. "Hello? Hello?"

Natalie realized he had hung up and slowly replaced the phone on its cradle. "Davina's gonna kill me," she said, and realized the shower had stopped.

CHAPTER NINE

What a Tangled Web We've Weaved . . .

Davina sat on the edge of the rumpled bed wrapped in a bath towel with her head on her knees. She considered curling up on the mattress in the blessed darkness and closing out the world. Everything had gone wrong; but she wouldn't give in. She slowly raised her head and turned on the bedside lamp. After finding a T-shirt among the contents tossed around the room, she wrapped another towel around her damp hair and began the daunting task of straightening the room.

She returned to the living room and was relieved to find that Natalie had restored a semblance of order there, too. Davina carefully sat on the sofa—too much movement made her head swim. Natalie had been right. She felt better and was thinking more clearly after the shower.

"I made some herb tea, okay?" Natalie called out from the kitchen.

"Great," Davina replied, her thoughts elsewhere.

She had shared the highlights of the dinner discussion with Natalie. But a new slant on the evening was looming in her mind: had Justin used the dinner as a ruse to have her apartment searched for the paintings he accused her of stealing? Davina touched her lips. The memory of his mouth lingered there. She had allowed herself to feel again for that small moment, she had wanted to trust again, to trust him—now she regretted it all.

Natalie interrupted Davina's musings when she came in with a serving tray and set it on the bare coffee table.

"Do you feel any better?" she asked, and peered into Davina's eyes. "You don't look too good." She placed a hand against Davina's forehead. "No fever, but I still think you ought to see a doctor."

"I look like I feel. Lousy. I've got to get those paintings back." She pulled her long, terry robe around her T-shirt and picked up a cup of the hot liquid.

"Davina, you don't think whoever did this will come back, do you?"

"This was no regular burglary. We know what they wanted." She looked at Natalie. "We're lucky you may have scared him before he found the last painting."

"Or harmed you. You have to hide it somewhere else."

"I know." Davina closed her eyes. "Who did this? Who else knew so quickly that I had the paintings—except for Justin Hardy, and he made a lucky guess?"

"I think it's unlikely Justin did it. He'd be the obvious suspect."

"Don't you read mysteries? The obvious person usually did it."

"David will help figure something out. After he blows his top, of course."

"He didn't call yet?" Davina asked.

"No; but, I didn't leave any details at the hotel either, just that he return an important call." She sipped the tea, then looked apologetically to Davina. "You did get another phone call."

Davina furrowed her eyebrows, but before Natalie could explain, the doorbell rang, which was soon followed by a series of impatient knocks.

Startled, the two women sat forward, then looked at each other before they put their cups down. "Who's that?" Davina whispered.

They both moved to either side of the door, as though their proximity would allow them to ascertain an identity. Again, the doorbell rang.

Davina placed her finger against her lips to signal Natalie. She then stared through the security peephole and looked into Justin's unmistakable dark eyes.

She covered her mouth in surprise and turned to Natalie. "It's Justin Hardy," she whispered. "What's he doing here?"

Natalie's mouth formed a circle. "That's who called while you were in the shower." At Davina's narrowed eyes, she explained. "I told him you were attacked after your date, but he hung up before I could tell him to stay away."

"It was dinner, Natalie, a business dinner, not a date," Davina exclaimed. This time, numerous knocks replaced the doorbell. "I don't want him here," she said, her anger rising. "I can't deal with him right now."

"It's too late for that. Find out if he knows anything."

"Knowing him, he won't leave until we let him in. And for heaven's sake, don't say anything about the paintings being stolen . . . again."

"Of course not, I'm not stupid." Natalie was indignant. "I'll disappear and let you handle it. Anyway, since you're dressed for bed, he'll have to leave soon."

Davina looked down at her robe. "I almost forgot. Let's get this over with."

Closing the robe with one hand, she motioned Natalie away from the door. She opened it to Justin's damp figure standing in the light drizzle. Although the door to her apartment had a small portico, it didn't provide total protection from the rain. He wasn't wearing a coat, and his shirt was plastered to his skin. The sight of him, in the flesh, was both disturbing and exciting, and she backed away.

Surprised that Davina answered the door, he entered without preamble. "Are you all right? Natalie told me what happened. Why aren't you in bed?"

Natalie closed the door and Justin followed Davina into the living room. Once there, Davina turned to face him.

"I'm fine now. I got a bump on the head, that's all." She crossed her arms. "You shouldn't have come here, and it would be best if you left." She tilted her head, and the movement made her wince from pain.

Justin saw the wince. "Not yet. You've got a head injury and you're not at the hospital? Have you called the police?"

Both Davina and Natalie answered, "No."

"Why not?" he asked, and looked from one to the other.

Natalie exchanged a glance with Davina and cleared her throat. "I'll go straighten things in the workshop," she said.

When she left, Justin drew a deep breath and openly studied Davina. The skin was puffy under her pink-rimmed eyes. Even so, with her face scrubbed clean and her hair hidden under a towel, she was still a beauty.

He looked around her living room for the first time, and though he admired the array of paintings that filled the pastel walls, he thought they looked slightly disordered. He suspected it had to do with why she was so upset.

"Davina, what happened here tonight?"

A flash of impatience crossed her face. "Are you always so overbearing? Do you know how many questions you've asked since you arrived a few minutes ago?"

At first, Justin was taken aback by her manner. Then, he realized what she'd done and softened his scowl. "As usual, you're changing the subject." He smiled now. "I'm sorry. Natalie wasn't making sense on the phone and I was thinking the worst while I drove here. But, it's good to see you're in fine form."

"How did you know how to get here, anyway?"

"Your letters to my office." His brows arched mischievously. "I have a good memory. If you want me to leave, tell me what happened here.''

"If you must know, a burglar surprised me when I came home. I was hit on the head and later, Natalie found me on the floor." At his questioning look, she added, ''She had promised to come by and used my hidden key to get in.''

He moved to her side in an instinctive gesture of comfort and anxiously placed his hands on her shoulders. "You were injured. Are you sure you're okay?''

"Yes. I do have a bump, but I'll be fine." She backed away from his hands. "Now, you've been told what you wanted to know, and I'd like you to leave."

Justin dropped his hands to his side. "If you won't see a doctor, at least let me examine your head. You may have suffered a concussion, Davina. I've had some experience with these things, you know."

"Are you a doctor now?"

He gave a quiet laugh. "No, but I've played football and coached little league and can handle most injuries. Now, let me see that bump."

Davina hesitated a moment, then reached up one hand and unfurled the towel. Her hair, unfettered by a band, fell down against her neck; some of the still moist ringlets had strayed to her face. She gently parted her hair near the crown.

"Natalie said the skin's not broken."

Justin leaned inward, his body brushing hers, while he carefully probed the area with sure fingers. Feeling through the thick hair, he applied pressure evenly across her head, asking questions and noting when she felt pain.

"You applied an icepack?"

"Of course," Davina replied, noncommittally.

"Good. If your headache has started to subside, that's a good sign. You should make sure someone keeps a watch on you through the night, and does not allow you to sleep more than a few hours at a time, just as a precaution."

"I don't need your help for that. Natalie will be with me."

Justin smiled. "Where's your brother?" He almost added "and that guy in the picture." "Shouldn't he be here?"

"David's out of town, but I'm used to taking care of myself."

"I'll bet you are." Justin took in the fact that she didn't offer an explanation for the other's absence. Her hair slid through his fingers as she stepped from him.

"Do you mind if I borrow a towel to dry off?" Justin wasn't ready to leave, and it was evident she wasn't going to invite him to stay.

"Sure, help yourself." She tossed him the towel from her hair. "You can probably find a drier one at your own house."

He smiled while he dried his neck and hair. The towel smelled of her. It was the same fragrance he remembered after the board meeting. He took in her bare feet that peeked from beneath her long robe she held tightly in place, and remembered the kiss they had shared only a few hours ago. She didn't want his help and, knowing her stubbornness, she would never ask for it.

"All right, so you won't call the police or see a doctor. Tell me why?"

"I'm not ill and no damage was done. Anyway, this is none of your affair. No one asked you to come here."

"I was concerned about you, Davina. Is anything wrong with that?"

"Plenty. We ... we're not friends, and it should stay that way."

"Surely you want to advise the police in the event they recover property or if the culprits come back." Justin watched her wrap her arms about her waist.

"Obviously, your dealings with the police are a lot different from mine."

He tried to fathom her mood. Again. "You are the moodiest woman I have ever come across. You run hot and cold from one minute to the next. I'm here to give you support and you act like I'm the one that hit you over the head."

Davina lifted her eyes to his. "Didn't you?"

Confused, he frowned as he stepped closer. "What are you talking about?"

"You're not the only one who can theorize. I find it pretty convenient that my apartment was vandalized the same night you find it necessary to talk business with me." Justin tried to interrupt, but she continued, her voice louder. "I've never had a break-in before, but I suffered one tonight, and after you accused me of ... of stealing." She breathed hard from the rush of words.

Justin tossed the towel onto a chair and closed the gap between them. "You think I planned something like this?" His anger was joined with disappointment that she thought so little of him.

"Why not? You're used to getting your way and making things happen." Her arms moved to emphasize her words. "What's a little bump on my head if you're ultimately proved right?"

They were barely a yard apart. She glared at him while he scowled at her.

"Since you know all the answers," he said, "tell me, was I proven right?"

"Check your man and find out for yourself," she retorted.

Justin's attention averted to her robe that fell open to reveal her T-shirt stretched tautly across her unbound breasts, the nipples prominently imprinted against the soft material. The sight was an electric shock; he couldn't believe this prickly woman had aroused him, and in the middle of an argument.

Davina followed Justin's gaze and, realizing her dishabille, snatched her robe together.

Justin swallowed hard to regain control, and returned his eyes to Davina's stormy face. In a deliberate, husky voice, he said, "Okay, I admit I said you took the paintings for your own, albeit misguided, reasons. That has nothing to do with what happened here." He held his hands out in supplication.

She refused to look at him. Instead, she turned and moved to the sofa. "I'd like you to leave, Justin. Now."

"Didn't we call a truce tonight?"

"A truce?" Davina intoned incredulously. She whirled to face him. "I was knocked unconscious!"

Justin could see she was upset; more upset than he had previously thought, and she was desperately trying to hold it in. But her eyes were quickly becoming moist. His first suspicion of why she was so distressed made sense.

"Something was taken, wasn't it?" He watched her raise her hand to the door. "Did they steal the paintings?" he persisted.

"I've told you to leave." She pointed a slim finger imperiously at the door, then laid her hand against her temple as she closed her eyes.

Justin saw the pain in that simple movement and, contritely, thought to help her sit down. "Davina . . ." But, as he reached for her hand, she opened her eyes and retaliated with a look filled with reproach.

"Don't. Just leave here." She spat the words at him.

Her words of anger stopped him cold. His own exasperation at not being able to figure her out made him want to return the hurt and shout that he knew she enjoyed his touch earlier; but, he didn't. Instead, he thought to neutralize her anger and said, "If you won't let me near you, how will I kiss you again?"

Davina's eyes grew wide at his words. "That kiss was a mistake and should never have happened."

"Whoa . . . what was that?" Natalie's reappearance caught them both off guard.

Davina looked heavenward as Natalie came from somewhere behind her. Justin stuck his hands into his pockets; his jaw was clenched and his eyes were slightly narrowed as they burned into Davina's. He frowned, not yet ready to give up on this discussion, but realizing not much else would be accomplished if Davina wouldn't cooperate.

"I think you both need to go to your respective corners and take a time out." Natalie turned to Justin. "That means you go home." She laid her hand on Justin's arm and ushered him out of the door.

Under the portico in the drizzling rain, Justin gave Natalie an earnest look. "I think she's still in shock. Put her to bed and—"

Natalie interrupted him. "Listen, I'll take care of her, but you have a lot of explaining to do, and tomorrow is as good a time as any to start." She gently closed, then locked the door.

When she returned to the living room, Davina had curled into the corner of the sofa, resting her head on the stuffed arm.

"Thanks for getting him out of here."

"Not so fast. You've got some explaining of your own to do." She stood in front of Davina. "You can either tell me, or I'll tell David. Which will it be?"

Davina sighed as she weighed her choices.

The voice coming through the phone was not happy. "There were only two. I looked everywhere, I tell you, and there were no more."

The man receiving the news wasn't happy, either. "You mean you could only find two. There were three, damn you. You were supposed to get them all.''

"I want my money for the job. No payment, no delivery of the merchandise.''

"If I find out you're holding the third as ransom for more money, you'll be sorry. Is that clear?''

"Yeah, yeah . . .'' the voice on the phone whined. "Same drop spot, right? I want to get rid of this stuff fast.''

"Same spot.'' The man dropped the phone distastefully onto the cradle. Sometimes you had to work with what was available. He drummed his fingers on the desk as he contemplated his next call. His contact would not take the news well. And now that the Spenser woman was alerted, she would be on her guard in the future. Something had to be done about her meddling. Something had to be done about finding that third painting.

Davina lay in the dark and waited for the call. It was after midnight and Natalie was asleep on the lounger across the bedroom. When the call finally came, the phone rang only once before Davina rushed to pick it up.

"Hello?''

"Vinny? Sorry I'm calling so late. I just got in and saw your message.''

She sat up in the bed and clutched the phone close to her mouth. "Thank God, David. I've been waiting for you to call.''

His voice was immediately charged with concern. "What is it?''

"Someone knows. I told you about the meeting with Justin Hardy. Well, when I returned home, I was surprised by a burglar.''

"Are you all right? What happened?''

Davina went on to give details of the encounter, Natalie's arrival, and their discovery amid the ransacked apartment that two of the paintings were gone.

David softly swore into the phone.

"There's more.'' She then told him about the five paintings missing at Hardy Enterprises and Justin's suspicion that she was somehow responsible.

"He wants them returned in two days or he'll tell his board everything he suspects," Davina continued.

"I was afraid this would happen. Our time is up, so we have to move."

"He came here tonight."

"To your apartment? Why?"

"I don't know." Davina swallowed hard on that effortless lie "Maybe to see if his handiwork was successful."

"You believe you were set up by him? Do you think he'd go this far?"

Davina's voice cracked. "I don't know, but it's the easiest answer right now. He saw some of the nude collection, too." She heard his deep sigh.

"In that case, we have no choice but to act in your best interest." Neither said anything for a moment, then David quietly asked, "How are you with all this?"

It was her turn to sigh. "So far, so good. I'm more upset that the paintings are gone again, and after all I went through to get them, than I am about my bruised head."

"Is Natalie still there?"

"Yeah. She's curled up asleep with a knife under her pillow."

"I'm coming home in the morning, Vinny. It's time I met the Hardy family."

CHAPTER TEN

An Unexpected Meeting of the Minds

The monthly breakfast with the Atlanta Businessmen's Association was over, and Justin entered his third-floor office from a convenient side door that linked to the parking lot. He was hanging his coat in the closet when Nora peeked in from the main door and closed it behind her.

"You'll never guess who's been waiting for you."

Justin turned to Nora. "Since I'll never guess, tell me."

"I tried to schedule an appointment for later today, but your book is full." She followed him to his desk.

He lowered himself into the big, leather chair. "Nora, just tell me who it is."

At that moment, the door yawned open. They both looked up to see a well-dressed man appear in the doorway.

"Excuse me, but I figured you were back," the man said. "I told your secretary I had to see you today." He stepped farther into the office.

Justin stood up and frowned at the intruder, whom he immediately recognized from the photo in Davina's office. His gut reaction was that her lover had come to exact some form of retribution.

"This is the young man waiting to see you," Nora said, gesturing in his direction. "He's Miss Spenser's brother, David Spenser."

When Justin heard the name, his frown quickly changed to one of curiosity. That bit of information brought an irrational flow of satisfaction through him.

"Young man, you should have minded your manners and stayed put until you were invited in," Nora added.

"That's okay, Nora. I have a few minutes for Mr. Spenser." Coming around the desk, Justin offered David a seat. Then, he proceeded to escort Nora from the office. In a low voice, he said, "Get my mother for me—she's somewhere in the building, and work out my next appointment to give me time with my guest."

"But . . ." Nora protested.

"Just do it." His voice persuaded.

She gave him her straight back and an indignant sigh before he closed the door. Justin turned to David, who stood in the middle of the room. He quirked his eyebrows at the neat ponytail against David's collar. *So this is her brother.*

He walked back to his desk before he met the younger man's intense scrutiny with equanimity. Although Justin was taller and possessed an athletic build, David's brawn was obvious, even in his well-cut suit. In the passage of a moment, the two sized each other up in an age-old male ritual.

Justin sat in his chair. "I thought you were out of town. What made you show up after keeping such a low profile?"

David moved to the wing chair and remained standing. "I returned this morning because my sister was attacked last night. I want to know if you had anything to do with it."

Justin's mouth thinned in displeasure. He leaned forward and rested his elbows on the desk. This was the third time he had been accused of hurting Davina. He hesitated a moment, then chose his words carefully. "I'm getting tired of that accusation. For the record, no, I had nothing to do with what happened."

David sat down and rested his ankle over his knee. "I didn't expect you to admit it even if you did, but I consider you a strong suspect after Davina told me you accused her of taking your paintings."

"How is she?" He had wanted to call her this morning, but decided her anger was too fresh for it to do any good.

"If you didn't do the damage, that's not your concern, is it?" David's voice openly challenged Justin.

Rudeness is rampant in that family. "I take it she's okay with the ever-watchful Natalie close by."

"You've met Natalie?"

"She's less prickly than your sister, but a pain, nonetheless. You were the only missing player."

"I didn't attend the meeting because Davina believed your board was reasonable and would agree to her requests. That's not the case anymore. She not only thinks you're unreasonable but dangerous, as well."

At David's pause, Justin urged him on in a sharp tone.

"She says you've offered her access to your storage records for research."

"You understand our conditions? We don't want the negative publicity."

"I suspect that's because of the rumors about a takeover?" David asked.

Justin exhibited a mild surprise. "They're rumors, and I'm sure you can understand why we've even entertained your sister's wild notions at all. It's to keep our company intact. My father built this company from a rickety building on Auburn Avenue. There's no way I'll allow anyone to come in and destroy it.''

''But, what if it was built with my father's input as well?''

''That can't be proven, and that's the whole point of this, isn't it?'' Justin's deep voice had become curt, and his words created a cool pause in the room.

''What do you plan to do about your missing paintings?''

Justin eyes were sharp as they drew David's attention. ''Your sister can explain a lot, but she's stubborn and won't. I'm going to keep my word and not say anything, but I won't keep quiet forever. You should encourage her to talk to me.''

''Your accusation can hurt her, and I'll do whatever's necessary to protect her.'' David straightened in his chair. ''It would help if we had something else that you might want, right?''

''I believe it's called quid pro quo.'' Justin's voice was sarcastic.

''Right.'' David put on his own sardonic smile. ''What would you say if we offered you the management of the Vinny Richards art show?''

Justin's surprise that it was in the open didn't show on his face. ''I'd say I'm amazed Davina didn't use it as a bargaining point when she met with the board.''

''We knew it was only a matter of time before you found out that she was the artist behind that show.''

''So, when was she going to say something? Is this another of her secrets?''

''It was no secret; we didn't know you were interested. She only recently learned that yours was one of the galleries that hoped to represent her. When she found out, she decided to let an agent handle it; but when the agent gave her the short list of the best offers, there was your name.''

''So, let me get this straight,'' Justin said. ''Davina will give Hardy the show if I keep my promise and let her browse my records to prove that my now missing paintings belonged to your father, whom she also believes to be a founding partner of this business and, as such, owner of half of the company.''

"They don't call you a whiz for nothing," David added his own sarcasm.

"We're giving up a lot for just a show and no negative publicity from her."

"Not if you don't believe she'll find anything to justify the claims. You'll get a show that'll pull in revenue, and her return percentage can be negotiated to Hardy's benefit for consideration of your, shall we say, 'good will.' "

"Will she agree and cooperate with us on a show?"

"I'll press her with the more salient points. The final decision is hers."

Justin frowned. "You don't have any . . . say in this? If my past experience with your sister is any indicator, I don't think she wants me to back the show."

"You have to understand Davina. She has a passionate nature. When she gets something in her head, she can be very headstrong."

"Opinionated and stubborn are better adjectives."

"That, too," David agreed. "But I support her. It's important to both of us, but to Davina it's a matter of honor when a promise is made. Your attorneys ignored her when she wrote them, and then you insulted her at the board meeting. She doesn't trust you, and now she believes that you may have orchestrated the break-in last night to prove a point."

"Did she explain why I accused her of taking the paintings?"

"You read a lot into the coincidence that the Maceo paintings are missing and she was interested in them. I think it's similarly coincidental that on the same evening you accuse her of theft, her apartment is broken into and ransacked."

"Touché. But, no more coincidental than my bumping into her as she left this building Thursday night with a bulky canvas bag."

Now, it was David's turn to raise an eyebrow in quiet surprise.

"So, she didn't tell you?" Justin laughed. "That sounds like her. I didn't know who she was at the time."

"No matter what your opinion of her, she's not involved in anything that would provoke an attack like last night's," David said.

"That's just it. Something's going on, and your sister may be involved. I don't want to see her hurt, but I'm going to get to the bottom of all of it. Tell her I'm not the enemy." He watched as David rubbed his chin.

A light knock sounded from the door. Justin looked up when it opened and Mrs. Hardy's head appeared.

"May I come in?" she asked. David turned to the door.

Justin stood and came around the desk. "Of course." He met her in the middle of the room. "Mother, I'd like you to meet David Spenser." Before he could complete the introduction, she had already made her way to David, who also stood.

"Nora has already told me who you are. I'm Elizabeth Hardy." She wore a smile, her inquisitive expression warm, as she tilted her head up to him.

David reached out and stiffly shook her hand. "It's a pleasure meeting you, Mrs. Hardy."

"You have good manners, young man. Now, sit down, both of you." She took the seat next to him. "Our meeting with your sister was under, shall we say, strained conditions, and based on the way it ended, things didn't look too good for a future one. Now, I've been given the opportunity to meet you. Tell me, are you as ardent about all this as she is?"

David glanced over at Justin, clearly caught off guard by her comments. "Davina told me your board would probably reject her request."

"She has strong feelings about this claim of your father's."

"Yes, she does. We both do."

Mrs. Hardy leaned forward in her chair. "I'd like to invite you and your sister to my home for dinner this week."

Justin smiled at his mother's invitation. "I think that's a great idea. Mr. Spenser and I were discussing amenable conditions for resolving our differences."

"Why would you want to invite us to your home?"

Mrs. Hardy leaned back in the chair. "Frankly, I don't know if I like you or your sister. It's not a pleasant thought that you want to take what we believe is ours and cause conflict. But, I'm an optimist, and through knowledge comes understanding. Maybe we can learn something from each other."

Justin enjoyed David's obvious discomfort with his mother's openness. Her frankness was something the family had long learned to expect.

Mrs. Hardy pressed her invitation again. "Will you accept, Mr. Spenser."

He let out a sigh before he spoke. "Please, call me David and, I won't speak for Davina, but if she'll agree, so will I."

Mrs. Hardy smiled at him. "Well, all I can do is expect that you'll try." When she stood to leave, both of the men did, too. "I only dropped in to see you, David. You can let Justin know about the dinner."

Justin came from around his desk and walked her to the door. When he closed the door behind her, he leaned his back against it, arms crossed.

"A warning—tell your sister it's in both your best interests to get to know the board members. If we back her show, I have a vested interest in keeping the police out of this. Unfortunately, the board may not see it that way. It's her call."

Later that evening, Justin found himself walking across the hot pavement of the apartment complex with Natalie, wondering if Davina made the call. The sun was a blister in the sky and baked the beautifully landscaped grounds covered with late summer blooms; plumage from exotic grasses undulated in the warm breeze.

When Justin hadn't received a message from David that the dinner invitation was accepted, he had made it his business to stop by and find out if Davina was the cause, since it was exactly what her contrary nature would do. Upon arriving at her apartment, he'd found Natalie there, who offered to show him the pool area where Davina regularly swam evening laps.

"I never thought of her as a swimmer," Justin said, slowing his pace for Natalie's shorter stride. He smiled to himself. A dancer, maybe.

"She swam competitively all through high school."

"You and Davina are pretty good friends, then," Justin said to Natalie.

"Very good friends, thank you." Natalie shielded her eyes from the sun.

"Do you really think I would harm her?"

She gave him a sidelong look. "Probably not, but I don't suppose it hurts to be careful." She stopped and pointed into the distance. "The pool is just beyond the tennis court, around the fence. Do you think you can find it from here?" She looked at him as she settled both of her hands on her hips.

He smiled at her deliberate impudence. "I believe I can. Thank you." He turned to continue down the path when she called out to him.

"Justin, listen. On a personal level, leave her alone, okay? I know there's business between you; but, Davina doesn't play games, and I'm sure you know them all. Anyway, David will never let you get near his sister."

He started to respond, but decided against it. It was best to keep silent after she'd made everyone's position crystal clear. He nodded to Natalie's expectant scrutiny, then continued on without a backward glance.

Justin thought about her comments. He did not intend to press anything of a personal nature. Well, there was that kiss, but it satisfied a curiosity only. He wondered if Natalie got that idea from Davina. Was Davina upset that she'd returned his kiss? Or upset that he knew she'd returned it?

As Justin rounded the fenced tennis court to the patio, the first things in his line of vision were two slender feet with coral painted nails hanging over the edge of a lounger. He moved farther into the area and the feet became part of slender ankles, then shapely calves. They in turn gave way to smooth, supple thighs that glistened like golden cinnamon under the sun. Justin's eyes propelled onward along the enticing form before they were abruptly halted by a white terry towel. His gaze traveled up to the face, and he recognized Davina, her eyes closed in sleep. Her bare shoulders glowed above a towel that covered her middle, and it rose and fell in rhythm with her deep breathing.

What a surprise hiding under the layers she always wore, he thought, and he definitely found no disappointment in the sight. He sighed, warmed by more than the heat of the day, and took a moment to study her resting face. Her lips had parted slightly and the nerve along the outer corner of her left eye jumped erratically. He smiled. Even in sleep, she wasn't relaxed. Her hair was wet from her swim and lay in a thick mass off her face; a few tendrils had dried and floated in the breeze.

He took off his coat and looked around before he sat in an adjacent lounge chair. The pool area boasted a number of adults and children enjoying the sun. A lifeguard watched lazily from his perch near the diving boards. A few queer stares were thrown his way, and emphasized how out of place he was in the business suit.

Justin leaned forward and softly whispered her name. "Davina?" He watched and was soon rewarded with a sleepy stretch as she adjusted her legs on the lounger.

When she didn't wake up, he placed his hand on her sun-warmed shoulder and gently shook it. She smelled of flowers. "Davina?" he called out much louder.

She opened her eyes, squinted at the man smiling above her, then bolted upright in the lounger as she recognized that smile. Her towel doubled over into her lap and revealed a white tank suit with the straps pulled down off her shoulders. The smooth mounds of her breasts kept the suit in place.

"Justin. What are you doing here?" She frowned as she rubbed her eyes, then squinted against the sun.

"Watching you sleep." He leaned back into the chair and comfortably rested his arms along the side. "Actually, I want you to accept the dinner invitation and thought you might need some incentives."

She drew her feet up and wrapped her arms around her legs. They provided her with a stationary post to which she could cling as she fought the discomfort of his intent gaze. "Don't you know the word patience?" Her eyes closed against the sun.

"I met your brother this morning in my office. After he accused me of masterminding your attack, we got down to preparing the outline of a business deal. Did you think about the offer? Do we have a deal?"

She opened her eyes and turned her head with an indignant swing. "I just swam a hundred laps and I was sleeping. So, give me a moment to think.'' She sat back on the lounger and carefully pushed her arms through the straps of her tank suit, all the while feeling the burn of his eyes with each movement.

''Don't you find this interesting?''

''What?'' she asked as she adjusted the straps comfortably on her shoulders.

''That we can be at cross purposes, yet find a way to work together.''

Davina looked at the cocked eyebrow of his chiseled face. ''Can we?''

''How are you after last night?''

Davina knew he referred to the attack, but her memory returned to the kiss they had shared, and she felt a languid heat creep upward to her face. She carefully touched the sore spot on her head. ''I'm okay. David lectured me on my quick assumption about you. So, if I wrongly accused you about last night, then understand why I made the accusation in the beginning.''

''Your brother is your biggest defender. He tells me I'm wrong about you, as well.'' He smiled. ''So, if I wrongly accused you, then understand why—''

''I know, I know.'' Davina had detected the hint of censure and mockery in his tone and glared at him. She swept her legs to the side of the lounger, across from him.

Justin continued. ''That doesn't mean I'm going to stop asking questions.''

''I never thought you would.''

''You were scared last night. I saw it in your eyes. Are you okay with being out in the open like this?'' He looked around the pool area.

Davina slid forward to retrieve her shirt hooked at the top of the chair. As she reached, her knees momentarily rubbed against Justin's legs. The contact caused an electric sensation. Afraid that it showed, she averted her face from his. ''Lots of people are around and, of course, David is back.''

''Good. Do you want to hear those incentives?''

''I have a choice?''

''My mother was around in the days Hardy started out, and she's probably a wealth of knowledge. Dinner would be a good time to find out if she remembers anything.'' He smiled broadly as he awaited her response. ''If you feel safer with Natalie, bring her, too.''

Davina slipped on the shirt. She knew he goaded her, but she couldn't help responding. ''You think you know everything, don't you? Your mother is the only reason I will come. If the truth be known, she's about the only one at Hardy I trust.''

''Great, Vinny.'' He made a point of using her nickname. The mirth showed on his face as he clasped his hands together. ''Do you want to work out the details of our arrangement now?'' He stood and held his hand out to her rising figure.

She avoided his hand and rose fluidly from the chair, irritated by his pleasant mood. ''I'm going inside. I'm sure you can find your way back to your car.''

Davina picked up her towel and slipped her feet into a pair of rubber sandals. She felt Justin's heated stare as she walked away, but dared herself not to look back, even as his deep laugh sounded in her ear.

CHAPTER ELEVEN

An Enchanted Evening

Davina had worked a compromise with David on the dinner invitation. She would get in his car to attend, and he would let her complain during the drive.

''Are you sure you know where you are?'' She had asked the question every five minutes since they had exited the perimeter highway. She peered through her window into the early evening where the homes were fewer and farther apart.

David threw her another dark look. ''His assistant gave me the directions. Here, you read them.'' He passed the scribbled note to

Davina, who didn't bother to look. "I think this is the last turn, and the house should be at the end of the street, behind a black, iron gate."

Davina steadfastly fought off the dread of the upcoming evening. She accepted her attraction to Justin, but she was determined not to act on it. Crossing her stockinged legs, she folded her hands in her lap and closed her eyes. While David chose a black suit and his de rigueur ponytail, Davina wore her only "little black dress," a knee-length jacquard print that hugged the curves of her slim frame. The long, tight sleeves buttoned at her wrists, and another set of covered buttons reached from her neck to the small of her back. Gold earrings matched the silk ribbon entwined through her thick, twisted braid.

"That's it ahead, Vinny. Look."

She opened her eyes and looked ahead at what resembled a beautifully lit castle, complete with a turret. The upper windows were tinted with a pale light and the second-story picture window above the entranceway showcased a chandelier that sparkled as though it were made of a thousand lighted candles.

"Good Lord, David. It's lit up like a Christmas tree."

"It's some kind of place, huh?"

"They're rich. The rest of Dad's paintings are probably holed up in there."

He slowly drove through the opened gate and onto the circular driveway. "Are you ready?" He looked at Davina, her arms crossed in defiance.

At this distance, she could see movement beyond the bright windows of the main floor. "No. But, I might as well make the most of the opportunity."

He reached over and squeezed her hand. "That's the spirit." He parked near three other cars that sat in a flood of soft light at the side of the house and got out.

Davina had not opened her door yet. Her attention was drawn to the wall near the front of the house where a shadow separated from the building and moved toward them. She watched David reach the front of the car, then halt as the shadow became Justin's tall figure. His hand extended in a greeting to David, and they both continued to her side of the car. She pulled in an anxious breath before scrambling for both her discarded high heels.

Justin spoke first as he opened her door. "I was telling David I'm glad you didn't have trouble finding us. The family is anxious to meet you."

Davina watched Justin reach to help her from the car. She frowned at his appreciative inspection when she swung her feet around and to the ground. "Let's get it over with, then." And she meant it.

A bricked walkway, marked by lamps that edged a border garden, led up to the front double doors. Davina preceded the two men up the walk, with Justin quickly stepping forward at the door.

"Allow me," he said, and pushed the door wide so Davina could walk in.

She immediately heard the laughter of children and adults to her left. As she moved into the foyer, she was mesmerized, struck by the beauty before her. Her stares took in the loveliest entranceway she had ever experienced. It was a long hall, and wide, with a proud staircase on the right that gracefully curved upward to the magnificent chandelier she had seen from the outside. Its tiny glass prisms threw off miniature shards of delightful color that danced against the bright surfaces of the room. Upon discovering the paintings farther down the wallpapered walls, her wide eyes softened to curious appreciation.

"You have a beautiful home," David said, as he, too, glanced about the room.

Davina had already strolled halfway down the hall, quietly savoring the eclectic blend of paintings and digesting the names of the artists who had created them.

"Do you see anything interesting?" Justin asked at her shoulder.

Davina turned abruptly. In the bright light of the foyer, she could see that he, too, wore a black suit and tie, and she was acutely conscious of his nearness. She looked up at his face. The warmth of his gaze felt good, too good, and for a moment she was shamed by the sum of her emotions since arriving.

"I was admiring the mix of work here." Her glance took in all the art. "Altogether, including this room, it's an amazing display."

He smiled with open candor. "I can't take credit for any of it. It's all my parents' doing. But I agree, it does grab you. I walk through here every day and I sometimes forget its effect." He walked back to the doorway from which she had heard the laughter. "Everyone is in the salon," he said, and strode into the room ahead of them.

Davina couldn't imagine getting used to beauty such as this. She decided to add "unappreciative" to his list of character flaws.

David joined her in the doorway and clasped her hand. Before they walked in, he whispered, "You're frowning again. It'll be over soon."

"Not soon enough, I'm afraid," was her withered response.

They entered and found themselves, once again, impressed by the quiet elegance that trumpeted around them. People were scattered about the large room that was decorated to perfection. Mrs. Hardy's tiny figure moved toward them, but Davina's eyes unerringly found Justin as he now gave his full attention to two young children that he lifted into his arms.

Mrs. Hardy's voice was demanding her attention. "Welcome to our home, Miss Spenser, Mr. Spenser. Let me introduce you to everyone."

"First names are fine," David said as he shook her hand.

"I'll make the first introduction," Justin said as he made his way to them. He bounced the two children on his arms while they chattered and squealed with joy. "This is three-year-old Isabel, and her brother, five-year-old Brian." The cute, well-dressed children giggled at the adult treatment. "Tell Davina Spenser, and her brother, David Spenser, hello," he urged.

Isabel gave a tepid wave as she clung to Justin's neck, but a smiling Brian blurted out, "She's pretty, Uncle Justin."

Davina flushed at the child's announcement, while everyone else laughed. It served well as an icebreaker, and she gave the children a smile. "What a compliment from such a little guy. Thank you, Brian."

Justin's smile was equally broad as he playfully whispered to his nephew, "You've got a good eye already. You're going to make your uncle proud."

Stephanie Rogers and her husband, William, had moved from the love seat and proceeded to remove their children from their perch, which had now become Justin's shoulders. "Justin," she exclaimed, "You spoil them rotten. Wait until you have your own, and you'll see what I mean."

As the grumbling children were pulled from Justin by their parents, Elizabeth Hardy made the remaining introductions. At each handshake,

Davina knew that she, along with David, was the object of avid curiosity. She recognized Carolyn and Alli from the board meeting, but was surprised to see Douglas Bradley. Justin quickly explained his presence, saying, "The house is matriarchal so, on occasion, William and I have to include Douglas to help balance the scales." Elizabeth smiled at her son's humor before excusing herself to check dinner.

Douglas slapped Justin's back. "Don't let him fool you. He holds his own quite well around here, and only includes me when he needs to pick my brain about a report or something."

Davina gave Justin an inquisitive glance, only to find his eyes on her.

"I'll get you and David a glass of wine before dinner. . . . Be right back." Justin walked off as Alli and Carolyn came up.

"You've been standing since you came in here. Don't you want to sit down?" Alli's innocent suggestion was aimed at David.

"Thank you. Davina?" His question to her was met with a nod. The four retired to a group of chairs while Douglas continued his conversation with Stephanie and William. Davina sat in a tufted armchair next to the sofa, Alli maneuvered to sit next to David on the sofa, and Carolyn was left to occupy the remaining chair. Davina watched Carolyn send her sister a cocked brow and smothered her own smile as she recognized Alli's actions were for David's amused benefit.

"So, you're the artist, Vinny Richards?" Carolyn asked Davina.

"Yes. Justin didn't waste time sharing the news. Do you know my work?"

"Linda made sure everyone saw samples of it," Carolyn said.

"Linda?" Davina asked, and looked from Carolyn to Alli. "I'll have to thank her." Davina saw a look pass between the two sisters.

"She handles new acquisitions and contracts," Alli explained. "But, trust me, you can wait for the introduction." She turned her attention to David. "And you're Vinny Richards's brother?"

"Yes," he answered, smiling. "I'm usually called David, though."

"Do you model for any of her nudes?"

Davina and Carolyn did a quiet squirm in their chairs while Alli smiled at an entertained David.

Before he could answer, Stephanie came up to the back of the sofa and tweaked Alli's shoulder. "Don't be rude, baby girl."

"I'm curious, okay, and stop calling me that around company." Her petulant words confirmed why her antics were indulged by her siblings.

Stephanie came around and wedged herself between David and Alli. Alli sighed and uncurled her leg to make sufficient room. Stephanie patted Alli's leg and said to Davina, "You and Justin seem to have worked out your differences since the board meeting?"

"Pretty much, I guess," Davina answered. "I'm here and we haven't cut each other's throat—yet."

"The evening's still young for blood," Alli said, and slanted a look in Stephanie's direction.

Carolyn ignored her sisters. "Why do you paint under a different name?"

Davina looked to David before she answered. "Vinny is a nickname only David uses, and there was a time when I needed a separate persona for my art. My father suggested it." Davina felt more than heard Justin's presence behind her.

"The name caught us off guard until David let us in on it," Justin said and handed David a glass of wine.

David stood as Mrs. Hardy, who had entered with Justin, came around to face the group. "We can go in to dinner shortly."

Stephanie rose from the sofa to leave. "In that case, I'll prepare the kids. Mama, you can sit here."

While David and Mrs. Hardy sat down, Justin returned to Davina's chair and handed her the other wineglass. Careful so as not to spill the pale liquid, Davina's fingers curved around his.

"Thank you," she said, fighting the impulse to jump away. He remained standing next to her chair, his arm stretching casually across the back of her seat.

"I'm happy the two of you decided to come tonight." Mrs. Hardy smiled at Davina. "I was caught by surprise at that announcement you made at the meeting. The fact that you know about Maceo after he disappeared is fascinating information. Do you have any idea how many people would be interested to know that story?"

"It was only recently that it became known to us." Davina shifted about in her chair and looked over at David.

He turned to Mrs. Hardy. "You knew him, too, didn't you?"

"Not as well as my husband did, but my impression of him from the little contact I had was that of a fun-loving and gentle man."

Davina's voice floated through the quiet that permeated the room. "Did your husband speak of their friendship at all?"

Elizabeth Hardy leaned back into the sofa's cushion. "You have to understand that Jacob started this business before we were married, and I didn't get involved until much later, after Maceo had all the trouble; but I never heard James Spenser's name mentioned regarding any deals or paintings, either. I'm sorry."

"Mom, why did Maceo disappear?" Carolyn asked.

David spoke first. "The newspapers sensationalized the trouble he was in and, given his choices, he disappeared."

"What do you remember about it, Mrs. Hardy?" Davina's eyes concentrated on the small woman.

"We—or at least close friends—never wanted to believe that he was guilty of anything except, maybe, passion, and the little I know came from Jacob and his close-knit group of artist friends." Her voice trailed off, as if her thoughts were elsewhere.

"Go on, Mom." Justin's deep voice urged her to continue.

Her voice was light as she recalled events. "The story that circulated after the paper's appetite for blood had cooled was that a well-known male patron of the cabaret club where Maceo's girlfriend sang was beaten—horribly. The man was left for dead; and if things weren't bad enough, he was white." She raised her eyes to Davina's. "What the papers didn't print was what circulated on the streets—that the patron had raped the singer some days before and Maceo, in love with the woman, had been set on revenge."

Davina stiffened in her chair and exchanged a glance with David. She felt Justin's hand brush her neck.

"Did you believe that story?" David asked.

"All of this happened just after his artwork started to take off with the critics. But, Jacob believed him, and what happened couldn't have come at a worse time. It all but destroyed Maceo."

"Was he ever arrested?" Alli asked.

"The next thing we knew, Maceo was gone. The papers followed it for a while; they loved calling him a fugitive, and there were sightings of him all over the U.S. for a while, but nothing ever materialized that resulted in an arrest."

Davina's lips thinned in a bitter smile. "Of course, his notoriety only made his paintings go up in value and they were snapped up everywhere."

"Whatever happened to the man who was beaten? What about the woman?" Carolyn asked.

Elizabeth Hardy sighed. "I don't remember, it's been so long ago. I do know that your father never willingly brought up Maceo's name again. He ignored the rumors but continually defended him, even after he disappeared."

"Was your husband questioned about Maceo's whereabouts?" David asked.

"I can answer that one." Justin's hand dropped from Davina's chair and he moved a step away. "He was questioned, all right. The police tried to accuse him of helping Maceo disappear."

"Then they were good friends." Davina spoke quickly. "He would have had access to Maceo's paintings, just as my father said."

"There is no evidence to support the accusation." There was a kindness in Elizabeth Hardy's voice, as though to let Davina down gently. "He never admitted to such, even to me."

Stephanie walked into the room and defused the strained moment. "Mrs. Taylor says dinner is waiting."

David helped Mrs. Hardy rise from her chair as everyone stood to leave for the dining room. Justin stayed near Davina, his hand lightly brushing her back as he prepared to show her the way.

"Davina," Elizabeth said, "my husband was the real link with Maceo, and unfortunately, he's not here to tell us what we need to know, and that is, whether Maceo and your father helped fund the business." The four now stood alone in the large room.

"Justin has agreed to allow me access to your archived files, and I'm satisfied with that, for now. I don't want to cause you any harm, Mrs. Hardy. I swear. But, I do want answers to the questions my father raised."

"It sounds like a noble cause, but I don't know if there are answers at this late date, child, and the ones there could affect all of us in ways we never thought possible.'' She gave Davina a cryptic smile. ''Even though we may never know the truth, I respect your desire to pursue it. All I ask is that you, in return, respect my family's desire to protect what we believe is rightly ours.''

Davina was impressed by Mrs. Hardy's words. Consumed by a need to explain away her guilt, she looked into the older woman's gentle eyes. ''I owe it to my father to at least try to prove his legacy, and my links are your husband and Maceo.''

''There is a price for truth, Davina, and you must be willing to pay it when the time comes. Remember that.'' She clasped her hands as she looked to her son. ''Enough of this maudlin talk. Justin, please escort Davina in to dinner and David will do the same with me.''

At his mother's suggestion, Justin caught Davina's elbow and firmly held her at his side. ''Let's eat.'' When Davina looked into his face, his eyes clung to hers, as though to analyze her reaction to all that had been said. She gave in to him and allowed herself to relax, letting him know the truce was on again.

David eased into a smile and nodded, first to Mrs. Hardy, and then to his sister, now ensconced on Justin's arm. Mrs. Hardy led the way to the dining room.

''By the way, Davina, Justin tells me how taken you were with the art displayed in the hall.'' At her words, Davina raised a fine, arched eyebrow in Justin's direction. ''So, I talked him into showing you around after dinner. That way, you'll get a chance to view some other rather lovely works.''

''Thank you, Mrs. Hardy,'' she said as she looked at a grinning Justin. ''I don't know what to say.''

The Hardy's formal dining room was both huge and exquisite. The curved wall was painted with a fresco of a Japanese garden scene. The deep, domed ceiling boasted a fresco of gaily colored papier-mâché umbrellas arranged in a circular pattern. From its center dropped another gloriously tiered chandelier that provided illumination to every corner. The enormous table had been rearranged to accommodate their relatively intimate group. Justin sat at the head, and Davina was at his immediate right, his mother on his left.

Davina's last glass of wine had sufficiently loosened her up, or at least enough to enjoy herself; she couldn't eat another bite of the wonderful dessert topped with whipped cream. The evening had been a new experience.

She found that she'd actually taken pleasure from the pleasant tinkling of dishes filled with good food, and conversation mixed with laughter that was shared with others. She had even delighted in the siblings' teasing of each other and the fuss the adults made over the tiniest of incidents from the children. And with no mention of business, the family had included her and David in their conversations, asking their opinions, and listening to their experiences. With her usual reluctance to admit changing feelings, she wondered what it must be like to share a life with such a large family.

"We should return to the salon," Elizabeth suggested, and stood from the table.

"Davina, we're going to freshen up. Would you like to come?" Alli asked.

"Yes, thank you." She left with the sisters and was shown a private bathroom along a corridor at the rear of the large house. She quickly freshened her appearance and reapplied the lipstick that was lost during dinner. When she paused as she stepped from the bathroom, unsure of the way to the salon, Justin walked up.

"Are you ready for the fifty-cent tour?"

She raised her brows. "Yes, but where's David?"

"He's occupied. It seems Alli has promised to do the honors for him if he wants to browse. Right now, she's going through the twenty-questions scenario. If the others don't rescue him, I'll have to apologize later."

Davina's gentle laugh, loosened by the wine, rippled through the corridor. When she saw Justin's curious expression, she put her hand to her mouth to suppress the remaining giggle. "I'm sorry, but you have to know my brother to appreciate the situation."

He shook his head, openly amused by her laughter. "I'm amazed at the change in you when you get rid of that frown you love to wear."

Davina thought she saw a spark of some indefinable emotion in his eyes. She couldn't quite place it, but she felt too good to get angry over his arrogance.

"Didn't you know? I only frown when you're around." Her eyes danced with mirth.

"I must be doing something right for a change. My goal is to keep you smiling, or at least for the rest of the evening. Come on, let's start on the terrace." He slipped his hand over hers and gently tugged her along with him down the hall and through the stained glass French doors, her giggles echoing behind them.

Their walk had covered some of the gardens, most of the spacious home's interior, and was coming to an end along the hall of the west wing's second floor. As they strolled along that hall, commenting on the last paintings, Justin allowed her to move ahead of his slower gait. It was refreshing to watch her excitement at seeing a piece she had personally coveted or was genuinely in awe of. He waited for her to come upon the surprise near his suite at the end of the row.

"Oh, my goodness," Davina exclaimed. She had come to a stop in front of a beautifully framed oil. "You have one of my paintings displayed on the same wall as a Lawrence, a Tolliver, and a Bearden. Where did you get it?"

Justin slowly walked up to her. "At the Art Expo in Charleston. One of our acquisition agents picked it up. You'll meet her later this week when we sign off on the contracts for your show." He leaned his shoulder against the wall, his arms folded across his chest, and looked at her. "When I saw it, my first thought was 'pure eroticism.' "

Davina smiled and followed the curving spine of the woman depicted on the canvas. "I know. I even blush sometimes." She pressed her back against the wall next to him and closed her eyes as she spoke of her work. "What I mean is, painting the human form liberates me on some level, and helps me throw off my inhibitions and fears."

As she talked, Justin's bold gaze caressed her face then slid downward. He knew what he wanted to do. He had known it when she first swung those beautiful legs from the car, and the anticipation was almost unbearable.

She opened her eyes. "I have no idea where my next focus . . ." The thought was never completed because Justin stepped in front of her and pulled her into the circle of his arms, one hand in the small of her back.

"Justin, we shouldn't." She whispered the words against his shoulder even as she wound her arms inside his coat and clung to his waist.

He tilted her face upward and brushed his lips across hers. "We can't seem to help ourselves, can we?" He moved his mouth over hers and devoured its softness. He wanted to exalt in the feel of her, and it became a slow, drugging kiss. Her hands clutched at his back for dear life while his dropped to her waist. With the help of the wall, her soft curves molded to the contours of his lean body.

When Davina felt his hard arousal press against her thigh, she was electrified and tried to move away.

"Don't pull back, Davina. Let it happen." His husky whisper was a command, and she obeyed. She relaxed and allowed his mouth to hungrily reclaim her; the sweetness of her breath beckoned his tongue. Davina returned his kiss with reckless abandon as the pleasure he gave her radiated outward. His hands explored the curves of her hips, then her bottom, and lifted her to fit neatly against his hard loins.

When his mouth left hers to shower kisses along her jaw and nibbles at her earlobe, Davina buried her face in his neck and breathed kisses there as she succumbed to the delicious domination. Her hungry response to his touch threatened to send Justin's world out of control; he realized that as he roused her passion, his own only grew stronger.

Justin gave a deep sigh and stepped back from her. Her eyes were half closed and she breathed lightly between her still parted lips. He slowly rubbed her arms. "Our timing is lousy, but—"

"We can't let this happen again," she stuttered breathlessly, and nervously smoothed her hair, then her dress.

"Something is happening between us. You feel it, too, don't you?" He gently tilted her chin up to him.

Davina ached at his touch, but knew such an attraction was both perilous and doomed to failure. She moved around him and walked a few steps away. "Yes, I do. It's only sex, though, pure and simple." She folded her arms across her chest. "I mean, the night was made for it—good food, wine. I'm even upstairs viewing your 'etchings.' How clichéd can this get?''

"You're right. It's sex.'' That she actually admitted to feeling something pleased him to no end, and Justin's mood was suddenly buoyant. He pushed his hands deep into his pockets, a satisfied light in his eyes.

"There's nothing wrong with being attracted to someone sexually.'' She said it as though to herself. "As long as it's not acted on.'' She looked to Justin for confirmation of this reasoning, but he seemed amused by her whole speech.

She pressed on. "We don't particularly like each other, so we'll just stay out of arm's reach.'' She pushed back a strand of hair that had escaped her braid.

Justin pulled one hand from his pocket and reached out to the lock of hair. He rubbed it between his fingers as he boldly looked into Davina's eyes. He tucked it behind her ear and allowed his hand to recklessly fall in a caress of her neck. Slowly, inexorably, he drew her to meet his mouth in a surprisingly gentle kiss. They both drank from its sweetness as if they knew it could be their last.

Raising his mouth from hers, Justin gazed into eyes that slowly opened and still brimmed with passion. "Your brother probably thinks you've murdered me by now. We'd better get back downstairs.'' She nodded in agreement and joined him in a quiet walk back down the hallway.

When they reached the bottom of the staircase, they ran into Carolyn.

"So, did you enjoy yourself?'' she asked Davina.

"Yes.'' They answered in unison before Davina turned to Justin. "Thank you for showing me around. If you'll excuse me, I have to find David. We really need to be going.'' She walked away in a direction she thought might be the salon.

Carolyn turned to Justin and adjusted his collar. "Anything going on I should know?''

He watched Davina disappear around the corner. "Not a thing.''

"So, why are you so quiet?'' David turned the car into the expressway traffic.

"I'm tired, that's all." Davina relaxed against the car seat, her face turned to the window. She didn't let him know she fought hard against the guilt that plagued her. What had gotten into her tonight? "We should never have come because we didn't accomplish anything."

"Sure we did," he said. "For one, I don't think Mrs. Hardy and her daughters have anything to do with this. Justin kept you occupied after dinner." He glanced quickly at Davina. "You were gone a long time with him. Did he say anything?"

Davina clenched her fists in the dark. "Nothing useful."

"We're going to have to be careful and guard what we say about Maceo."

"I know," Davina agreed. "Something tells me that none of the Hardy family will take lightly the news that Maceo and our father are one and the same."

CHAPTER TWELVE

The Deal for the Art

"What do you have, Connie?" Justin watched the PI take a seat in the office.

"It's pretty routine so far." Connie Preston's mahogany head resembled a carved African bauble under the light in Justin's office. His dark face was a perfect foil for the peppered gray beard that sprouted like two-day stubble. He was a big man, and years of eating burgers and drinking flat colas on stakeouts had begun to take its toll on his waistline. Still, it was his eyes that grabbed you. The piercing, hazel orbs usually won him a trust that produced information others gave up on getting. It had served him well during his years on the police force.

"They grew up in South Florida," he said to Justin.

"I didn't know that." He reached for the file Connie had placed on his desk earlier, and opened it. He had known Conrad Preston, called Connie by his friends, for years, and trusted him to obtain and handle sensitive information discreetly.

"David Spenser paid for college with football, then went on to law school. That took money, so he did it with part-time jobs, his sister's help, and loans."

Justin tabbed through the file notes. A quick glance at the crystal clock nearby told him it was early, which gave him plenty of time before Davina arrived to sign her contract that afternoon. "What about the sister?"

"Interesting. She was a good student, but didn't go straight to college. Later on, she attended and commuted." Comfortable in shirt-sleeves on the warm August morning, Connie referred to a notepad on his lap. "Let's see, she worked full time, went to school, and took care of her father." Connie looked up. "Which explains why it took her a while to get her art degree." He leaned back in his chair, his hands bridged, and waited for Justin's next query.

"That's it?" was the frustrated, though not unexpected response from Justin.

Connie smiled, and relaxed his hands. "After all these years, man, you're still impatient."

"Sorry." Justin raked his hand across his head. "What you learn is important to me. I was just expecting more."

"I ran into a brick wall with the father, James Spenser. The trail died after the usual yield."

"Nothing on his supposed friendship with Maceo?"

Connie shook his head. "Not a thing. Spenser was sick over the last ten years, and got progressively worse. It had to be hard on his daughter." He sighed and straightened in his chair. "There's no nice way to put it, Justin, but the man was a drunk."

Justin looked up from the file and frowned. "What about the mother? It says here she died when Davina was six years old."

Connie nodded. "The death certificate lists her cause of death as injuries suffered from a car accident. Which brings up something else. I'm researching the death record on James Spenser. I don't have anything on him, not even a picture."

Justin rubbed his chin. "See what you can dig up using the mother's name."

"I'm already on it. Oh, I checked like you asked and neither the brother nor sister is married, but the sister was engaged. The man's name is in your file."

Justin's fingers quickly skipped through the sparse report in search of the name. "Lawrence Parker, it says here. What happened?" He looked up.

"Nothing specific. It ended while she was in Florida, before she moved to Atlanta. That's about it so far. I'll have more soon."

Justin reared back in his chair and pondered all these pieces of the puzzle that made up Davina Spenser. "I appreciate your quick action on this, Connie. It means a lot to me."

Connie stood to leave. "I hope you know what you're trying to find, because I'll be damned if I do."

Justin grinned at his attempt to learn the why of the investigation. "That makes two of us, my friend. But, when you find it for me, I'll know it." He got up from his chair. "Can I ask you a question, off the clock?"

"Sure, man."

"Where do you look when you believe there's an inside leak?"

"Is that why you're playing this so close to the vest?" He gave Justin a knowing look before he stuffed the notepad back into his shirt pocket. "You look in your own backyard, then follow your instincts. You know, two and two does equal four more often than not."

Justin didn't correct Connie's assumption. "I'll remember that." He joined Connie around the desk and clasped the man's burly hand in a farewell shake.

A quick rap on the door was followed by Ray Miller's entry with a folded newspaper. He looked at Connie's departing figure. "What's Preston doing here?"

"Checking some things out for me." Justin raised knitted brows in the direction of the newspaper. "What have you got?"

He made his way across the room where Justin stood, and thrust the paper into his waiting hand. "Here's the story in the *Leader*. That pesky reporter took our threat seriously and didn't print the innuendo, but what he did print is damaging enough.'' He dropped his considerable girth onto the sofa.

Justin opted to lean on the edge of his desk and read the article. From the day his presidency was announced, Justin knew he would have to prove he was capable of handling the problems of a business in trouble as easily as he had managed stock portfolios on Wall Street. The story hinted of a business in transition, trouble with investors, and its vulnerability to a takeover. It left unanswered the question of troubles on the horizon for the young, untried president.

The paper hit the desk in a soft slap as Justin mused out loud. ''How did they get that information? Only the board and department heads know what's going on. Is the *Leader* paying someone for this stuff?''

Ray held up three fingers. ''There are three reasons to be concerned. First, these problems started with Jacob, but they picked up tempo when you came on, along with press interest. Second, did you notice there's been no mention of Ms. Spenser's claims in the paper? I'm not complaining, and she agreed not to go to the press, but if the paper finds out everything going on, why not that?''

Justin nodded at Ray. ''That crossed my mind, as well. Your last point?''

''What if Miss Spenser is our leak to the press? She could very well be—''

''Hold on, Ray. She doesn't know about our capital problems.''

''Maybe she knows someone who does. Remember, she came to us out of the blue after Jacob died and you took over. She said Jacob would've cleared up her claims. Convenient for her, he was dead.'' He shook his head at Justin's look of skepticism. ''I don't know, but it's possible that all this is somehow connected, and here we are about to enter into a contract with her.''

''One that'll bring us money and good press notices. With only a rumor that we have her show, *Atlanta Magazine* has approached us for a feature story.''

''We have to do this with our eyes open, and you, Justin, watch your back.''

''I appreciate the observations, and I've already considered some of your points.'' Justin returned to his chair behind his desk, and leaned forward. "This show will be good for us. We can squeeze in extra exhibit time without the related overhead and complete the gallery's calendar. We can even play up her Maceo connection . . . that is, if we can get evidence to back it up. It's risky, true, but it's what we do, Ray."

"Hello, guys." Linda joined them through the door Ray had left open, the scent of her expensive perfume already launching an assault. With a sheaf of papers in her hand, she beat a languid path toward Justin's desk. The soft, seductive swish of her short silk skirt against silk stockings cut through the room.

"Where's Nora today?" she asked. "She's usually blocking your door with her body." She sat in the armchair near Ray, and balancing the papers on her crossed knee, looked over at him. "Let me guess . . . you found something to worry over?"

"We were discussing your Miss Richards, or whatever she's calling herself today." Ray pulled himself from the sofa. "I see you have the contracts for the signing this afternoon, so I'll leave you two."

"I'll touch bases with you at the meeting." Justin picked up the folded newspaper and came around his desk to hold it out to Ray. "Drop this by Marc's office. Make sure the department heads see it."

"Done." He took the paper and left, closing the door behind him.

"Something interesting in the paper?" Linda asked.

'Another piece of crap from that reporter at the *Leader,*" Justin said matter-of-factly. "Are those the revised contracts?" He sat in the chair next to her as she nodded her head.

"They should be at Nora's desk, not mine," he said.

"I don't like the changes, and neither does Marc."

"I already made note of your feelings. What does Marc have to do with it?"

"He's always had contract approval. Jacob never concerned himself with new acquisitions and stuff like that."

"I don't think my father concerned himself with much of anything." Justin dropped his head to the back of the chair. "Marc knows why I'm involved."

"Are you still angry with me?" She moved the papers from her knee and turned in her chair to face him. "I'm sorry my proposal didn't reveal Vinny Richards and Davina Spenser as the same person. But, it did work out in the end, right?"

He raised his head and, with a deep sigh, turned to Linda. Leave it to her to always look for the bottom line. "You're good at finding talent, Linda. But, this was a case where precise information would have helped, and you have a habit of not being meticulous with your proposal packets."

"Everyone who saw the woman at the meeting says the same thing —she's unfriendly, and you two were at each other's throat." She leaned toward Justin's bent head with a hopeful glint in her eyes. "I know you love her work, and for the sake of the show, I really wanted you to have a good relationship with her. She seems such a harmless, sad little mouse from those pictures and articles. I'm sure you can handle her. Did I let you down very much this time? Am I forgiven?"

Justin's mouth twitched in amusement as she tried to press her point. He wondered what Davina would say about Linda's take on her. "Everything's been handled to our benefit, so you can breathe easy."

"And she doesn't have an agent?" Linda frowned in distaste. "Who was the person you talked with in New York if it wasn't her agent?"

"He was an agent, but only through a friend of a friend that owed her brother a favor, or at least I think that's how it was explained to me." Justin's smile warmed his face clear to his eyes as he thought of Davina and her odd way of doing things. He looked over at Linda. "You were right when you said talent is quirky."

A beep near the phone signaled Nora's return and a call for Justin. "Excuse me," he said, and returned behind his desk where he picked up the phone.

While he sat and quietly listened to his caller, he watched Linda leave her chair and place the contracts near a folder on his desk. Intent on his caller's words, Justin belatedly noticed Linda's interest in the folder Connie had clearly labeled ONGOING INVESTIGATION, with Davina's name on the jutting tab.

Without a break in his conversation, he set the contracts on top of the file, and removed both to the credenza behind his chair. A shadow of annoyance crossed his face as Linda returned to her chair.

When he hung up the phone, she spoke quickly. "Justin, you

said everything was okay with the artist. Why are you having her investigated?''

He leaned back and gave Linda a pointed stare. ''I'll look at the contracts before the meeting starts.'' His manner, now cool and aloof, was a silent dismissal. Rising from her chair, Linda started to speak. But, when she looked into his eyes, she said nothing and left the office.

Justin came around his desk and walked across the room to a large, intricately framed painting that graced the end wall. The painting was of his father as a younger man. He stopped in front of it and contemplated seeing Davina this afternoon. It was a remarkable painting, though not because it depicted the late Jacob Hardy. There were a few of those in the building, as well as at the house. Its uniqueness lay in the fact that it was a signed original by Maceo.

''Live a little, Davina.'' Natalie joyfully slapped butter on the soft, yeasty roll while she and Davina waited for David to join them at Houston's. ''You're going to sign show contracts in a few hours, Justin Hardy accepts your changes, and you get a chance to see his records.'' Her smile was sly. ''So what if you had a hot moment the other night and enjoyed it? Welcome to the living.''

Davina threw her a black look. ''This is serious, and you're making a joke.''

''No, I'm not.'' She slathered another piece of the bread with butter. ''I have changed my mind a little about him, though.''

''What brought that on?''

''He's the only man in two years who's gotten this kind of a reaction from you. Denzel on a movie screen doesn't count. Your mind may lie to you about what you want, but your body won't.'' She chewed the bread and eyed Davina. ''I'll bet he didn't make any bones about what he wanted, right?''

Davina looked away. ''He's a man. They seldom do. Anyway, I wouldn't give him the pleasure of knowing how much he affected me.''

Natalie was right. She had forgotten the exquisite sensation of becoming weak with want until Justin reintroduced it the other night.

She also remembered why she had closed off that part of her feelings, and the guilt returned.

"So he did want you, huh?"

Davina ignored the impertinent question. "I can't let him know how I feel—uh, felt." She darted a frown at Natalie's narrow gaze.

"Trust me, he knows. But, I think you should explore these feelings you're having." She reached for another roll. "What about David? He had to see you two looking hot and bothered when you returned from your walk."

Davina flushed from the picture Natalie's words painted. "He was occupied. I told you Justin's youngest sister, Alli, flirted with David all evening, but it was in fun. She's cute, quite petite, and just out of college."

"Cute and petite, huh? What did he do?" Natalie asked.

"You know David since he and Sheree broke up. He still prefers to make the passes." Then, they both laughed when Davina recalled some of Alli's outrageous comments.

"Are you going to talk to David about what's going on with you and Justin?"

"Stop saying that. Nothing is going on. And do you really expect me to tell my brother I have the hots for the man we believe is—" She saw Natalie's stare travel beyond their table.

"David's here," Natalie said, her voice low.

"Promise me you won't say anything to him," Davina demanded in a whisper. Before she could elicit the promise, David arrived at the table with a waiter in tow. Davina looked at Natalie, who smiled sweetly from across the table.

With the point of her shoe, and under the cover of the table, she kicked Natalie's shin.

"Ow!" Natalie screeched, and reached under the table to rub her leg. She looked at Davina, righteously indignant. "Okay, all right?"

"What's wrong?" David asked as he squeezed into the booth next to Natalie.

"What makes you think something is wrong?" Davina gave a bright smile to the young waiter who stood nearby. "We'd like another basket of bread, please."

* * *

This was Davina's third time entering Hardy Enterprises' office and gallery, and each time had been met with trepidation. She would never be able to enter absent the accompanying anxiety until she could be honest about all she had done. Her prior actions were an albatross that hung from her slender neck.

As she and David followed Nora Watts to Justin's office, Davina wondered if Linda would be present. She hadn't learned the woman's last name, but her shoulders straightened proudly at the thought that someone on Justin's side of the table had actually pulled for her.

The double doors to an office that lay beyond Nora's work area slowly opened when they drew near. As if by magic, Justin appeared from the other side, a formidable figure in his domain, and Davina faltered a step at seeing him so soon again. Nora efficiently handed them over and walked into the office.

"Right on time," Justin said as he extended his hand to David. When David entered the office, it was Davina's turn to shake hands.

When she looked up at him, his smile was a torch, and the passion they'd shared at his house flared into her memory.

"No smile for me today?" The husky whisper was for her ears alone.

She held her composure and returned a hesitant smile, saying, "Let's see how our meeting goes first."

"That's a deal," he agreed as he dropped his hand so she could enter.

It was a large office, broken into areas marked by sofas and chairs. A large desk, with an equally sized leather chair behind it, took up a wall. An ornate, antique cabinet near the desk did a magnificent job of masking its new function. With one of the doors ajar, it revealed a television, VCR, and assorted electronics.

There was a conspicuous absence of paintings and art objects about the room. The sole exception was a large, handsome painting, which she supposed was of a young Jacob Hardy. It commanded a far wall.

Another wall boasted floor to ceiling windows and was defined by a table where a man and woman already sat. Davina didn't know the beautiful woman, but her face was familiar. She felt Justin's hand as he led her to them and performed the introductions.

Davina had met Ray, and her curiosity had already turned to the worldly looking woman sitting next to him. The woman stood for the introduction.

"And this is Linda Daniels, from new acquisitions and talent," Justin said.

David shook her hand as Davina stepped forward. For a second or two, the women stared at each other. Davina, in that instant, recognized where she had seen her face. Linda, on the other hand, recognized something else and reacted.

Shaking Davina's hand, her eyebrows were raised a fraction as she said in a voice that didn't quite match her words, "I'm delighted to meet you."

"You're Linda Daniels, the fashion model," Davina bluntly responded.

Linda patted her hair and glowed in the recognition. "I am, but it's been a while since I did any modeling work."

"It's a pleasure to meet you. I understand you're the main reason Hardy Enterprises is interested in my art."

Linda's eyes stretched as she swallowed. "Yes. . . . It's good work."

"You also found my nude Justin hung on his wall at home. He showed it to me the other night." Davina smiled pleasantly as she shared the news.

"Oh," Linda said weakly. "It's at his house?" She fluttered a hand in the air as she reclaimed her seat. "You know, you're hardly recognizable from that Polaroid with your portfolio." She looked at Justin, but he was watching Davina take a seat next to David.

"Those old things? David took them years ago," Davina answered.

"She uses them because she won't take time to have professional shots done," David added with a smile.

Linda's smile didn't quite reach her eyes. "A little work on the hair and wardrobe wouldn't hurt either, don't you think, Justin?"

The comment drew a raised brow from Davina, and Justin quickly intervened.

"Let's get to business," he suggested. "Ray, you want to start?"

"All right," he said, and reached for a stack of sheets next to him.

He passed one to each person at the table. "This is a list of items we'll cover."

Davina felt David's squeeze of her hand under the table, and it shored up her confidence. She returned the squeeze, then gave her attention to Ray's voice.

After an hour, Davina's nerves were frayed, but she wasn't going to back down on this point. She wanted the right to set prices to the pieces, and for some reason, Linda had argued against each change Davina wanted in the contract. Galleries were notorious for boosting prices out of the reach of the average art lover, and Davina didn't want that to happen with her show.

Justin pushed away from the table. "I can assure you, the prices will be in line with both the market and product."

"If that's the case, then working it out together shouldn't be a problem," Davina pressed stubbornly.

"You're paid to paint the pictures, not set the gallery price," Linda retorted.

"There's nothing wrong, Linda, with voicing opinions," Justin warned.

"That's not the case here," David said. He looked from Ray to Justin. "You told me you'd agree to that stipulation."

Justin directed his stare at David. "I told you I would consider it."

Picking up the gauntlet, Linda continued the attack, her sneer marring her beautiful face. "We've been more than generous as it is to a first show artist."

Ray lay his hands against the table top. "We're at an impasse." He sat back in his chair and, like the others, looked to Justin.

"This is important to me." Davina concentrated her gaze on Justin. "I would be willing to make an adjustment elsewhere in the contract for this one." She watched his brows narrow as he looked at her with uncertainty. She removed his doubt with a subtle nod of her head; it was as if they were the only two in the room. She was drawn into his depthless black eyes before she blinked into reality.

"Give her what she wants, Ray."

"But, Justin . . ." Linda started, and looked from Justin to Ray.

"You heard him," Davina said firmly, and bestowed an eager smile to David and Justin.

"Not so fast," Justin said as he tapped his pen on the table top. "In return, your percentage reverts to the lower figure and your related overhead will be paid from your profits."

Davina looked at David, who nodded in agreement. "Fair enough," she said.

"We're holding you to the letter of this contract, so read it," Linda warned.

"That's it," Ray said, as he noted the last adjustment on the final page. "We have ourselves a contract." He motioned for Davina and Justin to initial the change. When they finished, Nora collected the papers and quietly left the room.

Justin lay the pen down and reached a hand across the table to Davina. "Welcome to the Hardy Gallery, Vinny Richards."

This time, Davina gave him a wide, open smile, and allowed him to encircle her hand with his. For a moment, she enjoyed its firm caress, then she returned to the business at hand. "Thank you. I'm glad to be here."

As she basked in a multitude of emotions, she noticed that Linda still sat in her chair with a decidedly unfriendly expression on her face. The look she wore carried a chill that cut through the warmth like a cold dagger. Davina shook it off, but wondered if it was a harbinger of things to come.

"One of your first appearances will be the annual charity auction and wine tasting at the Richmond Mansion. It's good publicity," Justin said.

"I've heard of it, but never attended any Atlanta art events." Davina saw Linda's eyes float upward, as if to attest to Davina's constant state of naïveté.

"Then you'll attend?"

Davina looked from David to the disdain on Linda's face. "Yes, I will."

"It's one of the better functions," Ray said. "They always have great entertainment. Most of the others are boring."

"Tomorrow morning," Justin said, "Linda will acquaint you with the gallery and art workshops. Can you make it?"

"I'll be here." The group moved from the table to leave when Davina's attention returned to the large painting on the end wall. As the others made small talk, she walked up to it. The artist's name was not so much a surprise as it was a joy. She wasn't sure how long she stood before the others were behind her.

"I was going to tell you about it at the end of the meeting, but I see you were drawn on your own," Justin said. "You really are enamored of Maceo's works."

"I'm only now learning how gifted he was. Look at the colors."

"Amazing," David said. "I thought you didn't have his paintings on display."

"Technically, we don't. The office isn't considered a show area."

Davina looked behind her and saw that Ray and Linda had left. "I'd like to stay longer," she said softly. "May I?" She returned her attention to the painting.

"Of course," Justin replied. "You can come any time you want. I'll tell Nora."

A proud, secretive smile softened Davina's lips as her eyes faithfully studied brush strokes she remembered from lessons learned at her father's side years before. *We're inside, Daddy. It won't be long now.*

CHAPTER THIRTEEN

A New Member of the Family

"I know why you're involved, Justin, but I think you should step back. Let me handle her." Marc faced Justin from across the small room. They stood in one of the two offices located in the third-floor art gallery. Separated from the exhibit area by a wall of glass, the offices were used by show artists to conduct business.

Justin held a tight rein on his rising anger. Davina wasn't the problem here. "Linda is ticked off because her discovery isn't as malleable as she'd thought."

"She's concerned about your intensity with the woman. I can't believe you gave an untried artist price approval." Marc shook his head and stepped away from Justin.

"You have a problem with that?" He watched Marc stiffen at his words and come to a stop. "You're doubting my decisions, too?"

"I didn't say that . . ." He turned and raised his eyes to Justin's.

"Sure sounds like it. In fact, you're sharing that opinion with everyone but me." At Marc's sigh, he knew his intuition was right. "Were those your sentiments Ray issued yesterday?" When he didn't respond, Justin quipped, "Thanks for the support." He touched his forehead slightly in a mock salute.

"I'm worried, Justin. When you're advised to do one thing, bam! You do the opposite." The two men were wound tight as a clock, and the strain of their discord was evident on each face. "What you're doing is suspect with everybody."

Justin slowly shook his head and allowed his heavy voice to boom. "My management style doesn't match my father's and that's too bad. Why do you think everything's falling apart around here? He should have made changes a long time ago and that advice should have come from you. Remember, I didn't want this job. He left me with little choice."

"Is that what this is about? You leaving your comfortable life?" Marc's voice rose, too. "I told Jacob you wanted to stay in New York and fry big fish, and running the family business down here was not in your cards."

"You want the job, Marc? You want the damn job?"

"If you can't hack it, yes."

Justin's mouth was a determined line. He knew where their anger came from. Marc had worked at Jacob's side for over ten years while Justin had come and gone several times during that time. If the truth be known, Justin carried a certain amount of guilt that Marc wasn't the sitting president. He took in a deep breath, and walked to the rain-splattered window.

"I'm sorry, Justin. I didn't mean that."

"Sure you did. We both know you'd be president if I had taken the expected route and declined, but Dad figured a way to control me, even if it was from beyond the grave. I was ready for a change, anyway. What else would I do?"

"You could have continued to be one of the smartest men trading on the Exchange. You had valid reasons for not joining Jacob here."

A grudging smile played across Justin's lips. "I guess we both got a royal screw." He looked at Marc. "I'm glad you stayed on."

Marc slowly made his way over to Justin at the window and sealed their understanding with his own hesitant smile. "Jacob wanted you here because he knew you wouldn't be afraid to push for change to save the company. You have a way of making things happen."

"And you see where it's gotten me. My hands are in everybody's department, but it's going to be that way for a while." Justin balanced an outstretched arm against the wall and looked beyond the rivulets of rain streaking the window.

"I may not like it, but I do hear you," Marc said and rocked on his heels. "Are you taking the lady around the gallery today?"

"No. That's Linda's job. Besides, I have meetings most of the afternoon. If she needs help, the support staff is there."

"That reminds me," Marc said. "The bank wants a meeting about extending our loan. The investment group I lined up wants to pitch their proposal as well. As soon as I can arrange the meetings, will you be ready to go?"

"If you think the deal is worthwhile, I can rearrange my schedule."

As Justin talked, he absently watched the early morning traffic along Piedmont Road. His eyes were soon drawn to a lithe figure darting along the sidewalk through the rain, and he promptly recognized Davina. Her warm, pliant body in his arms momentarily ruled his thoughts. "Davina is here." He inclined his head toward the window.

"You really think Linda will let you work closely with a good-looking woman like Davina Spenser?" He joined Justin at the window. "She's already figured your eye is wandering in that direction."

Justin's brows rose in surprise, but his eyes never left the figure below. "I expect Linda to do her job. Where'd she get that idea, anyway?"

"From your signing yesterday." A grin slowly replaced Marc's earlier smile. "I started to tell her your interest is there because Miss Spenser's isn't." He started for the door, but paused before he exited. "That is the case, right?"

Justin shot him a withering glance, but Marc was already maneuvering around the art displays, laughter left in his wake as he exited the gallery. Justin returned his gaze to the sidewalk, only to find she was gone.

Was Marc right? Was he getting too close to gauge the best benefit for the company? Davina was complicated, different, and totally unpredictable. And interesting. He was inexplicably pleased by the fact that he'd see her shortly. If he had to experience all of her aggravating moods to find out what she was after at Hardy, then so be it.

A steady drizzle of rain fell and Davina didn't try to avoid it as she made her way down the sidewalk. She was in a good mood, and nothing would change it—not even the fact that she was no closer than she had been last week to finding anyone in this city that could tell her about Maceo's early days.

She sidestepped a final puddle of water and sought the dry shelter offered by the lobby at Hardy Enterprises. The staid receptionist treated her with an obvious deference this time, and sent her directly upstairs to Justin's office. Once there, Nora presented her with a personal building pass.

"You're wet," Nora exclaimed, taking in Davina's linen blouse and slacks.

"I know." She looked down at her soaked hems and felt compelled to give Nora a reason for her unkempt condition. "I left my umbrella at home."

Nora clucked her tongue. "You should always keep one in your car. I do. Come on into the office. We'll get you dried off in there." She walked on ahead.

Davina stopped outside the double doors and wondered if Justin was in.

"Come on." Nora's trademark firm voice wafted back through the open door to Davina.

She walked through to the luxurious office but didn't see Nora. "Where's Mr. Hardy?" she called out.

Nora reappeared in the doorway of what Davina now saw was a bathroom that matched the office's polished wood and blue decor. She handed a blue towel to Davina. "When you're finished, just drop it in the hamper. Mr. Hardy is out, but Linda Daniels should be here any minute to take you around."

"Oh, boy, that should be fun," Davina mumbled and entered the bathroom.

"Oh? Why do you say that?" Nora asked. She walked to the windows and busied herself with the blinds.

Davina didn't readily answer, but reached up and pulled the headband from her damp hair. She peered into a wide mirror above the sink, her image small inside the framed glass. Nora now stood outside the bathroom door while Davina used the towel to blot the rain from her face. She would be frank with Nora.

"She wasn't too friendly at the meeting." Davina rested her hip against the counter and faced Nora. "It started off fine, but by the time it was over, she was snapping at anything I said." She started to blot her hair. "In fact, she acted like she had a personal grudge against me."

Nora snorted. "None of us thought too highly of you when we heard about your claims." When Davina started to speak, Nora held her hand up. "Don't try to explain, I know that's business. Linda, though, has a history with the boss, and my guess is when you showed up she took an instant dislike to you being around him."

Davina lowered the towel from her head, her dark eyebrows slanted in a frown. "You mean she and Justin Hardy are a, you know, couple?"

"No. I mean they aren't a couple anymore, and she's jealous. Of you."

Davina was both relieved and surprised. "Jealous of me? No way. I'm going to tell her there's nothing—"

"I wouldn't do that if I were you," Nora said, a smile forming on her sharp face. "A word of advice, young lady. What you say won't mean a thing to a suspicious person like our Linda, and it could hurt more by putting it in words. What I suggest is you and the boss watch your body language if you don't want to send the wrong signals." Nora walked across the room to leave. "When you finish, I'll see you outside." She closed the doors firmly behind her.

Davina stepped from the bathroom and stared at the closed doors as she considered Nora's words.

Did she suspect something more than business between her and Justin, or was it an innocent warning of caution? The frigid air blanketed Davina's wet blouse and a shiver snaked through her body. She drew her arms within the folds of the bulky towel and absently walked toward Justin's desk where his two framed diplomas hung on the wall. One was for an undergraduate degree in business; the other, an MBA degree from the Wharton School of Business. She raised a brow, disinclined to be impressed, but knew that was an accomplishment for anyone.

Remembering that Linda could arrive at any moment, she retraced her steps into the large bathroom equipped with a shower and Jacuzzi. A closet door was closed at the other end. The wet blouse was clammy and uncomfortable against her skin. She deftly unbuttoned, then slipped it off. A tan body-suit was all she wore underneath, and while it provided the modesty of a chemise, it clung like a second skin and disappeared into the waistband of her belted slacks. The towel would never dry the blouse, so she looked around for another solution, and found one. A hair dryer hung from a hook in the corner.

She plugged the dryer in. A raucous whir accompanied the rush of hot air she directed to the upraised blouse. The noise from the dryer, and the certainty that she was alone, allowed Davina to lose herself in the task. She was unaware that what she presumed was a closet door now opened from the other side.

Justin had left the gallery and stopped by Marc's adjoining office. Marc wasn't in, but Justin had heard noises from his bathroom. His reaction when he walked through the unlocked door was surprised silence, but his brows raised in immediate appreciation. There was Davina, her back to him and an arm raised high with a blow dryer. His first thought was to retreat discreetly because she was undressed from the waist up. A second, more careful glance revealed she wore a flesh colored chemise, and it held his attention. Too late. In his brief pause before leaving, she turned around. Justin braced himself for her venom.

Stunned by Justin's sudden appearance, Davina dropped the dryer to the counter, the clatter only adding to the din already created by the motor.

"What are you doing in here?" she demanded. "You just about scared me to death." She breathed deeply as her hand fell to her heart.

"What am I doing here? You're in my bathroom." He didn't turn away from the lush sight she presented and his eyes feasted on.

"I was trying to dry my blouse. Don't you know how to knock?" They both reached for the whirring dryer to cut it off.

"How did I know you were in here? You don't know how to lock a door?"

"I didn't know there was another door."

Justin pulled the plug from the wall. Instantly, the room fell silent.

"That's better," Justin said, and pushed the dryer away. He inclined his head to Davina. "You know, I could have sworn you told me that you would make it your business to avoid me—alone—and here you are, in my bathroom. Undressing."

Davina didn't think he was funny. She raised her chin and sent a cool stare in his direction as she crossed her arms over her breasts. That simple action only accentuated her cleavage. "You just don't quit, do you?" She looked around the room. "You always have to give the last word. Where's my blouse?"

"Over here." He picked up the material and held it out to her. "It's still a little damp."

She snatched it from his hand and gave a frustrated sigh while she pulled it on. Justin's eyes watched in fascination as her breasts strained against the soft fabric. "Need my help?" he offered.

"Over my dead body," she replied, and gave him her back.

Justin smiled at her discomfort as he finally allowed a buried thought to surface. He wanted to make love to her. She was demanding and complaining, but beautiful and complicated. He wondered if she knew how attractive that combination made her. She had been clear that she wanted nothing to do with him, and he'd have to change her mind.

It was the only way she'd lower her guard and let him make love to her. And it was the only way he'd be free of her.

The office door opened outside, and they both reacted to the sound.

"Someone's here," Davina whispered loudly, and quickly fastened the last button. "Go back the way you came in." She smoothed a hand over her damp hair and started for the door.

Justin put his hands on her shoulders to slow her down. "It's probably Nora."

He opened the door and they both looked out, Justin behind Davina, as Nora and Linda entered his office. In that second, all four sets of eyes locked, and the moment became a freeze frame.

Linda reacted first, her eyes burned into Davina's. "What are you doing in there?" Her query was more a demand than a question.

Davina gave Justin an accusing frown from over her shoulder before she joined the women. "I got wet coming in this morning, and Nora offered me a towel." She looked to Nora for help, but it came from Justin, who had joined them.

"Linda, you were supposed to greet the newest member of Hardy's family. Instead, Nora and I kept her occupied."

"I gave her permission to use your bathroom," Nora advised Justin before she turned to Davina. "And, you're still wet, you know."

"Yes, you are," Linda said through pursed lips.

Davina felt Linda's disapproving gaze sweep over her; she reached to smooth her hair behind her gold-hooped ear.

"I told her there was no rush, but she insisted she didn't want to keep you waiting." He smiled at Davina, a silent message for her only.

She was acutely conscious of his presence and looked up at him, thankful that he smoothed over the awkward moment, as well as put Linda in her place. She grimaced. That woman continued to step on her last nerve.

She studied Linda through more knowledgeable eyes. *I should have known he'd look for her kind of glamour and sophistication, and boy does she dish it out in spades. They deserve each other.* Linda strutted her femininity in a ruffled blouse, which made her resemble a petaled flower, her cleavage the sought after nectar. She doubted if Linda's hair ever dared stray out of place. Unconsciously, she smoothed her own hair.

Linda laid her jeweled hand prettily on Justin's arm, and stepped closer to him. "We should have lunch together so we can go over my plans for the show. Today would be perfect."

"You forgot you had me pencil in Miss Spenser for today," Nora said. "You wanted to discuss the charity benefit."

Davina, surprised, looked to Justin. "Oh?"

"I never confirmed it because something came up." He gently removed Linda's hand from his arm. "We can discuss the plans at the staff meeting."

Linda branded Davina with a stare before curtly announcing, "I have a lot planned this morning. Are you ready?"

"Whenever you are," Davina answered evenly. She clamped the inside of her lip with her teeth.

"Oh, one more thing," Justin said. As both of the women turned to him, he looked at Davina. "Before you leave today, see Nora. I'll make sure she has the schedule for you to begin reviewing the papers from the archives."

"I'm glad I didn't have to remind you of our agreement." She offered him her hand, which he firmly captured in his, and they both smiled in earnest. "Agreed."

Linda's hands rested on her hips. "Nora, I asked for an intern to help me out today. Did you find time to get someone?"

"I sure did," was Nora's unconcerned response.

As if on cue, there was a knock at Justin's door, and it was pushed open. Alli's tiny figure scooted through the door, hardly a quiet entry with her noisy jewelry. Her small voice cut through the room. "Hi, sorry I'm late."

Davina saw the sidelong glare Linda gave Nora and realized Alli was the intern expected to help. She smiled. She was learning to like Nora more and more.

"I think a perm and a good cut will do wonders for your hair, as well." Linda smiled at Davina for confirmation as they walked toward the gallery.

Davina continued to ignore her. She was glad Alli had been the one to show her around. For one thing, she surely would have strangled Linda, who only just rejoined them to take over the gallery tour.

"The current photography exhibit will close next week," Linda was saying, "And we have a short run with the European show traveling across the country. After that, you're on, Davina. Aren't you excited?" Linda pushed through the doors.

Davina caught Alli giving her a strained look behind Linda's back. She smiled and entered the gallery.

Remembrance of the night she hid here returned like a suffocating blanket. She recognized the photographs and knew that beyond the wall to the left was a metal door that led to the storage and work areas. As expected, Linda led them there. To her right, Davina saw an older black man sitting in a glassed office.

"Who is he?" Davina asked Alli.

"That's Morris Mangley," she said as they walked by. "His photographs are a part of the current exhibit."

They caught up with Linda and went through the double metal doors. The back of the gallery was set up much like a warehouse, with storage bins, shelves, and wired receptacles that held supplies, canvases, and much more.

"We have a restoration lab we're quite proud of that keeps our curator busy," Linda said. She moved deeper into the cavernous room and rounded a corner until she was out of view.

Davina and Alli slowed to a stop and looked around the huge work area.

"Aren't you excited?" Alli asked, obviously mocking Linda. Her laugh brought a smile to Davina's face, too. "So, really, how are you liking it so far?"

"Does she really expect me to do a makeover for publicity shots? I'm selling my paintings, not my face."

"Listen," Alli confided, "she's our resident prima donna." She tilted her head at Davina. "Relax, and don't let her get to you, because if she can, she will."

"This is all a first for me, and I'm impressed by the amount of what goes on here. I had no idea Hardy Enterprises did so many different things."

"Neither did I."

They were both laughing at Alli's observation when Linda returned. She was accompanied by a thin, middle-aged man in a white lab coat pulled over a shirt and tie. His serious mien was accentuated by his wire-framed glasses. A shock of dark brown hair hung across his pale forehead and gave him a boyish appearance.

Linda made the introduction. "Charles Albritton, I want you to meet Vinny Richards, the new artist we're showing. She's also known as Davina Spenser."

"Please call me Davina," she said to Charles.

"It's good to meet you, Davina," he said. "I've seen your work. It's going to be a pleasure working with you."

Davina looked at Alli, confused by his comment.

"Charlie authenticates everything," Alli said. Davina nodded her understanding as Alli continued. "He makes sure that what comes in is the same thing that leaves. Right, Charlie?"

He took off his glasses and wiped them on his lab coat. "Alli makes it sound like a lot more than it is. It can be monotonous work, actually, but it's important and I enjoy it." He replaced his glasses.

"I have to leave and handle some other things," Linda said. "Alli, I believe you and Charles can answer any remaining questions Davina might have. If you have a problem, don't disturb Justin with it; find me or Nora." She turned and left.

With Linda gone, Davina quickly learned the curator was better known as Charlie, and he showed off his lab like a proud papa. When they had walked the circular route through the lab, they returned to the workshop area where they first came in, and were met by a young man close to Alli's age, also in a lab coat, as he came through the metal doors. The first thing Davina noticed about him, after the short dreadlocks that bobbed across his head, was the engaging grin he wore.

Alli hailed the new arrival. "Hey, Robert, I wondered where you were."

Davina met Charlie's protege and lab assistant, Robert Montgomery.

"It's great meeting you," Robert said, offering her a strong handshake. "I can't wait to talk to you. I bet you could give me some great pointers."

Davina gave him a puzzled look.

Alli and Charlie both laughed. Alli piped in with, ''Robert's a local graffiti artist turned straight since joining us.''

''He's learning about restoration from me, and he helps with the gallery setups,'' Charlie added.

''I've got a lot to learn, though,'' Robert said. ''I'm okay with the art scene.''

Davina remembered some of the beautiful and elaborate graffiti murals she had seen in Miami and Atlanta, put together by so-called ''burners.'' She smiled at Robert. ''So, I'm talking to a bona fide burner, huh?''

''Yeah, I've tagged my name on a few walls. I gave it up when Mr. Hardy helped me avoid jail by learning the business of art. Now, I only tag canvases.''

Charlie slapped the young man across the shoulders. ''Who knows, you might have a show here one day like Davina.''

''Hey, you know about Maceo,'' Robert said to Davina. ''Now that's really something. Do you mind if I talk art with you some time?'' His eyes were bright. ''That's one of the perks I get around here . . . talking one-on-one with real artists.''

''I'd like that,'' Davina said, taken by his friendly attitude. ''Any time. I only wish I knew someone that I could talk to about Maceo.'' She turned to Charlie. ''Have you come across any artists that knew Maceo back in the fifties?''

''I can't think of anyone right off. I'm sorry.'' He walked over to one of the numbered bins stacked with canvases. ''Maceo was unique, you know. No one knows what he could have accomplished if he had kept on painting. It's a shame all of his paintings are in private collections.''

Davina spoke as they all followed Charlie. ''I know. They were bought up so long ago, it's hard to find one anywhere.''

Alli's voice chimed in. ''With the African-American art trade booming these days, you won't find an original by an acclaimed artist for sale under the medium five-figure range. And when you consider originals dated before the sixties, you're really talking money.''

The three of them looked her way, surprised by her informative comments.

"I did a research assignment for the accounting department a while back and, well, you learn things."

Everyone laughed. Davina, in spite of how the day started, was enjoying herself. Robert left to continue some chores, but promised to get together with Davina. Charlie assigned Davina a bin for storage, handed over keys, and showed her where she could set up her own private work area before the opening.

As the day quickly progressed, Alli took her leave, and Davina left the building for lunch, but not before Alli exacted a promise to meet her in an hour. With a bright sun greeting her after the gray morning of rain, she decided to walk up the street and eat at Salvatore's, a nearby Italian diner.

When she entered the quaint restaurant, she waited for her eyes to adjust to the dim interior. As she stood there, a waitress touched her shoulder.

"Miss," the waitress said, "I believe that man is signaling you to join him."

Davina followed her hand and saw Morris Mangley motioning her over.

Surprised that he knew her, she said, "I'll join him, thank you."

She walked to his small table, the wall behind it filled with wine bottles.

"Hello, Miss. Sit down with me." He spoke with a slow, friendly drawl as he pulled out the chair.

"Mr. Mangley, I saw you earlier in the gallery. And, please, call me Davina." She decided he was much older than she first thought, his salt and pepper beard was almost entirely salt. She sat in the pulled out chair.

"Only if you call me Morris. You're the new painter everybody's talking about." A waiter interrupted them when he set a plate of spaghetti on the table.

"You've already ordered," Davina observed. "I shouldn't disturb your lunch."

He waved off her comments and proceeded to spice up the plate of food with the assorted condiment shakers that sat at his disposal. "I hear from Charlie and Robert that you and your folks knew Maceo."

He looked up at her before he continued with his preparation. "Is that true?"

Davina tilted her head to the side, not sure how to take his blunt query. News traveled fast in that place. It's a wonder everyone there didn't know about the missing paintings. "Yes. But, why are you interested?"

"Well," he said, "I guess it's because I knew Maceo, too."

CHAPTER FOURTEEN

Footsteps in the Shadows

Davina couldn't believe her luck. She pulled her chair closer to the table.

"You . . . you've met Maceo before?"

"Sure did. Knew him when he used to hang out with me." While Davina gaped, Morris slurped a forkful of steaming pasta into his mouth.

"That had to be a long time ago."

"We were young, talented we thought, but poor." He chuckled at the description. "Course, I'm still around, but just barely."

Davina rubbed her arms, not sure if her chill was from the over-worked air conditioner or what she was hearing. "He did speak of old friends here in Atlanta."

Morris nodded his head. "I always wondered what became of him when he left. Do you know where he is now?"

"I can't answer that. The little I know is through my father."

"When Maceo disappeared with no word to us, we understood why he did it."

"Us?" Davina leaned forward on her elbows.

"There were six of us that called ourselves good friends."

Davina couldn't believe the luck she had stumbled on, and was caught in the rapture his words created. "Please," she urged him, "tell me about them."

He wiped his mouth with the red linen napkin. "Let's see, there was Maceo, Lee Randolph, Billy Bivings, Otis Carter, and Jake Hardy."

"Jacob Hardy?"

He nodded his head. "We'd shoot pool, play cards and checkers, and help each other out making a little money here and there."

"What was Jacob doing hanging around with a group of artists?"

"We all had our own talent. Me? I was a writer who loved cameras even more. Otis, Maceo, and Lee were the artists. Billy played saxophone, but he's dead now. Jake could handle a piano, but he was good with money. He always made it work for him, always the business man. Still was, until the day he died."

"How did the group's friendship fare after Maceo left?"

"We were on and off, through good and bad times, until we finally lost track of each other. Maceo's disappearance affected us, Jake the most, I think. He and Maceo were like that." He held up two fingers pressed against each other.

The waiter quietly intruded with Davina's menu, and left. She laid it near the silverware, unopened. She wanted to hear more from Morris.

He looked up from the pasta. "It hurt Jake real bad when Maceo got in that trouble and had to leave town."

"They must have been close." When Morris made no response, Davina pressed him with a question. "So, did Jacob help him get away?"

He put the fork down and gave his full attention to her. "There was no changing Maceo's mind about leaving because we all knew things were about to come down hard on him. I don't know," Morris said, and shook his head. "But, I always believed Jake helped him out."

"Did anyone else offer to help?"

He paused a moment before he answered. "No one else had the resources to do it, except maybe Lee, but that's another story."

"Lee?" She remembered he was the other artist.

"He was a little selfish and jealous—you know how that can be among friends—and wouldn't have helped. So, it had to be Jake." He grasped the sweating glass of iced tea and took a long swallow.

Davina fidgeted in her seat in anticipation. "Is Lee still around? And what about the other friend, Otis Carter?"

"Otis left for New York over twenty years ago. As for Lee, last I heard he was living over on the southwest side with his son." Morris looked up at Davina from under knitted gray brows. "You seem like a nice young lady, but I'd be careful before I go digging around and asking questions about things long buried."

The remnants of the penne pasta and herb sauce sat forlornly in the wide, oval dish in front of Davina. Morris had returned to the gallery and she was deep in thought. As her mind tripped through a gamut of questions that remained unanswered, she bowed to the overwhelming urge to look toward a lone diner sitting not too far away. Careful not to stare, she averted her eyes. He was in his thirties, Hispanic maybe, and his face was familiar, as if she had seen him before. And then it hit her. She had seen him before—at the grocer's last week.

He did it again. He stared in her direction a moment too long, and she was sure of it now—he watched her. She tried to remember if he had been seated when she first came in. He didn't have a meal before him, only a cup of coffee. A peek at her watch showed she'd been gone over an hour. Alli would be waiting; but she wondered if this man, indeed, watched her. And if so, why?

She paid the check and after a backward glance, exited the diner. Outside, the day was sunny and clear, and the street was an innocuous avenue that led to the gallery. She chastised herself for being apprehensive, but it had happened before. What were the chances of running into the same man at such divergent places? She looked up and down the street. Confident that everything was all right, she joined the lunchtime crowd and walked back toward the gallery.

Shortly after Davina departed the diner, the man who occupied the other table also exited. He stood on the sidewalk, near the black, lattice-iron fence, and pulled a cellular phone from the inside of his jacket. He efficiently punched in a number and then spoke into the receiver, his eyes ever vigilant of his surroundings.

"She talked with Mangley and left, that's all. I'm behind her now. Check with you later." His voice was low and concise, with no hint of an accent.

He closed the phone with a decisive click and returned it to his pocket as he, too, joined the leisurely traffic along the sidewalk, just behind Davina.

Opening the door to the Hardy building, Davina looked over her shoulder one last time. *See . . . no one is after me out here. I've got to stop imagining threats and danger everywhere.* She shook her head and walked through the door, flashing her badge as she moved past the receptionist to the elevator.

Davina knew if she shared this newest concern with David, he would try to end her involvement with Hardy Enterprises. And the game would be over without the prize being won. She wouldn't let that happen before they found what they were looking for. When the elevator arrived, and the doors opened, Alli stood there.

"I hope I didn't keep you waiting," Davina said, and stepped into the hall.

"No problem." Alli smiled and rearranged two packages in her arm. The movement caused her bracelets to sing. "Justin sent me on an errand."

"Justin?" Davina's brows lifted in surprise. She felt her heart beat faster.

"Yep. He's waiting for you in the gallery." Alli slipped into the elevator, then quickly leaned out again. In a conspiratorial whisper, she added, "It must be really important because he changed his schedule. Later." Her bracelets echoed a final goodbye as the elevator doors closed.

Davina didn't move immediately, but stood there and listened to her heart's rapid beat become a pulsing drum in her head. She was both excited and aggravated that she would see him shortly. *Why does the mention of his name do that to me? Get over it, girl.* A small group came toward the elevator. Davina corralled her resolve and started for the gallery, the stern reminder all that she needed. She had survived Lawrence and learned a lesson in the process, so surely she could handle the sex appeal that radiated from Justin Hardy. Men. You can't live with them and . . . she frowned . . . you just can't live with them.

The gallery was busiest from lunch hour to closing, and Justin appreciated the fact that it teemed with activity this afternoon. He leaned his suited shoulder casually against the wall and watched a group file through the exhibit.

The doors opened and Justin looked up in time to savor the entrance Davina made. She was a fine woman who easily consumed his senses. Her long legs performed a graceful strut in his direction. She stopped in front of him. Her thick, dark hair, parted in the middle, had dried and was a mass of tight curls that behaved behind her headband. Justin enjoyed the picture she made and didn't move from the wall.

"I saw Alli at the elevator. She said you're waiting to see me."

"We can go in the back work room and talk in private."

Davina turned around and surveyed the room. "It's busy in here."

Justin's appreciative gaze lowered to her round bottom presented to his view.

She turned back to him. "But, I'm sure that's the way you like it."

"I do like it that way." His eyes danced with mischief as they met Davina's.

"We can stay in here," she said with a slight tilt of her head.

He motioned to two chairs in a quiet corner. "We can sit over there."

She led him to the corner where she sat down and crossed her legs. Justin folded into the wing chair and leaned forward.

"I have to leave town for a few days. In fact, I'm leaving this afternoon." Justin thought he saw a flash of disappointment cross her features. "Douglas Bradley will make sure the files and papers you need are available."

"I thought Marc Randall was in charge when you're gone."

"Marc will be with me."

"So, why are you telling me this? Doesn't Linda handle your acquisitions?"

"Because I know you, and don't want you getting into trouble while I'm gone." He smiled. "Douglas will take care of any problems that come up, and I want your promise that you'll honor our agreement and not cause any."

They each regarded the other. Justin's eyebrows raised inquiringly at Davina for a response.

"All right, I'll work with your Mr. Bradley."

"Good. The other thing I need to mention is the charity auction."

Stubborn recognition lit her eyes, and she shook her head as she spoke in a runaway breath. "I warned you, I'm not good at formal functions. I don't like them, they're pretentious, and I'm sure Linda would love to go. Send her."

He ignored her resistance. "It's in less than two weeks. Your show starts in about two months. Perfect timing."

"I don't think I should go, Justin." Her measured words were mulish.

"Part of your contract is to sell your show. You have to go." Justin was firm.

The thought of the function caused Davina's stomach to churn, and her shoulders lifted in a silent sigh. "Fine. Fine. I'll get directions from—"

"No."

"No?" She shifted in her chair.

"I'll pick you up." He stretched his long legs before him. "We're both going." Before she could lodge the expected protest, Justin continued. "I know, it's strictly business and nothing else. I want you to meet the art critics and patrons that'll be there. You'll be introduced as our newest artist." When he saw the doubt written on her face, he almost laughed out loud. "Trust me, you'll do great. I've been to a lot of these events. They'll love you."

"Have you told anyone else about the missing paintings?"

Justin was caught off guard by her change of subject. "I have another board meeting soon."

"And then you'll tell them everything?"

"Hold on." Justin leaned toward her, and the fragrance he had come to know as hers pleasantly greeted him. "I've been open with you on what I'm doing on this thing. I haven't decided on the next step." His voice was a deep whisper between them. "I still have options open to me, but it would help a lot if you would share with me what's going on in that beautiful head of yours."

It had slipped out before he realized what he had said, and now it filled the air around them. Davina's brow wrinkled in contempt. Justin leaned back and observed how quick she was to anger.

"I don't appreciate the personal comments." Her expression had become closed.

He knew exactly what she spoke of, but he found her displeasure amusing. "What are you talking about?"

"You know what I mean—the smooth lines, that kind of stuff. I don't like it."

"Is it my imagination, or do you have a hard time accepting compliments?"

"I have a hard time accepting them from you."

Justin grimaced in good humor and clutched his chest. "You wound my pride, Davina, but I'll try to remember not to bother you with them."

"Do women really fall for that wounded heart line?" Her mouth curved, unconsciously, into a smile.

"Obviously, you won't." Justin was in good spirits and enjoyed their exchange. "You changed the subject again and, no, I'm not any closer to finding the paintings, but I'm holding that information a while longer. Not forever, though."

Davina turned her head from his unsettling gaze and saw David enter the gallery with Linda. She shifted to the edge of her chair. "David is here. He said he might stop by."

Justin rubbed his chin as he watched them look around, then walk in their direction. He was disappointed that his talk with Davina had been interrupted. Frowning, he stood and met them, his hand extended in a greeting.

Davina followed Justin's lead. The two men made a dynamic, handsome pair and turned heads in the gallery as easily as a beautiful woman. Their business suits did little to dilute their virility. This was not lost on Linda, and she managed to stand between them and remain the center of attention.

David gave his sister a peck on the cheek and loosely draped his arm about her shoulders. "I stopped in to see how things were going for you."

Linda directed her words to Justin. "I specifically told Alli not to disturb you." She looked around. "Where is she, anyway?"

Justin would have to speak to Linda about her attitude. His father had allowed her free reign and now she was close to uncontrollable. "She's running an errand for me and will be back shortly to finish her job." He looked at David. "Have you been in our gallery before?"

David smiled. "No, I haven't. Vinny hasn't dragged me in before."

"Dragged being the operative word," Davina teased.

"We admit when it comes to artistic talent, I was left out," he added, grinning.

Justin looked at his watch. "I'm expecting the limo to take me to the airport, so I'd better get going." He shook David's hand again. "I'll leave you with your sister to enjoy the exhibit." He turned Linda's shoulders toward the door. "Davina, I'll see you next week and we can talk more about the charity auction."

Davina acknowledged his goodbye. When she offered the same to Linda, she received a pair of finely arched brows coldly raised in disdain.

David watched Justin and Linda leave before he turned to his sister. "What was that about?"

"The auction?" She purposely ignored his referral to Linda. She led him by the arm to the chairs she and Justin had occupied.

"That and everything else. I walk in and you two are sitting in the corner, talking, and looking very comfortable together for a change."

"He has to leave town on business and reminded me of my promise to go to that auction thing in a couple of weeks. He thinks I should meet some of Atlanta's rich and famous art patrons and critics." She playfully mocked Justin's words.

"That makes sense, though I don't think Linda was too happy to find him here."

Davina leaned in close and whispered, "That's because she and Justin were dating each other until recently."

He smiled. "So he's moving on and she wanted to move in, huh?"

She punched him in the shoulder. "Don't be ugly. You may whistle the same tune when Alli gets back in here." Davina giggled when his eyes opened wide.

"You should've warned me she'd be here. Now, I know I won't be here long."

"I don't want to talk about them. I have good news. I want you to meet someone who knew Maceo James in Atlanta." She smiled in anticipation of telling him about Morris Mangley and all she had learned.

Linda walked through the door Justin held for her. Coming behind her, he slammed it shut, then walked briskly past her on his way to his desk. Nora had already packed his briefcase with the necessary papers and he saw it waiting, opened for him on the conference table. The woman was priceless.

Justin dropped into the leather chair behind his desk. He rubbed his face with his hand, then looked at Linda, still standing in the middle of the room.

"What is it with you, Linda?"

"I have no idea what you're talking about." She walked to his desk and half sat on the edge, facing him.

"You're belligerent, employees have started to complain, and we have a new artist under contract that you go out of your way to be rude to. This has to end."

Linda studied her nails. "You seem to go out of your way to be with her."

"She's part of what this company needs to survive right now."

"You don't trust her any more than the rest of us do," she quickly retorted. "You're having her investigated," she said and stood from the desk. "Are you seeing her, too?"

Justin also stood and pressed his hands against the desk top. He gave Linda his complete attention. "Let's get something straight one last time. Whatever I do, Linda, it's my decision, my business, and not your concern. For the record, I have a business to run, and I don't want to hear another word from you about an investigation. Your complaints to Marc, that things aren't what they used to be, won't change anything; and he surely can't get us back together.''

Linda's eyes had turned bright while she listened to Justin. ''What will get us back together, Justin?'' Her voice was low, pregnant with expectation.

He ignored her question and strode past her to the conference table where his briefcase rested. Finally, he spoke in measured words. ''I'll be gone a few days. When I get back, tell me if you can work with me and Hardy Enterprises on a business level. Otherwise, I'll be happy to accept your resignation, your contract be damned.'' He clicked the briefcase closed, then turned to her. ''Can I make myself any clearer?''

Linda didn't answer. She turned on her heels and left the office.

At the door's slam, Justin let out a deep sigh. She was good at her job, but he could no longer tolerate what she had become. He knew her well, and he didn't want Davina to be the recipient of Linda's particular brand of cruelty. His mind told him that would be bad for business. In his heart, he knew Davina had gotten under his skin, and he wasn't going to let anything happen to her.

CHAPTER FIFTEEN

New Players in the Game

''I think I'm being followed.''

Natalie's head jerked around. ''What?'' She sat cross-legged on the carpeted floor in black leggings, a pile of phone directories toppled in front of her.

''You heard right.'' Davina stood in the middle of her living room, surrounded by an array of painted canvases.

''Does David know?''

''No, and you won't tell him, either.'' She raised a small canvas to the light. "I think it's a good idea not to make the entire exhibit nudes."

"Stop changing the subject," Natalie growled, and scrambled from the floor to face her friend. "Do you understand what you're saying?"

Davina lowered her arms and shrugged off the qualms Natalie had awakened. She slowly traipsed to the window. "Yes, but I could be mistaken."

"When did you notice this?"

Davina set the canvas on the floor. "Twice. The first time was about a week after the break-in. Last week, when I talked with the photographer at the restaurant, I think I saw the same man again."

"It started three weeks ago?" Natalie shouted the question.

"Or, at least I think he was the same man," Davina said, ignoring the shout.

Natalie managed a deep sigh and joined Davina at the window. "If you won't tell David, tell Justin."

"No." She impaled Natalie with a stare before she turned away. "He's out of town. And it'll only confirm his already low opinion of me—that I'm somehow responsible for his missing paintings and everything that happened afterward."

"So what? You've nothing to lose by getting his help."

Davina gave her another daggered look.

"You know what I mean. We don't care what he thinks as long as he knows you could be in danger. Unless, of course, we do care what he thinks. . . . Do we?"

"I don't need the editorial."

Natalie held up her hand in peace. "Okay, okay, I won't go there for now." She crossed her arms and leaned against the wall. "The way I see it, whoever stole the paintings from you wants that third one. What better way to find it than to follow you around?"

"If I'm really being followed," Davina reminded her.

"You can't take chances. I'll keep quiet for now, but you've got to be more careful and tell me about any suspicions or, so help me, I'll tell David and Justin."

Davina turned to her. "I didn't want you to worry. I just needed to . . ."

"Share the burden?" Natalie looked at her friend closely. "That's why I'm here. You're my dearest friend."

"Why did the burglary have to happen on that particular night?" The words were muttered lightly, but her relief from sharing her thoughts with Natalie was immediate. "I don't want him to be the one who set me up. I know he says he didn't do it, and I said—" she broke off, unable to continue.

"You told him you didn't take anything from his office," Natalie finished her friend's thought. "Sounds like the two of you have reinvented the 'little white lie.' "

"It wasn't supposed to be like this . . . one lie leading to another. David doesn't want to trust any of Justin's people. And if I tell him I'm being followed, he'll confront Justin and mess up everything."

"A lot has happened over the past few weeks, Davina. You haven't had a chance to sort through it all, including what's happening between you and Justin."

"I forget to breathe when he's around." She brushed back her hair in frustration.

"Your hormones are waking up."

Davina turned away from Natalie's probing eyes. "Suppose he's the wrong man again?"

Natalie let out a deep laugh. "There's hope for you, yet. Three weeks ago, you wouldn't even admit there could be a man in your life." When she saw the stubborn slant of Davina's eyes, she quickly added, "Don't even bring up Lawrence's name. He hurt you and you're over him." She watched Davina's lips set in a hard line. "You are over that whole episode, aren't you?"

"How can you even ask me that?" She moved from the window and dropped to the sofa. "Of course, I am. I was foolishly in love, blinded by beautiful words that came from the devil himself."

"Don't say it like you were wrong, Davina. He was your first love, your first real sexual—" At Davina's groan, Natalie laughed and joined her on the sofa. "All right, let's just say you were young and inexperienced and gave your heart to a selfish man. The important thing is you saw him for what he was."

"I can't afford to repeat mistakes. It hurts too much. It's easier to ignore the emotion. But, when I'm around Justin, everything just . . .

comes out. And, Lord knows I try to keep them inside." Her head lolled against the back of the sofa. "I feel transparent around him, like he knows every thought I have. So, I keep my anger on the edge to block those dangerous feelings I don't want to experience, that I don't want him to know about."

"He could feel the same way. Look at how his attitude has changed since that first day we met him."

"Oh, please." Davina sat up straight and waved her hand, dismissing the idea. "The man loves his business, and is good at it. If I lower my guard, all I'd be to him is another conquest." She turned to Natalie. "My problem isn't him. It's me. I almost feel sorry for that bitchy Linda."

"Davina, you are one of the bravest persons I know; yet, here you are scared of your own emotions. You always sell yourself short. You did it with your art, too, remember? Maybe he's tired of chasing, or in his case, being chased. Maybe something more made him kiss you."

"That's right. The same thing that made me kiss him back. Hormones." When Natalie laughed, her own smile gave way to one, as well. "I wish I knew the truth about him."

Natalie kicked her flat slippers off and curled up on the sofa. "Some things are best not known and you have to just go for the gusto." She giggled at her joke. "Maybe that's not the best advice to a woman who hasn't had sex in two years."

"You give a good line but I don't see you going for it, either," Davina said in her best sarcastic voice. "You haven't dated anyone since Jonathan left town four months ago. At least I've been kissed— twice." She lifted her brow to Natalie.

Natalie smiled. "Long-distance romance is not for me. When Jonathan took that job in Portland, we both knew that was it. Besides, I haven't had time to get bored with you and David."

"Speaking of my brother, shouldn't he be back by now?"

Their heads turned in unison to the clock on the wall.

"Maybe his friend at the phone company couldn't get the addresses." Natalie reclaimed her spot on the floor amid the phone books. "Back to the phone," she whispered tiredly. "I've called every Randolph listed. No luck."

Davina sat up and stretched. "I've got to finish the price list, too. Linda will be all over my case if I so much as stray an inch from that contract. I'm glad Mr. Renfield agreed to let me work part time until the show closes."

"Huh," Natalie snorted. "Only because it'll look good for his agency to have a name artist working on the accounts."

A hard rap on the door, followed by the doorbell, commanded their attention. Natalie answered it by peeking through the eyepiece. "It's David."

She unlocked the door and swung it wide, but he stood there, with hands behind his back and hair loose in the warm air. His grin was wide and inviting.

Davina came to the door as Natalie inquired, "What's with the grin?"

He waved a sheet of paper in the air before he stepped inside and captured Natalie by her bare midriff. Effortlessly, he swung her around.

He set her down and Natalie breathlessly exclaimed, "It must be good news."

"You're right for a change," he said, his smile still broad. "My friend came through." His eyes traveled between the two women. "I've got the unlisted numbers and addresses for fifteen Randolphs, and three live on the southwest side."

"The only thing we want in return for the capital we'll provide to Hardy Enterprises is a new stock issue." Robert Stockman was a venture capitalist and well known for giving troubled companies what they needed. Cash. He sat across from Justin and Marc in the living room of the hotel suite.

"You know we won't agree to relinquish management control, and I know you don't want token stock. What are you really after?" Justin sat next to the desk and drummed his fingers quietly along the top. He had a keen dislike for this man who made his living from the misfortune of others.

"A simple promise to pay, backed by a large block of stock as collateral." Stockman leaned back in the big chair and ran his hand across his sleek, graying head. "I know you're here to meet with your bankers. I understand you've got a large loan payment coming up soon."

"You've done your homework." Justin's fingers abruptly stilled on the desk. He stood up from the chair and sat on the edge of the desk.

"You've done wonders to stabilize things in only a few months. But even you can't create miracles. Your father should have taken my offer six months ago when things weren't as bad as they are now and I was more amenable to negotiation."

"Is this the same offer you made to DuMonde Press, now one of your subsidiaries?" Justin folded his arms across his chest.

Stockman smiled and rose from the chair. "That was different. Your company is much better managed and I'm sure I'd never have to call in the stock."

Justin heard Marc shift in his chair, but he didn't look at his partner. "And what assurances do we receive that the same thing won't happen to us?"

"With your management and finance skills, Justin, we would definitely make allowances for your continued relationship with the company and any new management team." Stockman rocked back on his well-polished heels. "Anything else would, of course, be subject to further negotiation."

"Why are you after Hardy?" Justin asked. "Let's see, you've made two other offers in the last eighteen months. Both times you were refused."

Stockman smiled. "You're smarter than your father. He was a good man, but he had become too complacent for today's business world." He walked a couple of paces away.

"He was smart enough to smell a rat."

Stockman turned to Justin. "All right, let's cut to the quick." He clasped his hands behind his back and slowly walked to Justin. "We both know I can sit back and buy you out for a song when your loans are called in. I'm giving you the opportunity to at least buy some time and figure out how you want to go out."

Angered at Stockman's insistence that the company's collapse was a foregone conclusion, Justin pulled himself to his entire imposing height. "There is no way I will ever allow you to take over my father's company and hash it into your other subsidiaries. I'd go to hell and back first.''

"The decision could be out of your hands soon."

"Is that more information fed to you by someone inside Hardy?'' When Stockman's eye widened slightly, Justin added, "Surprised that I know it's you acquiring our stock and helping spread rumors of our demise?''

Stockman held his sleek head up to Justin. "I'll leave, but, I'm sure I'll be hearing from you.''

"I hope you have a comfortable wait." Justin's business smile was as false as Stockman's, who headed for the suite's door.

"He's a bastard," Justin said before he dropped tiredly to the sofa. "Dad was right about him. He tried this same thing before.''

Marc walked over. His hands were deep in his pocket and jingled the coins and keys there. "When were you going to tell me your suspicions about the guy?''

"I put it together with Douglas. When you urged me to meet him and consider his offer, it was just the opportunity to see him react firsthand. As you can see, he's too pompous to even deny it.''

"I didn't know Jacob had discussed Stockman's offers with you.''

"We had our differences, but Dad still called me and dropped ideas in my lap. It was a game we played pretty well. I'd give him advice and he wouldn't have to admit that's what it was." Justin laughed.

"That explains a lot," Marc said. "When Stockman talked with me, I believed he had changed his position on control of Hardy.'' When Justin said nothing, Marc continued. "He's got the money we need, and I thought we should at least hear what he had to say.''

Justin's gaze made a cut into Marc. "You heard him, didn't you?'' He looked away. "And, what he said is he'll kick your ass out on the sidewalk along with everyone else when he takes over. There's no way he'd ever let us off the hook if we coupled up with him for a deal. I warned Dad to stay away from him.''

Marc dropped onto the sofa and rubbed his hand across his flushed forehead. "Now what, Justin?''

Justin smiled, as though the crisis they faced was not monumental. "First things first. We meet with the bank and wait for their decision to extend the loan." He got up from the sofa. "Let's get moving. I want to go home."

Two days passed before Davina was sure they had located the right Randolph.

Garibaldi Avenue was never meant for two-way traffic. Barely the width of two cars, the narrow street was marked by broken asphalt and potholes. And those residents who boasted vehicles had parked along the narrow street, further reducing the driving area.

The wood and brick homes were relics of past middle-class splendor, built up from the street, close to each other, with small, squared lawns that had once been green. Now reduced to disrepair and neglect by both apathetic landlords and inattentive owners, the area had long gone to seed. The only people who remained in the neighborhood were those who could go nowhere else.

Davina walked closely behind David along the narrow, weed-infested sidewalk and up the steps to the screened front porch of the house numbered 2681; the six hung crazily from its nail and became a nine. It was near dusk. The brilliance of a bare lightbulb just above the front door and inside the porch lifted the otherwise gloomy surroundings. David rapped on the porch door's faded wood.

"Maybe no one's home," she whispered as they waited in the silence. She stood on the step just below David and looked around.

"They were when we called." He rapped on the door and called out. "Hello."

"I'm coming." A muffled voice floated to them from the inside of the house.

David smiled. "Bingo."

The front door squeaked open and a braided head appeared. The young woman's pretty brown face was immediately suspicious. "What do you want?"

David made the introductions. "I called earlier about Mr. Randolph. Are you his daughter?"

She stepped from behind the door to the porch. Barefoot, she wore jeans and an Atlanta Braves T-shirt. "I'm his daughter-in-law, Laquilla. Quilla, for short. What do you want with Lee?"

"On the phone, you said Mr. Randolph was an artist," Davina said. "We'd like to ask him a few questions about a man he may have known in Atlanta."

She offered a smile that revealed stark white teeth against brown lips. "I guess you can call Lee an artist. He hasn't painted in years, not since the stroke."

David glanced to Davina, still crowded behind him, before turning back to Quilla. "Can we talk to him?" His eyes pleaded. "We won't stay long."

She paused a moment to look at them before she gave a grudging nod. "He likes company." She walked to the screened door and unlatched it. "Come on in."

Lee Randolph was draped in a light blanket, seemingly unaffected by the stifling, un-airconditioned house. Davina thought he looked older than her father and Morris. His stroke appeared to have affected his left side, signified by his skewed mouth. A nearby fan hummed as it recirculated the humid air across the room. He sat in the corner of the sofa with Quilla behind him, perched along its back. Davina and David sat in straight chairs facing them.

The inside of the house was as clean and inviting as the outside was seedy and unsightly; but the stale, musty odor from years of dirt and mildew encroachment could not be covered with a window drape or nice rug. Davina noticed the man's fondness for mixed media abstracts. The painted walls were dotted with what she suspected were his own unframed creations; much of it carried a patina of anger with the primitive technique.

For all of fifteen minutes, they politely spoke of the weather and his health. Finally, an impatient Davina asked if he remembered his circle of artist friends.

"Jacob's place was our hangout, all right." He spoke in a slow, steady voice that was surprisingly clear. "I figured most of us would either be dead or doin' better things by now."

"Morris Mangley mentioned you were one of the few friends Maceo could ask to help him leave town."

"If he'd wanted my help, he'd have asked for it." Lee's words were belligerent. "I figured Jake was the one who helped Maceo. They were close, probably closer than the rest of us, but I warned Maceo about him."

"Warned him about Jacob?" Davina asked.

"I told him Jake was hungry to make something of himself and he'd better watch what he was doin', 'specially when the white galleries took notice and the papers started talking about Maceo being the next great Negro artist." Lee took great pains to speak clearly. "Maceo was laid-back, though, and he had to make sure things were taken care of before he made his move."

"What kind of things?" Davina spoke quickly.

"You know, his paintings, canvases he had started, that kind of thing."

David leaned forward. "Did Maceo and Jacob ever give the impression they were in business together?"

Quilla spoke to Lee. "That other man asked you the same thing."

Davina exchanged a look with David. "Someone else asked you about Jacob and Maceo?" she asked Lee.

Quilla nodded in response. "A man was here a few days ago. He didn't come in and I forgot his name."

"What did you tell them?" David inquired.

"The same thing I'm telling you," Lee said. "That I knew both of them and Maceo messed up his chance to make it."

"Who else did Maceo confide in?" Davina's question was met with silence, but she pushed on. "Did anyone have the connections to help him disappear?"

"Not for me to say after all this time. Maceo is dead and gone, so let the past die with him." He squinted at Davina. "You know, this was a long time ago. I don't remember so easy anymore."

"Damn right." A heavy voice boomed from the doorway. "What are you doing in my house bothering my father?"

David shot up from his seat as the lean-figured young man stomped to Quilla's side and placed a hand on Lee's shoulder. Davina also rose, surprised at the anger written on the younger Randolph's face.

"They're not bothering me, son," Lee offered in defense of his guests.

"C'mon, chill out, Nathan." Quilla calmly rubbed her husband's arm.

David stepped up and extended his hand to Nathan, who hesitantly completed the traditional handshake between black men. "I'm David Spenser. This is my sister, Davina. We were only asking your father a few questions."

"About what?" Nathan's frown held steady.

"It's a who," Davina offered. "An artist he knew a long time ago."

Nathan's eyes narrowed.

"Maceo James," David said.

"Who are you?" Nathan asked in evenly drawn words.

David answered. "We're trying to learn what happened to Maceo's paintings and property after he disappeared."

"Well, you got the wrong place. My father don't know anything about that." He turned to Quilla. "Take him to his room, baby." He patted his father's shoulders before he motioned for David and Davina to follow him to the porch.

Davina watched him leave and frowned at his high-handedness, but decided to abide by his wishes. She bent and spoke to the elderly man. "Mr. Randolph, thank you for talking with us. Maybe we can come see you another time?"

"My son thinks I'm weak and tries to protect me. He sounds rough, but he doesn't mean any harm."

Davina smiled. "If you think of anything you can tell me about Maceo or Jacob, call me at this number." She pulled a card from her pocket and was surprised when his hand snaked from under the blanket to take it. She slipped it into his grasp. "Goodbye Mr. Randolph . . . Quilla."

She walked out to the porch with David and Nathan Randolph.

"He doesn't want us back here," David said.

"But, we need your father's help," Davina explained.

The young man was adamant. "He's sick and needs his rest. Half of the time he doesn't know what he's talking about. He can't help you, and I want you to leave him alone."

"I think he's more lonely than sick. Quilla says he doesn't paint at all anymore, but his hand seems fine after his stroke—"

"Vinny, let's go." David's voice was sharp as he turned her to the screen door. "Leave it alone."

She didn't, and continued on even as David pushed her through the door. "The art on your walls proves how good he is. It's a shame he doesn't still paint."

"Those aren't his paintings. They're mine."

Davina and David turned to look at Nathan. "Oh," she said. And, with his comments serving as the last food for thought, they left.

The next day, Davina arrived at Hardy Enterprises and found a message from Douglas Bradley. The first group of Hardy records was available. She'd have to sign for them and they could only be reviewed within the office. It could wait until after lunch, she decided. Right now, she had the show's business to perform, including choosing frames and settings for the artwork. Charlie was busy authenticating the new exhibit, but Robert had been a constant at her side, asking his own questions and offering suggestions as problems arose. She hadn't fathomed the extent of the work required to put on a show. The gallery was between shows and quiet with no visitors, but workers noisily prepared for the new show.

Davina was settled on a high stool in the back of the gallery, engrossed in the sample catalogs and oblivious to the din beyond the metal doors, when she heard low voices coming from the direction of the lab. The filtered staccato voices drew her curiosity and she slid from the stool. She walked toward the lab and ran into Marc. He was back, and that could only mean Justin was back, too.

"How's it going, Davina?" He gave her a quick smile. Robert followed closely behind and also greeted her.

"Fine, thank you." Davina turned to join them. "I didn't know you were back in town. I thought I heard something back here. I forget how big this place is."

"Maybe you heard the carpenters," Robert suggested.

"That's probably it," she agreed. They had returned to her table.

"I wouldn't worry about it," Marc said, his hands deep in his pockets. "See you later."

She watched them enter the gallery through the metal doors. Shaking her head, she climbed back onto the stool. Once again, she lost herself in the work at hand until she was interrupted by another inward swing of the metal doors.

Davina looked up, and this time, her breath was sucked from her, but not by suspicions. Justin's presence filled the cavernous room as his long strides led him to her. She swallowed hard and raised her eyes to his gaze.

"I didn't realize you were back." *Yes, I did. Take a deep breath, and don't stare. Try to get through this without embarrassing yourself.*

"Douglas told me I'd find you in here." Justin's deep voice reverberated through the large room.

Davina was fascinated by the ease with which he carried his powerful body across the room to her, devilishly handsome in the dark suit, looking like a feast for the eyes. She swallowed again, and ignoring her own advice, lost herself in the provocative senses he awakened.

He stopped in front of the slanted table and studied the artwork photos clipped to its edge. His glance took in the clutter of open catalogs and note papers. "You look like you have a lot of work ahead of you."

She fumbled with the pencil and her notes. "Yes, but I'll get it done."

His sigh drew her eyes again, and he raised his hand to massage his temple. The gold bracelet he wore was in such contrast to his conservative business attire that it seemed a symbol of his smoldering decadence. "I've learned you've made an impression on a few people around here."

"Oh, and who would that be?"

"Robert, for one."

Davina cocked her brow and smiled. "Robert? He's curious, that's all."

"I saw him a while ago. He likes discussing art with you, but I believe he's become one of your biggest fans."

"He admires you for letting him work here despite his past."

Justin shrugged off the compliment and crossed his arms along the top of the slanted table as he leaned toward her. Her high stool put them at eye level. "Douglas said there were no problems. That means you kept out of trouble."

"It's pretty easy when you're not around to provoke me."

"So, you missed me, huh?" His grin easily reached his eyes.

"Hardly." She ignored his arrogance and forced her eyes to return to the catalog. "Like you said, I have lots of work to do."

"Such as . . ." The gentle timbre of his deep voice teased her.

"Choosing the frames for paintings." She looked at him, her brows furrowed. "I'm having a hard time choosing the right ones for the larger canvases."

"Let's see what you've got so far." He came around the table, rested his arm along the back of her chair, and looked over her shoulder. Davina pointed out her choices from the catalog.

The clean scent of his masculine cologne was seductive, and Davina was sure he could feel the heat emanate from her body. She fought the desire to close her eyes and languish in this mood.

"I see what you mean." Justin breathed in her fragrance, a combination of fruit and flowers, and managed to keep his eyes on the catalog as he indulged the pleasant tightening that built in his loins. From the moment he had walked through the doors, he was, again, taken in by her unique beauty. He had been out of the office less than a week, and upon returning had sought her out first. What he really wanted to do was bury his hands in her hair and . . .

"What do you suggest?" Davina's soft voice floated into his reverie.

"You might want to go without a frame on some," he quickly answered.

"That'll work for the more contemporary subjects." Affected by his proximity, she fidgeted in the high chair.

Justin reached across Davina to turn the page of the catalog. As he brushed against her bare arm, they both felt the lush stroke of current that jackknifed through their bodies. Caught by the jolt, they turned to each other, lips only a wish's breadth apart. In the span of the moment, they both knew what they wanted, and neither moved from the delicious place where they had arrived.

Davina slowly bowed her head and studied her hands.

Justin's fingers clamped over her chin and gently raised her face to his once more. He stroked her lips with one finger.

"You didn't miss me, Davina?" He whispered the words. "I missed you."

"Don't say that." She pushed his hand away and closed her eyes to the waves of desire that crashed deep inside her.

"All right, I won't say it." He dropped his hands to grip either side of her chair's seat and leaned in to kiss the tip of her nose, then her eyes.

Davina's eyes opened, as did her mouth, at his unexpected touch.

He met her open mouth with his own in a kiss that was more a caress than anything else. The gentle attack on her senses sent currents of desire through her, but she didn't return his ardor. She held on to her tattered sanity for dear life.

Justin pulled back and looked at her. "Kiss me back, " he growled.

The command worked. Davina's lips instinctively found their way to his. Now he smothered them with demanding mastery in a series of slow, shivery kisses. They were intended to make her want more, and she did. Of their own accord, her hands raised to his shoulders, and the kisses deepened as Justin's mouth pressed her further against the chair.

His hands moved from the sides of the chair to the waiting softness of her thighs. He massaged the pliant flesh in rhythm with the tiny sounds Davina emitted against his hard mouth.

They both heard the groan of the metal door, and abruptly moved apart. It was not before they witnessed the remnants of hunger in each other's eyes.

Davina pulled her hand across her mouth as Justin bit into his lower lip. He stepped back from her and muttered, "I have the worst timing with you."

The door opened wider as Carolyn entered, cautiously at first, until she spied Justin in the room. Her high heels clicked a counterpoint across the wooden floor.

"Hello, Davina. I don't believe I've seen you since the dinner party."

Davina nodded a greeting from her chair. "No, you haven't." Carolyn was dressed in a business suit and her long hair fell in curly waves to her shoulders.

Carolyn's eyebrows raised inquiringly at Davina before she made a slight turn to face Justin. "I didn't interrupt, did I?"

"What do you want?" His tone was patient, even though he looked irritated.

"Did you forget the meeting? Douglas told me you might be in here."

Justin rubbed his fingers against his temple. "I didn't forget, Carolyn. In fact," he looked at his watch, "it won't start for another fifteen minutes."

She laughed. "Okay, so I was curious about what you had to do that couldn't wait until later." A smile played on her lips when she looked at Davina. "I'm sure I'll be seeing you again. Don't be late, Justin." She left quietly through the door.

"I don't think she approves of you fraternizing with the help." Davina couldn't keep the amusement from her face.

Justin's wide, white smile relaxed his strong features. "Carolyn knows I never ask for approval."

"Maybe it's her way of warning you . . . protecting you."

Justin propped his arm against the table and looked into her eyes. "I don't think so, and I don't want to talk about Carolyn." He straightened from the table. "There is one thing to discuss before I go to the meeting. The auction."

Her eyes strayed to his lips. "What's to talk about?" She raised her eyes to his, only to find he had also found her own lips a worthy subject.

"We are going together. I'll pick you up at seven o'clock." His voice was firm.

"Do you always manage to get your way?"

"Only for things I really want." He winked at her before he turned to leave.

"Justin?"

He stopped and turned around.

"Thank you for keeping quiet with your board a while longer," she said.

"I'm doing it because I believe you'll trust me with the whole story soon."

She watched his broad back as he took his leave of the room in his usual, subtle grace. *Is that possible? Will I ever trust him that much?*

As Justin was leaving the gallery, he ran into Carolyn in the hall. She picked up his stride and accompanied him to the boardroom.

"I thought you were concerned about being on time for the meeting," he said.

"I'm more concerned about you making out in the back workroom."

Justin glanced at his sister's smiling face. "It's none of your business."

"Don't worry. I won't tell anyone you have designs on the enemy." When Justin didn't respond, she said, "Lighten up. You aren't angry, are you?"

"Not about what you think," was his measured response.

They reached the business offices, and he held the door open.

"You don't know her at all," Carolyn warned. "None of us do. Be careful."

"I always am," he said, and followed her in. "You should also know that I wouldn't do anything to jeopardize the company."

"We had a deal." The elegant, well-dressed man walked around the room and switched on lamps to scatter the darkness.

"I know. And I still intend to deliver. It's just taking a little longer." From his chair in the far corner, he watched his contact move from lamp to lamp.

"I understand she's asking questions, and we still don't have the other painting."

"We could always go through her apartment again." He knew it was a poor suggestion, but he'd offer anything to get the heat turned in another direction.

"No." The man sat near the last lamp he had switched on and crossed one leg over the other knee. "The place was torn apart the first time. Any fool would know she's moved it by now." He pulled a cigarette from a foreign-brand pack that lay nearby, then offered one to his guest, who declined. "But this new problem you tell us about is not good." He put the cigarette in his mouth. "What did you find out?" He bent his head to meet the flickering flame of the lighter.

"He's not going anywhere else with what he found out. I've made sure of that."

"Maybe we should make sure." The clipped words were uttered through clenched teeth. He leaned back in his chair and allowed an expansive belch of smoke to fill the air.

"Please, I can handle it," he said, and stood to leave. "No one has to get hurt. We have time before she's bound to make a mistake, and then we'll get what we want."

CHAPTER SIXTEEN

Getting to Know You

Justin straightened the black tie that went with his formal suit as he bounded down the main stairs and headed for the drawing room to bid his mother good night. His mood was exceptional for an evening that was about to be spent at another charity event. This was a more entertaining one, and he looked forward to escorting Davina. On the night he showed her the house, he had enjoyed her open and unabashed enjoyment of the things he had sometimes taken for granted. He wanted to see that look in her eyes again.

He walked into the room and was surprised to find Douglas sitting with his mother and Carolyn.

"Justin, come in," Elizabeth Hardy called from the sofa.

"You sure are dapper tonight. What's going on?" asked Carolyn, observing his black formal attire. She stood and straightened the tie Justin had managed to send even further askew.

"The charity auction and wine taster over at the Richmond mansion," Justin answered, and looked over at Douglas, pleased to see him at the house. "I didn't know you were coming over tonight. Are you three going somewhere, too?"

"We have dinner reservations later," Douglas explained.

"Are you doing the auction solo?" Carolyn asked, and patted her finished handiwork on Justin's tie.

"No," he ventured a monosyllabic reply, knowing she wouldn't leave it there. He joined her in the chairs opposite the sofa, where Elizabeth and Douglas sat, and stretched his long legs before him.

"Who are you going with, then?" she persisted.

With a trace of laughter in his voice, Douglas said, "You didn't tell them your feisty artist agreed to go with you?"

Justin smoothed the tie again and gave a pointed look to Carolyn. "I'm taking Davina Spenser." He silently dared her to make something of the pronouncement.

"I didn't think she'd be predisposed to going anywhere with you," Elizabeth said with a smile. "I enjoyed her and her brother at dinner the other night."

"Justin did, too," Carolyn said, her devilish smile meant for her brother.

He leaned forward. "We both have to promote her show while we're there."

"Do you think this whole thing—about the partnership and paintings owned by her father—will die naturally when she can't prove her point?" Elizabeth asked.

Justin stood up. "Only time will tell, Mom. My experience with the lady is that you never really know what her plans are until she shares them with you. I'd better go before she changes her mind about tonight. I'll see all of you later."

He gave his mother a peck on the cheek and said his goodbyes all around.

Davina stood in her bedroom and smoothed the long, black silk dress with her hands, then turned to view herself from all sides in the cheval glass. Leave it to Natalie to help her pick this one, she thought. Admittedly, the dress was beautiful. The straps fit off the shoulders and dropped to a low back; but the squared decolletage revealed the tops of her breasts and she was uncomfortable with that much exposure. From the cinched waist, the dress fell in soft folds to the floor. Davina frowned at her image. After the saleswoman's promise that the dress would make any man happy, and Natalie's comment that if this dress didn't get Justin to jump through hoops, nothing would, she wondered what Justin would think. How was she going to get through an entire evening with the man?

The silk skirt of the dress made a luscious swish with each step Davina took from her bedroom to the living room. She stopped in front of the sofa, where she indignantly placed a hand on her hip. David and Natalie lounged comfortably on either end of the sofa engrossed, respectively, in the newspaper and a magazine.

"Look at the two of you still hanging around. You should both go home." They looked up and eyed her dress before returning to their reading. Davina cocked an eyebrow before she pleaded. "Please don't sit here like chaperons."

David closed the paper and dropped a hand to his denim-covered knee as he stood. "Okay. I'll watch television in your bedroom, but I'm not leaving yet." His disapproving eyes momentarily settled over her gown before he maneuvered his frame down the hall and out of view.

She now turned her attention to Natalie.

"So, why are you looking at me?" Natalie peeked over the top of the magazine. "If he's not leaving, I'm sure not."

Davina hiked up the skirt of the dress and sat next to her on the sofa. "I've gone out before, you know. I'm not a child."

Natalie let out a giggle. "Now that he's seen you in that dress, I think David realizes that." She curled her bare feet beneath her and strained her neck to make sure David was gone. In a quiet voice, she said, "David has this need to protect you."

"He's my brother, not my parent."

"I think he's noticed Justin's interest in you."

Davina's brows raised. "You didn't say anything to David, did you?"

She shook her head. "Of course not. But, since you won't tell him you're similarly interested, he's going to make sure Justin doesn't take advantage of you."

Davina frowned. "See what I mean? I can take care of myself."

"Give him a break, girl. He knows Justin has been around, has traveled in circles that, well, you haven't, and you may not be up to his kind of charm.''

"I keep telling David not to worry about me. He makes me feel like every decision I make in my adult life will be as bad as the one I made with Lawrence.''

Natalie rested her elbow on the sofa's arm. "He's determined to watch out for you. He carries guilt around about leaving you to care for your father all alone.''

"He left to go to school—he had no choice.''

"You didn't leave,'' Natalie pointed out.

"That was different.''

"David doesn't see it that way. He knows the sacrifices you made. You put off school, your art. Most importantly, he doesn't believe Lawrence would have had the chance to hurt you if he had been around to protect you the way a big brother should. If he can help it, he won't let you get hurt again.''

Davina was surprised at the revelations. "And when did you and David get so chummy and talk about me?''

Natalie shifted on the sofa and tugged at the hems of her khaki shorts. "Good grief, Davina, you're so suspicious.''

She smiled. "It's a comfort to know that the most important two people in my life can stay in the same room without firing weapons at twenty paces.''

"What about tonight,'' Natalie interjected. "Are you okay with it after all?''

"Yeah, sure.'' She looked at Natalie, then turned away. "No, I'm not. I don't even want to go to this thing because I don't belong with the idle rich. And, what's Justin going to think when he sees me in this dress?''

"He's going to think it's wrinkled. You need to stand up,'' Natalie offered.

Davina looked at the face of the gold watch disguised as a bracelet around her wrist, and did stand. "It doesn't matter. He's supposed to arrive in a few minutes, anyway. And knowing him, he'll be on time.'' When Natalie didn't move, Davina said, "That's a hint to join David in the bedroom.''

"A girl likes to be asked first, thank you.'' Natalie's tone turned playful as she hopped from the sofa. "I want to know every last detail of what happens tonight, and be careful of your hair. It's already fighting the pins holding it up." She referred to the tendrils that floated around Davina's face.

Davina motioned at the gold sequined evening bag on a nearby chair. "I've got all possibilities covered. There's a silk scarf in my bag for emergencies."

The doorbell rang, and a lurch of excitement surged through Davina. At once, she patted her hair while Natalie whispered against her ear, "Have a good time." Davina smiled and watched her pad down the hall where David's head now stuck through the door. Natalie squeezed into the doorway, under his arm.

Davina motioned for them to move away from the door, but paused a moment when she saw David's wink and smile of encouragement. She smiled back. When they closed the door, she smoothed her dress again, counted to ten, and tried to appear composed as she went to answer the bell.

Justin looked at his watch. He had been standing under the portico a minute and no one had answered his ring. Surely, she was home. He could see her car parked nearby. He decided to ring the bell again when he heard the lock turn from the other side.

The door opened, ever widening until Davina was completely revealed in the orange glow of the late summer's setting sun. Justin wasn't sure if it was a trick of light, but as Davina was gradually illuminated, her cinnamon tinged skin bloomed into golden honey, from her shapely neck down to her ... Justin swallowed when his caressing eyes came upon the ripe, swollen skin of her breasts poised above the delicate neckline. Recovered, he swiftly continued his seductive perusal, down to her hosiery-covered toes that peeked from beneath the hem of the dress.

To his disappointment, Davina stepped back from the door and quickly turned her back to him. "Come in while I get my bag." She walked into the living room.

Justin closed the door and followed her. His eyes didn't stray from the new, pleasurable view she presented. Her unruly, curly hair had been coaxed into a French twist, leaving a wide expanse of golden shoulders and back open to his delighted stare. He noticed a faint swimsuit line on her otherwise flawless back. He watched her struggle with the long wrap and quickly moved to her aid.

"Here, let me help."

He drew the material from her fingers and, standing behind her, draped it low over her shoulders before crossing the ends over her chest. Her hands swooped up and over his, to hold the wrap in place, which trapped Justin's hands firmly against her cleavage. Firm breasts breathing under his hands, mixed with the heated fragrance of her perfume, was almost too much for Justin. His hands slid down to her arms and he turned her to face him.

"You look lovely tonight. I meant to tell you at the door. I was . . . distracted." He offered a small smile. "In fact, for a minute there, I thought you had skipped out on me." Reluctantly, he dropped his hands from her soft bare arms.

"I wouldn't do that after I gave my word." She took a step back from Justin. "You don't trust people, do you?"

Justin smiled. "Do you want to give me reason to?"

Davina broke her stare with Justin and fumbled with her wrap. "Maybe I do."

Justin liked the way her answer sounded. "I'm going to make it my business to know you better by the end of the evening." He watched her glance toward the empty hallway.

She lifted her chin in what looked to be a challenge. "In that case, I'll be doing the same with you." Her voice was almost a whisper.

He looked around the room. "You have a nice apartment. The last time I was here, I didn't notice it. Now, I can see your personality." He turned to her and remembered how frightened and vulnerable she had been the night of her attack. "Cool, but with a hidden passion; casual and relaxed, yet complicated upon closer inspection." Justin's grin was wide.

She smiled back. "Is that pop psychology?" She picked up her purse and checked its contents. "Be careful of judgments. I doubt if I'm any of those things."

Justin followed her through the front door and closed it afterward. "I'm going to find out, one way or the other," he mumbled to himself.

They walked across the pavement to Justin's car, a sedate black and charcoal gray Lexus. He opened the passenger side door and held it while Davina slid inside.

When he joined her from the other side, he handed her a sheet of paper that contained a list of names. "These are guests I want you to meet tonight."

Davina looked from the list to him, apprehension building in her eyes. "I thought we'd simply circulate." She now stared straight ahead. "I told you I don't like these affairs. I'll embarrass myself, and that sure won't help my art show."

Justin started the car, and the low, smooth sounds of jazz emanated from the stereo. "Art critics and reporters will be there, not to mention the mayor, his wife who, by the way, collects art, and other artists."

Justin stole a quick look at her beautiful, bent profile, and noted that she still clutched the wrap in place. He reached over and gently touched her arm. She turned her face to his, suspicion written on her features. "You'll be fine," he assured her.

As they drove from the apartment complex, Justin's last words were prophetic. "I have a feeling, Davina, that by the time the evening is over, we'll both be surprised by what we've discovered."

By the time they arrived at the Michael L. Richmond mansion in the Buckhead section of Atlanta, Davina had been relaxed by Justin's easy banter. Activities had already commenced inside the high fence. Colorful Japanese lanterns lined the long, curved drive to the front door; Davina watched a host of valets wait at the end to whisk the car off to yet another area out of view.

Everything moved so quickly. Justin brought the car to a stop at the same time Davina's door opened. Helping hands extracted her from the car and, almost immediately, Justin was at her side. He held her elbow as he led her up the stone steps through the massive front door flanked by Corinthian columns.

Davina stepped through the doorway and was besieged by the exhilarating atmosphere. The air teemed with the low hum of mingled conversations that flowed from rooms venturing off the hallway. Elegantly dressed men and women, a mix of races, walked across the expanse of the hall, exiting one room, entering another.

Davina's neck craned to admire the remarkable tapestries that dotted the entry, until she realized the intrepid black-and-white dressed figure she had mistaken for another guest was actually the butler in uniform, and he wanted her wrap. She wasn't ready to give it to him.

"That won't be necessary, thank you," was Justin's easy reply, and he expertly moved her along the hall.

"I knew you'd like it here, if only to see the architecture and artistry of the place." Justin greeted familiar guests that passed them in the hall.

"It's . . . fascinating." She looked at Justin. "The only way I can explain the emotion is to ask you if you've ever looked at a work of art and been moved to tears?" She searched his face for signs of condescension, and saw none.

"I think that observation says a lot about you." He smiled at her.

They continued through the hall, and entered the first doorway they came to. The room was immense, and the furniture had been arranged to accommodate kiosk stations for wine tasting. Justin explained to her how the wine tasting worked and that the kiosks were located all over the estate. Davina noticed that each location was attended by a beautiful woman who poured the different wines from linen wrapped bottles cooled in terra-cotta pottery. Large trays of exotic breads and cheeses, surrounded by chilled fruit, sat nearby to further the liquor's digestion, Justin explained.

His cool hand was electric against her back. "Let's start here with a red wine." As they held their glasses up for their first sample of a rich, dark liquid, the attendant recited a litany of information about the wine, most of her attention steered to Justin, Davina noticed.

With wineglasses in hand, they continued into an adjoining room. This one was an oak paneled billiards room where a number of guests were engaged in a lively game, with onlookers cheering on their favorite.

Justin introduced her to more of the guests as he led her through the room and out the opposite door where they found themselves on an open gallery. It was at least sixty feet long, and used settings of furniture to break up the expanse. A magician performed for a seated crowd at one of the settings.

A cool breeze swept over the low wall, bringing with it fragrances from the garden just below. They slowly walked to the other end of the gallery. The laughter and gaiety around them was infectious, and Davina smiled, as this was not the stuffy evening she had expected.

"Justin Hardy."

They had reached the end of the gallery and looked in the direction of the voice. It had come from the ballroom ahead. When they saw whom the voice belonged to, a wide grin creased Justin's face before he caught Davina's hand in his. "Come on, I want you to meet a good friend of mine."

"Justin, it's the mayor," Davina exclaimed in a low voice.

"I know," he laughed, "and his wife. Remember, she's a collector."

Davina breathed an anxious sigh and allowed Justin to lead her back into the recesses of this elegant mansion someone had actually called home.

Natalie looked up from her book. "For God's sake, David, pick a channel and stay there." She watched as he channel surfed from his seat on the chaise.

He settled on a nature show and set the remote down. "What time will she be home?" David looked at her as she lay on her stomach across Davina's bed.

She gave him a sidelong glance. "She's only been gone a couple of hours. Give it a break, okay?"

David watched her for a moment. "You think she was hacked off at us for hanging around earlier?"

"Of course. But what do we care?" She smiled impishly at David.

He laughed. "I'm still surprised at how close you two became after I left for school. And now, you're friends again in Atlanta, and it's like you were never apart. Amazing." He shook his head.

"You don't even remember me back in high school," she replied petulantly.

"Sure I do. You were this skinny little kid that was always mouthing off."

"And what's that supposed to mean?"

"You're not a skinny kid anymore." The words hung in the air, only to be punctuated by the voice from the television.

Natalie rolled from the bed. "I'm going to get something to eat."

He grinned as she walked nonchalantly past him and through the door in the tiny khaki shorts. "You do that."

Davina meandered along the aisles of the auction tables with the other guests and viewed the items for bids. A gold pencil was attached to a pad in front of each display. The trick was to have your bid recorded as the last highest one at the time bidding was closed. It was early, and the popular items had five and six bid entries already recorded.

"Anything strike your interest?" Justin whispered from behind.

Davina enjoyed the woodsy scent that announced his presence. He had been pulled away by a few business peers and she had browsed the various rooms on her own. "The starting bids on some of these are pretty steep for me, but I did offer a bid for the carved Bantu mask."

"Hmm . . . maybe your luck will hold. I saw the art critic for the newspaper in the main ballroom a while ago. She says she talked with you."

"That's right, I was going to tell you." Her laugh soared through the air. "She likes my work, Justin, and thinks my talent will only grow with time."

"See, they're not all ogres." His smile matched hers. "Let's eat."

"Oh, we get real food, too?"

"Wait until you see the spread in the dining room." His hand found its way to her bare back beneath the wrap as he led her from the room.

From his chair, David rapidly pressed the remote control buttons, as if the mere action would wake Natalie so she could complain about his channel surfing. She was sound asleep on her belly, sprawled on top of the covers of Davina's bed.

He looked at his watch. He had to go in to the office in the morning, never mind that it was the weekend, so he'd have to talk to Davina later. He stood and stretched, then walked over to the bed with his shoes.

Leaning over her sleeping figure, he gently shook Natalie's shoulder. "Wake up." She gave a slight grunt before she turned away from the nudge.

He sat on the edge of the bed and put his shoes on. "I'm about to leave."

This time, she rolled to her back and blinked open her eyes. She rubbed them and tried to focus on David's face. "Why?" Her voice was deep from sleep.

He smiled while he tied his shoes. "You've been telling me all night that I should give Vinny her space. Now you want me to stay?"

Natalie's eyes had fallen closed again. "I thought you'd stay with me tonight . . ." Her whispered words petered out.

David did a double take before he dropped his foot to the floor, then leaned over her. *What had she said?*

She yawned and finished her sleepy remark, "and we'd wait up together."

He shook his head and smiled at her lips pouted in sleep. Then, his gaze moved down her provocative figure.

She opened her eyes and her brows slowly narrowed. "What are you doing?"

"Are you awake now?" David grinned as he returned his eyes to her face.

She grunted a yes and pushed up on her elbows.

In the span of a split second, David lowered his head and met the lips that pouted so prettily earlier. Their initial touch was delicious, and when she rose to more fully receive him, he deepened the kiss, but for only a moment. Regretfully, he raised his mouth from hers.

"I'd better go," he said. "Tell Vinny I'll be over tomorrow."

He left her side and went to the bedroom door, where he turned once again. "You know, I can't remember when I last saw you speechless." He smiled as he dodged the pillow she threw at the door.

* * *

Davina and Justin were watching the African Walli dancers perform when he whispered he'd be back shortly. Engrossed in the performance, she didn't notice that his chair was occupied again until she heard a familiar voice.

"Justin is one great catch, and I see you're dressed with the right bait."

She turned at the words and found Linda next to her, twirling a wineglass between her fingers. Why didn't Justin mention she'd be here? Davina decided to ignore the woman and returned her attention to the African showcase.

Linda continued. "He's fun to be with, good looking, and great in the sack."

Davina looked at her closely. "You're drunk. I don't know why I didn't smell you first."

"I don't believe it," Linda giggled. "Our little mouse has claws." She dipped her finger in the red wine and stirred it, then sucked the residue from her digit. "Tell me, Davina, do you think we have a great love just once in a lifetime?"

"I haven't given it much thought, Linda," she said, "But if that's a referral to your relationship with Justin . . ."

"No, no, sweetheart." Her high laugh came from deep within. "It's a comment on you and Justin. There will never be a lot going on between Justin and any woman, so you shouldn't waste your one great love in a lifetime on him."

Davina swallowed hard before she faced Linda again. "I wish you would understand that there is nothing going on between us."

The purple chiffon and silk confection that Linda wore rustled in earnest as she twisted in the chair to lean conspiratorially against Davina. "Don't be naive, dear. It's unbecoming."

Davina's eyes narrowed at the attractive woman's words.

"He has his eyes on you," Linda warned. "But he always comes back to me after he tires of the chase. And you won't let him chase very long. They never do."

"Linda, I didn't know you had tickets for tonight." Justin had returned and stood with his hands on his hips. He looked from Davina's frown to Linda's smile.

Linda stood and the purple silk cascaded to the floor. "I'm here with George Moore. You know me, always working for the good of the company."

"And the company appreciates it." He watched her slowly parade into the throng that headed for the next scheduled entertainment.

Justin sat down and took Davina's hand between his two. "Are you all right?"

The gentle massage he gave her hand was as disconcerting as a stolen kiss in the moonlight. "I believe she's drunk, Justin. I hope she's not driving."

He looked in the direction Linda had headed. "The attendants won't serve her any more wine and I'll make sure George drives her home." He turned back to Davina. "Are you sure you're okay? Linda can be a little hard to take."

"I'm fine, but I probably should walk off some of that wonderful dinner."

"I've got just the thing." He stood and helped Davina to her feet. "I'm going to show you the gardens."

"At night?" she asked.

"Especially at night." He clasped her hand and pulled her through the crowd and onto the gallery, where he took two colorful coverlets from a stack near the stone steps leading to the gardens.

"I wondered what these stacks of quilts were for," Davina mused.

"They're for sitting in the moonlight on a night like this." When they passed a kiosk, Justin handed her the coverlets. He took a bottle of wine, an Italian merlot, and two glasses. Together, they followed the path that led to the gardens.

The massive garden acreage had numerous walkways that took Davina and Justin past statuary, a reflecting pool, and a few lighted fountains. They ran into a number of other guests who had also left the din of the mansion for the tranquility of the gardens.

Soon, they came upon a quiet spot on the sloping lawn near a magnolia tree. It offered a clear view of the sky. The Labor Day weekend had brought fair weather and the sky was moonlit to perfection. Justin spread the coverlets over the grass and reclined on his side, raising himself up on one elbow. Davina sat within arm's distance, her legs bent so she faced him as they talked.

He poured a small amount of the wine into each glass, and passed one to Davina. "Are you chilly out here?"

She took the glass from his hand and shook her head. "No, I'm fine."

He quickly transferred his glass to his other hand and reached over and pulled her wrap from her shoulders. "Then, give me this thing."

Davina was caught off guard, but didn't attempt to retrieve it. She sipped at the wine, observing him all the time over the edge of the glass.

"You've had that thing clutched to you like armor all night." His eyes boldly caressed her neck and breasts. "You're a beautiful woman. Why do you hide it?"

Davina knew she blushed red, and was thankful the moonlight wouldn't show the color. She was at a total loss for a response, not sure how she should take his words. Insult or compliment?

Justin tilted his head and sipped his own glass of wine. "Davina, are you afraid of being sexy?"

"Of course not," she said, unsettled by his question.

"Yes, you are . . . you're scared of your own sexuality. You hide it as much as you can, don't you?" He didn't wait for her to answer. "Yes, that much is obvious; but, the question is, why?"

Davina didn't like the turn of the conversation and immediately changed it. "I'm surprised at how loose you are tonight, all reclined on the grass. You seem caught up in Hardy's business most of the time. I've figured you for one of those workaholics who can't relax."

He laughed. "Oh, I know how to relax, but I rarely mix business with pleasure." Then, he added in a low voice, "Although, there's always a first time."

"Is it hard running a business in your father's footsteps?"

"If they let you run it; but, there's always opposition to change. You, on the other hand, are trying to sink me with your claims."

She turned away from his eyes. "That's not the whole truth. Against my better judgment, I've come to respect your family."

"They respect you now that you've told me off. In front of them, I might add."

They both laughed at that inauspicious meeting.

She sipped from her glass to hide her nervousness. "Have you had any luck in tracking those five missing paintings?"

"No, I'm working on it. I'll have to make some decisions about them soon."

"Maybe someone stole them for resale or forgery," she offered.

He looked at her. "I've had my share of that."

"You mean you've actually sold forgeries and stolen works?"

Justin laughed again. "What I mean is it's a part of the business if you deal in publishing, art, and music. The threat of plagiarism, theft, and forgery is always there. It's conceivable that I could have forgeries for sale now, and not know it."

"That's why you have curators, Charlie and Robert, right, to keep you honest for your buyers and artists."

He sipped from the wine and set it aside before answering. "Forgery is a white-collar crime that's low on the police's list of priorities, unless you mix some other interesting crimes with it. The best thing to do if you come across forgery is cut your losses and move on."

"I can't believe you take so lightly that kind of stealing," Davina said.

"And I can't believe you're that naive," he said.

If there was one thing she was sensitive about, it was being called naive, and she'd been called that twice tonight. "I'm going back for the auction." She put her glass down and tried to get up before Justin's arm snaked out to her waist.

"Wait a minute, Davina." As he held her there, he looked at her. "I'm sorry for upsetting our peace. Stay out a little longer with me, okay."

She looked at his hand still holding her waist, and enjoyed the sensation. "Men still like to dominate the easy way . . . strength," she said with a smile.

"Women dominate as much as men, maybe not with physical strength, but with something much more pleasant." There was an edge to his voice that she had not detected before. He raised his hand from her waist and caressed her neck.

The touch sent shivers of delight to the pit of her stomach. She leaned into his hand and closed her eyes. She knew they would kiss, and she wanted it. Justin pulled himself up so his mouth could capture the softness below her ears. His lips and tongue continued to sear a path down the side of her neck to her shoulders. There, he nibbled the sensitive pockets of skin that lay along her shoulders to the hollow of her neck.

His feather touches sent shocks of desire through her. Davina held on to him, and moved forward to embrace his neck.

He moved his mouth to her ear and whispered, "I want you to feel sexy tonight. Everything you're feeling, I'm feeling in spades. Lean back against your hands."

Davina did so, and allowed him full access to her burning skin. His mouth nuzzled her ear and returned to the base of her throat, where his lips moved lower and lower until they unerringly reached her breasts. She breathed lightly between parted lips and her breasts surged at the intimacy of his touch. While he explored the swollen flesh displayed above the dress, Davina was transported to the clouds.

His hand slid across her belly then slowly moved up to outline the circle of her breasts beneath the silk material. He lifted his head and moved his mouth over her open one, as if to devour its softness. Davina could no longer not touch him. She shifted, as did he, to use both of her hands. When she encircled his neck, Justin gently eased her down to the coverlet. This time, his kiss was hard and searching. His tongue explored the recesses of her mouth and left her burning with fire. He wrapped his hand tightly in her hair and slanted his mouth across hers again and again, with no restraint.

Somewhere in her consciousness, Davina felt his hand leave her breasts and move under her dress to skim her thighs and the swell of her hip. Justin was affecting her in ways that alternately thrilled her and frightened her. She remembered how this kind of abandonment had served her poorly before.

"Justin." He smothered his name on her lips. Davina moved her hands from his neck and cupped his face.

He looked at her, then drew his lips in thoughtfully. He pulled himself to a sitting position then helped her do the same.

"I want to make love to you, Davina."

A flicker of apprehension coursed through her. He misread her look and smiled. "Not out here, not now. But, we both know it's inevitable, don't we?"

Davina ran her fingers through her mussed hair and allowed the rest of the pins to fall out. Anxiety had begun to cool her ardor. "I told you, I don't take making love lightly."

"Meaning, you have to be in love?" Amusement flickered in his eyes.

She opened her purse and took out the gold scarf and twisted it into a band. "Meaning, you don't?"

Justin's eyes followed her movements as she tied the gold band around her head and under her hair. Once again, the tight, corkscrew curls were controlled.

"You look lovely. I like your hair free." She watched him rise fluidly to his feet, then reach out and pull her up, as well.

"It's almost time for the auction announcements," he said. They gathered up the coverlets, wine, and glasses. He reached for Davina's hand, his fingers warm and strong as they grasped hers.

"Let's take things a day at a time, Justin, and see where they lead us."

He didn't respond, but nodded his agreement, and led her back to the path that would return them to the festivities.

Davina closed the apartment door behind her and turned the lock. Afraid she would find David and Natalie asleep on the sofa, she had refused to let Justin see her safely inside the apartment. Walking down the dimly lit hallway to the darkened bedroom, she flicked the wall light switch several times, until she heard the answering bleat of Justin's car horn.

She leaned over the bed where Natalie quietly slept and clicked on the bedside lamp. "Natalie, wake up." She prodded her friend's shoulders before she put her purse, wrap, and the Bantu mask on the night table.

Natalie turned over and stared into Davina's face. "This is the second time this has happened tonight. What's going on?" She rubbed her eyes.

"What?" Davina asked with a frown as she sat on the edge of the bed.

"Never mind." Natalie turned onto her side and propped up on her elbow. "Uh-oh . . . your hair is down."

"I know. We've got to talk."

CHAPTER SEVENTEEN

One Step Forward, Two Back

Justin had blocked the release of the inventory report on two previous occasions and could no longer reasonably hide its contents. Prior to today, he had discussed the report with Rich Peterson, head auditor in Accounting. Now, as the meeting neared the end, Rich handed out the long-awaited report. A few board members were absent, but it didn't take long for the expected clamor to start.

"How long have they been missing?" The question came from his sister, Stephanie. She and Mrs. Hardy were the only other family members present.

"We're talking about the loss of valuable paintings," Edward interrupted. "The police should have already been called in."

Justin directed the meeting from his usual chair near the head of the big oval table and scowled at Edward's suggestion. He motioned for Rich to come up front. "Let's hear from Accounting first."

Rich's loping gait was at ease with his tall, gangly frame. He joined Justin at the head of the conference table and started the presentation. The group remained quiet as he explained the meaning of the report.

"Police involvement would be premature because we're still analyzing the information we collected." He looked briefly to Justin for confirmation before he returned his attention to the others. "Although my staff prepared the inventory we no longer believe the report will stand up to the necessary scrutiny "

"What is that supposed to mean?" Ray Miller asked. He busily flipped through the pages of the report. Words of agreement came from others.

"We can't confirm the last inventory's veracity, and we can't reconcile the new one," Rich said. "We don't know how long the paintings have been missing."

With that admission, more conversation ensued around the room. Justin looked at Marc and Douglas, shared commiseration on their faces.

Justin quickly addressed the assembly from his chair. "A great deal of time has passed since the last complete property inventory took place, and by these results, it was long overdue. There are absolutely too many inconsistencies to validate the new one, so we won't. I've discussed it with Marc and Douglas, and we've agreed to start fresh."

As the room settled down, Rich referred to his papers. "If you'll turn to the reconciliation report for artworks, you'll see that not only is that figure less than it should be for the paintings category, but we have higher than expected numbers for other groups of items." The crackle of turning paper swept through the room.

"Mr. Hardy has instructed my department to recertify the report," he continued. "We've already started, but it'll take at least two to three weeks."

Justin quietly thanked Rich, who returned to his seat in the back.

Ray closed the report. "Well, let me ask this," he said. "Do you see a correlation between these odd numbers in the inventory reports and Davina Spenser's claim that her father owned some of our paintings?"

"Maybe we should start an investigation anyway to coincide with the new report," Edward added.

Justin's dark eyebrows slanted in displeasure. "Until we know what we're looking for, there won't be any investigations or police involvement." He glanced in Marc's direction and saw his subtle nod of agreement.

"Security gave us a report." Douglas spoke from the other end of the table. "There's no evidence of a breach in the storage lockup, so we don't know whether, or at whom, to point a finger yet."

"Will the delayed report affect our balance sheet for the extension on our bank loan?" Elizabeth Hardy asked.

"For now, it won't. The inventory report was supposed to boost our value on paper. If the loan extension comes down to us establishing an even better financial picture than we've shown them, then we'll shore up the inventory report."

Justin answered the remaining questions, then adjourned the meeting. As the conference room slowly emptied, he repacked his briefcase and glanced at his watch. It was late, but he had to seek out Davina in the gallery workshop before she left for the day. He wanted to share the meeting results with her and give her some relief. He also wanted to see her again.

"Your plan worked, Justin," Douglas said walking toward him. "It was a good idea to ask Rich to reconcile that old inventory report with the new one."

"Your opinion about him was right, too," Justin responded. "He's a precise man and was understandably upset with the conflicting results."

"I appreciate you taking me into your confidence, but I hope whatever decision you're trying to work out resolves itself in the next few weeks." Douglas joined Justin in the front of the room. "I wonder how Rich will react if he gets the same results from the second report?" He rested a hand on the table. "Will he get the same results?"

Justin smiled and latched the briefcase. "I needed to buy a little time, that's all. With your help and advice, I was able to pull it off."

"I trust your judgment, Justin. You know what you're doing."

"Marc isn't pleased about that second report. At least you brought him around to our way of thinking." He laid a hand on Douglas's shoulder. "Thanks." He strode through the door and down the hall.

"Mr. Hardy—"

Justin's head turned to the voice. "What is it, Nora? If it can wait until tomorrow, let it." She caught up with him as he headed toward the gallery.

"Mr. Preston called twice to get on your calendar. What should I tell him?"

Justin slowed. "Give him any day this week." He paused a moment, then added, "Tell him to meet me at the house. Right now, I've got to catch someone else." He reached out to open the gallery door.

"If you're looking for Miss Spenser, she's working at home today."

With his hand on the door, Justin turned to find her regarding him from under raised brows. "Thank you, Nora."

She smiled before starting back to her office.

He moved quickly through the mingling board members and headed for the relative privacy and quiet of his office to think things out.

Entering the side door to the business offices, he walked between the pooled desks that belonged to the secretaries. It was now after five o'clock, and most of the support staff had gone. The cubicle offices along the outer wall still held a couple of sales managers and staff, but even they seldom stayed beyond six.

He walked into his office and found Linda behind his desk. He could see her legs crossed high as she reclined in the chair. She had turned on the bookshelf stereo and a slow blues dirge wailed away the silence. He pushed the door shut.

"The meeting is over already?" Linda asked. "I thought you'd be there for a while longer." She got out of the chair and came around to the front of the desk.

Marc's hands found their way to his pockets and he jingled the coins and keys there. It was a bad habit he had tried to lose, but it would surface of its own volition. He moved to his now vacated chair and sat down, but not before he pressed the power button on the stereo. Silence. He slid his hands across his head and sighed. "What are you doing in here, Linda?"

"I want to know what happened at the meeting."

Marc rubbed his neck and leaned into the chair. "What did you expect? They didn't complain about a second report."

"Did he tell them he was investigating her?"

"Hell, no. But the audit report was thrown out. I still don't know his plans."

"That woman means trouble for him." She paced in front of his desk.

"And you want to rescue him." He shook his head in wonder. "What is it with him and women?" The last comment was almost a mutter.

Linda narrowed her eyes. "Why would he investigate her and not tell the board about it?"

"Figure it out for yourself. He doesn't want us to know."

She stormed her attention on Marc. "You need my help, so don't be a smart-ass." Her hands rested on her hips. "I didn't have to tell you what I knew."

"Don't hand me that." Marc's boyish grin was gone. In its place was a thin frown that reached his eyes. "You told me so I could help you get Justin back one more time. I guess you know this time it won't work. Either you really pissed him off this go round or his eyes are turned in another direction."

"He's infatuated, that's all." Linda's eyes grew dark with anger.

"You don't force him into anything. And, if you try, he'll fight it on general principle." He watched her digest his words. "I told you to ease up a little."

"I'm not going to just sit around while he chases that minx, Davina."

"You should have backed off months ago."

"As if you know all the answers," she said, and stopped in front of the desk. "If you did, you'd be the president of Hardy and I'd have Justin back in New York where I want him. All of your years of allegiance and hard work didn't replace him in his daddy's mind, did they?" She smiled cruelly.

"Like I said, it's not over with yet. The board still has to vote him in."

"Yeah, sure." Linda walked to the door and left without a backward glance.

Marc laughed. She should be more patient. The best revenge in this case was to get even. Reaching for the phone, he quickly tapped in a number and leaned back in his chair.

"Yeah . . ." A male voice on the other end answered.

"It's me," Marc said into the phone. "There's a change in the deadline."

"What kind?" the voice asked. "I thought you said there wasn't a rush."

"It doesn't matter. We've got to replace the originals we just delivered."

"I'm not finished. I just started on the new one."

"I figured that," Marc said. He leaned back and swiveled in the chair. "We'll worry about that when we get to it. For now, we work with the ones we have."

"How do you expect me to deliver when you keep changing plans?"

Marc abruptly stood from the chair and pressed a hand into his pocket. "Just do what you were hired for, Nathan, and let me take care of the rest."

"And you keep that lady and her brother from snooping around here."

"I'll talk with you later." Marc slowly hung up the phone. Deep in thought, he rubbed his brow. "Forget the problems," he muttered. "When it rains, it pours."

"Think about it, Vinny. If he's not behind the forgery you found, then who else would be?" David's voice was rough with anxiety. "He has the originals."

"You forget someone turned around and stole them from me," she countered.

"You used to think that person was one and the same . . . Justin."

She sighed. "I know, but I asked him what he thought about the whole idea of forgeries, David. And, like I told you, he didn't seem concerned, evasive, or even suspicious. He just went on about how the police hardly consider it a crime." Davina stood before her work-shop easel and drew patchworked strokes of liquid color across the canvas that depicted a nude woman stretching in the sun.

"You aren't upset that we're no closer to proving our theories against Hardy?"

"It's early yet, David. I'm not giving up." She stepped back and looked at the effect of the translucent color on the canvas. "There, that should finish it off."

"Are you going out with him again?"

Puzzled, she turned to look at him as he leaned against the wall. "Why?"

"Because I know you don't like being nice to him to get information."

"Believe it or not, he's not quite as vain and overbearing as I first thought." She stole a look at David over her shoulder as she swirled the brush in the medium. "He was even gracious the other night."

"You don't see it. He's a player and knows how to use his charm. He's always in the gossip pages with different woman. He's got you in his sights now."

Davina's fingers fumbled the paintbrush and it slipped into the cleaning solution. "Damn." She swore under her breath for more reasons than one.

David walked away from her in the small workshop. "He's on the prowl. I noticed it the day you signed the contracts, and again when I met you at the gallery. You have to be on your guard, or he'll try to get you involved with him."

She didn't deny what he said. "My eyes are wide open, David. I know his reputation. The fact that he could be dealing in illegal art to save his company hasn't escaped me, either." She wiped a paint-smudged hand on her already spotted smock, and looked at David. "Don't worry about me. I'm the one that suggested this plan, remember?"

"I do worry, though. He'll read you like a book, Vinny, if you're not careful. He's not stupid and, I can guarantee you, he's not going to miss an opportunity to learn something to his advantage if it'll get rid of us."

Davina turned to glare at David, annoyance evident on her face. "So, why are you so scared he'll take advantage of me? You know I wouldn't do anything to jeopardize what we're doing."

"Because I also see how you've been looking at him."

Davina's ears rang at his words and she felt herself grow warm. She allowed anger to supplant her embarrassment. "What's that supposed to mean? Do you take pictures and analyze our every move?"

''That dress you wore the other night, you've never worn anything like that.''

Forget Natalie and the dress, she thought. How could she explain to him what she felt when she wasn't sure herself. ''David, I went to a party.'' Her voice was calm as she tried reason. ''Would you rather I had worn a paint smock and jeans to preserve your ideal of me? I am not a young innocent and I know everyone can't be trusted, least of all Justin Hardy.''

David had the good sense to look sheepish. ''I know.''

''I love you, but if you continue to treat me like some untried virgin, I'm going to have to kick you.'' She playfully punched his chest with her fist.

He held his hands up in defeat. ''Okay, I'm sorry. I got carried away.''

She turned her back to him, effectively closing the subject and the argument, when the doorbell sounded.

''That's Natalie,'' Davina said. ''She's early.''

While David answered the door, she returned to cleaning the paint-brushes.

Davina never thought of her workshop as particularly small. It had a large window that allowed plenty of light to enter, and it was the size of an average bedroom. With Justin standing only a few yards away, he filled the room until she felt she'd suffocate in the small space. Her rapid heartbeat didn't help, either.

Justin's appearance at the front door had been a total surprise. David had presented him to her in the workshop like some prized painting for display. Now, from her high stool, she saw that David watched Justin like a hawk from the only other seat in the room. Justin had declined to sit preferring, he said, to stand.

''What brings you all the way out here?'' she asked.

He shifted his weight and pressed his hand on the nearby worktable. ''Actually, it's because of you.''

His words and cool appraisal gave her a private thrill; but, acutely aware that David watched, she gave him an impatient shrug to continue.

"The board met today and I was able to put off any direct action on the missing paintings for at least another few weeks."

"And that means—?" David asked.

Justin turned to him. "It means Davina still has time to come clean."

Davina exchanged a glance with David before she met Justin's eyes, eyes that shared none of the warmth from their prior evening together. "I've told you. There's nothing to explain. Hopefully, the paintings will show up soon."

"I don't know why I keep protecting you." He started to speak again, but stopped. Instead, he sighed and turned to leave. "One step forward, two steps back. Both of you realize that's about how our trust works."

Davina was uncomfortable with acknowledging the delicate understanding she'd achieved with Justin, and felt David's watchful eye from across the room. She slid from the stool and pressed her hands into her back pockets. "Thanks for stopping by to tell me about the meeting. Come on, I'll see you to the door." She threw a glance in David's direction that hinted volumes. He stayed put.

Justin followed her to the front door. When they reached it, she turned to face him.

He spoke to her in a low voice. "I should never have come over here."

Davina felt like the betrayer of their newfound understanding, but David was right. She must be on guard, no matter what direction her heart wanted to take. She didn't respond, but tilted her head up to his.

He moved in close, and his hand reached out, and beyond, to the wall behind her. Davina turned and saw that he touched the Bantu mask from the auction. She turned to him as the memories washed over her.

"Some part of me thought we had begun to trust the other," he whispered. "I considered the odd possibility that maybe you would tell me the truth without being coerced to do it. I see I'll have to wait another day for that to happen."

He bent his head and brushed his lips against hers, a fleeting, feather touch that made her heart leap. Then, he was out of her door and gone. As she stood there quietly, next to the mask, she became aware that her rapid heartbeat had been replaced with the thud of a dull pain.

CHAPTER EIGHTEEN

Investigations and Insinuations

Two days came and went and Davina's heart raced each time she heard the gallery doors open at Hardy Enterprises.

She hoped—no, expected—that Justin would appear, but he didn't. In the halls, she was sure they would run into each other, and it never happened. To have found themselves in each other's company so many times in the past few weeks, she knew he was purposely avoiding her. He had more records delivered to the gallery, reneging on his own directive that she review them in his conference room.

She admitted, grudgingly, that a part of her reveled in Justin's open admission that he wanted her. That unnerved her, and not because of her own burgeoning emotions, but because of the price she'd pay if she acted on them. And then, there were David and Natalie. While Natalie urged her to enjoy herself, David, at every opportunity, preached caution. Leaning her elbow on the desk, she rested her chin in her hand and considered her dilemma.

Davina stretched in the chair and looked at her watch. It was late evening and most of the staff had left. She had officially moved into one of the vacated gallery offices, where she could prepare and work on the details for the opening. She would continue to use the workshop to prepare the remaining paintings.

Davina looked beyond the glass window and saw that Rosa Gallegos, the gallery secretary, was still at her desk in the corner on the gallery floor. She could also see the new paintings Robert had recently hoisted in place in the gallery. The new show would open next week; then, it would be her turn.

She also looked at the box of archived records. So far, they had yielded few secrets that she and David could use to prove their case against Hardy. To date, their best leads had come from an old man with a sketchy memory. Soon, she'd have to return the box to security for lock up, so she turned her focus to the files.

Elizabeth Hardy handed Justin a cup of tea from the tray. They both enjoyed the cool breeze wafting through the screened patio salon that wrapped around the back of the house.

"Douglas thinks you've become Davina's protector, of sorts."

He smiled. "And you're his confidante, huh?"

"Justin," Elizabeth said in a shocked voice, "Douglas was your father's best friend and I treasure his friendship as well. I thought you liked him."

His eyebrows shot up in surprise. "Of course, I do, Mom. That's not what I meant."

She looked at him in mock severity. "I know exactly what you meant, and Douglas is a good friend. I'd rather talk about you and the young Spenser woman. I know you're not seeing Linda." At his mild groan, she smiled. "It was no secret that she wasn't my favorite person; but unlike your father, I've always allowed you children to lead your own lives, mistakes and all."

"Davina is . . ." He searched for the right word.

"A beautiful girl, quite different from others you've known," she suggested.

"Mom, do you know I've never once seriously entertained the thought of marriage and children. Until now."

When his mother's eyes grew wide, he laughed out loud. "Hold on, I didn't say I wanted to marry her. Frankly, I doubt if she'd have me; but being around her has made me look at my own life differently."

"How is that?" She watched him with interest.

"It's easy to take advantages for granted when you're blessed with them. Lately, I find myself looking at things through her eyes. She's managed to stay clean and unspoiled even though she had a rough time coming up. When I see her standing up for her convictions, I respect her for it, even if I don't believe in them."

"So, Douglas was right. You do want to protect her."

"I'm trying. I want her to trust me. If I can get her to do that, maybe it'll explain some of the craziness going on."

Mrs. Taylor quietly appeared on the patio. "Justin, Connie Preston is here."

Justin set the teacup down. "Thank you. Show him to the library and I'll be there in a moment." He tilted his head at his mother. "Are you going to ask why I'm seeing him here?"

She smiled. "Does it have anything to do with your young lady?"

He liked the way that sounded. "Let's hope so." He left the patio and headed for the library on the other side of the house.

Connie was standing near the cold fireplace when Justin walked in.

"Have a seat," Justin said as he walked to the side bar to fix a drink. "Can I get you something?"

"Whatever you're having is fine for me, man." He sat on a nail-studded leather chair. "Getting in touch with you was rough. You need to slow down."

"It's been a bear ever since I got back in town. You just don't know." He handed one of the glasses to Connie and sat across from him.

"You expected it would be like this if you took over. Are you sorry?"

"No," Justin answered. "I took the job out of respect for Dad because he wanted me to. But I never realized I'd have so much trouble changing things." He noticed the ever-present notepad in Connie's shirt pocket. "Are you going to tell me what was so important?"

Connie put the glass on the table, and fished the pad from his pocket. "I've been following up on bits and pieces of information that didn't make sense, but put together, they create an interesting picture. You wanted me to be on the lookout for anything that might be connected with the Spenser woman and her brother."

Justin leaned forward. "True. What did you find?"

"First," he started, "there's no paper trail of Maceo after he disappeared."

"Not unexpected, since that was his intent."

"Exactly. But, when he changed towns, who did he become? The popular rumor that spread, maybe on purpose, was that he was dead. Davina Spenser says her father knew Maceo sometime during the past few years. Why would someone who had stayed hidden for thirty years show up using his correct name?"

Justin nodded as he listened to Connie.

"When I asked James Spenser's old neighbors about his habits, they remembered him as an occasional drunk, but they also said he liked to paint, and he was always painting with his daughter."

"She never mentioned that," Justin mused.

Connie flipped the page of his notepad. "I started rethinking what we'd been led to believe. James Spenser and Maceo were both artists, good friends, and, as Davina Spenser claims, connected with the beginnings of Hardy Enterprises."

"They're all irrevocably linked." Justin rubbed his chin in thought.

Connie opened a small manila folder Justin only now noticed on the table before him. "Death certificates are protected by the privacy act and when my sources couldn't find one in Miami for Mr. Spenser, presuming that's where he died, I researched his marriage to one Estrella Montero, Davina's mother. We got his social security number that way." He handed Justin two photostat documents.

"What's this?" Justin looked at them, a social security card and number, and a photograph of a young white male.

"One is a copy of the card issued to James Spenser."

"Is this a picture of her father?" Justin's voice registered surprise.

"No, that's the owner of the social security number. He died thirty-seven years ago in Ohio when he was fourteen. His name was James Spenser."

"Well, I'll be . . ." Justin exclaimed. "I know the answer to my next question. You didn't find a picture of the man known as Davina's father did you?"

"You got that right. I'm still searching," Connie said. "But I'll lay even money that James Spenser and Maceo James were one and the same person."

* * *

"I promise this is the last time, baby. I promise." Nathan held onto Quilla's hands, but avoided looking into her tear-stained face.

"You said that before, and now you're doin' it again. Don't you see you're getting in too deep? Walk away before it's too late," she cried.

He dropped her hands and pushed back from the dinner table, disgusted with himself. "I can't. I already committed myself. I'm doing this for the baby. We'll have enough money to move out of here and I can take you, Pop, and the baby to a better place. For now, I can't back out." He looked at her. "They won't let me."

Her bitter tears mixed with her words. "That's what I'm scared of, Nathan. That's what I'm scared of."

David hoisted the gym bag onto his shoulder and pressed the ringer on Natalie's door. He had just left Davina's apartment in the next building, and she wasn't home. After a hard workout at the gym, he had planned to meet his sister, shower, then the two would get something to eat. He decided he'd wait for her.

For months, he had never noticed Natalie, except to complain about her irreverent style. Now, all he did was notice her. The kiss had been unexpected, and thankfully, she hadn't made anything of it. That was Natalie for you. It wasn't a good idea to have designs on your sister's best friend, anyway.

David rested a bare, brawny arm against the door frame and tilted his water bottle to his mouth just as the door opened to Natalie. She was dressed in a black leotard with a towel draped around her neck. He had not expected to be confronted with her hourglass figure so quickly after deciding she was off limits.

He slowly lowered the bottle, brows raised in appreciation. "I'm not interrupting, am I?"

"What are you gaping at? If anything important was going on, I wouldn't have answered the door." She matched his smile and left the door open while she returned to an exercise mat in the middle of the living room floor.

David followed her into the expensively decorated contemporary apartment where he noticed the exercise video playing on the television, the volume turned down. "I was looking for Vinny. Do you know where she is?"

"She's probably still at the gallery." She glanced at the gold clock sitting on the mantelpiece before she looked over her shoulder to David. "Nope. It's after seven. She's usually left there by now."

"That was my point." He dropped his bag in the corner and retrieved a delicate wood-slatted chair from the breakfast area. When he returned to the living room, Natalie was kneeling on the mat watching Victoria Johnson gyrate through floor exercises on the muted television.

"You mind if I crash here until she gets home? I was supposed to shower before we go to eat." His words trailed off as he turned the armless chair and straddled the seat. He folded his arms across the back.

"That's what you get for living across town from us," she said.

"I wouldn't bother you, but she moved the spare key after the break in."

Natalie sat in a lotus position. "Of course you can stay. She's probably on her way home now. Just don't get in my way."

He watched the women on the television perform the exercises, and a devilish glint flared in his eyes. "Hey, do you need my help? I can spot for you."

Davina could find no mention of Maceo in the written historical account of Hardy Enterprises. Browsing through early brochures in a box filled with an assortment of items, she came across pictures of Jacob Hardy as a young man. She could see the resemblance in those early pictures to Justin today.

She gathered up the materials from the desk, but as she lifted them, the ungainly folders and books became too much and spilled from her arms. They dropped to the floor and spread like a great paper fan.

"Man." She crouched down to gather the mess. As she pulled the folders together, one of them dragged unevenly from a corner weight. Taking the time to investigate, she saw that it was weighed down by a small, bulky package secured to its back with staples and rubber bands.

"What's this?" she asked aloud. Sure fingers pulled on the folded envelope until the staples released their hold. Quickly, she removed the rubber bands and discovered a cache of photographs.

They were old, black and white prints of men she suspected were friends of Jacob Hardy. Some were individual shots, others were in groups. Davina dropped to the floor, momentarily forgetting the papers that still fanned around her, and studied the pictures.

She examined them in hopes of seeing her own father. He had shunned cameras. Now, of course, she knew why. She felt lucky to have found the ones she used to work on his portrait. They had been found stashed among his things after he became too ill to care for himself.

She couldn't identify anyone from the first six photos, and the next two were of Jacob. In a stroke of luck, the next one had the name of its subjects scribbled on the back: Jake, Lee, Maceo, and Otis, a name Morris Mangley had mentioned.

Through the process of elimination, she recognized her father, and smiled to herself. He had a wide grin on his face, a happy face, and was dressed to the nines, as he'd have called it, including a brimmed hat. The men were lined up and clasped shoulders. Next to him stood a young Lee, the spitting image of his son, Nathan. She thought it interesting that father and now son created paintings, like herself and her father. Even Justin followed the path of his businessman father.

The last photos were similarly themed. It showed some of the men as they hovered over a table and laughed while they played a game of cards in one, checkers in another shot. Davina knew these pictures. They were the subject of one of her father's paintings, one she had removed from Hardy's that night.

A muffled thump sounded through the silent gallery. *What was that?* Davina looked up and around, but heard nothing else.

She looked at her watch. *Good Lord, it's late.* She scrambled from the floor and stretched her cramped legs. Looking out into the gallery, she saw that Rosa had left. That meant someone in the lab was probably patiently waiting for her to return the box of records for lock up. She hurriedly stacked the folders into the cardboard box, but she placed the package of photos aside on the table. *I have to show these to David.*

The box was too heavy to carry to the lab, so she walked across the gallery to get Charlie or Robert to take it to storage. The empty room was strangely reminiscent of the night she took the paintings, and the similarity spooked her.

The windows showed the darkness outside. She had promised Natalie she wouldn't take chances by staying too late. As she pushed through the metal doors toward the lab, she made a mental note to have the security guard escort her to the parking lot.

"Charlie . . . Robert," she called out, stepping through the doors. The first thing she noticed was the main light was off. The storage bins cast long shadows in the dim room. Only the wall sconces were lit, throwing off enough light to maneuver through the room. She wondered where the main light switch was located.

As she moved farther into the room, the quiet became a menacing presence. She called out again, "Charlie, are you back here?" No answer. "Robert?"

She quickly made her way to the lab. The door was slightly ajar, but cool, clean light poured from within the room to lighten a triangle of darkness in the hallway. Davina breathed a sigh of relief that the lab was not locked up. Charlie or Robert would be inside. She briskly entered the doorway, an apology on her lips for losing track of time.

The room was quiet and there was no one in sight. Davina turned in a complete circle. "Charlie? Robert?" Concerned now, she looked more carefully around the room. The normally pristine lab had obviously not been closed for the day. Something was not right. She walked around a wide partition that separated the work counter from the rest of the room and immediately stumbled into something on the floor. Davina caught her balance, then peered down to see what had blocked her way.

"What in . . ." Davina's eyes stretched as she staggered backward. It was a body, with Robert's face. Panic, like she had never experienced, welled in her throat. Her eyes wouldn't leave the deathly still body that lay comfortably on the floor. Robert wore his white lab coat, and his face was turned away, but his dreads were unmistakable.

"Oh, my God. What's happened?" She uttered the words out loud.

Within seconds, she had taken control of her terror and walked slowly toward him. She had to feel for a pulse. *Maybe he's not dead, only knocked out.* She stooped close to his body and pressed her thumb against his neck. As she felt for a pulse, she noticed that a spot of blood peeked from the edge of his lab coat. Her heart thumped madly but she forced her other hand to push the coat aside. Then, she jammed her hand against her mouth to hold back the threatened bile.

The spot became a wide circle of bright blood that saturated his shirt. She gasped, then panted in sheer horror as her heart hammered into her head. "Oh, God, no," she cried out.

"What are you doing?" A security guard had silently entered and come up behind her.

Tears had already begun to form in Davina's eyes when she looked up at the guard. "Quick, call 911. It's Robert. I believe he's dead."

CHAPTER NINETEEN

Murder Most Foul . . .

Justin was furious with Davina, and did a slow burn below the surface. His meeting with Connie had turned into dinner as they discussed details of his investigation.

"Did you hear me?" Connie was staring into Justin's face.

Justin frowned and returned his attention to the business at hand. "I'm sorry, Connie. I was gone for a minute."

"I know," he said with a smile. He dropped his napkin on the table and pushed away from his empty plate. "I was saying I still don't have anything to explain why someone would want to harm her."

"Unless it has something to do with Maceo being her father."

Connie nodded in agreement. "Except for that disturbing the peace citation when she was in college that I told you about, there's been no trouble with the police. What about the internal leak you mentioned? Did you find the source?"

"I took your advice and kept my eyes and ears open." He, too, dropped his napkin and leaned back in his chair. "I've spent the last few days closed up in my conference room with some of my staff. I did learn a few things." He stared hard at Connie. "Like before, your information is confidential, and I want you to continue to report to me. What we need now is a picture of James Spenser and his death certificate."

"Are you going to confront her with all this?"

"No. I want her to keep thinking her little secrets are safe." The words were ground out between his teeth.

Connie started to speak but was interrupted by a commotion outside the dining room door. Both men turned at the sounds.

Elizabeth Hardy made an abrupt appearance in the doorway; a bleak expression creased her brow.

Alarmed, Justin rose from his chair. "Mom, what is it?"

"There's been a terrible accident at the office."

Natalie inched through her door with arms loaded with take out food. She heard the sound of the shower as she kicked the door closed. David had decided to take her up on the offered shower while she went for the food. Walking toward the kitchen, she passed the answering machine and noticed the message indicator's red blink. She pressed the play button and continued on to the kitchen. After the familiar beep, she heard Davina's voice.

"Natalie, if you're there, pick up. David is not answering his phone, either. Please come to the gallery. An employee was killed and the police are on their way. Hurry."

Natalie, momentarily stunned, stood frozen. Then, she dropped the bags of food to the table and rushed down the hall toward the shower. She snatched open the bathroom door and met a billowy cloud of steam.

"David," she screamed into the clearing mist.

"What's wrong?" His head stuck around the glass shower door; he blinked through the rivulets of water that flowed down his face.

"Davina left a message on the machine." She forced the breathless words out and crossed her arms to quell her building panic. "There's been an accident at the gallery. Someone's been killed. The police are on their way and she wants us there now." She stopped for a breath.

"What?" David yelled incredulously. He pushed the glass door aside in the steamy room and stepped from the shower, grabbing a nearby towel as he moved past Natalie for the door. "What else did she say?"

"That was it." She crossed to the shower and cut the water off, then followed him into the hall. "She tried calling you first, then she called me."

"Damn." He was already at the door of the guest room, the towel now draped around his waist. "See if you can get her on the phone, and be ready to leave in five minutes."

Shakily, Natalie went to the phone. "Oh God, Davina," she said out loud, "What have you gotten into?"

Justin arrived at the gallery entrance and identified himself to the uniformed police officer even as his eyes sought out Davina. All he remembered of the call from the security guard was that she was unharmed but shaken up by what had happened. He thought of his earlier anger. Now, all he could think of was her safety. Then, he spied her, curled in a chair in the office. He strode across the room and paused at the doorway.

"Davina . . ."

She looked up, then in a swift movement, rushed into his open arms.

"I'm so glad you're here." Her words were muffled against his coat as she clutched him.

Justin leaned his chin against the top of her head and held her tight. He closed his eyes and breathed in her fragrant essence. The last time she'd looked this frightened was the night of the break-in. He'd wanted to protect her then, too.

"Are you all right?" he asked gently.

Davina answered with a nod and raised her head. Justin studied her intently, feature by feature, as she pushed her hair back from her face and exhaled deeply. Devoid of makeup, except for a remnant of lipstick, her beautiful face carried a look of pure innocence, but was she?

"Robert is dead. I found him, but they haven't told me anything. He had a horrible wound in his chest." Davina's eyes were bright with unshed tears. "It's been a nightmare here, with police all over. And I can't reach David or Natalie. I've left a message for them."

Justin pulled her into his embrace and slowly rocked her. "Tell me what happened." His deep voice was gently bidding.

She told him about hearing a noise and, ultimately, her literal stumble onto Robert's body. "The detectives questioned me, told me not to leave, and to wait here while the medical examiner removes the body." A tremble swept her body. "They asked so many questions, Justin, some of them over and over."

He leaned back and let his hands drop to her waist. "Don't worry. It'll all work out." Tilting her chin up, he watched her dark lashes rise. "David will get your message soon, but I'll make sure you're not here alone."

She let out a physical sigh. "Thank you, Justin."

"Why don't we try and talk with the detectives now."

She quickly agreed. He draped an arm around her shoulders and led her through the gallery and into the work area in the back.

The area was now brightly lit and crime scene technicians, along with uniformed officers, studied the room for evidence. Farther down the hall, a police photographer exited the lab while other personnel, hands encased in gloves, moved in and out of the door.

"They're not finished, so maybe you should wait here." Justin walked the short distance to the lab and went in. He looked around the room, and immediately spotted two men he suspected were the detectives on the case.

They both wore business suits, but the similarity ended there. Standing together, the older man was overweight and had thin, gray hair with brown streaks. The other was closer to Justin's age and nattily dressed. His black skin had a spit polish shine that was accentuated against the light-colored shirt. His frantic gum chewing was totally incongruous to his appearance.

Justin looked around but didn't see Robert's body. He noticed activity near the partition and walked to it. Behind it, four men wore jackets emblazoned with the coroner's office emblem. In various squat positions, they ministered to an inert figure on the floor. Justin gritted his teeth. The lifeless body belonged to Robert.

"Who are you?"

Justin turned to the voice. With another backward glance at the body, he swallowed hard and met the older of the two detectives across the room.

"I'm Justin Hardy. The young man over there," he motioned with his head, "was my employee."

The man introduced himself as Detective John Jaragoski. He pointed out his partner, Detective Frank Lovett, who busied himself inspecting paint samples on a shelf.

"What happened?" Justin asked. "My security service called me at home."

The detective propped his foot on the rung of a nearby stool. "We don't have much. No one saw the crime being committed. The dead employee has been identified as Robert Montgomery. He suffered a mortal puncture wound to his chest. We'll get a more detailed report from the coroner's office later. An artist, Davina Spenser, found him. One of the security guards, Mitchell Timmins, found her leaning over the body. Can you vouch that these people work for you and had reason to be in the building this time of night?"

"Yes. Two guards cover the interior and exterior of the building. Davina Spenser's show will open here next month. She works late, on occasion, preparing for it. Mr. Montgomery worked in the lab."

"The gallery closes during the week at six. Is it normal for people to hang around here this time of night?"

Justin frowned as he answered. "I wouldn't use the word 'normal.' Miss Spenser is authorized to stay as late as she deems necessary. Charles Albritton runs the lab and can better explain Mr. Montgomery's schedule." He watched the detective take notes. "Do you have any theories on how this happened?"

"That's what we're trying to put together, Mr. Hardy. Was anyone else in the building tonight?"

"After six, there's a sign in and out register kept with the guard downstairs."

"All right, I'll check that out before I go."

"Is Miss Spenser free to leave?"

"After she comes to headquarters for a written statement."

"Tonight?"

"Tonight," the detective repeated, looking up at Justin. "We need her official statement while it's fresh. Your security guard has already gone down to give his."

"It's all right, Justin. I want this over with." Davina had come up behind him. "The sooner it's done, the quicker these detectives can find out who did this."

"In that case," Justin said, "I'll drive you there." His voice carried no room for compromise on her part.

The detective looked over at his partner. In a silent agreement, he turned back to Justin as the other detective joined them. "That's fine. Detective Lovett will take your statement at the office."

"Will you finish here tonight?" Justin asked. "We have a new show opening."

"We may need to come back and question other employees," Detective Jaragoski said. "I'll be staying until the ME carts the body out. But, we'll leave officers here to patrol the building until your security staff returns from the station."

Justin nodded his agreement.

Detective Lovett closed a small flip notepad and placed it inside his coat. "I'm finished for the time being. Homicide headquarters is over on North Avenue."

"I know the building," Justin said. "We'll follow in my car."

"Good. We can go now."

The three of them retraced their steps through the lab and out to the gallery. But, Davina abruptly stopped when they reached the door.

heart & soul

1 year (6 issues) $16.97 plus receive a FREE HEART & SOUL
Healthy Living Journal with your paid subscription.

YES! I want to invest in myself and subscribe to HEART & SOUL, the health, fitness and beauty magazine for savvy African-American women. I'll get a year's worth of helpful information that will inspire me to discover new ways of improving my body...my spirit...and my mind. Plus, I'll get a FREE HEART & SOUL *Healthy Living Journal* to keep a daily record of my wonderful progress.

Name _____
　　　　(First)　　　　　　　(Last)

Address _____ Apt # _____

City _____ State _____ Zip _____ | MABI3 |

☐ Payment enclosed　　☐ Bill me
　Rush my HEART & SOUL
　Healthy Living Journal

Please allow 6-8 weeks for receipt of first issue. In Canada: CDN $19.97 (includes GST). Payment in U.S. currency must accompany all Canadian orders. Basic subscription rate: 6 issues $16.97.

BUSINESS REPLY MAIL

FIRST-CLASS MAIL   PERMIT NO. 272   RED OAK, IA

POSTAGE WILL BE PAID BY ADDRESSEE

heart&soul

P O BOX 7423
RED OAK IA 51591-2423

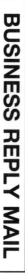

"Detective Lovett, I'd like to try and call my brother again, before we leave."

"Can we meet you at headquarters?" Justin asked.

"Sure. Ask for me when you get there." He left them.

Justin slowly paced across the gallery floor in between glances thrown at Davina as she used the office phone. Noise at the entry garnered his attention, and he saw David and Natalie hailed through by the officer. David's eyes were stormy under knitted brows as he looked past Justin in search of Davina.

"Vinny." David called to his sister, visible through the glass wall.

She turned at her name and, dropping the phone onto the cradle, sped into the gallery to hug David. "I just tried calling you again. Where have you two been?" she cried. Her arm reached out and pulled Natalie into the embrace.

Justin didn't disturb them. He looked away and noticed a familiar cardboard box on the floor of the office. He walked in, gathered up the records he suspected Davina had forgotten about, and secured the box in a cabinet.

"What's happened?" David asked. "We called here, but no one answered."

"The lab assistant, Robert Montgomery, was killed, mur . . . murdered." Her voice caught in her throat.

Justin walked back out to the small group and stood behind Davina. He gently placed his hands on her shoulders. "Davina found Robert's body in the lab"—he paused at Natalie's gasp—"and the security guards called me and the police. They're still handling the investigation in the back, but we were on our way to the police station to give an official statement."

David's stare moved from Justin to Davina's eyes. "Are you up to going . . . ?"

"Yes, I want to get it over with." She looked from him to Natalie. "I'm okay."

Justin took her hand, pleased that she didn't pull away, and started for the door. Natalie and David fell in step with her.

"We can talk about everything in the car," Davina said.

"And we can all go in mine," Justin added.

* * *

Shock was written across Marc's face as he listened to Justin's voice through the phone. "Davina has given her statement, and we're about to leave homicide headquarters."

"Do they have any idea who did it?" Marc asked.

"No. They'll be looking into Robert's background, but it could also have been an intruder in the gallery. Nothing appeared to be disturbed, and no one saw anyone enter or leave suspiciously."

Marc swore into the phone. "What do you need me to do?"

"Call Nora and fill her in. She'll know how to prepare. There'll be lots of press at the office tomorrow. Also, get Robert's next of kin address from Nora. Then, call me on the cell phone so we can both meet with his family tonight."

Marc held his head in his hand. "We didn't need this. I'm sorry."

"What are you apologizing for?" Justin asked. "We're in this together and we'll get through it that way. Get on those details and I'll talk with you later."

A click and the call was over. What happened? He replaced the phone and looked at his watch. He'd better get moving. A lot had to be accomplished tonight. He left the house, slamming the door behind him.

Natalie paced across the small bedroom floor and looked over at Davina, curled around a cushion on the chaise. They were waiting for David to return from Natalie's with the food. "When David gets back, you've got to tell him you're being followed." When Davina remained silent, she said, "For God's sake, someone was murdered tonight. This is too serious to ignore."

A shiver seized Davina as the events of the evening replayed in her mind's eye. She rubbed her forehead with both hands. "Don't you think I know it? Someone I knew and befriended is dead. I can't let myself even consider that the things happening to me are, in any way, related to his death." She dropped her hands as her eyes widened and the tears of frustration finally broke loose.

Natalie moved to the edge of Davina's chair and embraced her.

"You're right. It may have nothing to do with you, but you can't take chances."

Davina heard the sniffs and realized Natalie was crying, too. She reached into her pocket for a tissue. "Something tells me that I wasn't the target tonight. I could easily have been harmed, just like the night my apartment was broken into." She brushed over an object in her pocket and fished it out. It was the packet of pictures she came across earlier.

"I almost forgot, look at this," she said between sniffs. "I found these when I went through those records at the office." She presented the bound packet to Natalie, and explained how she came across them. "With everything happening, I forgot I'd left them in the office. Afterward, when I tried calling David again, they were on the table. So, I slipped them into my pocket."

Natalie flipped through the photos. "They're just old pictures. What do you think you'll find?"

"I don't know," Davina said. "Maybe David will have an idea."

"Don't you think you ought to tell Justin everything? Maybe he doesn't know what's going on himself?"

"I don't know. It was all supposed to be so simple. We would prove Hardy sold forgeries of Dad's paintings left with them for safekeeping as part of some type of agreement." She sat back, cross-legged on the chair. "And now, I don't think I ever felt more comforted and safe than when Justin was with me tonight."

Natalie dropped the pictures to her lap. "I know. I could see it all evening."

Davina looked straight ahead; her face shining from the tears. "Now, if only I can believe that feeling will last more than a moment."

"It can if you'll admit that you care about him. I'm not talking about admitting it to some deep part of yourself that you can hide at will, but admit it to him."

"I can't." She looked at Natalie. "Not now, not until I'm sure about what he feels and wants in a relationship."

"Relationships are about trust. One of you will have to be the first to admit you want to explore this thing. If you want it, why not tell him?"

"Because I will not let another man use me." She looked away from Natalie and wiped her face. "What if he's not the right man?" she whispered. "What if he really is selling forgeries and, worst of all, what if that's why Robert was killed?"

It was much later that same evening when Marc entered the Marriott Marquis lobby. He was tired, but he had to do this one last thing tonight. He had to know. The express elevator to the suites was hypnotically quiet. What he would give right now to have his life return to the rut he used to complain about. His knock at the suite was answered by a coarse voice from the other side.

Before he was barely in the room, a tall silhouette against the window barked, "You shouldn't have come here." The accent had its usual clipped sound.

Marc swallowed hard, and launched into a wary explanation. "I need to know if you intervened tonight at the Hardy Gallery?"

"If you're asking if we took care of things when you wanted to include your entire company in our business arrangement, the answer is yes."

At the man's unmitigated gall, Marc threw his usual caution to the wind. "You made a final action without telling me?" At the man's casual stance and continued silence, Marc's anger spilled over. "You went too far this time. Even your boss didn't plan for this. No one was supposed to get killed," he yelled.

"Don't ever speak of him again," the man roared. "Next time you will take better care of your details, won't you? That includes the Spenser woman."

Marc blanched at this threat to Davina. He swallowed his reply behind a mouth pressed tight with anger. Turning on his heels, he quickly left the suite.

It was the middle of a new week and Davina was a prisoner to her bed. The alarm preyed on closed ears. After hitting the snooze button a tenth time, her aim was finally true as she managed to shut it off. Light had begun to filter in behind the blinds at the window. What time was it? She didn't want to know.

Davina rolled in a restless twist to the other side of the bed, entangling the cotton sheet about her body like a mummy. She lay on her back and stared at the ceiling. Things had been worse in her life, but they never seemed so hopeless as now. And she missed Justin. So much. She wanted to see him, touch him, smell him. She let out a groan and turned again, landing on her stomach.

She had bravely returned to the Hardy building the day following the murder, and it had been a nightmare. The gallery was temporarily closed due to media coverage, a steady stream of grief-stricken employees, and the detectives. To make matters worse, the local media made the murder their top story, causing Davina to be hounded by reporters both at home and at the gallery. Altogether, it made working impossible. On the one occasion she saw Justin, he was with others, and his only acknowledgment had been a nod.

For nearly a week, she had done nothing on the show and, instead, had alternately pined over Justin, been saddened by Robert's death, and fretted over the lack of evidence to sustain her father's claims. She groaned again as she rolled in the twisted sheets.

"Arrgh!" she screamed, and tumbled over the side of the bed. At the same time, the bedside phone rang, trumpeting the fact that she was finally out of bed.

Davina sat up on the floor, groggy from sleep, and picked up the phone.

"Hello," she whispered.

"Davina, is that you?"

She frowned before recognition shone through like a bright light. "Yes, Rosa, it's me. I was still in bed. Well, sort of."

"In that case, you'd better get it in gear and get down here. Linda is on the warpath about the specs for the printer. You were to give approval, remember? She also wants your final list of paintings. That's not confirmed, either."

"Oh, Lord. I can't deal with anything right now, least of all her." Davina rubbed her eyes, thankful that Rosa was an ally in these battles with Linda.

"Sure you can. I told her you've been working at home, and you'd be in this afternoon. It's around ten. You've got a few hours to put something together."

Davina groaned and climbed back onto the bed. "Thanks for warning me, Rosa. I'll see what I can do." Davina replaced the phone and sat on the edge of the bed. She threw off the sheets followed by her sleepshirt. *When things are at their worse, suck it in and get on with life.* If she was going to deal with Linda, she'd better move. She crept toward the shower and wondered what tricks Linda had up her silk sleeves today.

CHAPTER TWENTY

Moving Forward One Push at a Time

Linda's office was located on the second floor. The door was ajar, but Davina knocked on it anyway.

"Come in."

Davina walked in. Linda sat behind a cleared desk. An in-basket that held a sheet of paper was the only thing on its surface. A quick glance revealed a small, neat office decorated with glass and delicate botanical paintings. There were also framed photos of Linda with, Davina presumed, celebrities she knew. The adage, "clean desk, warped mind" stuck in Davina's head. "You were looking for me?"

"Yes," Linda said. She stared at Davina a moment before she added, "Have a seat." A well-manicured hand motioned to a Queen Anne side chair.

Before Davina could sit down, Linda launched into a critique. "Mike in Printing buzzed me not long ago. He has your initialed specs for the program sheet." She leaned back and tightly crossed her arms against the smooth, electric blue material that hugged her chest. "You can move fast when you have to."

Davina's nose wrinkled indignantly. "You're disappointed?" She rose from the chair. "I have work to do."

"You sure do." Linda picked up the sheet of paper from the basket and studied it. "I know you've been upset about Robert, and the media is an aggravation, but your contract calls for all the work to be ready at least ten days before the opening. Only the basic preparations should remain beyond that point."

Davina sat back into the seat and squinted at Linda's words, painfully aware of their import. *So, this is her angle.* "I'm familiar with my contract."

"Then, you know about the penalty clause if you renege on your agreement?" Linda paused a moment. "You pay for all expenses incurred as a result of your failure." The beginnings of a dark smile played on her face.

"Of course," she continued in a light voice, "I've informed Justin of your show's status, and he raised no objection to invoking the failure clause."

Davina's nails slowly pressed into the soft material. To be told of Justin's indifference after pining over him that morning was like water splashed in her face.

She took a deep breath. "There won't be any reneging. Both you and Justin can rest assured that the exhibit will be on time." Again, she stood to leave. "I'll have the list of paintings for you tomorrow." She left without a backward glance.

Davina was seething as she stomped down the hall. She was angry with herself for giving Linda the opportunity to confront her about the contract, but she was hurt that Justin agreed to the penalty. The least he could have done was ask her to explain the delay. As she neared the stairwell, she ran into Alli.

"Oh, I'm glad I found you," Alli said as her bracelets jingled briskly. "Rosa said to warn you about two reporters hanging out in the gallery. They want an interview, and it's not about the show, either."

When Davina let out a groan, Alli said, "Why don't you work at home?"

Alli's words made Davina give in to a smile. "I don't do much better there."

"Justin can have security boot them out. Do you want me to get him?" she asked, and turned, ready to find him.

"No, no." Davina's hand snaked out to stop her. "I don't want to bother him with this. But maybe you can help me."

"Sure. What can I do?"

"Is there another way out of the building without using the regular entrance?"

Alli's eyes sparked with an idea. "I know what we can do," she said eagerly. "Come on." She linked her arm through Davina's and continued down the hall.

Justin sat with Marc and Douglas at the conference table. Nora was nearby taking notes. The meeting was to update the men on a few immediate matters.

"At least the police have completed their investigation," Douglas said. "If the reporters would lay off, things might get back to normal. The international exhibit should open without a hitch and the Vinny Richards show is on schedule next."

Marc lounged in his chair with an elbow propped on the table. "Did you see Linda's status report this morning?" His question was directed to Justin.

"I scanned it," Justin said. He also leaned back comfortably in his chair, having long since shed his coat. "The past week has been particularly rough for Davina; that's probably why she's behind on her work schedule. But, I'm not concerned that she won't meet the deadlines."

"Linda doesn't see it that way," Douglas responded.

"What do you mean?" Justin's eyes narrowed.

Douglas shrugged matter-of-factly as he placed his arms on the table. "I saw her earlier. She complained that Davina hasn't met some interim deadlines and is throwing everyone else off. Linda was looking for her to discuss the delays."

Marc gathered his papers together from the table. "You know Linda. She likes to use that penalty clause in the contract as a scare tactic to pressure her artists." He stood up. "If we're finished, I have some things to get to."

"That's fine. I'll catch you later." Douglas said.

"Sure, Marc," Justin added. He tapped his pen on the table's edge, somewhat aware that Marc was leaving the room.

"What are you thinking?" Douglas asked him.

Justin looked up, his expression blank from deep thought. He turned to his assistant. "That's all Nora. You can leave, too." While Nora gathered her things together, Justin lay his head against the back of the soft, leather chair.

"You're preoccupied by a lot more than hovering police," Douglas said. "When was the last time you took a break from everything? You haven't taken any days for yourself since you became president, and that was months ago."

Justin rubbed his chin. "I can't do it now. Too much is going on."

Nora's loud, contemptuous snort was heard from the door as she left the room. Both men turned at the sound and smiled, used to her occasional disdain.

"I agree with Nora." Douglas leaned toward Justin. "Now is the best time. The bank has us on hold for the extension, and the new show is on. Stephanie's magazine is off and running, and the police are handling their investigation."

When Justin said nothing, Douglas laughed. "Don't tell me a young buck like yourself has forgotten how to have fun in the course of a few months. You're not that old. I'm not that old."

Justin stretched his legs out and laughed with Douglas. "Sounds like you're trying to get rid of me."

"No, but your mother and Carolyn have noticed the hours you're putting in to straighten out this place, and they worry. You are wound too tight, and a few days away just might do it for you."

Justin thought carefully on his next words and, spreading his hands regretfully, shrugged. "Unfortunately, Douglas, what I need is a lot more complicated than a few days away from the office. My salvation, if that's what you want to call it, is wrapped within a beautiful, complicated package called Davina."

"I don't think we should go in, Alli," Davina said.

"I told you, Nora said he's in a meeting this afternoon. She's still with him, see?" Alli referred to Nora's empty chair.

Skeptical, Davina walked with Alli past the vacant desk and through the double doors that led into Justin's office.

"I just don't want to run into him," Davina said.

"You won't." Alli took the lead as they walked across the carpet toward the wall behind the desk. "There's an exit in here that leads directly to the parking lot."

"And I keep it locked against intruders."

Davina knew that voice and froze in her tracks. Alli, on the other hand, whirled at her brother's words and, with hands on her hips, immediately challenged him. "What are you doing sitting in the shadows like some vampire?"

"Watching you sneak around."

Davina turned and saw Justin sitting alone at his conference table. He didn't wear a coat and papers were spread before him. A delicious warmth spread within her when his eyes moved from Alli and captured hers. Even as her heart hammered in her chest, she steadied her voice. "Alli was helping me avoid reporters by using your private exit to the parking lot."

"I see." His eyes returned to Alli. "You can go back to work. Aren't you helping Stephanie with the magazine this week?"

"Hey, I'm on a break, okay?" She walked to the door. "See you later, Davina. Sorry we ran into him."

"Close the door behind you," Justin reminded her.

"Sure," she said. A solid click sounded before the door closed.

Davina watched Justin sigh as he rose to his feet. The rich outline of his shoulders strained against the soft fabric of his shirt. It had been a while since she had been able to covertly observe him, and she tried not to get caught staring now. She enjoyed the view, vaguely remembering that she was angry with him.

He strolled toward her, each stride a fluid motion, before he continued past, the heady scent of him strong in his wake. Davina swallowed hard as she smoothed her palms against the soft material of her slacks.

"The door you were looking for is over here." He walked to his desk and sat on the edge, facing Davina's slowly approaching figure. "It's kept locked, so running into me was inevitable." A crooked smile crept onto his face.

Davina's ears pricked at his reference to her earlier words. "It wasn't meant that way. I know you've been busy and I didn't want to bother you."

"I thought I made it clear that you could talk to me if something came up." He crossed his arms. "How are the show preparations coming along?"

Davina felt his eyes upon her, but she wouldn't meet them. Instead, she turned to study the diplomas on the wall. "I'm sure you know the answer already."

"I want to hear it from you."

She turned and watched him with a critical squint. His black hair gleamed under the recessed lights. His equally dark eyebrows slanted above piercing eyes. It was then that she became keenly aware of his equal scrutiny of her.

"Surely you've discussed this with Linda and she told you it was behind schedule?"

"No, I haven't talked with Linda," he said.

Davina cocked her head as she walked over to Justin. She should have known Linda would exaggerate. "Oh," she said quietly. "Things are being pushed right now, but the show will be on time. You know what a madhouse it is around here with the new show starting, detectives, not to mention the reporters. Even when I try to work at home, the reporters still call and ring my doorbell."

"What you need to do is get away for some quiet work time, right?"

"That would be nice, but I don't have that option. I'll have to make do with the interruptions and start jumping." She gave an uneasy laugh. "I don't know that I'm going to make much money on this first show, and I sure don't need to pay the little I make back to you in penalty fees."

Justin frowned at her words. "You can use my cabin in the mountains."

Davina's look turned curious as his words registered. "I can't do that."

"Why not?"

"It's . . . I don't know . . . unseemly?"

He laughed out loud. "You're asking me to define appropriate behavior?"

She liked when he laughed. It made him less intimidating, softening his otherwise stony features. She laughed, too. "You're right, you're the wrong person to ask that. But surely, you know I have to refuse your offer."

"All I'm doing is providing you a work facility as the owner of your contract. Nothing more. I'll deposit you at the cabin's front door, and return to deliver you, safe and sound, back to your apartment door." He shifted his weight on the desk. "Anyway, that muscle-bound brother of yours plays the part of guardian very well. Do you think I want to deal with him?"

Davina laughed again. "David's not that bad."

"You're right," Justin added. "Natalie's bite is probably much worse. Those two really look out for you."

"I know," she said.

They both smiled at each other, enjoying the respite from their sporadic disagreements. "So what do you say?" Justin asked. "The location isn't common knowledge, and I'll keep your whereabouts under wraps so reporters can't find you."

"Why are you helping me? The last time I checked, we were at cross purposes." The warmth from his eyes played on her face.

"I don't know, Davina, but for some godforsaken reason, you seem to be in my blood, and I can't leave you alone or bear to see you in trouble."

"I still believe in what I learned from my father . . ."

"And you don't trust me enough to tell me the whole story just as I don't trust what little you tell me. But I have to know if you're a common thief who took my paintings and wants my company, or simply a misguided daughter." His eyebrows arched in a question. "We make some pair don't we?"

"As long as we know where we stand."

"So, do you want to use the cabin? I can drive you up there tomorrow."

"It's tempting, Justin, but let me think about it, okay?"

She watched him reach across the desk for a pen, and then scribble something down on a nearby pad.

He folded the sheet and handed it to Davina. "This is my private number. Call me tonight and let me know your answer."

She took it and slipped it into her pocket.

"To business." He held his hand out.

Davina reached out and gave Justin her hand, expecting a handshake, and was gently drawn into the space between his legs.

Justin reached for her other hand and held them both within his. His lean, brown face was close to hers, and her heart fluttered wildly in her chest.

"I haven't spent any time with you since the auction, except the night you found Robert. But, seeing you is all I can think about some days." His eyes moved to her lips. ". . . and kissing you."

Davina felt the same way and became lost in the way his eyes savored her. "You say these things because you know they'll shock me."

"I want you to become used to hearing them."

They were definitely a turn-on. Her heart beat at a rapid pace, and she was shocked by her own eagerness to taste his now certain kiss.

Justin pulled her closer and brazenly nibbled the soft flesh of her mouth as his hands found their way to her bottom and pressed her against him.

The first impact of the kiss and the feel of his hard flesh against her own throbbing need left Davina weak, and her hands gripped his shoulders for support.

She pulled her head back and whispered, "Someone will come in."

"Alli locked the door when she left." Justin's voice was rough with passion when he moved his mouth over Davina's again, his kiss urgent and exploratory.

Davina's hands slowly found their way to his chest, where she stroked the tight muscles beneath his shirt. Her lips opened to his thrusting tongue, and it sent shivers of desire racing through the very center of her. She let out a tiny moan.

Justin's lips left hers and, between sensual words, pressed kisses along her jawline. "I like that sound you make, Davina. Can you feel how I want you?"

In answer, she moaned again and turned her head in search of his lips.

"Do you want me?" He whispered the question against her cheek.

Davina was drowning in the sea of long-stored emotions Justin had unearthed. Her very being existed for the circular motions his hands made when they pressed her, again and again, to his growing hardness; and she, hungry for him, could no longer deny that fact. She raised her hands to his neck and lay her weight against his chest. Before she could answer him, he captured her mouth.

A rattle from the door handle froze Davina's fingers in Justin's hair. Justin ignored the intrusive noise and embraced Davina closer to him.

"Don't stop," he implored, breathlessly.

Linda's muffled voice rang out from the other side of the door. "Why is the door locked, Nora? I thought you said he was in."

Davina's hands dropped to Justin's shoulders, but he held her captive with his arms and muttered, "Damn you, Linda."

They didn't hear a response from Nora, and Linda's voice became faint and unintelligible. The damage to the moment had been done, and reality came screeching back to Davina.

She slowly pushed from his embrace, but relished the electric feel of his muscular arms as her hands slid down their length. He quickly caught her hands up into his, and brought them to his lips, his eyes delighting in her every move.

"Things happen so fast with you, Justin, I don't always think clearly." She pulled her hands free and rubbed her forehead. "And believe me, knowing that Nora guarded your locked door when you and Linda played here is not a turn-on."

Justin leaned back and peered at her. "So, you know about Linda? Then, surely you know that's been over for months, ever since I stepped in at Hardy."

"I don't think she sees it that way, but you're missing the point. And that's why I shouldn't take you up on your cabin offer. I may want to make love to you, Justin Hardy, but that doesn't mean I will. You and I said we'd explore this attraction thing we have slowly and carefully."

"That's what I've been saying." He fingered a loose tendril of hair that lay on her cheek. "I want to explore you slowly and carefully," he teased.

"You're unbelievable." She playfully slapped his hand away.

"Despite all that, you'll still consider using the cabin, won't you?"

She smiled and reached for a tissue from the box on his desk. "You have my lipstick on." She wiped the smudged color from his mouth.

"Now that you've managed to cool my ardor"—he took the tissue and enveloped her hand in his—"do you still want to leave the building through here?"

"Yes." She smiled. "Unless I want an audience."

"One day, I'll have to show you what we missed here today."

He stood wearily from the desk and placed his arm around her shoulders. "I'll lead the way down. That way, I won't be tempted to suggest making love in the stairway. I doubt you'll agree to that, either."

"The stairway?" She laughed. "Justin, you're incorrigible."

That night, Natalie watched as Davina pushed the remnants of her food around her plate with the fork. "Alright, tell me what really happened before David gets back from the salad bar," Natalie said. Her eyes darted to David's back at the island of food in the crowded Steak and Ale restaurant.

Davina ignored her table manners and sat propped by an elbow on the table, chin in hand. "It's just like I told both of you. He offered me his cabin. And, since there's no phone or television, I can escape to work."

"Oh, and what will he be doing while you're working?" Natalie's brow cocked in interest.

"He won't be there."

"You sound disappointed."

Davina looked up to find Natalie happily chewing a shrimp. "For that, I'm thankful. He says he needs a break himself. That's why he wants to drive me there and return to pick me up."

Natalie tapped the knife on the side of the plate. "He's driving, both ways?"

"Yes, and don't look at me like that. So, what do you think?"

"I think you should call him, accept the offer, pack those canvases, and go." Natalie plopped another shrimp into her mouth.

"I'm still not sure. David will suspect the wrong thing if Justin is there, too."

"But, Justin's not staying. Go on, girl, and have some time to yourself. You deserve it after all that's been going on here."

Davina gave a doubtful groan as she expertly speared a piece of broccoli and led it to her mouth. "Suppose we get there late and he has to sleep over until the next morning?"

"That only happens in romance novels." Natalie raised her brows unconcernedly. "Of course, everybody needs a little romance now and again. Even you." She gave Davina a pointed look. "You don't have to sleep with him." When Davina didn't respond, she sharply added, "Right?"

"Right," Davina quickly agreed.

"Then it's settled. Tell David you're going to work at the cabin and you'll talk to him Monday. Call Justin tonight and confirm for tomorrow. Are you going to eat that last roll?"

Davina sighed as she passed the bread to Natalie. "There's nothing like having a heart to heart with you." She smiled as David returned to the table.

"So," he said, arranging his napkin, "Did you decide about using the company's cabin?"

Davina glanced at Natalie before answering. "Yes. I think it's a good idea."

"Natalie and I can drive you up there, or come up on the weekend to help you get back."

Natalie choked on her tea.

Davina avoided her brother's eyes. "There's no need for you to miss work. Everything's taken care of." She lay her fork and napkin beside her plate before she looked from Natalie to David. "I've got to go and get some things together if I'm leaving tomorrow. I'll call you both later tonight, okay?"

Out of the corner of her eye, she saw Natalie's wink. Before anything more could be said or asked, she scooted her chair back from the table and maneuvered around it before she headed for the door.

*　*　*

Three hours later, Davina sat cross-legged in the middle of her bed and stared at the phone resting in front of her. She had dug Justin's discarded number from the nether regions of her purse. The crumpled slip of paper that carried his block print had been straightened out and placed near the phone, as well. All that was necessary now was her willingness to make the call that would most assuredly take her to the next rung of a relationship with this man.

She took a deep breath and held it. She quickly punched in the number from the paper and only exhaled when the phone on the other end began to ring.

"Hello?"

Her body actually vibrated when she recognized his low voice. Did she wake him up? Oh, great. Wake him up to ask him to drive her a hundred miles tomorrow. Surely he didn't punch out at ten o'clock? *This is a bad idea. I should never have called him.*

"Hello?" his voice repeated. "Davina?"

Her eyes stretched when he said her name. Too perturbed to hang up the phone, she answered, "Yes, how are you doing?" *God, I'm acting like a schoolgirl. I sound like a dunce.*

"I'm okay. Why didn't you say something? I've been waiting for your call."

"Oh." So, he wasn't sleep, she thought. *Say something, anything.* "I didn't recognize your voice at first. I thought maybe I dialed the wrong number." When he didn't respond, she cleared her throat. "I only called to ask if your offer of the cabin was still open. And, if it is, I believe I could use the time alone"—she stressed the last word— "to get the work for the show back on track."

"Great. What time is good for you? I'd suggest we leave no later than early afternoon. I've already called the property managers and told them to get it ready."

Oh great, he's already planned everything as if he knew I'd go. So, why should she be surprised by his continued arrogance, she told herself. "Tomorrow, any time after noon is fine."

"I'll see you about two o'clock, then."

"Thanks again, Justin. Bye." Shakily, Davina placed the phone in the cradle, then dropped backward to the bed. With arms stretched

out, she lambasted her decision. "What have I done?" she moaned
out loud.

CHAPTER
TWENTY-ONE

The Pain in the Pleasure

"I won't forget. I'll call you the minute I get back on Sunday."
Davina eyed the clock on the wall as she repeated to Natalie the same
thing she had told David over the phone. She dragged a group of
bound canvases to the front door.

"Where's the list I have to deliver to Rosa?" Natalie yelled from
kitchen.

"It's on the table in the folder. And, don't forget she has to give
it to Linda today. Also, don't mention I'm—"

"I know," Natalie interrupted. "Don't say you've gone to the
mountains for the rest of the week." She walked into the living room
and just managed to avoid Davina, who now dragged a travel case
across the room to add to the other bags.

"I wonder if I packed enough clothes. Is this too much stuff?"
Davina's musings were spoken aloud as she pushed the case against
the others. "Maybe I should take a couple of sweaters, just to be
safe."

Natalie put her hand on her hip. "Is it me, or do you need to chill
out, girl?"

Davina smoothed her hair and took a deep breath. "I'm fine."

"In that case," Natalie said with a crooked smile, "it must be
me."

The two women squeezed each other in a warm embrace. "Work

hard, but enjoy yourself okay?'' Natalie opened the door. ''And call me if you need advice.'' She looked over her shoulder. ''Oops, I forgot, there's no phone. Lucky you.''

''Bye, Natalie,'' Davina gently chided, and closed the door behind her friend.

Alone, she stole another look at the clock before she checked over the apartment to make sure nothing was forgotten before Justin arrived. No sooner had she walked from room to room than the doorbell rang. She knew who it was. Before she darted for the door from her bedroom, she glimpsed herself in the cheval glass. The clean, faded jeans fit snugly below a white cotton shirt that stopped at the waist. Her crop of unruly hair had already become disarrayed. She picked up a leather headband from the dresser and slid it across her head before she left the room. The familiar pound in her heart had begun.

Davina opened the door. ''Hi,'' she said, greeting him gaily. He wore a sleek pair of Ray-Bans, which he now pulled from his face.

''Hi back to you,'' Justin answered. His smile was wide as his white teeth gleamed in the sun. He hooked the glasses in the opening of his polo shirt tucked inside linen slacks. A pair of deck shoes completed the picture. ''Are you ready?''

Davina felt the caress of his eyes and the color rose in her cheeks. ''Yes. I'll need help getting a few things to the car.'' She moved so he could follow her into the room. ''I don't think I've ever seen you dressed out of business clothes.''

''And what's your opinion?'' Justin's rich voice floated through the air as he gathered up her luggage.

''Are you fishing for a compliment?''

He laughed with her. ''I forget you once called me an arrogant bastard.''

''Something like that.'' Davina's words teased, and the anxiety of the trip began to dissipate.

She opened the door and followed Justin, but didn't see his car. ''Where are you parked?''

He nodded toward a Land Rover parked across the aisle and led her to it. He opened the rear door and began storing her bags next to another sitting there.

''What's that?''

Justin leaned against the door and crossed his arms, readying for a battle. "It's mine." He gazed hard at Davina. "I can also use a few days away."

Davina drew in a swift breath, and a warning bell sounded in her head. "That was not our deal, Justin." Her frown clearly showed her distaste to the idea. "I agreed to use the cabin because I'd be alone to work. When were you going to tell me your change of plans? When we got there?"

"I didn't decide until late last night, after I talked with you. I admit I wanted to surprise you today, but I was going to tell you . . . now."

"You're manipulating me for your own benefit. How dare you? You can just take my things back inside." Davina walked quickly towards the apartment before she heard his swear as he gained on her.

"Davina, will you wait a minute?" He grabbed her arm and spun her around.

She angrily shook free and continued up the steps to the apartment door that was still ajar, with Justin close on her heels. When she turned, they almost collided. He placed a hand on her arm.

"Will you hear me out, please?" Justin's voice was conciliatory, but his brows tilted uncertainly. "This is the very reason I didn't tell you over the phone."

Davina clamped her jaw tight and stared at him.

"You won't even know I'm there. I started thinking how you won't want to cook, so you'll need a car for food. I could do that, catch up on my reading, do a little fishing. We'll only see each other when we want to." His words were met with silence and her tight glare. Justin looked at her grim face. "Say something."

"I was right. You are an arrogant bastard." She leveled a stare at him and, against her better judgment, asked, "How many bedrooms are there?"

He started to smile. "Two. They're on opposite walls with the bathroom in the middle. I'll sleep all the way over on one side, and you'll sleep all the way on the other side. We'll be light years apart."

"Don't start smiling yet. I'm still not convinced. This trip was supposed to relieve the pressure I'm under. With you there, there'll still be tension, but another kind. You know what I'm talking about."

Justin's eyes narrowed slightly before he stepped away, then faced her again. "Do you think, because I said I wanted you, I'd trap you away from home to seduce you?" His words mocked her comment.

She shook her head, amazed that he had managed to put her on the defensive. "I didn't say . . ."

He spoke what his eyes made clear as he closed in on her. "When I make love to you, Davina, believe me, you'll want it." She saw the smile that overtook his features. "In fact, you'll welcome it." He bent slightly and placed a soft kiss on her cheek. "We're wasting time arguing. Let's put the rest of the bags in the car."

Davina watched him pick up the bundled canvases and paint bag and go out the door again. She closed her eyes and touched the cheek where his lips had sealed her fate. The problem wasn't that he'd seduce her. Her fear came from the fact that she would consent to it.

The trip through the mountains took only a couple of hours, though it seemed much longer to Davina, who was conscious of Justin's presence every moment. Their conversation was careful, specific, and bordered on the ordinary topics of weather, scenery, and plans for her show.

When they neared their destination, Justin pointed out the small, Swiss style town at the base of the mountain trail. Davina was tired and anxious to settle in at the cabin, so they opted to order sandwiches for later. Soon, they were headed back up the mountain road to the cabin.

After a short drive, Justin turned off the main road and onto a single lane path through the woods. The trees and undergrowth abruptly cleared and there at the end of the lane was a small, ranch house, built of fieldstone and wood. Davina didn't think it was a cabin, or at least not what she thought of as one.

"Justin, it's lovely." She glanced at him and could see the pride in his eyes.

"I get here as often as I can." He opened his door. "I'll show you around before dark."

* * *

Detectives Jaragoski and Lovett sat across from each other in the congested, noisy room on the first floor of homicide headquarters. As was their usual pattern, they played devil's advocate to each other's questions about whatever case they were currently working on. Right now, they studied the coroner's report of Robert Montgomery's murder and bounced their questions off each other.

"No extraneous wounds, and the mortal blow was true. The victim knew his attacker," Jaragoski said before he reared back in the desk chair.

"So we're looking for someone that was a friend of this kid's?"

"Not necessarily his friend. Just someone he knew and wasn't wary around," Jaragoski added. "The attacker also knew exactly what he was doing when he delivered the fatal wound."

"He?" Lovett asked.

"Okay, so it could be a woman. Whoever did it was tall and strong. No upward shift in the wound entry."

"And," Lovett added, "still no murder weapon." He searched his crowded desk for another report. "Where's that sheet on the crime scene search?"

Jaragoski reached into a basket at the corner of his desk filled with papers. He handed the one on top to his partner. "Here. There's not much to go on."

"We had to overlook something." Lovett's jaw worked on a new wad of gum as he read the report again. "It's there, I know it's there. The coroner's report suggests a sharp weapon with a pointed end that's, maybe, at least six inches long, like a thin knife or similar type instrument. You know, there were all kinds of tools and implements in that lab and work shop."

With a groan from his chair, Jaragoski sat up to look at his partner. "What do you say to going back over there and giving the area our personal once-over?"

"I was waiting for you to get around to that, old man. You're slipping in your twilight years," Lovett joked in between chews. "Let's go over there first thing in the morning."

* * *

Davina had expected rustic quarters and basic amenities, but was surprised and delighted to find an inviting living room with a raised hearth wrapped about a wood-burning fireplace. A small kitchen adjoined the living room. The bedrooms were on opposite walls, as Justin had said, with a common bathroom in the middle. The floors were hardwood with colorful, woven rugs dotted throughout the house.

She now stood in the bedroom Justin had shown her to, and unpacked her bags and easel. Unkind visions of Justin and Linda, cavorting through the wilderness, meandered through her consciousness. Davina frowned, reluctantly recognizing her jealousy. She decided to set the easel near the bedroom windows.

The room was comfortable, but sparsely furnished. A small dresser with a matching vanity accompanied the four poster double bed covered with a stitched quilt. The managers had placed bouquets of fresh flowers in all the rooms. She wondered if that had been Justin's idea.

"That's the last of the bags," Justin said from the door. "Are you hungry?"

"I'll prepare the sandwiches if you get the canvases from the car," she suggested.

"I've beat you to it. Your canvases are in the living room and the food is on the table. All that's missing is you."

Davina went to wash up and, upon reaching the kitchen, realized that Justin had been busy. He had found candles, silverware, and linen napkins for the table, the sandwiches were cut and arranged on a platter, and a Caesar salad sat nearby. A bottle of red wine had been poured to round out the setting.

"I don't remember that we bought wine in town," she said.

Justin smiled and grandly threw open a door to the side of the cabinet in the kitchen. Inside, two shelves were fitted to store wine. All seven portals, with the exception of two, contained a bottle.

Davina accepted his challenge and did the same with the refrigerator door. Except for a spigoted container of bottled water, and a half-filled carafe of wine, it was empty. "There's no food here, but the wine shelf is stocked." Her eyes twinkled as she looked at Justin. "I wonder whose idea that was?"

He held Davina's chair out. "Come on, we'll deal with the food one day at a time. Right now, these sandwiches are calling."

Davina sat down, but gave herself a good talk. *Keep everything light, girl, and don't fall for his easy charm. What are you going to do if he's behind the forgeries and swindled your family's legacy? Don't let him get under your skin.* Turmoil notwithstanding, she casually reached for a wedged roast beef sandwich.

"A penny for your thoughts," Justin said over the salad greens.

She raised her eyes to his and smiled. "They're not worth that much."

"They're worth more if they shed any light on you, Davina." He looked at her. "You know, I wonder, who are you below that careful surface you present?"

"I could ask the same of you, Justin Hardy. Is there more to you than the reputation you enjoy?"

"I don't know if I enjoy it, but maybe we'll figure things out over the next few days. A toast"—he held his wineglass up to Davina's— "to those answers." A cocksure smile played on his face before he sipped the liquid.

Davina didn't say anything as she, too, sipped from the wine, a penetrating stare leveled at Justin over the edge of the glass.

Justin leaned into the soft back of the sofa and contemplated the cold fireplace through shrewd eyes. A glass of the wine from dinner kept his hand occupied while the oak and glass coffee table supported his legs. He heard the sounds Davina made as she moved about her bedroom. He turned in that direction. When she excused herself after dinner, he hadn't stopped her. Instead, he'd used the time alone, and in the quiet, to consider how he'd approach her about her past without revealing his ongoing investigation.

That was the main reason he'd made the trip, right? Of course it was, he reminded himself. One thing he knew for sure. He'd keep his word that he wouldn't force a seduction that she didn't want. But, he also wouldn't turn away if she welcomed it. The thought of that possibility awakened his body.

He shifted on the sofa to take a deep draft from the glass. He was convinced Davina took the paintings from him that night, almost two months ago, just as he was sure that theft was the reason her apartment was broken into shortly after. So, why did she continue to keep this a secret from him, especially about her father and Maceo being the same person? Right now, he could only rely on Connie's detective work. He emptied the wineglass in one swallow. The woman could drive a man to drink.

Rising from the sofa, he returned the glass to the kitchen before turning out the lamp in the living room. Feeling a buzz from the bottle of wine they had consumed, he headed to his bedroom. When he entered the hall, he stopped and looked toward the other end where Davina's room lay. The door was open; he would tell her good night.

He rapped lightly on her door. A low lamp light was on and Davina was peering through the window screen. Though she didn't look back to him, her hand behind her flapped up and down frantically as she signaled Justin to keep quiet.

Bemused that she found something interesting outside, he watched her a moment before he joined her at the window. Her shapely bottom strained against the denim and was stuck out saucily as she continued to gaze outside. The short shirt exposed her cinnamon skin at the small of her back. And she was barefoot, up on her toes, as she pressed against the window.

"What's going on?" Justin asked. He kept his voice low as he came up behind her and pressed his hands to the window sill on either side of her. He looked out the window over her head. Not quite touching her, he enjoyed the fruity fragrance he remembered she used in her hair.

"Look," she uttered in a loud whisper. "It's a deer."

Justin saw the deer bathed in the shadowy edge of light that came from the floods installed on the corners of the cabin.

"It's just a baby," he whispered back. "The bucks are twice that size. You'll probably see one before we leave."

Davina did a half turn into him. "You mean they come this close to the house all the time?"

Justin had the distinct pleasure of finding her close and within his arms again, and savored the moment. He wondered if their proximity affected her as it did him. "I should have warned you, Davina." She brushed against his chest when she looked up at him. "We're in the mountains, so you could see bobcats, even bears, near the house. That's one of the reasons we don't leave food inside when no one's here. The animals will break in to get to it."

"I'm a born and bred city girl. You can bet I won't stray far from the house."

She turned back to the window and Justin didn't move, enjoying the dangerous contact their bodies made.

"The deer is gone." Her tone was regretful as she turned again to face Justin. She stretched her arms out along the sill, too, above his hands.

"I only stopped in here to tell you good night." His eyes didn't leave hers.

"Sleep tight," she added with a smile.

"And don't let the bedbugs bite," he finished. They both laughed at the silly children's rhyme. He watched her eyes lower shyly, the dark lashes long against her cheeks.

"Great minds think alike," Davina said. "So, what will you do tomorrow while I work?" She raised her eyes to his again.

"I'll trek down to the lake and fish. First, I'll pick up some breakfast." Justin's stare was drawn to her mouth where her tongue flitted along her lips.

"I should call it a night." In the dim light, her eyes twinkled above her smile. "I'm a little sleepier than usual, but I'll be wary of you and a bottle of wine."

Justin thought she had a buzz going, as well, and dropped his gaze from her overly bright eyes to her parted, moist lips. He bent his head and kissed her. Her tongue, pressed against his lips, was an electric shock, and he allowed her entry into his mouth. At her signature moan, he slowed the tempo, and lingered at the heady taste of the wine there. He pulled away and watched her eyes slowly open.

"Why don't you get some rest?" He brushed a soft kiss against her eyes. "I'll see you in the morning."

Justin pushed away from the wall and left her. He entered his own darkened room and, kicking the door shut, made short work of stripping down to nothing. Crossing to the bed, he pushed back the quilt and crawled beneath the sheet. He stared at the ceiling as he rested his head on his bent arms, his thoughts centered on Davina. He squeezed his eyes tight and genuinely hoped her body felt as miserable as his did right now.

The morning sun poured through the window and onto Davina's legs exposed beneath the oversized T-shirt. As was her habit, the covers were kicked away and twisted, her body curled around the pillow. Slowly, she opened, then closed her eyes a few times before it hit her. She wasn't home.

Davina sat up in the bed and pushed her hair from her face. She noticed that her travel alarm showed it was well after nine in the morning. Her train of thought shifted to last night, the wine, and Justin. She blushed at the thought.

She dropped her feet to the floor, pulled on her robe, and stuck her head through the door. The house was quiet. She wondered if Justin was gone. She padded into the kitchen, and found his note: he would return at the end of the day. However, he also left fruit, juice, milk, tea, an assortment of breakfast items, and a couple of sandwiches to go with the leftover salad. He ended his scribbled note with the comment that "man and woman cannot live by wine alone." She smiled, then prepared to shower and start on the work that had brought her up here.

When Justin returned that night, Davina couldn't be coerced into leaving her easel. She had become single-minded in her zeal to make headway in the show's work, and wouldn't be bothered for anything. A shared dinner was tabled for another night and Justin went out alone, bringing a boxed dinner back for her.

In the early hours of the morning, she ate the cold dinner alone and got a few hours of sleep before she started her process of working all over again.

Justin parked at the same edge of the lake as the day before. First, though, he returned Nora's page. He dialed from the cell phone and waited for her voice.

"Hello?" she answered.

"Nora, it's Justin. I got your message. What's up?"

"I figured you had your phone turned off." Her voice held a note of censure. "Those two police detectives were asking questions yesterday. They took some things from the gallery and lab, and said it was evidence."

Justin rubbed his forehead. "I thought they were finished. Did Douglas or Marc say what they took?"

"No. Mr. Bradley didn't think their appearance was important enough to interrupt your vacation. And I didn't offer to tell them where you were, anyway. You told me to inform you directly of anything out of the ordinary."

"You did the right thing, Nora. Has Connie Preston tried to contact me? Any word from the bank on the loan extension?"

"Mr. Hardy, I would've told you."

"I know." He smiled at her annoyed tone. "I was checking just in case."

"Do you still expect to return on Monday?"

"Right. I'll see you then." He ended the call and replaced the phone beneath the seat. He moved to the rear of the Land Rover and took out the fishing tackle. There was no point in dwelling on what the police were doing in Atlanta while he was up here. Instead, he decided he'd surprise Davina by cooking dinner tonight.

Davina was tired, physically and mentally. Two full days of work had shown results, and she appreciated the fact that Justin had left her to use the time as she saw fit. He had kept his word when he so easily could have pressed her into making love that very first night.

She had felt badly about refusing his good-natured offer to go out for dinner, but when the work was intense, she didn't like stopping.

Dusk was finally settling in, and Justin had not returned since leaving before she had risen that morning. She began to peek out the window at every sound.

Shortly thereafter, she heard him drive up. It wasn't long before he made his way to her room, but what she heard when he arrived was a deep wolf whistle.

Davina turned to him from her easel. He wore a rugby shirt under a canvas fishing jacket. His khaki shorts revealed muscled thighs and calves that disappeared into thick socks and boots. "What was that for?" she laughed.

Justin nodded at the painting on the easel. "The sister on the canvas." He came into the room.

Davina looked at the canvas she had just touched up. It was a provocative painting of a nude woman sitting on a mussed bed. It was one of her favorites.

"I take it you like it, huh?"

"I might buy that one for myself."

"In that case, I'll revise the price upward for this one. You can afford it."

"You finished the price list? Great. I want to take a look at it later. Does that mean you have time for dinner with me tonight?"

Davina hesitated, disappointed that she would decline again.

"Before you say no to going out, how about I fix dinner in?"

She turned and stared at him, a smile slowly forming. "You can cook?"

He laughed. "You be the judge. After I take a shower, give me a couple of hours, and then we'll see."

He winked at her and left the room, leaving the slight smell of fresh fish in his wake. With a soft giggle, she wrinkled her nose. He'd been fishing for two days and she wondered what he'd been doing with his daily catch.

As the time passed and Davina worked in her room, she heard Justin rattling about the kitchen, a swear punctuating the air every so often. After a while, mouth-watering odors wafted in from the kitchen and fed her hunger. When he finally announced dinner was almost ready, Davina took the time for a quick shower, and changed into a blouse and shorts before joining him in the kitchen.

"I can't eat anymore." Davina laughed as she avoided another spoon of the strawberry shortcake that Justin held out from across the table. He had prepared the dessert with healthy dollops of whipped cream, which he remembered was a favorite of hers.

"You're sure?" he asked, his grin wide as he continued to threaten her with the overflowing spoon.

"Positive. No more." She watched him lower the spoon to the plate. "Everything was delicious, Justin. You're a good cook after all."

"Lobster is easy. Just drop them in a pot of hot water." He rested his arm on the table.

"No, I can tell you know your way around the kitchen." Davina also relaxed in her chair.

"I learned to fend for myself when I lived alone in New York. And you?"

"I had no choice in the matter." Davina looked away from his probing eyes and studied the bowl of strawberries nearby. "David played a sport every season and was never home. So, if we wanted to eat, and I did, it was on me."

"Did you get to do anything special?"

"I swam in high school, even competitively for a while, but I also took care of the house and my dad. I kept busy. What about you?"

"Football, basketball in college," he said. "You lost your mother when you were very young," Justin said quietly. "A lot of responsibility rested on your shoulders, I imagine."

Davina looked up, only to find she was still under his careful stare. It was disconcerting. "I suppose." She reached over and put a strawberry on her plate. With the sharp knife, she expertly sliced it in two. "David and I adjusted okay with just Dad. It made me realize life wasn't a bowl of berries, so don't expect it." She offered a smile to him as she plopped the sweet fruit into her mouth.

Justin's dark eyes studied her kindly. "So, painting became your release?" At her puzzled stare, he added, "Your biography says you started painting early."

Davina faltered a moment before she answered. "My father suspected I had a talent early on, and made sure I received training. I imagine it's a boon to have both parents around to feed you words of encouragement and wisdom." She changed the subject to him. "Your father was a well-known, respected man and must have made you very proud." She reached for more strawberries.

Justin's laugh echoed through the room. "My dad and I argued at every opportunity. It can be a burden trying to live up to everyone's expectations. I even believed for a time that I hated him." He reached over and spooned a great helping of whipped cream beside her fruit.

Davina eyed him with a critical squint. "You don't hate your father, Justin. Don't ever say that. Anyway, you've more than met any expectations, real or imagined, that were forced your way."

"Just because your father was great doesn't mean mine was." Justin smiled at her confused expression. "My mom knows what's in my heart and allows me the space to find it with my head. Dad, on the other hand, wanted all of his children to make their future with him in the family business. When I chose my own road, he took it as a direct insult."

"And you took that as a direct challenge," Davina countered. She thought of her own father's failings, yet the knowledge of them didn't sully her love for him. "Even though you didn't agree on things, do you believe your father loved you and did his best within his capacity?"

He nodded. "Yes. We always managed to find common ground to agree on . . . except for this last time." At her raised brow, Justin explained. "He died before we could reconcile our last difference."

"Justin, I'm sorry. But I'll bet he knew that your argument would be resolved like all the ones before." She dipped the sliced strawberry into the creamy concoction and slipped it into her mouth.

"I guess he did." A quiet passed over them before Justin spoke again. "I've learned that my dad was right, you know. I should have become involved in the business from the beginning. In fact, he probably had more faith in my ability than I sometimes did. Over the last couple of months, I've come to realize that's why I didn't join him. I didn't want to fail and come up short."

"Don't dwell on regrets." She picked up the knife to slice another piece of fruit. "Look to the future."

"What about you? Do you have any deep regrets, Davina?"

She pressed hard on the knife, her attention momentarily diverted by Justin's words, and sliced into her finger.

"Oh, no," she muttered out loud. The knife clattered against the plate as she concentrated on her index finger that dripped spots of bright red blood across the expanse of white whipped cream.

Justin's reaction was immediate, and he came to her. The cut was small, but deep. A thin rivulet of blood flowed from the cut finger onto the back of her hand. Davina stood and turned toward the bathroom, but Justin scooped her up by the waist and sat her on the kitchen counter next to the sink. Within moments, he had the damaged finger elevated under cold running water. Stretching to the refrigerator, he got ice cubes to use as a cold compress.

"That's a deep cut." Justin wrapped her hand in the ice cubes and clean cloth. "Hold this while I get something to wrap it with."

"I spoke too soon about knowing how to cook, huh?" She offered a weak smile as she watched him take a few steps to a kitchen drawer and come up with a first aid kit. "It only hurts a little. I should be glad it's my left hand. At least I can still paint. No iodine, please. It'll burn." Davina realized she was babbling.

Justin returned and set the box on the counter. He stood in front of her and gently unwrapped her finger. "I don't know, but you didn't cut your finger to get out of answering my question, did you?" He shot her a look of amusement before he lathered her finger with an antiseptic ointment.

The throb in Davina's finger now competed with a decidedly sensual glow in the vicinity of her stomach. Her knees gently brushed his sides as he worked diligently on her finger. She looked at his hands, big and strong, that so easily stirred her senses. Davina wasn't immune to his considerable attraction, and it was disturbing to be so close to him. Suddenly, she was anxious to escape.

Davina swallowed hard. "I forgot the question."

"I asked if you had any regrets from the past?" He wrapped a clean bandage around the cut finger.

"Not that I remember." She pushed her hair back from her face.

"What about the diamond you wear on your right hand. Is that a regret or fond remembrance?"

Davina shifted her weight uneasily on the counter before bringing her right hand in front of her. She looked down at the ring. "It was my mother's. My dad saved it for me after her death." Her eyes lifted to Justin. "What did you think?"

He glanced at her while he completed work on her finger. "That you were hiding a fiancé somewhere."

"No." She studied Justin's handiwork, then looked at him. Now was a good time to open to him. Tell him about Lawrence so he'd understand her reservations. "I was once engaged, but it's over with."

"Is that why you keep me at arm's length, why you won't let me make love to you?" He took her injured hand in his, and kissed the bandaged finger, his eyes narrowed and hardened. "Are you still carrying a torch for him?"

Davina tried to pull away, but Justin's hold was like a vise. "His name is Lawrence and no, I don't carry a torch for him. I never will, for anyone."

He took her hand and placed it to his heart. Davina felt the fast pulse inside his hard chest. As they held the other's gaze, Justin placed his hand in the valley between her breasts, and curved it against her own fast beating heart.

"We know what we want, Davina. We want each other. Which heart beats faster?"

She was succumbing to the truth of his words. Slowly, his hand slipped from her breasts to her waist. The other joined in to encircle her. Weary from denying her feelings, she whispered, "What do we do about our problems, or differences?"

"We'll figure something out."

He spread her knees to either side of him and pulled her close to his chest. As his mouth hungrily covered hers, his hand slipped under her blouse and explored her back. Davina's lips parted and, at once, she was filled with both relief and anticipation. What she wanted, more than anything else at this moment, was right here.

CHAPTER TWENTY-TWO

Love . . . Where There's Smoke, There's Fire

The pleasure radiated outward as Davina luxuriated in Justin's embrace. His arms moved seductively over her back—it was so male, a magnificent bliss she had denied herself for a long time.

Justin's hands seared a path to her waist and then around to caress her stomach. She gasped as the trail of his fingers continued downward until the waistband of her shorts unsnapped and he freely explored the silky skin along the curves of her waist and hips.

"We won't be interrupted this time, Davina." His breath was hot against her ear, and when his hands unbuttoned her blouse, there was no protest. "I want you in my bed."

Caught within her own heated emotions, she couldn't respond.

"How long will you refuse me?" he asked. Her hands came up over his as the buttons, one by one, came undone, until the blouse fell open and revealed her lacy bra. With each breath, her breasts threatened to overflow the fragile cups.

"Do you want me to do this?"

Before she comprehended his words, his thumb flicked the front clasp open and her breasts spilled free of their frilly barrier. He brushed aside the lace, his ardent gaze burning into her exposed flesh, and outlined their tips with his fingers.

"You're more beautiful than I imagined." Justin's voice was husky with passion as he stared openly, hungrily. Cupping her breasts, he kissed, then licked the tight nubs her nipples had become. Her heady fragrance completed the assault on his already ravished senses.

Jolted by spurts of desire, Davina's head lolled back as she closed her eyes. "Please, Justin . . ."

"Tell me what you want."

Davina yearned to touch him as he did her. She pulled his shirt up and found the warm skin underneath—Justin's flinch was unmistakable. She rubbed her hands across his hard, hair-roughened chest and was exalted by her power. How long had it been since she had touched and was touched like this?

Justin raised his head from her breasts. "I want to make love to you, and I don't think I've ever craved anything more." When she looked into his dark, hooded eyes, he asked, "Do my words still frighten you?"

Davina's pulse raced. "Not anymore. I want you, too."

"I'm close to making love to you right here on the counter." Justin groaned as his hands caressed the bare skin that tapered to her waist. He kissed the soft spot below her ear and whispered, "We'll do that another time."

He swept her into his arms and headed for the bedroom. His bedroom.

Justin sat her on the edge of his large bed. When she reached to remove her sandals, he stopped her. "I'll do that." He sat next to her and slipped her shoes off before he kissed her again.

He pulled Davina to her feet and slowly undressed her, savoring every revelation of beauty he had noticed from the first day he bumped into her. When she was naked, and his eyes roamed her woman's body, his voice, low and raspy, commanded, "Now, undress me."

With his help, Davina pulled the shirt over his head. She stroked her hands through the light smattering of hair that favored the middle of his chest. "You're a handsome man, Justin Hardy." Her hands lowered to his intricate belt buckle.

Justin caressed her arms. "I want it to always be this way between us, Davina. Open, and no secrets, just like when we share our bodies."

"I'm a little rusty at this," she said as she fumbled at the belt. Justin's hands slid over hers and made quick work of it. Her eyes, unwavering, held his as she pulled the zipper down. "Promise you'll be patient with me.'' She brushed against his erection, and Justin held her hand there.

"I can be patient.'' His eyes smiled comfortably. "But only for so long.''

She hooked her fingers into the band of his black briefs that rode low on his hips. "It's been a long time.'' She didn't tell him she was unsure of her abilities and uncertain of his expectations.

His words and smile were encouraging. "You're doing fine.'' Justin swallowed hard when she pushed the underwear below his hips. With Davina's help, the rest of his clothes disappeared. He pulled her into his naked embrace and kissed her a long time before he drew her to his bed. He stretched out beside her on the mattress and pulled his hands through the tangled length of her hair. He realized he needed her—more than he had ever needed a woman before—but after her words of self-doubt, he knew he would go slowly.

Justin kissed her deeply before he left her lips to capture a dusky rippled breast. Davina's sighs of ecstasy became moans for relief as his hands and mouth began a slow exploration along her length— from her neck, over her breasts, down her thighs, between her legs, to the tender skin on the soles of her feet, his love for each part of her body whispered along the way.

In one fell swoop, Justin had managed to shatter the hard shell of indifference Davina had built around her emotions. She could only describe the hungry desire that ate through her as blind lust, and she feared she had lost her soul to Justin. She didn't care, and was surprised by her own unbridled cries of passion in response to his exquisite lovemaking.

Justin was spurred on by the sounds of her need and spread her knees to receive his lowering body. He prided himself on his control, but he was on the verge of losing it. He took her hand and guided it to himself. "Davina, I need you now.''

His hardness electrified her. "I need you, too.'' She saw him stretch his arm to a wooden box that sat on the nightstand. When he drew his arm back, he had a small, silver packet in his hand. He tore it open.

"Put it on me.'' He placed the condom in her hand, then pulled her to her knees as he sat back on his.

Davina had never done this before, and it became a totally erotic experience for both of them. As Justin planted kisses along her face, she slowly unrolled the thin membrane onto the length of his erection. Once it was in place, neither of them held back, and Davina welcomed him into her body. She clung to his back as he became a part of her, again and again. Stroke after deep stroke, she held on, her body arched intimately to his. Finally, the passion within her rose like the hottest of fires, and she was hurtled beyond the point of return. At Justin's last hard thrust, she let go completely, and he limply collapsed onto her.

After a moment, Justin raised himself on his elbows and pushed Davina's hair away from her damp face. "I've got a screamer on my hands," he teased. "No matter how much you tried to hide it, I knew the passion was there." He kissed her eyes before he realized they were tear filled.

"Davina, what's wrong? Did I hurt you?"

"No, of course not," she said as she looked at him. "I . . . you . . . it was perfect. Almost too perfect, Justin. I don't want this to be a one-night stand."

"Do you really think I'll let you get away now?"

She saw desire in his face, but did she also see tenderness and warmth? Was it possible that he also cared about her, or was this her imagination? "What happens when we return . . . ?"

Justin pressed his finger to her lips. "We'll work it out." He pulled her into the curve of his body, spoon-like, and draped a possessive arm under her breasts. Davina clung to his arm, as she wiggled comfortably into the covers. "I'm not made of stone," he said. "So if you want a few minutes of rest, I suggest you keep your rear still." He kissed her shoulder and relaxed against the pillows with her.

Davina smiled and closed her eyes. Trouble might be on the horizon, but for now, the small amount of bliss she had harnessed was worth it.

David parked in front of Natalie's apartment, then opened her car door.

"I told you I'll be fine." She swung her legs around and stepped down.

"Vinny would never let me hear the end of it if I didn't make sure you got inside safely." They had just come from checking on Davina's apartment and eating dinner. He followed her up the few steps to her apartment, his eyes, more than once, drawn to her delicate sway.

Her hands dug inside her bag for her keys. "I don't want to impose since I know I tend to rub you the wrong way."

"That's not true." He crossed his brawny arms as he leaned against the portico's railing. "I've never really known you, and you're different from my sister."

"Is that good or bad?"

He was mildly amused as he watched her continue to search her large bag for her keys. "Neither. Of course, your help is appreciated to help keep her out of trouble, and she still seems to find it."

Natalie looked up from her search and raised a brow. "That's your problem, David. Get a life and let Davina run her own."

He threw his head back and laughed, the evening breeze catching his loose hair. "See what I mean? Short of your tendency to speak your mind a little too often, you've started to grow on me."

"When you expose yourself to me in the shower, where else can the relationship go?" She slanted an impish look in his direction as she finally hoisted the keys from her bag.

"Turnabout is fair play," he grinned.

"You wish," she retorted and turned to unlock the door.

David pushed himself from the railing and walked to her. "Sure do," he muttered under his breath.

"Are you flirting with me, David Spenser?"

He put his hand over hers, still on the doorknob, and halted her entrance into the apartment. "Trying my best."

He bent and tilted her face to his. Wearing flats, she was shorter than usual. "I'm just realizing how short you are." Anticipating a smart response, he buried it under his kiss. When her lips softened to his persistent pressure, he knew he'd won the battle of wills. The kiss ended as softly as it had started.

They stood apart and regarded the other at length.

Natalie brushed a short curl behind her ear. "Do you want to come in?"

"Not tonight." He said, enjoying her agitation. "But, I'll hold you to the offer another time."

Natalie smiled. "I wonder if Davina's weekend has been as enlightening as ours?" She cocked her head at David before she went inside.

As he walked back to the car, he glanced over his shoulder at the apartment and saw Natalie peek from behind the blinds. He shook his head and smiled.

It was already seven in the evening and time to leave as Justin pulled the vehicle up to the cabin. He had gone to pick up a few things for their journey home and Davina would be waiting. When he entered the house, he was met by silence. Their bags were stacked near the door, but where was she? As he walked toward the bedrooms, a storm of pleasurable memories from last night filled his head.

They had made love again and again before dawn, and each time he had learned something new about her wants and desires. He had left her, asleep and sated, early this morning, and returned with breakfast. From the bed, they had fed each other by the emerging morning light, before feeding their passions once more.

When he had left their bed for the last time this morning, it was only to give her time to complete any work that remained on the show before they left tonight.

They had agreed to keep their changed personal relationship private until they worked out the quirks in their business one. And they made a pact that, for the remainder of their stay, they would not talk of what awaited them back home. . . .

Thoughts of the untied ends in Atlanta interrupted his pleasant memories. He looked in each bedroom and Davina was in neither. He walked into the kitchen, then he saw her through the window.

The green grass sloped away from the back of the house and ended at the edge of a small lake. Davina stood at that edge where the sun was dropping from sight. She thought the view was absolutely beautiful here. Behind the lake, the distant mountain range rose majestically across the landscape, their colors reflected in the water. She rubbed

her bare arms absently as she composed a painting of the scene in
her mind.

"Beautiful, isn't it?"

Davina turned to see Justin come up behind her and drape his arm
about her shoulders. "I didn't realize you were back," she said.

"I saw you from the window. He followed her eyes to the mountains.
"This is why I wanted a place up here."

She nodded in agreement. "I'd love to set up an easel out here and
paint through the different lights."

"You can. There'll be other trips to the cabin for you."

Davina looked at Justin and let his gaze warm her. "I'm not ready
to leave."

"Neither am I."

"There's no putting off the real world, is there?" she sighed.

They walked back up the slight incline to the house, hand in hand.

CHAPTER TWENTY-THREE

Interruptions, Interactions, and Misinterpretations

For an early Monday morning, Davina's step was light and breezy.
She made her way confidently to Linda's office with the reports she
had completed over the weekend with Justin. Each time she thought
of those extraordinary days, she couldn't stop the blush that warmed
her all over.

He had introduced Davina to a side of herself she had reserved
for—and thought existed only in—her paintings. Natalie's reaction

upon learning the general details of the weekend was as expected—
supportive. David, she knew, was another story. She decided to put
off telling him that Justin had stayed the entire weekend.

She knocked on Linda's closed door.

"Come in."

Davina's surprise was appropriately understated when she opened
the door and found Justin's tall, suited figure standing near a chair.
The delicious eddy of passion she experienced whenever she saw him
whirled through her body. She could tell he was surprised to see her.
Linda, beautifully composed as usual, held court from behind her
desk.

"Well, well, well," Linda said, "Our missing artist has decided
to show up." Her words were as cool and smooth as the silk she
wore. Davina, nonplussed by Justin's presence, ignored her sarcasm.

"I didn't know I was interrupting." She looked from one to the
other. "I can return later." Her blithe mood had faded as her mind
raced in a jumble of thought. Embarrassment, jealousy, and curiosity
battled within, but she tamped them back.

"No, don't leave on my account." Justin moved to stop her exit.
"I was on my way out." His hand brushed hers on the doorknob,
and hesitated at her bandaged finger. "Linda tells me you've been
away for a while. Welcome back." Amusement flickered in the eyes
that met hers.

Davina picked up on the game and confidently straightened from
the door, the beginnings of a smile on her face. She cleared her throat.
"Thank you. It was . . . stimulating."

"Can you stop by my office this morning, before lunch?" he asked
Davina.

She nodded. "I can make it within the hour."

"Perfect." He looked at Linda. "Thanks for the update. We'll talk
later." With another nod to Davina, he closed the door behind him.

Both women's eyes had followed his departing figure. They now
fell on each other for a long moment before Linda spoke first.

"I'd guess that's for me?" Her eyes cut to the folder Davina held.

"Last time we talked, you threatened me with a penalty," Davina
said as she sat down. "Now, I'm happy to report I'm back on sched-

ule.'' She gathered up the papers from her folder and pushed them across the desk.

Linda thumbed through the sheets before looking up. ''Everything's here, even the price list.'' She sat back in her chair and regarded Davina from under a slanted brow. ''I know our relationship is purely contractual, but you could have told me you were going off somewhere.''

''It was a quick decision. I didn't know myself until the last minute.''

''So, tell me, where did you go?'' A smile gathered across her face.

Davina stood up, suspicious of the sudden friendliness. ''That's not important.'' She walked to the door. ''What's important is that your insurance will kick in when my art work is officially delivered for the show. So, I need the transport schedule date.'' She opened the door to leave and mischief came to mind. ''As soon as possible,'' she added.

''Hello, Davina.''

Marc's voice at the door was a surprise. Confronted with his pleasant smile, she smiled back. ''It's good to see you.'' She held her hand out to him.

''Your show will open soon. Jitters yet?''

Davina shrugged away her qualms. ''There's so much to do that I don't have time to get nervous. That'll happen the night before, or opening day if no one comes.'' They both laughed before she said, ''See you around,'' and walked off.

Marc came into the office and put a set of stapled papers on Linda's clean desk. ''My notes on the new projects you're trying to line up,'' he explained as he dropped into a chair. ''You don't want to make too many promises before getting Justin's okay. Budget problems, you know. We're all holding our breath while he tries to work out new financing with the banks.''

When Linda didn't give her usual quick retort, Marc cocked his head to the side and watched as she tightly crossed her arms. ''What's with you?''

''Justin was in here earlier and, instead of the champagne reception we give at openings, wants a big fête to honor Davina.'' Her lips thinned in displeasure. ''Since I usually arrange the receptions, he wanted me to be aware of what he was doing." She looked at Marc. "Can you believe it? He's going to spend a lot of money on a whoop-de-doo party for a woman who's been nothing but trouble for the company." She propped her elbows on her desk. "Men can be so stupid."

"He already ran the idea by me," Marc said, amused by Linda's annoyance. "Plus, he's paying for the bash himself."

Linda was taken aback by Marc's words and repeated them. "He's paying?"

Marc nodded. "If you want anything out of Justin, now is the time to act. Since he got back from his little vacation, he's in an excellent, laid-back mood. Whatever he did, he should do it more often."

"Vacation?" Linda leaned forward in her chair. "I thought he was meeting with the bankers out of town. That Nora. I should ring her scrawny neck."

"He didn't want anyone to know where he was, but Alli let out that he took the Land Rover and his fishing gear, which means he was probably somewhere in the mountains at that cabin he owns."

"A cabin? In the mountains?" Linda's voice was small as she repeated Marc's comments.

"I guess stupid men can still have secrets."

"Like hell." Linda tapped a sharp, red nail against the desktop. "Davina was gone the same weekend as Justin." Then, her hand slapped down on the desk. "You don't think . . . ?" She stopped in midsentence, as though to continue the thought out loud was unthinkable. She raised her head and looked at Marc.

"Face it, Linda, the man has moved on." He leaned forward and looked at her earnestly. "And so should you."

Linda pressed into her chair in a huff. "No one drops me until I'm ready, Marc. No one."

Douglas Bradley's tall frame was folded onto Justin's comfortable love seat while Justin, himself, fitfully occupied one of the chairs that sat in front of his desk.

"So what?" Justin was angry at the news Douglas shared. "The only reason they came back is they don't have anything. There's no reason why Davina should be elevated to a suspect. Didn't they notice how upset she was at finding a body? The security guard can attest to that. What reason would she have had to harm Robert? Charlie told them she had a good rapport with the kid.''

Douglas held his arms wide. ''Justin, you don't have to convince me. And, she's automatically scrutinized because she found him.'' At Justin's silence, he continued. ''I'm sorry I ended our meeting on this note, but I don't think you can ignore the direction of this investigation.''

He picked up his coffee cup from the mahogany table and took a deep sip. Still faced with Justin's silence, he said, ''I trust you had a good weekend. Up until a while ago, you looked pretty rested.''

Justin was busy considering how he might further protect Davina from this new threat. Vaguely aware that Douglas was talking, he looked over at him. ''I think she'll eventually trust me. It's only a matter of time.''

''You're different with this woman, Justin—more introspective.''

He remembered their weekend and exhaled a long sigh of contentment. ''She's complicated as hell, I'll grant you that. Cautious one minute, reckless the next; but, she needs my help.'' He stretched his legs out. ''And she's sticking to that story about her father and the company.''

''Choose your battles, Justin. Don't forget in two months your term as interim president will be over, and the board will vote in a permanent president. Don't get sidetracked with solving every little battle, and lose the war. You can't help anybody that way. Marc or Ray won't mind winning the presidency by default if the board loses confidence in your leadership. There's a lot riding on your reputation and ability to put us back in the black. If you fail, and I don't think you will, the board may be unforgiving and put someone else at the helm.''

''I know, I know.'' He leveled his stare at Douglas. ''If I'm voted out, I'm going to recommend you for the job. It's what I want, and you have the family's best interests at heart.'' When Douglas shook his head, Justin said, ''You would've been Dad's next choice.''

''When Jacob learned of his heart condition,'' Douglas said, ''he wanted you to head the business. I told him to make it clear that he wanted you for the job, and that you would do the right thing. And you did.'' Douglas raised himself from the sofa and gave Justin's broad shoulders a rough slap as he passed to the silver coffee service. ''I also told him I would be here for you. And I am.''

Justin's eyes followed Douglas across the room. So, his father had believed in him, huh, and knew he would comply with his wishes about the company? He smiled. The least he could do was not let him down.

Steam rose from the china cup Douglas filled with coffee. ''Ray told me that pain-in-the-butt reporter over at the *Business Leader* is trying to get a behind the scenes scoop on the murder and everything else that's happening here.''

''No chance,'' Justin said. ''Legal already advised his editor we'll sue them for libel if they print anything but facts.''

''The reporter, Patrick Chavis, is trying to tie everything that's happened here with one neat bow. Ray talked with him, off the record, to find out what he knew.''

Justin lifted his head alertly and asked, ''And what's that?''

Douglas retraced his steps back across the room. ''Ray says he spouted theories, nothing substantial.'' Taking a sip from the cup, he joined Justin in the vacant chair. ''You know how blunt Ray can be. He told the guy to blow it out of his ear, or something to that effect.''

''It sounds like the reporter has a source.''

''That's not good, Justin.''

He laughed. ''Yeah, but I like what Ray told him. Ray may not be everyone's favorite person, but you can't deny he always stands tall for this company.''

''And Marc?'' Douglas asked.

''That's a hard one these days. We lost contact when I was in New York. He's capable, a little intense sometimes, and he put a lot of time in with Dad when I wasn't around, and that should count. But, I don't know if I could throw my vote behind him to lead the business.''

''I don't believe it'll come to that. Time will prove you're doing a good job.''

Justin smiled. ''Then Lord help us if that reporter knew the real story going on, not to mention the screwed up inventory reports.''

''Speaking of which,'' Douglas said, ''Have you talked with Rich?''

Justin left his chair and moved behind his desk. He pulled a memo from a silver-plated basket on the credenza and handed it to Douglas. "He expects the new results to be certified before the next meeting."

"Good," Douglas said as he read the memo. "That should end the speculation once and for all." He reached out and replaced the memo on Justin's desk. "Do you still leave tomorrow for South Africa with the mayor and his business task force?"

Justin rubbed his forehead tiredly. "Yes. After my schedule rearrangement last week, I've still got two or three things to handle before I leave, including the meeting Nora scheduled into the evening."

"As long as the time off was worth it," Douglas said. He stood and drained the last of the coffee from the cup.

Justin's thoughts returned to Davina, his mouth curving into an unconscious smile. "It was."

At that moment, his phone buzzed. With an apologetic look in Douglas's direction, he answered it through the speakerphone. "What is it, Nora?"

"Miss Spenser is here. She says you're expecting her."

"I am," he responded. "Send her in, please."

"Have you looked at your calendar at all this morning?" Nora pointed out. "You have another appointment shortly."

Justin rubbed his chin as he glanced at the closed, leather-bound book on his desk. "I'll check it in a few minutes, Nora. Thank you." He clicked off the phone.

Douglas was already at the door. Chuckling, he said, "She kept Jacob in line, and I see she's got her job cut out with you, too."

When he reached for the handle, the door pushed open from the other side.

"Mr. Bradley." Surprise lit Davina's face before she looked beyond him to Justin, who stood across the room at his desk. "Is this not a good time?"

"No, no," Douglas said, "I only visit Justin to drink Nora's coffee, then I leave." He smiled down at her. "I saw some of your work scheduled for the show. Impressive."

Davina peered up at Douglas's stately, gray-headed figure and smiled. "Thank you, sir."

He moved on through the door. "Justin, if I don't see you before you leave, have a safe trip.'' As Justin acknowledged his words, he left.

Closing the door, Davina clasped her hands behind her and made her way toward Justin. She blushed from the heat of his stare. ''Are you leaving now?''

Justin also strolled forward to meet her halfway, holding her gaze. ''Not before I do this.'' He held his arms out and she walked into them. The familiar, rich smell of his cologne surrounded her as he enveloped her.

Her body bent slightly backward, but Davina felt comforted within his arms, and wrapped her own around his neck. Tiny hums of pleasure floated from her throat as Justin smothered her lips with his hard ones. Her hands stroked his neck above his collar, across, then down his shoulders, until they found his chest. She slowly pushed out of his embrace, their lips reluctantly coming apart.

''Is this why you wanted to see me?'' she asked, breathlessly.

''Partly.'' His hands dropped to her waist. ''I miss you already, and I haven't left the country yet. We should have stayed together last night.''

''We have to keep up our strictly professional appearance, remember?''

''I know, I know.'' He raised his hand to her hair and sank his fingers in the thick curls. ''But, we've got ten minutes . . .'' His lips brushed against hers as he spoke, ''and I think we should use them wisely.''

Davina giggled and dodged his lips. ''You look pretty professional wearing lipstick,'' she teased as she wiped a spot of it from his mouth. Then, cupping her hands against his jaw, she pressed a chaste kiss there. Spurred by her action, Justin nestled his own kisses along the smooth expanse of her neck.

She closed her eyes at the exquisite sensation. ''Rosa just told me the detectives investigating Robert's murder were here again.''

In a regretful sigh, Justin set her from him. He pushed his hands into his pockets and looked at the expectant expression across her beautiful face. ''That's what I planned to tell you. They seem very interested in you.''

Davina's eyes grew wide. ''Me?''

"Come over here." He drew her to the love seat and turned to face her.

A frown had quickly transformed Davina's earlier glowing face. "Rosa said they searched my office in the gallery."

He caught her hand between his. "It gets worse."

The phone buzzed—twice this time. Justin didn't get up, but looked toward the door and explained. "That's Nora's signal that an appointment is on the way in. Since you're in here, why she didn't announce them first?" A rap came at the door.

When Justin told the caller to come in, they both blinked hard at the visitor.

"David, what are you doing here?" Guiltily, she snatched her hand from Justin's and scrambled to her feet. Justin rose up behind her.

David closed the door and continued into the room. He was dressed in business attire and appeared just as surprised to see Davina. He looked from his sister to Justin, and in that instance, comprehension of their deepened relationship showed on his face. "Your assistant gave me an appointment for today. Excuse me if I interrupted anything. Did I?"

Davina didn't think he looked apologetic at all.

The two men warily watched each other from across the desk: David with ill-disguised hostility, Justin with amused tolerance. Davina sat next to her brother and gritted her teeth in frustration. She had learned his appointment with Justin had everything to do with his position as her legal advisor, and nothing to do with the past few days. That was the source of Davina's private guilt and the genesis of David's current antagonism at seeing her so intimately posed with the man they had agreed to distrust.

In an effort to deflate David's rancor, Davina had spent the last ten minutes turning the subject to the stepped up police investigation. Justin had also thrown in the idea of a celebration for her opening. With a mutual stake in these events, the men declared an unspoken truce, and at least on the outside, civility prevailed.

"I'll talk to the police if it'll help," she said, and darted glances to the men.

"Let's not jump to conclusions," David said. "We'll assume you're their chief suspect because you found the body. That's the natural course of things." He saw Justin's quiet nod. "They're still collecting evidence in the hope that it'll point somewhere, not necessarily to you, Vinny."

"If there's nothing suspicious in Robert's personal life," Justin added, "they'll turn to his business contacts."

David angrily responded to Justin and sat up in his chair. "Davina isn't a business contact. You are. She shouldn't be under a microscope over a murder that happened in your business." He settled back. "I hate ever suggesting she align herself with you."

"That was my decision." Davina barked the words at her brother.

Justin calmly reached for a chilled glass of water from the nearby tray. "You mean the company, don't you? And, if I remember correctly, you had no choice. Your secrets precluded that." He sipped from the frosted glass.

"Both of you stop it." Her frown stopped David's retort, while Justin's mouth went grim. "I found Robert, and that's a fact. The police are only doing their job."

"He's right on one point," Justin said. "If I had enforced my own rules on the records, you wouldn't have been there."

"Vinny could've been the one hurt," David said, "And, you didn't protect her."

Davina, irritated by their obvious friction, stood and crossed her arms before walking away. "I feel much better now that both of you have laid blame for my situation." Her words dripped of sarcasm as she stopped at the love seat and sat on the blue cushions. "I can take care of myself, and without either of your help."

"It wasn't meant that way," David said, turning to her.

Justin came around his desk, and sat against the edge in front of her. "All right, Davina. We'll wait and see what the police do." David also nodded.

"Let's discuss this opening party," Davina suggested.

"What do you think of my idea?" Justin asked.

"It's all a little overwhelming, don't you think?" she asked.

"That's a lot of people and planning," David chimed. "And, won't it be expensive?"

"Davina's show is important, and we want the word out to the art community and critics," Justin explained. "It'll be worth the cost. My mother is an expert at planning these things, and I've left the details to her. She'll fill you in, Davina, as the plans progress. And, of course, you're welcome to make suggestions."

"I don't know, Justin. I'm comfortable with the more intimate type setting."

"Yeah." David looked at his sister. "What you're talking is pretty big."

"Only because of the guest list, but the occasion requires it," Justin insisted. "Mom has hosted much larger parties at the house, so location won't be a problem."

"With the opening a few weeks away, interviews scheduled, and the police snooping around," David pressed, "you don't think we're asking for trouble?"

Justin turned to him. "That's the advantage of having it at the family estate. We control everything with our security."

Davina watched as the men talked civilly. She had to explain to David the complicated mess her feelings had made of their once simple plan. She had to explain Justin.

"What do you say to this, Vinny?" David asked as they both looked to her.

"I . . . yes, okay. I'll give it a shot." She pushed herself off the sofa when, as Justin reached for her hand, he mistakenly squeezed her bandaged finger.

At her yelp of pain, he instantly released his grip. "I'm sorry, Davina. I forgot about this. Is it any better?"

"Yes, but sore," she answered, and drew the hand behind her back.

"What happened to your hand?" David asked, curiosity sharp in his stare.

"Oh, it's nothing," Davina said warily.

"She tried to slice it off at the cabin," Justin casually announced. "So, I put my dormant Boy Scout skills to use."

"It's just a cut." Her voice had become curt and she turned to leave. "I've got to get back to the gallery."

"Wait a minute." David's words cut to Justin. "You were at the cabin, too?"

Justin looked at Davina before he answered. What he saw in her eyes spoke volumes. She hadn't mentioned to David that they had spent the weekend together. "I made sure she arrived and returned safely." He put his hand to Davina's back and guided her to the door. "Didn't you say you had to return to the gallery? David and I have a few more things to discuss."

"David," she called out, "we'll talk later." They continued on through the doorway and into the relative privacy of the foyer. "Justin . . ." she whispered.

"I want to see you tonight, before I leave town." He was drawn to the warm pools of her brown eyes. "I'll call you at home."

"About David, he's probably angry . . ."

"He'll be fine." He briefly kissed her mouth. "I promise I won't hurt him."

Davina sighed as he squeezed her hand before he returned to his office.

Justin closed the door behind him and strode to his desk, his mouth a straight line. David had not moved from the chair in front of his desk.

"I want you to stop messing around with Vinny," David said darkly.

"Why are you so hard on her? Don't you think it's time she stopped trying to live up to everything you and your father required her to be?"

"What? You don't know what you're talking about."

Justin sat behind the desk. "I know she puts her own happiness last, and she's spent her life up to now caring for you and your father. Yet, she can't bring herself to tell you she had an enjoyable weekend. What is this guilt she carries?"

"Where did you get this from? Vinny?"

"Some from Davina, and some I figured out myself."

"Is that why you're going through with this big opening party, to show the talented but poor artist that life is wonderful, and you can buy her a corner of it?" he sneered. "You think she can be bought that easily? She'll see through you."

"The answer to your first rambling question is no. To your second one, I say anyone can be bought. You just have to know the price. And, David, it's not always money."

He leapt from his chair. "You slip my sister off somewhere over the weekend and now you think you know her and own her? Damn you." David's jaw muscle pulsed. "That's what you call seduction, an enjoyable weekend?"

Justin, incensed by David's words, also stood. "That's not true. I would never take Davina so lightly. Why don't you come out and say what it is that's bothering you? You've had a burr up your butt and a chip on your shoulder about me since we first met."

David took a step at him and pointed an emphatic finger. "You'll know soon enough. But, if you hurt my sister, emotionally or otherwise, you'll find more than a burr up yours." He turned and left the office with a resounding slam of the door.

Justin drove his fist into the palm of his hand in frustration and dropped into his chair. *I sure handled that well, didn't I?* And, what did he mean by "I'd know soon enough"? He rubbed the back of his neck with one hand and reached for the leather appointment book with the other.

"I read the memo on his desk." David's voice was terse as it came through the phone that night. "In a week, everyone there could know the paintings are missing. So what, you ask? For one thing, Hardy and the insurance company will give you up to the police, that's what. Justin's tracks will be covered with you as the scapegoat and no one will believe you didn't take all of his missing paintings."

Davina sat in the chair of her workshop and twisted the phone cord in thought. "If the worst happens, we'll tell the whole story." She bit at her lower lip.

"Justin and the rest of his people know more than they're letting on, and they'll protect their stake. You have to be careful."

"You were the bull in a china shop today."

"How did you expect me to act when you didn't tell me before-hand?" His brusque voice barreled through the phone.

Davina let out her own impatient sigh as she pushed her hair from her face. "Exactly the way you did, which is why I put it off." The day, long since kissed goodbye, had started with such promise, and David's anger had still not dissipated.

"How can you trust him? You know what he is, and God knows what else he's involved in. All he's doing is feeding you a line, and a company line, at that."

Davina squeezed her eyes tight before she dropped her head. "Am I so horrible, David, that there could be no other reason he wants to see me?" She pressed her fingers against her pulsing temple. "I know my score with men or, at least I should by now, right?"

"Damn." David was contrite, but it was too late. "I did it again, didn't I?"

She stood up. "We can talk again tomorrow. Right now, I'm tired."

"Vinny, I'm sorry . . ."

"Bye, David." Davina hung the phone up on the wall, then slowly sank to the floor, her knees pressed into her chest.

He was her brother, she loved him, and he would make sure things were right between them tomorrow. Now, she was hurt by his cruel words. Actually, scared was more like it. Scared that truth was intricately threaded within them. Had she fooled herself again? Was she so destitute for touch and affection that she ignored the sum of Justin's actions?

It was late, and Justin hadn't called as he'd promised. Was that a sign she ignored, that she was another of his easy conquests? Maybe it was best that he didn't come here tonight. She needed to talk with Natalie, but not tonight. Her dear friend was away at a CPA conference all week.

Davina opened her eyes. They settled on the shimmering satin nightshirt she wore. She had dug it from the back of her closet, a Victoria's Secret purchase made long ago for some forgotten reason, but never worn. Anticipating Justin's visit, she had put it on. She smiled ruefully and, in the aftermath of her brother's caution, felt embarrassed by her own naïveté at becoming the seducer for a night.

Feeling no restraints, she pulled herself up and headed to the kitchen for a feast of Neapolitan ice cream and potato chips.

* * *

Justin's mind was not on the slide show Stephanie presented for her magazine. He peered at his watch in the conference room's flickering light. It was almost ten o'clock and it looked more and more like he wouldn't have time to see Davina later tonight. The chairs had been arranged in short rows so that all twenty participants could view the screen. He leaned over and whispered to Nora to find him in his office before the presentation concluded.

He quietly exited through the anteroom only to run into Linda, also at the meeting. She caught his stride as he continued a path to his office.

"I saw you leave. We have to talk," she said.

Justin held in his sigh, but kept the pace. "You've got a few minutes."

"Are you really going through with this preopening gala for Davina?"

"I thought I made that clear in your office this morning. Next question."

"You didn't suggest this extravagance for the Barnes exhibit or that huge Russian show we took on when you first came. Both were bigger than this one."

They reached Justin's office. He stopped outside the double doors and faced her. "The Barnes exhibit was celebrated in each city before us and they agreed it had become anticlimactic, and I didn't like the Russian art. If that's it, I have to make an important call." He pushed open the door, but Linda slipped in ahead of him.

"You're so infatuated with this woman that you'd pay for the thing yourself?"

Justin shed his coat and threw it across a chair as he walked to his desk. "Linda, you're treading old ground. Dangerously, I might add." He sat behind his desk. "If there's a point, hurry and make it."

She casually pulled herself up onto his desk and allowed the short skirt of her black linen suit to ride across her thigh. Her crossed legs exposed a creamy expanse of flesh encased in silk stockings that broke Justin's line of vision. Leaning back on her hands, she studied his furrowed brows. "She's not for you."

Linda's antics were futile, but Justin allowed her to play out her point. "And you know who is?"

"Sweetheart, we've known each other for years. We know what we are. We live and love in the fast lane." Justin's eyes floated along the curved planes of her legs. "There was a time not too long ago when you wouldn't let an opportunity like this prevent us from having a feast." Her arm stretched to touch his chest.

Justin leaned beyond her reach. "It won't work, Linda. It's over."

"No," she pouted. "You'll think differently when you're out of this place." At Justin's raised brows, she explained. "You were easily worth a million a year as a Wall Street trader. I'll bet you don't get half that here. Everyone knows you're doing this out of obligation to Jacob, and you won't stay long. Give these problems to someone who wants them."

He narrowed his eyes. "What does all that have to do with Davina?"

"Don't you see? You and I are two of a kind. She wants to make you domesticated and boring, like she is—everything you tried to avoid by not coming back to Hardy. Get her out of your system, sweetheart. If you must, sleep with her." She smirked indifferently. "I'm sure the urge will die soon after that."

Justin smiled and pushed away from the desk. "Your claws are showing, sweetheart." He mocked her use of the endearment. "Lay off her."

"You're her protector, too? Seems I've hit a sore spot." She sat up and touched her finger to her lips. "Hmm, let me think. Does that mean you're still chasing her to the bedroom door, or did you finally get through, literally?"

Justin stood up. "You've crossed the line, Linda. Out."

Linda, though, had guessed the truth and wasn't through. She raised her voice. "Good Lord, are you crazy?" She slid from the desk and staked him with her gaze. "It's true, isn't it? You two were together last weekend. And I know you . . . you got what you wanted."

"I'm not discussing her with you, so cut your bull."

"And you're a bastard. Surely you wouldn't humiliate me by sleeping with that . . ." She sputtered for the right word, but gave up as she glided across the floor in an angry pace. "Can't you see what's happening? This place is destroying you and what we have. We know each other too well to be separated now.''

"No, we don't, and maybe that's why nothing came of us." Justin walked to the row of windows and watched the evening lights over midtown. "There was a time when I enjoyed flaunting convention and taking unnecessary risks. Now, it doesn't have quite the same sweet taste—not since Dad died and I returned home."

"You really believe you'll save your guilty soul by saving Jacob's company?"

"It's more than that." He turned to watch her restless pace. "I'm sorry if I've hurt you, Linda, but we've always been frank with each other. I don't love you."

She stopped her pace. "Who's talking about love?"

"I am," he said.

Her shoulders dropped. "Well, I'll be, Justin. You've actually rendered me speechless." She swept past him, her mouth set in an angry line.

He pressed his hand across his hair. "Linda, I'm the one you're pissed with."

"I don't forget much," she said, her head tilted high. "You should know that."

Justin watched her leave the office and shook his head. He made a mental note to keep Linda under a wary eye until she was over this perceived slight. A glance at the crystal desk clock showed he didn't have much time left. He punched Davina's number into the phone before he sat in the chair at the front of his desk.

"Hello." Her voice had an expectant quality to it.

He inhaled deeply and rested his head against the chair, enjoying the sensations her sleep-tinged voice aroused. "Were you in bed?"

"No. I waited for you. What happened?"

"Meetings. In fact, I slipped out of one to call you. Unfortunately, I'll be here for a while and have to cancel tonight." Justin's words were met by silence on the other end and he guessed what was wrong. "You talked with David?"

"Briefly. He suggested I stay clear of you."

Justin closed his eyes. *Damn David,* he thought. "I didn't think you would bolt and run at the first sign of opposition."

"I warned you," she continued, "about my brother, and your family, too, when they suspect something between us. Is there something between us, Justin?"

"Tell me, Davina, do you regret our making love?"

Her answer was immediate. "No, but—"

"Then, as long as you're sure about it, that's all that matters to me. I don't regret one minute I spent with you. And, we're not finished either. I'm going to make hot, passionate love to you again, and again, and . . ."

"Pretty soon, rumors will start at the office . . ."

"I want to kiss that tiny birthmark I discovered near your waist . . ."

"Justin, you're not listening." The humor had returned to her voice.

"Because you talk too much." A noise near the door drew his attention. He turned in the chair and noticed the open door. "That's Nora looking for me. I'll call in the morning before I leave for the airport." Then, in no uncertain terms, he told Davina exactly what he planned on doing to her at their next available opportunity.

Finally, satisfied that he had lifted the mood David had surely lowered, he listened to her quiet goodbye before he added his own, then hung up the phone.

Marc was sitting through the conclusion of the presentation when he looked over at Nora. She would be leaving to get Justin shortly. He also remembered Linda had left the room and a smile grew on his face. He wondered about her success at winning Justin back.

The door opened in the back and ushered in a wedge of pale light from the anteroom. Marc turned and saw Linda, momentarily illuminated, slide through the space. Rather than take her vacated seat near the front, she slipped into one at the back. He returned his attention to the speaker. The distress on Linda's face told him a lot. Obviously, she had not won Justin over, but that was fine with Marc.

CHAPTER
TWENTY-FOUR

And a Good Time Was Had By . . .
Most Everyone

Justin and Davina stood together in the salon where they greeted the last of the guests arriving for the preopening gala. Elizabeth Hardy and Marc were close by and completed the reception line. For the third time in less than a minute, Justin stole a glance at Davina as she made quiet conversation with guests.

She was exquisite tonight. Her hair was free, the way he liked it, and decorated with a gold braided pin. Her slate gray evening dress caressed her slender figure. The soft, shirred material accentuated the fullness of her breasts as it crossed her chest and disappeared behind her neck. His own heartbeat quickened at the thought that they had not made love since their return from the cabin. He would remedy that tonight.

He reached down and, behind the cover of their bodies, gave a quick squeeze to her hand. Justin's reward was a quick upward glance from her, and a smile that reached clear to her brows. Now that most of the guests had been welcomed, her face was a picture of composure, unlike when she first arrived, when she seemed daunted by the task. His mother had put her at ease and, unbeknownst to Davina, had barked orders to all of the family as well as the company executives that they were to do the same.

The rooms sparkled with energy. They were alive with the crackle of conversation and laughter. Justin looked around, pleased that no expense had been spared for Davina's evening, from the huge buffet set up on the twenty-foot tables in the dining hall, to the ice sculpture of a nude form that graced the table's center, to the entertainment in the gardens.

Behind them, the stained glass French doors were thrown open and tempted the guests to walk onto the wide terraced veranda that shaped the back of the house. There, selected pieces of Davina's work were roped off for display, along with a few of her personal favorites not in the show. Strains of heady, upbeat music flowed into the living room from the garden patio where a band of musicians played from an eclectic set guaranteed to touch on the tastes of everyone present.

Justin mused on the privacy the patio afforded. It was the perfect spot to linger with Davina for a moment. He turned just in time to see Natalie pull her away.

"Don't forget the photo session on the terrace," Mrs. Hardy called to them.

Justin smiled as Davina threw a helpless glance over her shoulder while Natalie prompted her in the other direction.

Mrs. Hardy patted him on the arm. "Son, she'll be fine. Don't worry."

He turned to Marc and grinned as his mother disappeared among the people dispersed about the room. "I don't look worried, do I?"

Marc laughed. "You shouldn't be. So far, I've only heard good things from everyone tonight. We should get a generous ride off this publicity. Let's hope everything holds up."

"It had better. We're giving the critics a good time for a good review." Justin saw David leading Alli their way. "Here comes David Spenser." He blinked in surprise when he got a view of Alli's dress. "What is that she's wearing?"

Marc rubbed his chin as he watched them approach. "I'm sure David appreciates the escort."

Alli spoke first. "Hi, Justin, Marc. We were looking for Davina. Have you seen her?"

Justin exchanged a curt nod with David and noticed Alli's bright smile and flushed face. He wondered if David caused it. He frowned at the revealing dress again; she had obviously avoided their mother's notice that evening.

"You just missed your sister," Marc said. "I believe she walked out to the gardens." He nodded in the direction she had taken earlier.

"Thank you." David said before he turned to Alli. "I'll catch you later," he said, and left them.

"Did I feel a chill roll in, brother dear?" Her eyes narrowed with suspicion.

Justin crossed his arms over his chest and looked down at his youngest sister, the picture of innocence in the bold dress. Its color and fabric, a wine-colored watered silk, was safe enough, but the style was not. To Justin's mind, the front was little more than a revealing bustier. There was no telling about its back.

"Did you actually buy that gown?"

"Uh-huh." She crooned proudly, and did a slow pirouette to reveal no back. "It resembles one you bought Linda for the New Year's Eve party. Do you like it?"

At Justin's resigned sigh, Marc threw back his head and laughed out loud.

Natalie's arm linked through Davina's as they strolled through the crowded room. "This place is fantastic," she whispered to Davina. She expertly balanced a glass of champagne in her other hand as her eyes widened with each new sight. "Justin and his family must be loaded."

"It's still early, and if you don't watch the champagne, so will you."

"I deserve to have some fun after last week. You have no idea how boring a convention of accountants can be. Anyway, you can drive home. Or, David, if he isn't still occupied by that little flirt Alli. When we got here, did you see how she grabbed him up while we were ushered to the suite upstairs to get dressed? And that was three hours ago."

"Why should you care that he's being manipulated by a flirt? He's a big boy."

"I'm sure she noticed that. And did you see that dress? If you can call it that." She sipped from the champagne glass. "It was just an observation."

Davina smiled at her simple observations.

Their walk had led them outside and into the garden. A part of the area was tented for the entertainers and a dance floor covered some of the flagstone walk.

Natalie slowed her steps. "Speaking of observations, don't look now, but that's one fine specimen straight ahead." She unlinked her arm from Davina's.

Davina followed her eyes to a man propped against a garden wall near a trellis of roses. Used to Natalie's chameleon moods, she laughed. "And you call Alli a flirt?" she teased.

Natalie smiled. "See you later." She floated ahead of Davina.

Davina stopped and grinned while Natalie walked the short distance that took her past the stranger; the long, black evening skirt with its form-fitting bodice emphasized her striking figure, to say the least. As Natalie crossed his path, the inevitable occurred. The stranger stood straight as he took notice of her and appeared to introduce himself.

Davina, always amazed by Natalie's intrepid spirit, sighed and spoke out loud. "We should all be so confident."

"About what?" David's voice came from over her shoulder. "Who's that guy bothering Natalie?"

Davina turned to find him peering at Natalie. She was proud of the elegant figure he cut in the tuxedo, although the ponytail against his mandarin collar did give him an edgy air.

"I don't think he's doing anything she minds," Davina said. "Where have you been, anyway? We thought you were lost with Alli somewhere."

David squinted into the light as he watched Natalie. "She's a kid."

"True, but she neither looks nor acts like one."

"Tell me about it," he whispered absently. "Looks can be deceiving."

Davina followed his stare to the rose trellis. Her brows furrowed as a kernel of knowledge tried to burst free into her consciousness. She turned to him again and punched his arm playfully. "Who are we talking about here? Pay attention."

"Sorry, Vinny." He smiled and complied. "Are you having a good time?"

She nodded. "It's . . . exciting. You're not angry that I am, are you?"

"Not a bit," he said. "I have to hand it to Justin, and you know I don't want to give him credit for much, but this party was a good publicity move. Everyone is talking about you." They moved to a bench under a tree bough and sat down.

"If everything is going so well, David, why do I have a sick guilt when I think about where things are now? Maybe it was better when we all hated each other out in the open. All the good things get in the way." She studied her hands.

"Hey"—David turned to her—"brighten up. You've worked hard for this, Vinny, and you deserve to enjoy yourself tonight."

She lifted her eyes to his. "It's all the deception, David. I didn't think before I took the paintings, and you warned me that one lie would lead to another, but it seemed so simple then . . ." She looked away.

"You're seeing him, and you want to tell him everything, don't you?" He picked up a leaf that fluttered into his lap from overhead.

"Neither of us is rushing into promises. But, I can't continue to keep so much from him, especially when his guesses are so close to the truth. I need you to trust my judgment on when he can be told what we're doing."

David tore the leaf into small shreds and tossed it on the path. "Does he share your penchant for honesty?"

"He's come to our defense too many times to be all bad. If we were to enlist his help, maybe we could find out more."

He took a deep breath as he looked at her. "I trust you, Vinny, but I don't want to take the chance of showing our hand until we know you won't be implicated in anything illegal."

"Okay." She entwined her fingers in his. "I won't say anything, for now." When their eyes met, they both started to smile, then it turned into a laugh.

"We must be the two saddest sacks here," David said. He helped Davina up from the bench and they walked back toward the patio. "Where did Natalie go?"

Davina followed his stare into the crowd. "There she is, on the dance floor."

"You want to dance?"

"No, Mrs. Hardy's agenda has me on the terrace with a photographer right about now. But, you go on." He was already headed for the dance floor. Davina watched him walk away, not sure if he even heard her. "Have fun," she called out.

Justin stood on the raised stage and surveyed the growing crowd that had gathered on the terrace. They all waited for Davina's arrival to discuss pieces of her work displayed there. A photographer nearby was setting up for publicity shots. As he nodded greetings to friends and business acquaintances, he saw Linda at the far end of the exhibit. She talked with Marc; but what caught his attention were her animated motions. Her expression was also curiously ominous for a party atmosphere.

Interested now, he watched Marc's hands grip her shoulders, as if to calm her down. A man walked up to them, a tuxedoed guest Justin didn't recognize. Marc nodded to the man and left, but Linda's expression had become a smooth smile again. Justin thought he'd ask Marc about her. He didn't want her to cause a scene. On second thought, he decided the less mentioned about Linda, the better. He'd keep his own eyes open.

The sound of claps and cheers brought his attention back. Davina had arrived on the terrace and the crowd parted to allow her to join Justin on the stage. Her smile was just as broad as his, and lit her eyes.

When Davina stood next to him, he whispered under the noise from the crowd, "Are you ready to meet your public?"

"Only if you stay nearby, like you promised," she whispered back.

Justin squeezed her hand and prepared to introduce her to the crowd. As he waited for their claps and cheers to subside, he looked into the crowd and met Linda's eyes. She still stood next to the same man, but her dark eyes were narrowed and stared through Justin.

* * *

The photography session was over and Justin had left Davina with her guests. Now, he strolled with Carolyn along the rear hall of the house.

"Did Davina mention a conversation we had at the house last week when we were planning the opening party?" Carolyn asked.

"No. I've only been back in the country forty-eight hours and we've just spoken briefly." When he glanced her way, he saw that she chewed at her lip, the same habit Davina displayed when there was trouble. He stopped at the staircase and turned to her. "All right, what happened?"

She pulled in a deep breath and smoothed her hands along the jade green of her gown. "Alli and I sort of ganged up and asked her what was going on between you two. And, she wasn't too pleased with the question."

Justin regarded his sister quietly. "You didn't." He watched her wince, then nod her head. "Why?" he asked.

"You know I don't usually go for Alli's harebrained schemes, but we were curious about the two of you, particularly when Davina made it so plain at the start that she had a problem with this family." She crossed her arms when Justin gave her a silent glare. "Alli and I really don't have anything against her. She's different from your usual fare and, I might add, a lot easier to swallow than Linda."

"So, you like her?" A smile slowly grew on Justin's face.

"How do we know she's not using you to get what she wants?"

"I could be doing the same to her."

"You defend her so easily." Carolyn tilted her head and looked into Justin's eyes. "I thought you'd be a lot angrier."

He stood from the railing and they continued their walk. "I want you to be nice to her, okay?" He glanced at her, the smile still on his face. "Did you and Alli ever find out what you wanted?"

"No. In fact, she told us where to get off."

Justin laughed. "Sounds like her, and she's right. It's none of your business." Ahead of them, Alli and Stephanie were coming their way. "There's your partner in crime."

"Good, Lord, where did Alli get that dress?"

"Don't bother asking about it," Justin said, his voice heavy with sarcasm.

"Congratulations on tonight," Stephanie said when she reached them. "Everything's perfect." Resplendent in a gold two-piece gown fashioned in a suit, she remained the businesswoman.

"Thanks, sis, but Mom planned it all. Where's William? I haven't seen him since he got here."

Alli started laughing. "Our brother-in-law is outside with the music. You should see him, Justin . . ."

"No doubt, dancing," Carolyn laughed, too.

"Leave my dancing machine husband alone," Stephanie teased, referring to William's known penchant for the dance floor. She turned back to Justin. "It's early, but everyone thinks the exhibit will be a success. Rosa told me she's already collected a stack of interest cards from the guests."

"Davina should hear that. She's the artist of the hour," Justin said.

"We told her when we left her outside dancing with William," Alli said.

"In that case, I'll go and join them." Justin looked at his sisters, amused by their identically quirked brows. "I don't want to feel my ears burn when I leave, okay?" He chuckled heartily as he turned on his heels and walked away.

From the edge of the patio, Justin stood against the garden wall, unnoticed by Davina, and watched her sensuous moves to the fast dance music. Although William was her partner, they moved separately as he performed modern versions of seventies moves. Her simple gyrations tantalized; the soft material of her dress flowed across even softer curves, and seduced Justin.

"You should join her," Douglas said, and joined Justin at the wall.

Justin expertly swooped a drink from the tray of a passing waiter. He took a full swallow before he answered, his eyes again on Davina. "Sometimes, there's just as much fun in watching."

"I don't think you believe this is one of those times."

"You're right." He took another drink.

"Drinking and staring won't make the feelings go away, either.

It's the natural order of things, you know, to feel the way you do about a special woman.''

Justin jerked his head around to Douglas. "Who says I'm feeling anything?"

"Well good, then," he said, "because when it happens, you won't have any choice in the matter."

Douglas gave Justin's puzzled face a parting smile before he left.

Justin looked at the remnants of the drink in the glass. He recognized he was consumed by thoughts of her, and not making love to her since the mountain trip had not exorcised her from his soul. Yet, he didn't trust her—wasn't that why he was investigating her? And now, the police were in this. She was trouble, all right, with a capital T. He knew it, but didn't care. Was that what Douglas meant by not having a choice? He watched as she stretched to the rhythms of the music. With a grimace, he tossed the rest of the drink down his throat.

"Dance with me."

The rich timbre of Justin's voice was a ribbon that undulated within Davina. She smiled as he linked her fingers in his and pulled her back to the dance floor. As if on cue, the band started to play an instrumental version of a popular ballad. The couples already on the floor parted to make space for them. He folded Davina into his arms and slowly began to sway with her body to the music.

Justin pressed his cheek against her ear, and into her hair. He closed his eyes as he took a deep breath of her hair's lush fragrance. He pulled her closer.

Davina luxuriated in Justin's arms as she was engulfed by his familiar scent. It was almost too much. She lay her head on his chest and allowed the sweet music to guide them across the dance floor. They threw caution to the wind in their innocent dance, but neither wanted to give up this palpable pleasure.

The song ended too quickly, and Davina raised her head and met Justin's eyes. He gently pulled her in the direction of the flagstone walk on the other side of the dance floor. Once there, he drew her into a short path hidden in the shadows of the nearby shrubbery and flowers.

With no words spoken and out of view, they fell into each other's arms. Justin's mouth covered her parted lips, each of them hungry for the taste of the other. As his tongue explored her warm, willing mouth, his hands massaged the pliant curves of her hips while her body tingled from his touch. Her arms about his neck, she pulled him close as she struggled to contain her soaring passion.

Slowly they floated back to earth, out of breath. With heads tilted back, they regarded each other.

In the pale light that filtered through the leaves, Davina couldn't see his eyes, but she saw the beginnings of his white smile.

"I've wanted to do that all night," he said.

"What took you so long?" was her playful response.

Justin's smile became a wide grin. "When you talk like that, I'm liable to throw you over my shoulder and take you upstairs, and to hell with what anyone thinks."

"Promises, promises," she whispered. A warm glow, like golden honey, flowed through her. She raised her eyes to his and moved her hands to the front of the starched dress shirt. Her hands stroked his chest. "Won't you care what your family thinks . . . a common, conniving artist carrying on with the distinguished son?"

He caught her hand in his, and put an end to the distracting motions she made. "Stay with me at the house tonight, Davina." His voice was thick and heavy. He raised her hand to his mouth and placed a kiss on her fingers.

Davina's heart sang with delight. "All right, I will."

Justin had spent the evening making sure Davina had been given the opportunity to personally speak to many of the guests. Her work was good enough to sell itself, but this was a business after all, and the marketplace could be fickle. A conversation with the artist could make a work all the more desirable if owned. At some point, they became separated, and now he mingled alone.

A glance at his watch told him the buffet had opened. He returned his attention to the two gentlemen who talked with him in the living room when he felt a tap on his shoulder. He turned and found David standing with a drink in each hand.

"I didn't say it earlier," David started, "but, you were right about this preopening party. It's going to start the Vinny Richards show off with a big bang." He handed one of the drinks to Justin. "Congratulations."

Justin accepted the drink as a toast and nodded to David. "Thank you." He sipped from the glass before he excused himself from the two men. Then, he and David strolled to the other side of the room.

"David, I'll cut to the chase. You and I don't agree on a lot, but I think a lot of your sister, and I would never hurt her." He watched David's jaw clench at the touchy subject. "Let her make her own judgment of me."

"You've known a lot of women," David said. "My sister isn't like them."

"You're right. She's like no one I've ever known."

"Opposites won't last unless they find a common bond to build on, and I believe you and Vinny reside on separate poles."

"So much for the measure of confidence," Justin said. "I'll just have to prove you wrong."

David nodded. "Fine. Again, congratulations." He sipped the wine and watched Justin walk off.

"You two could make excellent relatives," Natalie said, walking up to him.

"Did you hear him?" David asked, between clenched teeth.

Natalie punched his arm. "David, you're such a . . . man sometimes."

"What are you talking about?" His voice rose in surprise.

"Get in touch with your emotions. You two are acting like asses because he's interested in your sister. He acts the same way when it comes to his own sisters."

"David, I've been looking all over for you."

They turned and saw Alli making her way to them.

"He needs to keep that one in storage," Natalie said, under her breath.

Alli laid bright, Hard Candy lacquered nails on David's arm before she looked at Natalie. "You're Davina's friend, aren't you? We haven't been properly introduced. I'm Alli Hardy."

"Nice to meet you, Alli. I'm Natalie Goodman."

David cleared his throat. "I think we're all supposed to meet for the buffet."

"I didn't get a chance to show you the entire house, David." Alli pulled his arm in her direction. "Come on, we won't be missed," she said.

"Yes, you will," Natalie piped in. "I'll tell them you purposely left."

"Excuse me?" Alli's eyes narrowed as she now gave her attention to Natalie. "You wouldn't. That would be rude."

"I know," Natalie smiled, "but no more rude than you waltzing up and carting David off when we're talking."

Alli now looked at David. "Did I miss something here?"

"Not if you'd take a moment to listen." Natalie answered for him.

"Ladies," David cut in quickly. "Natalie, you've admired the house, right? We can all go together."

"Well, if you insist," Natalie said.

"I don't think so." Alli responded as she stiffened at the challenge. "The invitation is for David only."

Natalie hiked her skirt slightly and took a long step forward. "It doesn't work that way . . ." She stopped when Alli gasped and pointed a finger. "What's wrong with you?"

"Your shoes, where did you get them?" Alli pointed to the black and gold heels Natalie wore under the evening dress. The shoe was striking in that the heel and toes were left exposed, while soft straps wrapped intricately about the foot and ankle, and closed with a covered button.

"Snooty Hooty's. Why?"

Alli lifted her skirt to reveal the same shoe in a wine color. She raised her eyes to Natalie's. David cringed as he looked from one woman to the other, expecting a blow out like none he'd heard before. Then, both women started laughing and talking at once.

"I love that store," Alli declared.

"Me, too," Natalie said. "Have you been to that new shoe place over on Peachtree Industrial? I hear they get most of the designer shoes first."

"You'll have to tell me about it," Alli said.

"Imagine that," David said as he looked at Natalie, then Alli.

"Now that I think about it," Natalie said, "I promised I'd meet this guy I danced with earlier. So, I really can't go with you two."

"Who?" David regarded her testily.

"His name is Chazz. We're supposed to meet in the arbor about now."

"Chazz?" Alli asked. Her eyes slowly widened. "Listen, maybe we can do the tour thing after we eat. I just remembered I have to take care of some business for my mom." She turned to Natalie. "It's nice meeting you. You'll have to tell me about the shoe store." She hurried off through the French doors.

Natalie rubbed her hands together. "That settles that."

David looked at her. "What are you talking about?"

"I danced with Chazz earlier this evening. He mentioned he was little Alli's date. It's a shame she's not paying attention to him tonight. So, I thought I'd help."

David smiled. "I didn't know you could be so devious, Natalie."

"She's an example of the curse of youth, David—wanting to partake from too many plates at once. Experience will tell you to savor one dish to its fullest before moving on." She offered a champagne-edged giggle in his direction.

David tilted her chin with his finger and looked into her eyes. "Speaking of food, I think we need to get a dish of it in your stomach to balance off the champagne and wine. You're beginning to dispense philosophy like a two-dollar gypsy, and the scary part is, it makes sense."

He dropped his arm to her shoulder and they started out for the dining room.

It was past eleven and while some guests had called it a night, the majority remained to fill the house and grounds. Davina had sneaked away from the noise of the house to enjoy the cool breeze and quiet near a lily pond she found in a side garden. She sat on the bench while she collected her thoughts.

"I've been watching and trying to catch you." The voice came from a face that seemed to materialize from the shadows. Wrinkles were set in his features, but a thick, salt and pepper goatee distinguished the face. Even so, the old man still possessed enough style to wear a black velvet beret atop his gray wooly head as he lean upon a carved wood cane.

Davina figured she must have stopped to offer a personal word to every art aficionado and patron at the house, as well as give short, impromptu interviews to critics, yet unknown faces still stopped to congratulate her on the upcoming show.

"Did we meet earlier tonight?" As he advanced on her, she noticed his diminutive size and remarkably clear, almost shrewd eyes.

He leaned his head back and, likewise, studied Davina's face. "No, but Lee Randolph said I should look you up if I came to this shindig tonight."

Davina straightened from her seat as recognition came like a punch in the stomach. He was one of the men in the photos. She stood and looked around to see if anyone could hear her next words.

"You're one of Maceo's friends, aren't you?"

Justin excused himself from the group on the patio and left with Marc.

"What's so important that it couldn't wait until tomorrow?" Justin was impatient to get this business over with, and led Marc into the house.

"It's not good news," he said. He stopped Justin when they stepped into the privacy of the hallway. "We've been tipped about a lead story tied in with the celebration tonight and the show tomorrow. It's coming out in the morning edition of the paper."

To Justin, Marc's tone was ominous. "Nothing unusual about that," he said. "We want the publicity."

"Not this kind, Justin. It's that same reporter that's been hounding us from the beginning. He claims to have found an impeccable inside source for the truth."

"Go on," he said and steeled himself for more bad news.

"His editor wants your comments run with the story as some sort of validation. The reporter is our old nemesis, Patrick Chavis. He's going to name Davina as the basis for Hardy's recent troubles and probable future ruin."

CHAPTER
TWENTY-FIVE

After a Party, There's Always
the Mess

"How did you come to be here tonight, Mr. Carter?"

Otis Carter bent to claim the bench seat Davina had vacated. "I don't paint much anymore, but I collect. That means my name appears on lists when somebody wants to sell a painting." When Davina raised a brow at his cynicism, he added, "Of course, tonight's been enjoyable for a change."

She smiled at his charming disdain for the affairs. "I'm surprised Mr. Randolph's son allowed him to mention my name. What all did he say?"

He let out a laugh that imitated a cackle. "Like me, Lee wonders why you're so interested in Maceo? That's a name I hadn't heard in years. I figured he'd been dead for years."

"I need information for a research project I'd rather not reveal right now." The facile lie slipped effortlessly off her tongue—a fact she was uncomfortable with. "Anything you can tell me about the man would be helpful."

"Nothing much to tell that you don't probably already know. He was a gifted painter, and an all right fellow. A good friend."

Davina nodded at his words even as she tried to contain her eagerness. "I understand you were a part of his circle of friends, but Jacob Hardy was probably closest to him. In fact, that's who helped him disappear after the police charges."

Otis looked at her in surprise. "You've done some homework, I see. You know, Maceo always did right by his friends, whether it was in his best interest or not, and Jacob was always right there."

"You don't sound like you approved. Did Jacob take advantage of him?"

The small man offered a knowing smile. "That's a tricky question, and probably only Maceo knows that answer. You see, Jacob was shrewd and smart. He was a visionary and Maceo, like the rest of us fellows, lived in the here and now. It was nothing to Maceo to trade a painting for a place to stay a month, stuff like that. Now, there was this one painting he did of Jacob. It was big, maybe five feet tall. I don't know why he did it, probably to settle a debt, but it meant something to them and Jacob didn't want him to end up trading it off. He gave it to Jacob afterward."

Davina had seen it, the one in Justin's office. "What happened?"

"Somehow, Jacob ended up with it and stuck it up on the wall before the thing was even dry. Hung it in that old drafty building of his off Auburn Avenue that we used to hang out in. Afterward, Maceo even carved and built the frame for it."

"I guess it was a good thing that Jacob took the painting, huh?"

"When Maceo's work started to get noticed, and the white galleries wanted a piece of him, he tried to get some of his pieces back that he'd traded with earlier. Word was Jacob got a good number of them back for him."

"But Jacob kept the portrait?"

Otis nodded. "After Maceo disappeared, Jacob got a lot of offers for that thing. I even wanted it. It was one of the last pieces of Maceo's work and Jacob wouldn't sell it. Last I knew, it was still around. Did you talk with Jacob before he died?"

"Unfortunately, no. There are only a few of you left from those days. Morris wasn't around that often and Lee doesn't remember much since his stroke."

Otis cackled again. "You probably heard that from Nathan. I don't think he believes Lee can do anything, and there's not an ounce of truth to it. Lee's as capable as me." He crossed one leg over the other, his gesture defiant.

Davina smiled at this oddly gregarious little man. "He's protective."

He gave a snort. "He wants Lee to forget the past, forget his friends." He smiled wide. "Quilla, that's Nathan's wife, she's okay. I go by and see Lee when the boy's not home, probably out trying to figure an easy way to make it."

"Did Jacob take the easy way and use Maceo's talent to start his business?"

"If you ask me, it was more complicated than that." He raised himself from the bench with the cane and looked up at Davina. "Maceo didn't expect all that trouble to come calling at once. When that kind of thing happens, it's only natural that you turn to someone you trust and respect the most—your partner and friend."

"I told Chavis to leave when I realized Linda had invited him as her guest," Marc explained to an angry Justin. "She left with him."

"Not before he had a chance to talk with people who didn't know he was a reporter." Justin swore long and hard.

"I didn't think anything of Patrick Chavis being here until I got the call about the story not too long ago."

When they reached the door of the study, Justin stopped. "Find out what you can from the staff still here. Learn what they said, if anything, to him. I'd lay bets that Linda has done the real damage."

Marc left and Justin went into the study to the phone. In short order, he cajoled his contacts and discovered some of what he needed. Although strong allegations would be made in this story, Justin learned few details. He had to talk with Chavis.

Finally, he got him on the phone. The man made no apologies for the underhanded way he got his story, nor would he offer a clue to his unnamed source, but he had the gall to ask Justin for an interview to run concurrently.

"You expect me to give you more copy? Bull." Justin's voice exploded into the phone.

"I've wanted to interview you since you took over Hardy in the spring," Patrick wheedled. "I know there's another point of view. There always is. I'm willing to give you the chance to tell yours."

Justin bit the inside of his cheek to check his anger. When he thought of how Davina would be hurt when this story came out, he knew he had to halt it. "I'll make you a deal. Kill the story for tomorrow's edition and I'll give you an exclusive with Davina and me. I'll also give you first shot on future interviews." There was silence on the other end.

Patrick finally spoke. "That's a tempting offer, Justin. But, I'm committed to the story. My credibility will be shot if I pull back now. I can still do the interviews with both of you and run them later. I can make it a two-parter."

"No deal unless it's pulled for tomorrow. And I want to know the content. If you don't take this, I'll make sure you never get an interview with either of us."

"I can't take it, Justin. There's nothing in my story I can't back up."

"You'd better hope that's the case." Justin slammed the phone down. Still sprawled in the chair at the desk, he rubbed his hand across his chin. Linda. He needed his suspicions confirmed. Maybe in the process she'd admit more.

Justin dialed her private line. After a few rings, she answered softly.

"Why did you leave tonight without a word to me?" he asked, a smile in his voice. "After the publicity shots were done, I looked around and you were gone."

"Justin," she exclaimed in surprise. "I . . . I don't know what to say. You've been blowing hot and cold lately."

Linda's throaty voice swirled through the phone, but Justin remained immune. He wanted information, and if it meant gentle persuasion, then so be it.

His voice became enthusiastic, possessive. "I saw you with someone else tonight. Is he there now?"

"You're jealous," she pronounced proudly.

"I'm sorry about the way things have gone lately. I'm under a lot of pressure to make things work. That means doing what I ordinarily wouldn't do. One is keeping you at a distance."

"Oh, sweetheart," she began. "I knew something was wrong, and our misunderstanding would blow over. Why didn't you tell me this before?"

"Linda, Linda . . ." He ground her name through his teeth. "How could you have ever doubted how I really feel? The business has to survive at all costs, and I'll do whatever is necessary to keep it going. So, who was the guy?"

A faint click sounded from behind, and Justin glanced over his shoulder. Seeing no one, he returned his attention to the phone, already tired of this charade.

"Patrick Chavis." She drew the name out in a tease. "Are you upset?"

"Over a reporter?" He grunted the question and continued the game. "Only if you were angry or drunk and said the wrong thing. Was he asking questions?"

"He wouldn't be a reporter if he didn't, now would he?" She laughed. "I handled him, though. I want to see you. Can you slip away and come over later?"

Justin stood from the chair, the pretense dropped. "What did you tell him? How much damage will his story cause tomorrow?"

Nervous laughter floated through the phone. "What are you talking about?"

He paced a short line in front of the desk, his hand flexing open and close. "Are you the source he won't name?"

"What are you saying, Justin? I was drinking, but I didn't tell him anything that's not already common knowledge. You believe me, don't you?"

"Linda, you knew about his stories against me and the company, yet you invited him to a private party where he most probably got information that could do the company irreparable harm. You were irresponsible, and if his story causes trouble for Hardy, or Davina for that matter, and even if I can't prove you're culpable so I can freely fire you, your contract won't be renewed."

"You bastard." Her venom rose to the occasion. "You don't care about Hardy, just her. How dare you lecture me on integrity. You're right, you can't prove anything and, frankly, she deserves whatever she gets." The phone clicked. Linda had hung up.

Justin looked distastefully at the phone before he calmly laid it in the cradle. Once again, he sat at the desk and considered damage control. He picked up the phone and quickly punched in Connie's number.

Davina stood frozen on the other side of the study door, as though perched on the precipice of some great abyss that any moment would suck her into its yawning darkness. Had she really heard Justin talk to Linda and admit he'd do anything to save the company? In her mind's eye, Davina could imagine anything. But to hear him say the words struck her like an ax to the chest.

Blindly, Davina pushed away from the door and rushed down the hall. She wanted to leave here, to breathe, and to think. There was no way she could bear Justin's face, not so soon after hearing him speak the damning words.

She turned into the first open door and found herself in the library. "Vinny, over here."

She looked across the room and saw the back of a leather sofa where David motioned to her from the other side. The head of a figure was slumped in the sofa's corner. Davina managed to conceal her pain before she joined her brother.

When she reached the sofa, she saw that the slumped figure was Natalie. She wasn't sleep, but neither was she fully awake. "David, what's wrong with her?" She bent over her friend and smoothed her forehead.

David smiled. "She's had a little too much to drink. Can you believe it? Natalie is the last person I figured couldn't hold her liquor."

Davina glared at him, unreasonably incensed at his quick judgment. "Why do you say that? She seldom drinks, especially expensive champagne." She turned back to her friend and gently shook her shoulders. "Natalie, I'm taking you home."

"No, this is your party," David said. "I'll take her home."

Davina began to panic. She couldn't tell him her reasons for wanting to leave. Hadn't he warned her this would happen? "I was ready to leave anyway."

"What's this about leaving?" Mrs. Hardy walked up and saw Natalie on the sofa. "Is she okay?" She also bent and touched Natalie's forehead.

"A little too much champagne," Davina offered. "We're taking her home."

Mrs. Hardy turned to Davina. "But you can't leave just yet. You must stay and see to your guests." She looked at David. "I want you to walk Natalie out to the kitchen and I'll minister to her there before you take her home."

"She's right," David said. "You can't leave. I'll come back and pick you up."

"Oh, don't worry about Davina," Mrs. Hardy quickly added. "It'll be a while before the last of her guests leave. We'll make sure she's all right."

"I'll get Natalie's wrap from upstairs," David said, and stepped away. "Stay with her, Vinny."

Davina watched him leave before she made a plea to Mrs. Hardy. "I appreciate your kindness, but I have to leave."

"Why? I knew it would be late when everyone left, so I told Justin to ask you to stay the night. He told me you would."

Davina teetered on the edge of the abyss again. How stupid could she be in one evening? Justin didn't ask her to stay because he wanted to throw caution to the wind and let everyone know about their new relationship. It had been his mother's idea. She cringed inwardly at her own naïveté.

"It's settled then," Mrs. Hardy continued. "You'll stay with your guests and David will take Natalie home. I'm going to give her my special remedy that'll make her feel better after a good night's sleep in her own bed." She turned to leave.

Davina rested her hands on her hips and watched Natalie's eyes flutter open above a crooked smile. "You picked a hell of a time to get sauced, girl. I need to talk with you."

Natalie's unfocused eyes squinted in Davina's direction as she tried sitting up. She managed a giggle before she sunk back to the sofa and closed her eyes.

Davina glared at her friend as her frustration built. "Oh, Natalie, I don't think I'll ever forgive you for this. Never."

When David returned from upstairs, he and Davina pulled Natalie from the sofa. With a slight weave the only hint, her condition went unnoticed by others.

Davina gave them a grudging smile. "Take care of her, David, and I'll see you both later today, at the gallery."

"Sure thing, and I didn't mean anything by that earlier crack." At her nod of understanding, he leaned over and kissed her cheek before giving her a peculiar look. "Are you all right?" Once again, at her insistent nod, he returned his attention to Natalie. "Come on, let's visit Mrs. Hardy in the kitchen before we go."

Davina watched them maneuver across the room and through the door, only to see their casual figures replaced in the doorway by Justin's more formidable one.

She held her breath and watched him scan the room in that arrogant manner that she recognized as his alone. Davina swallowed hard. Remaining near the sofa, she watched him, the experience akin to a raw, aching passion that cut like a knife. He had yet to see her while a slight tilt of his head and the rise of an eyebrow acknowledged others in the room. Davina wanted to turn and leave before he saw her, but some perverse part of her continued to study him. She imposed an iron control on her will not to pick up the brass paperweight on the coffee table and hurl it at him. And she would not give him the satisfaction of a confrontation about what she heard before she decided her own course of action.

Her anger grew as she watched him search the room. Finally, when his eyes met hers, she looked away and quickly slid her mask of indifference in place.

Justin watched Davina from across the room and, in that instance, knew he wouldn't tell her about the news story right now. His brows drew downward in a frown. It would be an awful way to end her beautiful evening.

Experience had taught him that bad news will always keep; so, he would put it out of his mind and worry about it in the light of morning. After all, she'd be with him tonight, all night. He smiled at the thought. And, first thing in the morning, before they came downstairs, he'd tell her all about Chavis and the story. She'd understand and they would tackle the problem together. He liked how that sounded. He skirted the edge of the room as he made his way to her.

He came up to Davina from the back and whispered close to her ear. "We should send everyone home so we can call it a night."

Davina slipped from his touch when his lips brushed against her ear. "Where did you disappear to?" she asked.

"There was business to take care of, but I'm yours for the rest of the night."

Justin frowned at her expression and asked, "Is something wrong?" He glanced toward the door David and Natalie had recently vacated. "Natalie's okay, isn't she? Mom told me she had a little too much champagne."

"David is taking her home." She took another step away from Justin. "I almost forgot, I promised a guest I'd discuss one of the paintings on the terrace. I'd better get going. I . . . I'll see you later."

Justin watched her make a regal retreat to the door, her head held high. Confused and surprised by this change in her mood, he let out a deep sigh. She was, if nothing else, totally unpredictable.

David pulled into the parking space in front of Natalie's apartment. "You're home," he announced, and got out of the car to help her inside.

He maneuvered her sleepy form out of the car and up to the front door. With the key conveniently ready, he unlocked her door, then hit the light switch.

Natalie danced past him and across the floor as he closed the door. He watched her drop onto the sofa in a spent heap.

"David, I can't dance anymore. You're spinning around," she slurred. "The whole room's spinning." She giggled again.

David tossed the keys in the air and caught them, again and again. He considered whether he should leave her there, knowing full well that she was too wasted to do much for herself. It felt like a bad idea, but he'd put her to bed anyway.

He walked to the sofa and hoisted her up into his arms.

"What are you doing?"

David walked down the hallway. "I'm going to give you a couple of aspirin, and put you in bed before I leave."

"You're so sweet," she crooned.

The largest bedroom at the end of the hall was hers. A small bedside Tiffany lamp illuminated the room with a golden glow. He sat her on the edge of the bed where she promptly fell backward across the queen-size comforter.

"Let's get this over with," he said to himself. He lifted her limp calf in one hand and released the button on her shoe with the other, and slipped it off. He did the same for the other foot.

She shifted on the bed. "I don't want to move. My head hurts."

"I'll bet," he said absently, as he tried figuring how her evening clothes were fitted together. He pulled her by the arms into a sitting position before he grasped the hem of her top and tugged it over her head.

"What are you doing, choking me?" Her voice was muffled under the fabric.

"Trying to get you in bed," he said, not sure how that sounded. Free of the material, he watched her fall back to the bed. The straps of her black lacy teddy dropped from her shoulders.

He sighed and unzipped the long skirt, then pulled it down. When it cleared her hips, Natalie pedaled her stockinged legs in the air to facilitate its removal.

"Do you like me, David?" she asked.

"Be still my beating heart," he mumbled, and tried to avoid staring at her silk encased legs in the air and the straps of the merry widow that peeked from the edges of the teddy. "Let's see what you say tomorrow." He tossed the skirt aside.

"Why put off for tomorrow what you can do tonight?" Natalie reached up for David's coat lapel and, with surprising strength, pulled him close.

David fell against her, but caught himself on stiffened arms, only to find a bent silky knee that floated precariously close to his face. He placed a kiss there. With no objections from Natalie, he placed another on her belly, and finally one between her breasts. He raised his head to her smiling face. "There's something I've wanted to ask you, Natalie."

"Uh-huh," she mumbled.

"You wondered whether I liked you. From the way things are progressing, I think you know the answer. How do you feel about—"

David's words were cut off as Natalie gave him a great push that rolled him onto his back.

"Oh, no!" he heard Natalie utter as he lifted his head and watched her spring across the room and through another door.

David dropped his head back onto the bed and smiled as he listened to Natalie's wretches from the bathroom. He decided that when something is a bad idea, there's no changing it.

Justin shrugged from his jacket and tossed it on the sofa before he walked through his rooms. He didn't think Davina would be here, but he checked just the same. Odd, but he hadn't seen her since she left him in the library. Now that the last guests had gone and the house was closed for the night, she had to be in the guest wing suite waiting for him. He loosened the formal tie and the top buttons of the dress shirt. Pulling the door closed behind him, he headed for the south wing.

Davina sat near the window in her dark suite, still dressed for her party, and looked down into the gardens stroked with highlights from a moonlit paintbrush. The room's darkness matched her gloom. She had been sitting there a long time, but he would come soon. Every nerve in her body tensed for it.

A rap sounded at the door. Davina closed her eyes tightly and didn't move.

Another rap was followed by his distinctive voice. "Davina, it's Justin."

Davina didn't want to talk with him. The emotions were too raw for talk or confrontation. She didn't want a glib explanation easily bought from the one you love when the moonlight is in your eyes and a strong body is intimately entwined with yours. She shifted, uncomfortably aware that the word *love* had flowed through her thoughts. No, she'd face him in the clear reality of day.

This time, he rattled the locked doorknob. "Davina, I know you're in there," she heard him say. "Is something wrong?"

Tears burned for release, but she didn't dare let them fall. He would leave as quickly as he'd arrived. He was not the sort that would pine away at a door closed to him. And, as she predicted, he moved away and down the hall, his brisk steps on the hall's parquet floors heard through the door.

Davina rested her head on her folded arms, neither Justin nor her tears a threat. She would sort things out later, and most importantly, on her own terms.

The house was quiet. Justin poured a drink from one of the bars stationed near the patio and walked outside in the garden. He sat on one of the metal chairs near the pond and took a long swallow. What had gone wrong? He dropped his head against the back of the chair and looked at the stars.

He blamed himself and a host of what-ifs. Maybe she wasn't ready to reveal their relationship to his family, or her brother, and he was moving too fast. But, didn't she see that he loved her and wanted everyone to know? He smiled. *I love her.* Surprisingly, the admission didn't scare him. He'd talk with her later.

He closed his eyes. He had already begun to feel good.

"Wake up, Justin."

Justin opened his eyes, groggy from too much drink, too little sleep, and, now, too much light. It took him a moment to realize he still wore his tuxedo and had slept in the metal chair by the pond. He leaned forward and buried his face in his hands, but not before he saw Carolyn patiently standing nearby, her hands behind her back.

"What do you want, and what time is it, anyway?"

"It's after nine, and I think you'd better wake up, fast."

Justin raised his head and slowly squinted at Carolyn. "Why?"

"Davina just left the house in a cab."

He lifted himself from the seat. "What are you talking about?" He turned toward the house, hidden by rows of shrubs and flora, as though to see for himself.

"She came downstairs early this morning to read the reviews . . ."

"Oh, hell." Justin knew what had happened.

"Take a look for yourself," Carolyn said, and thrust the newspaper from behind her back into his stomach.

Justin's jaw muscle twitched as he read the three-column headline on the front page. HARDY'S MUCH TOUTED NEW ARTIST UP TO HER EARS IN BLACKMAIL/MURDER INVESTIGATION.

CHAPTER TWENTY-SIX

The Turning Point

The cab ride from Justin's house had been long and troubled, and a war of emotions raged within Davina as she now wandered restlessly around her apartment. Her anger was directed at Justin and his company because only they could have provided such detail for the news story.

And then, just as quickly, her anger gave way to mortification. She was flooded with shame from the reporter's accusation that she knew more about Robert's murder than she admitted, and that her first art show was steeped in blackmail threats to the Hardy company. Of course, the reporter didn't reveal his evidence, but simply wrote that his source talked because of concern for the company and family's well-being. What gall! That ridiculous comment, coupled with her recent defense of Justin's actions, completed her humiliation.

She tried to find reason in the maddening events. The scheduled show opening that afternoon, and another reception at seven was all but forgotten while she figured how to best defend herself from the story. She should warn David before he was caught by surprise. It would be a long day to endure unfair stares.

As she paced the hall, the doorbell's unexpected ring jarred her thoughts and brought her to an abrupt stop.

She pushed her hair behind her ear and anxiously moved on bare feet toward the door. David and Natalie wouldn't expect her to be home. And surely, Justin didn't have the temerity to show up. Oh, yes he would. Fueled by the certainty that the source of her anger was just steps away, she looked through the door's fisheye. It was David.

She released the breath she had so expectantly held and unlocked the door. David pushed into the room and closed the door.

His untidy appearance immediately caught Davina's eye. His hair was pulled into a band at the nape; and albeit wrinkled, he still wore the shirt and pants from his tuxedo of the night before. And then she saw the livid bruise near his cheekbone.

"David, what happened to you?" She reached up to touch the distended, bluish skin, but he brushed her hand away.

"I know about the story," he said as he looked at her. "Are you all right?"

Davina turned and walked into the kitchen. In a voice filled with regret, she said, "You were right. I shouldn't have trusted any of them." She busied herself at the counter.

"You mean Justin?" He followed her into the kitchen. "He told me about the story."

"He did? When?"

"After you left his house this morning, he called me."

Davina turned to him, her eyes widened in surprise. "You two aren't exactly best friends, so why did he call you?" As the import of his words sank in, she frowned. "You never said how you got that bruise."

David cocked a brow in her direction and, in a sheepish voice, said, "After I talked with him on the phone, we agreed to meet and exchange opinions."

"You didn't."

He nodded his head and gingerly pressed the bruise. "We got some talking done, and I think what he said is worth a listen." He returned to the living room.

Davina followed him. "What are you saying? That I should give him the chance to explain and lie again?"

He turned to Davina as he neared the door and gently shook her shoulders. "I don't want you blaming yourself for a decision you made without at least considering what he has to say. I'll do anything to keep you from hurting; even if I'm not thrilled about it. I know you want to believe in Justin. So, the two of you have to talk. It's that simple." He dropped his hands and reached for the door.

"Maybe later, David. I need to think. Where are you off to so fast?"

He opened the door and, to Davina's chagrin, Justin filled the threshold.

"What are you doing here?" was all she could manage to sputter as he sauntered in, casually dressed in an open-neck shirt and slacks. Her heart lurched madly with each step he took deeper into the foyer.

"Here's your chance to make things right," David cautioned him.

Justin acknowledged it with a nod. "Thanks. I owe you one."

Incredulous at their words, Davina looked back and forth at the men. "You brought him here?" she yelled at David.

"Yep. And after he explains his side, you're welcome to kick him out if you want. Natalie and I'll see you at the gallery later." He stepped onto the porch and pulled the door closed behind him.

Davina turned her hostile stare on Justin. "You used my brother?"

"You wouldn't answer your phone and I sure wasn't going to put an apology on the answering machine. David was the only way."

"Don't even try to tell me you were surprised by that story."

"Okay, I won't." He walked past her to the living room. "Can I have a seat?"

"No," she responded angrily and followed him. "You won't be staying that long. You picked a fight with David and hit him," she accused.

He gave her a sidelong glance. "That brother of yours has some temper, but he came at me. I only defended myself." He fingered the skin near his chin where she could see a cut below his lower lip. "I've had a hell of a morning, Davina, so I'll have a seat and I'm telling you what happened whether you like it or not."

Justin claimed a chair as Davina uneasily leaned against the wall and looked away.

"Marc received a tip during the party that the story was coming out this morning. He told me about it late last night," Justin said.

Davina clenched her teeth and avoided his gaze. "Why didn't you warn me?"

"The simple truth is I didn't want to spoil your evening . . . our evening together. I tried to stop the story before—"

"Stop it?" Davina's voice was raised as she glared at him. "You expect me to believe that?"

"Yes." He matched her volume. "I found out that the reporter responsible was at the party."

"You are responsible," she cut in. "Are you so afraid of my father's ownership in your company that you would tear me down in the press to get the upper hand?" She whirled off the wall and strutted toward the kitchen, not waiting for an answer.

She only took a few steps before she was halted by an iron grip to her wrist that twisted her around to face Justin's scowl.

"Would you listen and think for a minute? I know you're upset, and rightly so. But why would I try to destroy my own interest in your art show, or give inside details of my business to my competitors? It doesn't make sense, Davina."

He was right, none of it made sense—but she was hurt and all because she had allowed herself to feel again. He had done that to her and she had let him. She looked away to hide that truth from his stare.

"It was easier convincing David."

"He didn't sleep with you." The words were spoken flatly as she pulled from his hold and sped into the kitchen. She leaned against the counter, her back to the door when she felt his presence in the narrow room. "You've hurt me, Justin."

"I know."

"No, you don't." She turned around, her brows raised. "How do you benefit if I'm arrested for Robert's murder and portrayed as a liar and a blackmailer?"

"If I wanted you arrested, and God knows I don't, larceny would've been my choice of charges, and I would have done it a long time ago."

Davina blinked at his not-so-subtle reminder of the secret she had yet to admit to and, gritting her teeth, turned back to the counter. "What was your point in getting me into your bed?"

"You didn't want to be there?"

Damn his arrogance! "I heard you talk with Linda on the phone last night. You said that you were prepared to do anything to protect your precious company. Did that include sleeping with me and smearing my name?''

Justin moved closer to her. ''You were in the study?''

Davina's eyes flared at the off-handed way he asked his question and, unexpectedly, angry tears welled in her eyes. She threw a glance at him over her shoulder and with an effort, tried to make light of his comment with one of her own. ''I guess you make it a habit of juggling lovers.'' When Justin reached out to her, she flinched as she avoided his hand. ''Don't touch me.''

Justin stepped back. ''You think . . . you thought I was serious . . . good Lord, that's why you wouldn't open the door.'' He started to smile. ''You didn't hear the entire conversation. It's not what it sounded like, Davina.'' At her silence, he continued. ''After Marc told me about the story, I learned it was Linda who brought the reporter to the party as her guest.''

''I didn't see her at all last night.''

''She saw you, though, and wasn't happy. Later, in the study, I played a game to learn what she knew, and you heard that charade. I had to tell her what she wanted to hear so she'd open up. You see, I'm pretty sure Linda gave information to the reporter. We can't prove it, but she's one of his sources.''

Davina slowly turned and raised her eyes to his. ''Linda? I know she doesn't like me but I can't believe she'd be so cruel and hurt me this way.''

''Linda and I had a big row before I left town, and we cleared the air on a few things. One of them was you.'' He held Davina's stare. ''She knows how I feel about you.''

Davina looked away. Her mind whirled with this information she wanted to believe, but she tried to get a fix on her anger. She heard Justin's voice through a fog of thoughts.

''It was wrong not to tell you what was happening, but I knew you'd be with me until morning. I didn't think you'd refuse to see me when I came to your door.''

''I no longer thought it a good idea to stay overnight with you.''

''Why not?'' Justin asked.

"Because I had just overheard you talking to Linda and then I learned it was Mrs. Hardy's idea, not yours, that I stay at the house."

"Mom's idea? She suggested it, but only after I'd already asked you. I told her you'd agree because I had your promise to stay. For me."

Davina thought back to the conversation with Mrs. Hardy. Maybe it was as he said. She took a deep breath and shook her head to clear the confusion. Just as she'd feared, he had all the right answers.

"I thought things were beginning to fall in place for us, Davina."

She raised her eyes and studied him carefully. And, for the first time since he came through the door, allowed herself to really see him. His handsome face was drawn and tired, and there was some swelling at the corner of his mouth; but even that superficial damage didn't diminish the dangerous sexuality he exuded. She could feel the heat from his eyes as they searched hers.

"You had no right to keep quiet about information that concerned and affected me," she said quietly.

"I know."

"We have a contract, and are partners in the show."

"I apologize," Justin said. "I admit it was wrong. But, you couldn't have done anything, anyway. I was only protecting you—"

"I neither want nor need your protection. I much prefer your respect."

"You know the two aren't mutually exclusive." He smiled at her.

"Not in my experience." She rubbed her arms as she thought on the decision she had to make. "I'm not your experiment, Justin. Everything that happened last night affected me, and you should have informed me. Until you accept me as your equal, and not something to protect, and unless your attitude changes, this will keep happening. We'll never work things out."

"Okay, it won't happen again." He ventured a smile and another step toward her. "No matter how bad it is, I'll make sure you know everything. Do you believe me about what happened last night?"

She nodded. "I don't have a reason not to, and I want to believe you." When he started for her, she shook her head. "That doesn't mean we can pick up where we left off."

"Why not?"

"I realize now it would be a mistake."

He ran his hand across his head. "This news story, your misunderstanding of the phone call, of my mother's suggestion—those were mistakes."

"They happened for a reason and are signs of a deeper problem. We knew this wouldn't work. Riding home this morning I felt betrayed in the worst way." In a whisper, she added, "It felt just like before."

"The engagement you spoke of—is that the betrayal?"

"It's a story not worth repeating." As she pressed past him, he stopped her.

"I've got the time. What happened?"

Davina circled opposite him, to the other side of the table. "It was a long time ago, over two years in fact. Why it was called off isn't as important as the fact that it was." She looked at Justin. "The good thing about the experience is that I know what can happen when people aren't honest about their relationships."

"We're as honest as they come about our problems. It's your stubbornness that gets in the way. You see any attempt to help you or any kind word as manipulation. That's not always the case."

She looked down at her nails, scrubbed clean, like her body, of their patina and polish of the previous evening. "We're a crash waiting to happen." She slowly paced near the table. "And if you can't see it, I do. We'll betray each other and our affection will turn to hate at some point."

"Why are you so bent on believing that?"

"Because I made a promise to my father and I'm going to succeed."

"I'm willing to take a chance on the outcome."

"If you lose, you still have some semblance of your father's dream. But if I lose, I've lost my father's only chance at a respectable legacy, and that's everything. I'm keeping the promise I made."

"But not at any cost. I know you."

Davina thought of the lies she had told and the theft she had committed in the name of her cause. "Don't presume so much." She frowned at his raised brow. "Given the choice, I wouldn't choose you over my father's legacy no more than you would choose me in the same circumstance."

"Now who's making presumptions?" Justin asked.

"For sure, you won't give up the family store for me."

"I don't know, Davina. Maybe you're worth it." He pushed his hands deep into his pockets. "You're not the only one taking a chance here, and you act like you're the only one who hurts."

"Someone has to be realistic and it's better to avoid the pain down the road."

"I don't know what's in store either. I was torn up inside this morning because you were hurt. Both of us were betrayed. But we can get through it by relying on each other."

"Didn't you just hear me? I don't want to rely on you. I don't want to love you or be responsible for your love." She had said it again. Love.

"What happened in the past has nothing to do with us right now, this minute." He scratched his head in bewilderment. "You know it, too, don't you?" With an air of finality, he dropped his hands. "All right, I've given it my best shot, and you win. You push until you find an excuse, any excuse, Davina, not to feel. Nothing is guaranteed, least of all relationships, and you're taking the coward's way out."

"Why won't you understand—"

"I don't want to anymore. I won't keep trying to figure out where I stand with you day to day. If I walk out right now, you're safe. You haven't risked anything, and you can keep your little secrets and go on being angry with the world. So, I'm out of here." He gave her a long stare before he turned around and walked toward the front door.

Davina panicked as she watched Justin walk from her life one step at a time until he was out of her sight. What was she thinking? She loved him. All the excuses she gave were for her benefit. They had been the mantra she needed to keep him at arm's length. And damn if they hadn't worked. If he left now, she would never know what might have been. She rushed after him.

"Justin, don't go," she called out, and turned into the foyer.

She ran directly into his open arms at the door, where he had quietly waited for her. He looked down at her, and they both saw hope bright in the other's eyes.

"I'm not a coward."

"I knew that would tick you off."

"I'm not sure about a lot of things," Davina said. "But, I do know that I dream about you. Constantly. And you're in my thoughts when you're not in my sight.'' She lay her head against his chest. ''I don't know what to do about you.''

Justin tightened his arms around her and looked into her eyes. ''You're doing just fine.'' He covered her mouth with a gentle kiss that slowly became deeper. When the first sigh escaped her lips, he picked her up.

Davina's arms were gathered around his neck as she whispered between kisses, ''It's down the hall—''

''Don't worry, I'll find it,'' was his emphatic reply as he buried his mouth in the tender skin of her throat.

Detective Jaragoski leaned back in his chair in the squad room and stared at the blackboard that boasted a chalked flowchart that resembled a mutant stick man. The snaking lines that extended from the circles ran in no certain pattern, but they all flowed to a much larger circle that so far contained one name: Davina Spenser. He called out to his younger partner at the next desk.

''What time is it?''

''Almost three o'clock. Too early for dinner,'' Detective Lovett answered without looking up from the newspaper spread over his desk. He continued to highlight excerpts from the newspaper about the Vinny Richards art exhibit.

''Too early for an arrest, too.'' Jaragoski twisted his heavy bulk in the chair to look at his partner. ''Interesting, huh, that she wanted more than just a show from Hardy Enterprises. The paper says she claims she owns the company and some of the paintings. Even threatened them. You believe that's how she got the show?''

''Mr. Hardy sure didn't seem to mind her being around.''

Jaragoski returned his attention to the blackboard. ''The fingerprints we lifted from the murder weapon need to be identified first. Maybe we'll get lucky with an ID on the first run-through.''

''And then we can pay her another visit,'' Lovett said as he found another interesting passage and marked it.

* * *

"What are you thinking?" Davina asked Justin.

She reclined, in spoon fashion, on top of him in the square, garden-style bathtub. Filled with warm water, its sudsy warmth enveloped their spent limbs. Both enjoyed their lassitude, the consequence from a day of lovemaking.

"That you're insatiable, and I'm the luckiest man in the world." His voice was low and smooth. He raised his head from the towel on the tub's edge and placed a kiss on her wet ear.

Davina turned onto her stomach and pressed against his chest. When the scented, oily waves threatened to upset their precarious arrangement in the tub, Justin's bent legs tightened about her and held her steady while he absently stroked her back.

"I was thinking the same of you," she said. "Of course, I've been celibate a long time. What's your excuse?" She cleared the soap from his chest and planted a kiss on his nipple.

"You." Justin rested wet, slippery hands under her arms and slid her body up so that her breasts hung tantalizingly close to his mouth. He took each, in turn, into his mouth and suckled the taut, dark centers.

Davina grasped the sides of the tub as her control ebbed away under the assault by his mouth and, again, abandoned herself to the whirl of sensations she knew Justin would give her. She anticipated his slow, intimate exploration as she was pulled higher from the water. His nibbles to the sensitive underside of her breasts became a white heat as the air cooled the swollen peaks he had just left.

Pulled to her knees, Davina balanced trembling hands on his shoulders as he licked a path across her abdomen to her belly. Her hands stroked his shoulders, his neck, his head, and pled in their own fashion for him to continue.

Steadily, as he raised her higher from the water, Justin's hands slid down her sides and cupped the firm flesh of her bottom. He kissed the small birthmark that hid at the curve of her hips.

"Say my name, Davina. Tell me what you want." His lips, his tongue returned to the sleek, soft skin at the top of her thighs and moved upward to the juncture where they met to form the triangle of wet curls.

Davina was paralyzed by gusts of passion. Her head lolled against a boneless neck as she accommodated his erotic indulgence in this raw act of possession—and she said the words that would guarantee her release from the agonizing heat.

"Justin," she moaned loudly, "Don't stop now."

"I don't intend to."

She couldn't stand anymore, and her release was sure as she pressed against his mouth. Clutching Justin's head for strength, Davina toppled over the edge of sanity and into the bliss of stars, lights, the heavens . . . and finally earth.

Davina was pulled into the warm water where she came to rest on Justin's chest again. She quickly became aware that his hard body was still aroused, and opened her eyes to his.

He kissed her lightly and smiled. "We're not through yet." Justin stepped from the tub and reached for the towel nearby. He wrapped Davina in it, and carried her from the bathroom and into the bedroom.

"Will we make it to the reception tonight?" Davina asked skeptically.

"We'll see," was Justin's equally skeptical response.

"No, man. You wait a minute." Nathan stressed each word as he pointed his finger at Marc's chest in the dwindling twilight of Piedmont Park. "I thought I worked for you, and before I know it, I'm being strong-armed by these guys."

"I'm sorry it's come to this, but they want the rest of the paintings before the month is out, Nathan. You have to deliver."

"I only got the underpainting done on that last one," he said in a strained voice. "How do I finish it when the original is missing, huh?" His voice held the frustration his hands exhibited.

"We're still trying to locate it. What about the others?" Marc pressed the recalcitrant Nathan for an answer.

He held his head down. "All but three are ready. They still need curing."

Marc reached up and, with a thin smile, slapped Nathan on the back. "That's good. Just remember, all those dead black artists—Coppler, Edwards, Maceo—equal good money from greedy collectors. We're giving them what they want."

Nathan shook away Marc's hand. "I hate that I ever did this for you. I was good, but instead of creating my own art, here I am copying other folks' labor." He spit at the ground and stepped away. "No more."

A deep sigh escaped Marc. "I need to pick up the rest of the originals from you and replace them in the Hardy vaults this week. Are they at the warehouse?"

"Yeah." He turned to leave without saying goodbye.

"It doesn't have to be too late for you," Marc called out to him.

Nathan paused and turned back to him, regret in his eyes. "Sure it is." He continued his trudge down the path.

It was the second day of Davina's exhibit and things were going nicely in spite of the news article. Justin was pleased as he looked around the gallery.

"Hi, Mr. Hardy." Rosa offered a big smile to Justin from behind her desk.

"Hello, Rosa. I was looking for Davina. Is she around?"

"She's not back from lunch with her brother. But I expect her any minute now." She leaned across the desk and whispered conspiratorially to Justin, "That man over there is anxious to see her, too. He wanted to wait."

Justin followed Rosa's gaze to a man in a business suit whose back was turned to them. The man intently examined a small woodcut of a nude on the wall.

"He probably wants to buy something, but only after he gets a chance to meet her." He looked to Rosa for confirmation.

"I don't think so," she whispered. "He says he's an old friend . . . from home."

Justin frowned as warning bells sounded in his head. Again, he looked at the man who had now turned to give his attention to another piece of art. Justin studied the man's lean, dark-skinned face that sported a stylish mustache. He guessed they were near the same age.

Without taking his eyes from the man, Justin cocked a brow. "Did he give you a name?" He heard Rosa shuffle papers on her desk.

"Yes, sir. It's on his card. Lawrence Parker of Miami, Florida."

Justin blinked at the name. "I think I'll wait after all, Rosa," he said smoothly, as the bells now rang in earnest.

CHAPTER TWENTY-SEVEN

Past Havoc Revisited

David slowed his car to a stop in front of the gallery. "You want to get out here, Vinny, since we're late?"

"We'll park and join you inside," Natalie added.

Davina looked at her watch as she unbuckled the seatbelt. "I didn't realize the time," she said, and got out of the car. "I'll see you both upstairs." She stepped onto the sidewalk and entered the building as David pulled away.

The recent murder had brought about changes to security. A guard's post was now stationed in the lobby, and an additional security officer, Bobby Norris, was stationed there. The post was manned twenty-four hours a day with the other two shifts split by the remaining two guards.

"Good afternoon, Miss Richards."

Davina smiled as she greeted the newest guard with a wave of her badge before she entered the elevator. She'd have to get used to being referred to as both Vinny Richards and Davina Spenser.

She stepped from the elevator and made her way to the gallery, anxious to lose herself among the artwork and gallery visitors. It was her way of closing out impending problems that the newspaper story had made clear. Losing herself in Justin's capable arms was the other way. She smiled as she entered the gallery.

Rosa looked up from her desk and, before Davina could turn into her own office, called out to her. "You're back. There's someone waiting for you."

Davina looked through the glass walls of her office and saw Justin leaning inside the doorway, arms folded across his chest. Her heart made its familiar leap at the sight of him. She smiled and moved in his direction. "Thanks."

"I didn't mean Mr. Hardy," Rosa quickly pointed out.

"Oh?" Davina slowed down. "Who?"

"The other gentleman. He says he's a friend." Rosa's eyes shifted to a point beyond Davina. "There he is."

She turned and was immediately engulfed in a bear hug.

"Davina, how long has it been?"

A soft gasp escaped her as she recognized the face, heard his voice. *Oh, my God. It can't be Lawrence.* Her body stiffened in stunned shock as he continued to squeeze her.

Slowly, he released her frozen body and stood back. His hands still grasped her upper arms as he studied her with an appreciative eye. "You still look good. Just as beautiful as I remembered. Maybe more."

His words did it. She was thawed into action and twisted from his touch, her breathing now heavy with anger. "What are you doing here?" she demanded, her voice low. "You have some nerve showing your face." Her words were accompanied by anxious glances from the scattered visitors in the gallery. The world had begun to spin out of control again, and so soon. How could this be happening to her?

"You can't blame me for trying to see you again. The way we left things between us was pretty ugly."

"Ugly? Is that what you called it?"

"Davina, is there a problem?"

She looked up to find Justin at her elbow. He wore a frown on his face and his snarl of words were directed at Lawrence.

"I can handle this, but I need some privacy." Her mouth tightened when she returned her glare to Lawrence. She briskly walked away, expecting him to follow. In the short walk to her office, she tried to figure out what she felt. The initial shock of seeing him again after all this time had begun to subside. In its place a dull ache long ago buried started to build. *Who does he think he is that he can grab me like . . . like nothing ever happened? Does he think I still want his attention?*

Davina marched into the office and spun around on her heels to find Lawrence already in and Justin bringing up the rear.

"Justin," she began, "please, let me handle this."

Lawrence smiled at Justin. "You're a friend of Davina's?"

Justin ignored him. "Are you sure?" he asked her.

She nodded. "I am. I'll talk with you later."

"I'll be in the gallery. Just say the word and I'll have him out of here." Justin's eyes narrowed as they settled briefly on Lawrence, then he left the room.

"How did you find me here?" She felt as hollow as her voice sounded.

"I'm in town for a few days on a sales trip and saw your show in the paper. I mean, I was knocked for a loop when I saw your picture." He offered her a wide grin. "From a woman that I know has a warm heart, I didn't expect this cold treatment to an old friend."

"You're no friend. What do you want?"

They both stood there, Davina near the office's far wall, her arms crossed, and Lawrence at the door. At that moment, David and Natalie entered the gallery. Through the glass, Davina watched in surprised silence as David, recognizing Lawrence, charged toward the office. Things proceeded so quickly from that point that, later on, Davina could barely recall the order that events unfolded.

"You lousy bastard," David growled as he pressed into the room. "What are you doing here? I told you if I ever saw you again I'd kick your butt to kingdom come."

Lawrence backed farther into the room, his eyes warily on David. "Now wait a minute. That was a long time ago. I thought we were past that."

Davina recognized the fire in her brother's eyes and moved to him. "David, don't do anything crazy. There are other people here."

And then, everything happened at once. David backhanded Lawrence, who fell onto a nearby chair. Natalie ran into the room and, along with Davina, implored David to stop. Testing his jaw, Lawrence scrambled to his feet and made a wide swing at David, who easily ducked the punch. The two men then grappled in the small office, amid protests from the women, where David finally pinned Lawrence against the wall and held him in a chokehold.

"You're going to suffer for what you put Vinny through."

"Still a hothead, huh?" Lawrence baited him through gasping breaths.

"David, don't do this," Davina cried. As she and Natalie tried to pull him from Lawrence, Justin rushed into the room.

He curled his arm around David's neck and crooked it against his windpipe. "Break it up, David, turn him loose."

"No. I've waited too long for this opportunity," he said. Lawrence's grunts of pain were getting louder.

Justin slowly tightened his own hold. "Come on, David. You're upsetting your sister and you're pissing me off."

"I thought you cared about her, Justin. This lowlife called off their wedding a few days before it was to take place and then disappeared. You know why?"

"David, stop it." Davina's sharp voice gave a warning.

But David ignored it. "Because his other girlfriend was pregnant and he had to marry her or go to jail. Now, you want me to let him go?" Lawrence emitted another painful grunt as David pressed his arm into his throat.

Justin turned his grim face to Davina, and for a moment, his grip around David's neck relaxed.

"You've got to stop him." Davina's voice was urgent.

"You heard her, David." Justin pulled hard against David's neck and leveraged his hold with his other arm. "Do it now," he demanded.

With his own breath cut short, David released a gasping, coughing Lawrence. Justin, in turn, released David.

"He's not hurt," David said as he stepped away. "But, I don't know about the next time."

Lawrence rubbed his neck as he backed away from David. "You're crazy, you know that?"

Davina concentrated her attention on Lawrence. In a voice shakier than she would have liked, she said, "I want you gone. If you'd like, you can buy all the paintings you want, but there's nothing to be said between us. Just go.''

All eyes turned on Lawrence. ''Davina, I only—'' He took a step toward her but stopped when Justin and David made to take a step also. ''I'll leave. I'd like to buy a painting, but I guess it's best if I come back when none of you are around.'' He backed up to the door. ''Believe it or not I am sorry, Davina. About everything.''

He turned and rapidly cleared the gallery doors, then disappeared from view.

Davina separated from the little group and sank against the edge of the desk. Exhausted, she closed her eyes as she let out a ragged sigh and dropped her head into her hand.

''Why don't you guys disappear for a while, okay?'' Natalie suggested, before she sat next to Davina and squeezed her hand.

When Davina heard them leave, she looked up and let a shudder flow through her. ''Thanks, Natalie.'' Her voice was small and strained.

''What a bummer. Are you okay about seeing that rat again?''

She let out a dry laugh. ''Why is it that, when I'm on the verge of enjoying some measure of happiness, something horrible drops down out of nowhere, as if to say, 'Oh no, Davina, not today'?''

''Tell me about it,'' Natalie sighed in understanding.

Davina gave her a tired smile. ''I have to hand it to fate, though. His showing up makes me see things clearly.'' She gazed ahead. ''It's finally hit me that I've been living this fantasy of what I'd imagined we had.''

''And?''

''We never had anything. It was all a lie. I'm sure I recognized that when the truth started to come out. But somehow, this marvelous fantasy plays out in your mind and replaces reality.''

''Maybe the mind protects you from pain. Good is easier to handle than bad.''

''Yeah,'' Davina agreed, and studied her hands. ''How could I lose what I never had with him? I suspect he doesn't realize that yet.'' She looked at Natalie. ''He dropped in here as if nothing had happened, like we were old friends. The whole episode is embarrassing now.''

''Why do you say that?''

''These last two years, I pretty much martyred myself when I turned that fantasy inward, wouldn't date, and didn't trust anyone. All of that helped to make David's guilt more pronounced.''

''That you made it through the experience is the important thing. It took the right man, though, to make you rethink it all.''

''He did, didn't he?'' Davina marveled at that fact and turned her stare beyond the glass wall where she saw Justin and David approach the office. ''I should thank Lawrence for jilting me.'' She giggled. ''I could be married to him.''

They were both smiling when Justin reached the door and stuck his head inside. ''Is it okay to come in?''

''Sure,'' Davina answered. She joined him at the door. ''I think I've experienced every emotion there is these last few days.''

He caught her hands between his. ''Unfortunately, there's more.''

''What do you mean?'' She looked from Justin to David, who had now come around to flank her other side.

''While all the commotion was going on, Detective Jaragoski called,'' Justin said. ''He wants to question you again.''

Davina tried to back away from the news, but Justin held her hands tight. Her eyes questioned as they moved from him to David.

David nodded and spoke in a regretful tone. ''I agreed that you'd show up at their office, Vinny, and cooperate for now.''

David and Justin accompanied her to homicide headquarters. The meeting with the two detectives was brief, yet specific in the questions, accusations, and concerns they presented to her. The meeting left no doubt in any of their minds that Davina had become a prime suspect in their investigation.

Afterward, when Justin recognized two reporters in the downstairs lobby, he played the game of bait and switch. Since he had to leave them for another appointment, he left through the lobby and fielded the reporters' questions while David and Davina made their exit through a side door.

Back at the gallery in the nearly vacant parking lot, David turned the car off.

''Justin's suggestion that you stay at his house a few days, while I'm out of town, might not be a bad idea. The police and reporters can be persistent, and I'll feel better knowing they can't get to you so easily and," he looked at Davina and smiled, "you can keep an eye on him."

Davina didn't return his good humor. "Natalie will be around."

"She's got clients and this is a busy tax quarter for her."

"The police think I murdered Robert." Davina swallowed hard as she pressed her fingers against her brow. "They're not letting it go."

"Eventually, they'll have to. Remember, they have no motive, only hearsay from a newspaper story. So what if your fingerprints were on the murder weapon. It's a painter's tool. Justin told them you and everyone else with access to the workshop had the chance to touch it. Even they admitted they found other unidentified prints."

David got out of the car, and Davina followed suit. "I'm leaving in the morning," he said as they took the short walk to the building. "Promise me you'll call Justin if Lawrence bothers you again."

"Lawrence's showing up wasn't all bad, you know."

"What do you mean?"

"You can let go of that guilt you've been carrying around." At David's puzzled glance, she explained. "The tragedy is not that you weren't there to make the marriage happen. The tragedy would've occurred had I married him."

"But you loved him, Vinny. He broke your heart."

"I'm grateful I learned what he was before it was too late, and I'm not looking back." She playfully entwined her arm with his when they reached the building. "Come upstairs while I help Rosa close up."

"I can't." He looked at her. "I've got to go by my office before I leave. So, you're okay with everything? No regrets?"

"None where Lawrence is concerned. Justin is another matter." Davina straightened and looked her brother in the eye. "I've been thinking, and I've decided to tell him the truth about some of the things that have happened."

David nodded in acceptance. "It's your decision." He pulled her into a hug. "Please, don't stay late, and let the guard walk you to your car. I'll talk with you later and give you my schedule."

She waved him off and walked into the building. When Davina

entered the third-floor gallery, Rosa was preparing to close for the day.

"Your friend came back and bought a painting," Rosa said. At Davina's frown, she continued. "The nude woodcut on paper. He also left a note for you. I put it on your desk."

Davina went into the office and saw the white gallery envelope. She picked it up and turned it over in her hand several times before she slid a finger under the sealed flap and removed the sheet of notepaper inside. In a neat print, unsigned, it read, *I'd like to explain some things to you. Meet me this one time at the coffee shop across the street. I'll stay until six. If you don't come, I'll understand.*

Heaving a great sigh, Davina tucked the note inside her purse and stole a glance at her watch. It was ten minutes before six o'clock. She rubbed her mouth in silent thought.

Justin twirled the long-necked beer bottle between his two fingers before he lifted it to his lips and drained the remainder of its contents. "You believe this syndicate could be funding my problems?"

Connie sat across from Justin in the small bar near the gallery. They occupied a table near the front window, where the light was much better. Connie's meaty fists stopped halfway to his mouth with the remnants of a roast beef sandwich while he nodded his large, bald head.

"There are a few big-time dealers who specialize in this," Connie said. "They bring together respectable clientele with deep pockets who want to own certain works of art that just aren't available through the regular markets.

"By any means necessary, like stolen pieces and forgeries," Justin said. He looked at the sheet of notes Connie had given him earlier.

"Exactly. Unfortunately, they want to own the stuff so badly that they end up with more forgeries than originals. It's a big business."

"And that's where I come in?"

"They pressured Jacob. That's one of the reasons he wanted you in here."

"I know," Justin said. "So they threatened me by trashing my company in hopes that I lose the confidence of the board and investors and ultimately, control. I just don't buy your theory that Davina may be a part of their plan.''

''You pay me to theorize. You have to admit she's in the thick of things.''

''But what about the murder? If she's their plan, why are the police trying to pin a murder on her?''

''I haven't figured that part out yet,'' Connie said between chews.

Justin rubbed his brow tiredly. ''The board meets again in two weeks.''

''You'll get your break when someone talks. They always do.''

''I already started the rumor the way we worked it out,'' Justin said.

Connie looked up from his sandwich. ''Good. We can see where it leads.''

Justin pushed the empty bottle aside and picked up his pen. ''We should plan our next step.'' He tapped the pen against the paper as a figure on the sidewalk crossed his view through the bar's front window. It was Davina, oblivious to Justin and Connie sitting only a few yards away inside. As she walked on by, he abruptly stood, impervious to the chair's loud scrape against the linoleum floor.

''Connie, I'll be right back.''

A few steps and he was at the door. He looked down the sidewalk and saw Davina turn into the coffee shop two doors down. He quickly strode toward her. She should have left to go home by now, and she'd been through a lot this week. He'd just make sure everything was all right and then encourage her to stay with him while David was away this week.

He pulled the coffee shop door open and almost immediately spied Davina with her back to him in the center aisle, next to a booth. As she lowered herself behind a table, he saw that the booth's opposite seat was already occupied by someone. Lawrence Parker.

Frozen in the doorway, Justin's dark eyes stared at the pair, baffled. *What is he still doing here? And why is she with him?* He flinched as he recognized his own insecurity. Each time Connie had introduced a new, troubling fact about her, Justin had managed to explain it away. Was he a fool to believe he would ever have her trust? In that moment, he watched Lawrence's eyes sweep over Davina, and had his answer in the strange emotion he knew to be jealousy. Suspicion and anger fought to control him; he quickly backed out onto the sidewalk and returned to the bar where Connie waited.

"I knew you'd come," Lawrence said to Davina.

She felt the touch of his eyes as she eased into the booth opposite him and shivered with distaste. "By the time I leave, maybe you'll wish I hadn't."

A waitress offered a menu, but Davina waved it off. "I won't be long."

Lawrence leaned forward on bent arms. "So, you hit the big time with this gallery show, huh? Very nice. I knew it would happen one day."

"I think of it as an opportunity. No more." She motioned at the brown-paper-wrapped package that rested next to him in the booth. "Is that why you wanted to see me? A personal thank you for buying a piece of artwork?"

Davina leaned back in the padded booth and studied his face. He looked like the same Lawrence—an attractive man, but in a soft way, what with his flawless, dark brown skin. The meticulous mustache added a required masculinity, though nothing like Justin's strong, angular planes. Lawrence clenched and unclenched his hands, and she realized he was nervous—this from a man Davina had always thought of as self-confident. She wondered about the young girl he had married and who had borne him a child a few months later. That had been a sad affair and was neither her business nor her problem anymore.

"After I told you why we couldn't get married, I tried to see you again, to explain, but David made sure I didn't get near you. I wanted you to know I never meant to hurt you."

"You never meant for me to find out." Davina's eyes hardened. "If you're seeking some grand pardon for your past sins, I can't give it to you. You have a wife and child now, and you did the right thing. Ease your mind with that."

"Cheryl and I are separated."

Davina couldn't hide the surprise on her face. "You were married less than two years. What about your baby?"

"Still taking up for everybody else, huh? You know I only married Cheryl because her daddy threatened to file charges against me. I loved you."

Davina shook her head and frowned at his words. "And you're the same Lawrence, looking for immediate gratification. She was seventeen years old and pregnant, for God's sake. What did you expect her parents to suggest when they found out what was going on? She loved you."

"So did you at one time, Davina." He leaned forward across the table. "We made a mistake . . ."

"Hold on right there," she interrupted. "It took me a while to realize your specialty was snaring loyal, needy women. And the mistake was mine. But I didn't come here to reminisce."

"I tried to find you again when I heard about your daddy's illness. I know how devoted you were to him."

"Don't speak of my father. He hated you." Davina reached for her purse. "I shouldn't have come here. You're talking in a time warp, like nothing happened. You haven't learned anything from your mistake." She slid to the end of the booth when Lawrence reached over and touched her arm.

"You're telling me you've forgotten about us, and what we shared?"

Davina slapped his hand away. "We shared misery, you fool." She saw genuine surprise on his face at her reaction. "I guess you don't have a clue about why I decided to see you this last time, do you?"

"I hoped it was because we still meant something to each other after all."

Davina slid back into her seat and smiled as one would while indulging a child's odd query. "Wrong. I'm here because I can face you, and that's the beauty of it. The fog has lifted from the time you were in my life. I do feel an infinite sadness for the young girl you married . . . it was all for nothing." This time, Davina did get up from the booth.

"Oh, and I also wanted to say thank you."

"For what?"

"For not marrying me." She smiled broadly and without a word, left, not once looking back.

"Natalie Goodman speaking, can I help you?"

"It's me," Davina said in sheer relief. "Thank God you're still at the office."

"Hey, what's up? Are you home?"

"I saw him again." The words tumbled out in a rush.

"Whoa, calm down. Saw who?"

"The man that's following me."

"What—when?"

"I was leaving the coffee shop near the gallery," Davina said. "I looked across the street and there he was, watching me."

"What happened?"

"I didn't want him to follow me to the car so I decided to go back to the coffee shop. But in the time it took me to look up the street and back, he was gone, out of sight. So, I took off to my car and came straight home."

"Weren't you with David and Justin?"

"They were gone." Davina paused a moment. "When I returned to the gallery from the police station, Lawrence had left a note and asked me to see him at the coffee shop."

"Don't tell me, let me guess. You met him?"

"I'll tell you about it later, but some things were cleared up. He's probably on a flight to Miami by now." She heard someone call for Natalie in the background.

"Listen," Natalie said, "I'll be stuck here for a while, and this stalker sounds pretty damn serious. It's time to tell David."

Davina knew she should agree, but she couldn't right now. "We don't know if the man wants to hurt me. Maybe he's the police."

"Did you forget? You've been followed since before the murder."

"I'm careful, Natalie. So, please don't say anything yet."

"At least, while David's gone, take up Justin's offer and stay at his house."

"Maybe I'll do just that."

"Never mind the maybe," Natalie said with a laugh.

"Thanks." Davina's smile carried through the phone.

"What did I do?"

"Nothing . . . and everything. You're a friend. And that's what I need."

Alli floated on stockinged feet down the back stairs where Justin waited for her at the base. His arm rested lightly along the balustrade.

"You buzzed me?" she asked.

Justin had showered and changed into a comfortable pair of jeans and sweater. "Davina may be staying over for a few days."

"And?" Her face brightened with a curious anticipation.

He gave his sister an indulgent smile as he shifted his weight to the other leg. "I think she can keep out of the way of reporters and police from our house. Mom is fine with it. Do you have a problem?"

"Hey, you don't have to explain. I'm cool. So, when is she coming?"

He pressed his hands into his pockets. "It's an open invitation. She can come at any time, whenever she's ready."

"You don't know if she's coming, do you?" Alli's knowing smile grew. "Let's see . . . you're not taking that fact too well, either." When Justin didn't respond, she peered into his eyes. "You care about her, don't you?"

Justin was surprised at his sister's insight. He glanced at his watch. It was already past nine and he hadn't heard from Davina. Although he pushed aside the troubling scene he had witnessed earlier that evening, it was burned in his head. He needed some measure of explanation from her, and preferably an offered one rather than one forced from her.

"Just try and be nice, Alli. A simple request. No bull, okay?"

Alli sat on the stair step and leaned back on her elbows. "I'll bet Mom put her in the wing on the other side of the house, as in away from you." When Justin's brows narrowed, Alli laughed. With a flutter of her hand, she said, "Don't worry. You'll figure a way around it."

"You have no manners." Justin mussed her hair amid her loud protest.

The doorbell's ring stopped their joking. From another part of the house, Mrs. Hardy called out, "I'll get it."

Mrs. Hardy's light voice could be heard as it drifted from the foyer. Indistinct at first, her words became clear as she turned onto the back corridor where Justin and Alli stood.

"We wondered if you'd come tonight," Mrs. Hardy was saying.

The moment Davina came into view, Justin experienced a surge of affection mixed with relief, and started toward her. His dark eyes searched her face for some immediate assurance that everything was fine. As each step brought them closer, he saw her smile become broader. Her face was clean, void of makeup, and her hair was strangely in place, as if it had just been tamed into restraint. She carried a travel bag in one hand and clutched the strap of her purse with the other.

"I didn't arrive too late, did I? There were some errands I had to run."

Justin took the bag from Davina's hand, vaguely aware that his mother had already left them. "No, you're fine. I'm glad you decided to come." The scoop-necked white ribbed sweater she wore tucked inside black trousers left bare an expanse of silky skin that glowed under the luminous lighting in the corridor, and his eyes drank her up.

She broke into a wide, open smile that put a gleam in her eyes. "It wasn't a hard decision." Davina looked past Justin to Alli on the stairs. "Hello, Alli."

Alli waved to her. "I'm glad you made it, too. It gets boring around here."

In a joking aside to Davina, Justin said, "Of course, with Alli around, we're never bored."

"That's what I usually say about Natalie," Davina replied.

His fingers pressed possessively against her back. "Come on upstairs and I'll show you your rooms." As they started back down the hall to the front stairs, he glanced around and noticed Alli still watched them from the staircase.

He smiled and called out to her, "Later."

Alli winked and smiled as she gave him a thumbs up.

* * *

Justin stopped at a double set of doors on the second floor. "We're here," he said as he turned the doorknob and stood aside so Davina could enter first.

She found herself standing in a beautifully appointed sitting room with creamy walls and chintz-covered sofas made even more cozy by warm and inviting rosewood, duplicated in the tables and fireplace mantle. Davina watched Justin walk past her into a connecting room she suspected was the bedroom. When she followed him, she found she was right. It was a breathtaking fantasy that boasted a four-poster canopied bed with curtains tied back to reveal a matching teal and cream coverlet. He set the travel bag on the bed and turned to Davina.

"It's hard to believe people actually live in this house. It's beautiful, Justin."

"Good. Maybe I can get you to come over more often." With an easy gait, he slowly walked back to her.

She said her next words lightly. "Maybe you'll withdraw the invitation when you hear what I have to tell you." She watched his relaxed face grow serious.

He stopped in front of her and, braced for bad news, inhaled a deep breath. "What could you possibly tell me that would make me do that?"

"That you were right all along." Davina looked into his eyes, determined to end some of the lies, and spoke in a stoic voice. "I took the Maceo paintings from the gallery that first night we met."

CHAPTER TWENTY-EIGHT

Confessions and Suppressions

Davina slowly released her breath under Justin's stare. With a slight lift of her chin, she held his gaze, determined not to look away.

"What took you so long to tell me?"

"I never meant to keep the paintings, just threaten you with the fact that I knew they were in existence. But then, everything went wrong. You saw me in the building, I was invited to the board meeting . . ." She watched as his brows drew together in anticipation. "The paintings were stolen from my apartment . . ."

Justin whispered into the air. "I knew it."

". . . and the lies started to pile up." She swallowed the lump in her throat and stepped away. "There's more."

"At the board meeting," she continued, "what I said about my father and what I learned about the paintings from Maceo was all true, but"—she turned back to Justin, "I left an important detail out."

"What?" Justin's scrutiny was sharp.

"James Spenser was the alias my father used from the time he fled Atlanta years ago." Davina's eyes blazed in defiance as she waited for Justin's anger to explode. "Maceo James is his real name."

To her surprise, it never came. Justin strode away from her before turning back. He spoke matter-of-factly. "Maceo James was your father and you didn't think that was important enough at the time for us to know?"

Davina's relief that he took the news calmly was palpable. She answered in a rush of words. "I couldn't tell you everything, not then.

I didn't know what to expect. When he told us your company had his paintings, he said Jacob Hardy would help us get them back. But, Jacob was dead, and your lawyers lied and ignored me, and I believed you'd do the same.''

He quietly studied her. "So, you took all of them?"

She had almost forgotten that little discrepancy and vigorously shook her head. "No. I only took three. I was as shocked as you that others were missing."

Davina watched Justin absently rub his chin and walk to the window.

"I've waited too long and now you don't believe me. I should leave."

"That's not it. I'd already figured it out that you took the paintings. I was just waiting for you to admit it. And your father . . ." He scratched his head and darted a glance her way. "That wasn't quite as obvious."

"You do believe me?" She asked the question hesitantly. "I should have told you earlier at the cabin, when we first talked openly, but I wasn't sure about us."

"Let's say yes, I believe you. What made you change your mind?"

"I decided I had to trust you. I wasn't comfortable with so many barriers between us." She watched his broad back flex under the sweater as he straightened his shoulders.

"Have you considered the other reasons I should have known this sooner?" He turned to her from the window. "What if the theft from your apartment and the murder are somehow connected?"

"My only link to the murder is that I found Robert. No one should have suspected I took the paintings or that they were in my apartment, except for you." She thought about the man who followed her and wondered where he fit in.

"Someone knew. Did you run into anyone else that night we met? Could you have mentioned your past link with Maceo to someone?"

"I don't think so." She searched her memory. "I did talk with Mr. Mangley during his photography exhibit, but that was because he knew both our fathers in the early days of the business." Davina sighed. "It's strange when I openly admit to my father's real identity. David and I still aren't used to it."

"How long have you known?"

"A little over a year and a half now, just before . . ." She calmly knit her fingers as her words trailed off.

"I lost the chance to fully appreciate my father before he died. I guess you would argue the same, only the circumstances are different. I wasted my time—but it was time you never had."

"He made the choice to run, but that meant he'd never get the chance to tell what really happened that night in Atlanta."

"My mom said rumors circulated about a girlfriend of his who had been raped. Maceo severely beat the man, who died from his injuries later on."

"She was my mother, Justin." A chill coursed through Davina and she rubbed her upper arm. She could see that Justin, too, was affected. "Dad was so distressed by her pain and shame that he committed a violent act and then took off with her. He never forgave himself and reasoned, why should the justice system?"

"At least they had each other."

"Not for long. A few years later, David and I were born while they lived in Florida. They had changed addresses so many times. And after my mother's accidental death while we were small, Dad was never the same again—he started to drink." She looked away. "Some time during elementary school, we finally settled in one place, but it was the beginning of my father's descent into his personal hell."

"Davina, I'm sorry. That explains a lot of your anger and tenacity."

With a tilt of her head, Davina sloughed off the sympathy. "It's why I intend to keep the promise I made to him. David is quietly researching the charges against him and our legal options. It felt good when I talked with Robert. He understood and enjoyed the impact of Maceo's art. I think Dad would like to be remembered for that."

"You didn't tell me you and Robert discussed Maceo."

Davina nodded. "That's all we ever talked about. He heard about what I'd said to the board, about being familiar with Maceo's work firsthand, and he was curious for any information I had."

"What did he want to know?" Justin's strides brought him back to Davina.

"Oh, things like if I'd ever seen any of the original works, which ones, that sort of thing. I didn't say a lot because I didn't want it known that I took the paintings. He was awfully proud of the fact that he had cleaned and authenticated an original Maceo that was to be loaned to an off-site exhibit.''

''When did all this happen?''

''I think it was the day I signed the contract with you. I met him as I toured the gallery with Alli and Linda. Why?''

When Justin didn't respond, Davina interpreted the enigmatic expression below his knitted brows. ''You don't think my conversations with Robert had anything to do with . . . anything?'' She spread her hands wide as her own mind skipped about for answers. ''What are you thinking?''

He pulled her close to his side; they walked into the sitting room where he sat her down on the sofa.

''I honestly don't know, but it won't hurt to turn every idea over to see if it fits our puzzle.'' He claimed the cushion next to her. ''We've got to find the paintings, Davina. I've got to give my board answers that don't point to you.''

''Otherwise, you'll have no choice?'' There was a hint of humor in her voice.

''That's plan B.'' He gave her a crooked grin. ''Is there anything else you need to get off your chest?'' he asked as he drew her to him.

At her slow nod, Justin frowned. ''I only meant that hypothetically. There's more?''

''I saw Lawrence again, earlier this evening.''

Justin straightened in the chair. ''I see.''

''No, I don't think you do.'' Davina touched his arm to keep him at her side. ''It was a necessary chore. Seeing him again in the gallery was a shock, but I needed closure on that part of my life. Once and for all.'' She looked Justin in the eyes. ''And, that was all to it.''

''Why wouldn't you tell me the whole story between you two? Did you love him very much?''

Davina's smile conflicted with the roil of emotions he'd summoned. ''You don't ask easy questions, do you? I didn't tell you because I wanted to forget. I wanted it to fade along with all the other pathetic choices and memories that harbored in my past. I loved him in that time and space. He protected my exposed soul, and paid attention and compliments to me when I had no concept of my feminine persona.

I gave him control and I mistook it for love. In retrospect, it was reliance more than anything else.''

''What about David and Natalie? Were they around?''

''They'd left home by then, though at different times, to go to college. And I was alone, struggling and overwhelmed by my father's mounting health problems and his incessant drinking.'' She looked at Justin. ''I was going to school at night, working all day, and holding together the threads of my family in between. Then Lawrence entered the picture. He said and did all the right things, or so I thought. Before I knew it, I had become dependent on him. We were together for three years. You see, I was so desperate to give up control of my wretched life, even if for a little while, that when he asked me to marry him, I didn't hesitate to accept. What more could a girl want?''

''Her love returned?'' Justin's hand caressed Davina's.

''No such luck for me.'' Davina gave a wry smile. ''It turns out he was sleeping with at least two women at both the high school and college. It all caught up with him, though, just days before my wedding. Lucky me. You can imagine what it did for my confidence. In my own way, I probably used him just as badly.''

''You were vulnerable, innocent, and he knew it.''

''But, I learned from the experience.''

Justin raised himself from the sofa. ''I'm glad you've closed the chapter on Lawrence because David was right—he's a bastard. I understood David's rage this afternoon. There was a moment when I didn't care if he beat the guy to a pulp. Because you deserved better, much better.''

Davina also stood. Her body was achingly close to Justin's and she drew in the scent she had come to know as his. ''I feel better.''

''Confession cleanses the soul,'' Justin said as he raised his fingers to stroke her cheek.

''So, what do you have to confess?'' Davina basked in his attention.

Justin pulled her into his arms. ''That I didn't know if you'd come tonight. That I've wanted to kiss you since you got here,'' he whispered, his breath hot against her ear.

He tilted her chin up so that his mouth covered hers in a gentle kiss that was as intoxicating as fine wine. Both of them drank in its sweetness, savored its velvet warmth, and reveled in the comfort it offered.

As they came apart, Davina burned under the heat of his gaze.

His fingers moved from her chin and tenderly traced the line of her cheekbone and jaw. "Why don't you get comfortable and I'll close out some business I started downstairs. Have you eaten yet?" At the shake of her head, he said, "I can get something to drink, whip up a couple of sandwiches from the kitchen, and join you back up here in a while."

Davina nodded her agreement and watched Justin leave. As the door closed behind him, she dropped back onto the sofa and, nervously, chewed her lip. A flicker of apprehension coursed through her as her mind relived the heady kiss.

"Christ," she whispered through her sighs, and tried to relax. "How comfortable can I get when I still have more to tell you, Justin?"

Meanwhile, Justin had already retraced his steps to the other wing, but Davina's earlier words still rang in his head: *Robert had just cleaned and authenticated an original Maceo that was to be loaned out . . . It was the day I signed the contract with you.* He had not approved any Maceo artwork for off-site exhibits, so who did? Marc? Douglas? By the time Davina had signed her contract, the auditors had already discovered the paintings missing in the inventory report. So, why does a painting that's missing from the count show up in the lab to be cleaned, only to quickly disappear again?

Then, a possibility occurred to him. Since the precise timing of the inventory count wasn't generally known, the paintings unofficially removed would have been lost in the count. All he had to do now was find out why a painting would be removed and returned outside the proper channels? He remembered what Connie had said about stolen art and forgeries and cleared his head with a shake. This had been some day for revelations.

The grating racket of the buzzer was relentless, and Davina finally turned over in the bed toward the abrasive sound. Peeking through sleep-tinged eyes, she recognized the brightly lit intercom button on the phone, and pressed it.

"Yes?" she mumbled.

"Good morning, Davina. I'm sorry to wake you, but your brother is on the phone. It's the blinking line." Mrs. Hardy's voice was a cheerful salute to the day.

What time was it? It had been a night that didn't include much sleep. She looked to the other side of the bed, expecting Justin. Then she remembered his kiss before he returned to his room only a few hours earlier.

"Oh, and Justin left for the office some time ago," Mrs. Hardy was saying. "He didn't want to wake you so early, but said he'd see you there later."

"Thank you," Davina managed to say. She pulled the sheet against her nakedness and flushed over the thought that his mother might have guessed why she was still in bed at so late an hour. She touched the blinking light, then pressed the phone to her ear as she dropped back onto the pillow. "Hi, David."

"Hey, what took you so long?"

Davina heard a cacophony of stereophonic noises in the background and deduced he was at the airport. "I was just getting up. Are you in Chicago?"

"I'm still waiting for my flight to be called so I can leave. I forgot to ask you last night when you think you might make the trip?"

Davina rubbed her eyes. "Some time this week. You thought I forgot it was my turn, didn't you?"

"No," he said. "It's always rough on you, that's all. With Lawrence showing up, I figured it'd be especially hard this time."

"I'm okay with it, especially since I told Justin last night about Dad's real identity and the paintings I took."

"How'd he react?"

"Surprised, and a little angry that we kept it from him, but I think he understands why."

"And you sound too calm and rested. You didn't tell him all of it, huh?"

Davina rolled onto her side, uncomfortable with the question. "No, but I will. It's best that I break it gradually. You think I should've told him everything?"

"I told you before, it's your call." He paused a moment. "Vinny, they're announcing my flight. Call me with Keller's latest evaluations.''

"Okay, and I'll make sure Natalie knows when I leave.''

They said their goodbyes and David clicked off the line. Davina lay motionless as she stared into the ceiling of the dusky room. She considered how she would leave town for a day without arousing Justin's suspicion and thus avoid questions she couldn't answer right now. *Didn't you just learn anything, Davina? Tell him the truth before it's too late.* A jarring screech announcing the phone off the hook shattered her disquieting thoughts, and she quickly replaced it in the cradle. She was now officially awake.

Davina stopped at Nora's desk on her way to Justin's office.

"Is he in?'' Davina asked, gesturing toward the closed double doors.

"He had to stand in for one of the other managers in a meeting at Callaway Gardens,'' Nora explained. "He won't return until tonight, probably after ten. Can anyone else help you?''

Davina couldn't believe her luck. He'd be gone all day. She gave Nora a broad smile. "No, I'll see him tomorrow.''

She returned to the gallery office and, as quick as one-two-three, made plane reservations for the trip, called Natalie, and told Rosa not to expect her at closing that night. She jotted the flight numbers on a notepad, and calculated she could still make it back to Justin's house before he returned that night, thus avoiding his questions.

Since her flight would leave in less than two hours, she appealed to Natalie's sense of drama, and arranged an airport curbside drop off. The navy slacks and sweater she wore under her red blazer would have to do for the trip.

Davina had stuffed her papers into her tote bag, explained away her hasty departure to Rosa, and now waited for Natalie to arrive. She had pulled off a perfect plan. As the purpose of this monthly journey started to push its way forward, though, her light mood became increasingly morose. To chase off the growing shadows, she picked up an artist's pencil and put it to a sheet of rag paper. And as impressions surfaced of the man who had followed her, she sketched them on the sheet.

Nora looked up into Justin's face as he strode past her desk on his way to his office.

"I thought you were gone for the day?" She was around her desk in a flash and followed him through the doors. "It's only noon."

"Change of plans," Justin said. "Actually, Ray was able to make the meeting after all, and I had a lot to do here, so here I am. Anything come up?" He shrugged from his coat and opened the armoire for a hanger.

"The reports you ordered are on your desk ready for your signature. Stephanie wants you to go over the new circulation figures. She thinks they might be helpful when you meet with the bank. And, you still haven't called the bank."

Justin frowned as he hung the coat inside the closet. "Maybe I should have stayed. Anything else?"

"Miss Spenser came by and I told her you'd be gone all day. She's in the gallery, but she said it could wait until tomorrow. And, Mr. Preston called."

Justin looked up as he closed the armoire door. "Important?"

Nora smiled. "He thinks every message he leaves is important. He said to make sure you call him on his cell phone as soon as possible."

"I'll go to the gallery and see Davina. In fact, I'll call Connie from there."

"She's in the ticket line at the airport. Do you want me to follow her to the gate?" The words were rushed as the man spoke from a wall of telephones inside the main terminal. He could see the woman from a distance as she stood in the long queue to await a ticket agent.

"Go ahead," the voice on the other end of the phone urged. "Get a flight number and call me right back."

The man hung up the phone, and checked to make sure the slim woman in the red jacket was still in line. He spied a chair near a huge potted ficus; it faced the lobby that led to all gates. Pulling a newspaper from under his arm, he carefully postured a stretch before he sat down. He presented a picture of a man engrossed in the sports page, but he kept a watchful eye on his quarry.

"Where's Davina?" Justin issued the words to Rosa when he noticed the gallery office was empty.

"She's out for a while. Her friend Natalie came by and they left together."

Justin smiled and turned on his heels. "I'll just use the phone in her office."

He walked around the desk to the phone and punched in Connie's number. The office was fast becoming hers as personal items graced the desk's surface and the nearby console. A small sculpture had been conformed into a paperweight, and it rested on top of a sketch of a man's face. Justin tucked the phone between his neck and shoulder as his attention turned to the drawing. He picked it up. The man depicted was young, of foreign descent, and wore straight black hair. A question mark had been drawn under the picture. Connie's familiar voice interrupted Justin's thoughts.

"Investigations, Connie speaking."

"Hey, it's me." Justin turned to the other side of the desk and replaced the drawing there. But before he turned away, his eyes were snared by an innocuous white pad with a delta symbol boldly doodled at the top.

"Justin, I've been trying to reach you since last night."

"Nora told me you called this morning." He stared at the pad. Below the symbol sat two sets of numbers with clock times written across from them. With his thoughts divided between the scribbled numbers and Connie on the phone, Justin's words were drawn and slow. "Do you have something for me?"

"Man, I've got new information and I didn't want to wait too long with it."

Justin wasn't listening to Connie. He concentrated on the numbers before him and what they meant. *Delta Airlines flight numbers, the top one a departure at twelve-fifty in the afternoon. Did that mean*

the lower one was a return flight? From where? Was Davina planning
a trip? Had she taken one? He remembered Connie was on the line.

"I'm sorry, I didn't hear you. What did you say?"

"Her father's not dead, Justin. Davina Spenser's father is alive."

Justin's shock was swift and sure.

Davina rose from the center seat in economy class and gratefully
stretched her legs as she waited her turn to step into the narrow aisle
to deplane. She was glad she didn't have to go through baggage claim.
A quick stop at the car rental counter and she would be on her way.

As she briskly exited the jetway and entered the terminal, she felt
the strong surge of air-conditioning that attempted to conceal the
familiar mugginess that told her she had come home again, to Miami,
Florida.

CHAPTER
TWENTY-NINE

You Can Go Home Again

The Florida afternoon had been overcast when Davina stepped
through the automatic sliding glass doors of Miami's International
Airport terminal. She had hustled through the throngs of passengers
to anxiously claim her rental car.

Now she drove the compact north along the smooth corridor of
Interstate 95, the palms and scattered islands of flora on the wayside
still sultry and green in October. The road led her from the chaotic
bustle of the airport and closer to the efficient calm of the chronic

care unit at North Beach Hospital and Medical Center where her father lay comatose.

Davina thought about that fateful night early last year when so much had happened to change her and David's life. To have her father confess on his expected deathbed that he was someone else, someone she had never imagined, was an enormous shock to her soul. And to then have him slip into a coma soon after that confession effectively numbed her spirit for some time.

After tests showed their father's coma was irreversible, David had urged her to move to Atlanta where he was employed. With the deterioration of their father's health following so closely on the heels of her disaster with Lawrence, Davina knew her brother worried about her. So, upon arranging long-term placement care for their father, she finally agreed. With David and Natalie's help, she slowly rose from the depths of her own apathy, and a plan to confront Jacob Hardy and pursue the legacy her father had spoken of took root.

She and David alternately made the "trip" to their father's bedside once each month. It was a simple vigil and conference with either the nurse manager or doctor; but it was a satisfying time for Davina because each visit assured her that he was safe in that peaceful limbo that existed between life and death, and she was given more precious time to continue her quest to bring his legacy to fruition.

As Davina smoothly changed lanes and turned off the expressway at the 95th Street exit, it all became familiar again. How long had it been since she had left this city for Atlanta? Almost a year? As she traveled the secondary road, she moved deeper into the economic oblivion of North Miami's inner city. There was a continuous stream of last-chance, one-story strip mall establishments that had seen better days: pawn shops, liquor stores, quick grocers. . . .

She remembered the area as rife with opportunistic crime. But out of the heart of this rough and tumble community that had known better days rose the beautiful and stately art-deco building known as North Beach Medical Center. With its majestic seven stories gracing the skyline, perfectly manicured lawns, and lush, exotic flowers and trees, it seemed some great joke played on the otherwise sad surrounding community.

Davina turned into the parking area and quickly found an empty space. As a courtesy, she had called the hospital from the airport since it wasn't necessary to stand on formality due to the state of the patients housed in the long-term care unit. She could drop in whenever she chose. Her only concern was whether she'd catch up with the physician on call for the day.

Davina pushed past the main doors and walked through the atrium to the elevators. The hospital tried hard to look anything but what it was. And it succeeded. It brazenly wore the mask of an avant-garde museum with its murals, back-lit paintings latched to the wall, and larger-than-life sculptures. Even the people who stopped to enjoy the art looked neither sick nor desolate. In fact, they were quite taken by the artsy ambience.

She entered the elevator behind two other women and pressed the second-floor button. When the doors opened again, she stepped out onto her floor and paused in the empty corridor. The ambience of the first floor had traveled no farther. This was the hospital. She swallowed her dread and moved purposefully down the institutional gray carpet into the adjoining hallway.

To her left, she heard the muffled shouts of voices that came from behind the barred gates of the psychiatric care unit. It was unnerving, juxtaposed across from the peaceful unit where her father slept—an oddity to visitors at this otherwise state-of-the-art hospital, but not necessarily the occupants.

She reached the wood and metal doors of the chronic care unit and, through the webbed glass pane, could see the workstation in the center of the huge ward. Several uniformed nurses worked at the pushed together desks. Davina pressed open the doors and walked toward the group.

"Can I help you?" A young nurse looked up from a stack of papers.

Davina couldn't recall her face and started to state her business when another nurse came over to join them.

"Miss Spenser, you're here already to see your father."

Davina turned to the older, gray-haired nurse, and immediately recognized her as Mrs. Keller, the amiable nurse manager she and David knew from previous visits and the one she had telephoned from the airport. Her presence gave Davina's spirits a boost.

"Yes," she answered. "Traffic wasn't too bad this time."

The two women engaged in a warm hug. Eleanor Keller had shown extraordinary kindness and understanding from the beginning as Davina and her brother dealt with the gravity of their father's condition. From a shared empathy, a friendship was forged.

"How long will you be here this time? And how is that brother of yours?"

"I'll only be here for the day, and David is fine. He's in Chicago on business. I was hoping I'd see the doctor, but I missed him, huh?"

"He made rounds earlier this morning," Mrs. Keller said. "I'll put a call in and we'll see if you can talk with him before you leave. How's that?"

Davina smiled again. "Thank you, I'd like that. Can I go back now?"

"Sure. I'll go with you."

Davina walked around the desks and headed for one of eight cubicle spaces in the large, open ward that had been set up for the bed-ridden patients. Each cubicle accommodated two to four beds.

Mrs. Keller took the lead and talked as she walked. "Mr. Spenser's been doing great this month. He did have a bout with pneumonia, but the antibiotics did the trick almost immediately, so we didn't see a reason to alarm you with a call."

She stopped at the door of a room that contained three beds, all separated by ceiling-hung curtains. Mrs. Keller briskly walked in and pulled the curtain around the two beds farthest away. The remaining bed held Davina's father.

Davina no longer wept when she saw him. In that respect, time had become a friend and she had grown accustomed to his disturbingly quiet body. In other aspects, time was a nemesis that exacted a loyal pain from her still grieving heart.

The concrete walls were painted pale yellow, and the high window was never meant for viewing outside. Davina was used to the inhospitable interior and paid it no mind as she walked to her father's bedside. She stood near the ventilator that beeped near his head. The trachea tube that snaked from his neck to the machine had been pinned out of the way so that beyond the austere conditions, he could have been asleep in his room in their old apartment. She pulled a chair close to the bed and sat down.

As if on cue, Mrs. Keller quietly stole from the room as Davina reached out and touched her father: his arms, hands, brow, and finally, she smoothed his wooly, unruly hair. She leaned back into the chair and stroked his cool hand.

"Dad, a lot has happened since my last visit." Her voice was small, yet strong with the conviction that her words did not fall on deaf ears.

"David told you some of it last month, but there's more," she continued. "I've met another of your old friends." And, as if she were sharing stories over tea, she proceeded to bring him up to date on all that had happened since her last visit.

Justin was restless as he sat in his office. He wanted to act on the information Connie had brought him, but patience was the key.

"How sure are you about your sources, now that someone else is asking them the same questions we are?" he asked Connie.

Connie sat across from him at the conference table. "Damn sure. And we're on the right track. You'll have your bombshell by the time we're finished."

Abruptly, Justin stood from his chair. "I almost forgot to show you this." He went to his desk and came back with a pencil sketch of a man.

Connie looked up from the table. "Show me what?"

Justin held out the sketch for Connie. "I found this in Davina's office."

The overcast sky had finally released its promised rain when Davina left the hospital that evening. Calculating that she had roughly two hours before her return flight to Atlanta, she drove the car to her next stop.

Within ten minutes, she saw the bright orange sign of the public storage business emerge through the shadowy evening mist. She drove through the main gate and to the building she had rented when she first left Miami for Atlanta.

She parked the car and sprinted through the rain drizzle to unlock the door. She pushed the creaky metal door wide and clicked the light switch inside the dark space. The twelve-by-twelve room became flooded with bright, incandescent light from a bare bulb fixed in the ceiling.

Awesome shadows grew from cardboard boxes stacked tall near one wall, furniture against another, and canvases of all sizes propped along the remaining two. The last tangible memories of her bittersweet family days had been reduced to fit this room and lived alongside the mildew and musty odors. She left the door open, partly as a precaution, but also out of fear. Davina carried a childhood phobia of crawling insects, and imagined that multilegged bugs lurked simply to give her a good scare.

Davina shook off the fear and turned to the nearest stack of canvases. She sorted through them in search of the one she wanted. Some of the paintings were her own, others were her father's. She could see that his fascination with color continued from his early work, though the later work was darker themed.

"Where did David put it?" She spoke out loud to break the eerie silence as she sorted another stack. And there, she found it.

It was the Maceo painting of her mother in a garden, the one she had taken from Hardy and that had been miraculously overlooked by the miscreant who ransacked her apartment. It was still wrapped in the brown paper and oilskin. David had stored it here on his last trip but Davina wanted it back in Atlanta. Visibly relieved that this chore was done, she gave the room a last glance before she escaped through the door.

The drag from the cigarette felt good in Marc's lungs. It had been a long time since he had indulged in the habit, and it was proper that he do it in the dark. Recent times had been trying, and he had fallen into a lot of old habits, dirty habits.

He stood in the dirt and overgrown weeds at the side of the warehouse on Old Marietta Street downtown and waited for his contacts to show up. The three-story warehouse was a gargantuan eyesore among others, with its blackened rows of squared windows across the top story and brand new padlocked security doors at the front and back. The city wanted it torn down, but the taxes were always paid, in advance, and the owner never seemed to be available for negotiations.

Marc blinked from the oncoming lights of a slowly approaching car. He threw the cigarette down and crushed it with his foot. He walked out to meet the car that stopped in front of the building. The back window of the towne car floated down. Marc bent his head and peeked into the dark car and saw the man who had been able to purchase his soul.

"Is everything ready?" the man asked with an incline of his head.

"I believe so," Marc said, with only a moment's hesitation.

The man's chuckle had a cynical sound. "Meet us at the back entrance." He leaned back in the seat and motioned to the driver to pull into the rear.

Marc stood back from the car as it turned into the lot and drove through the weeds to the back and out of sight. Expelling a heavy sigh, he quickly followed on foot. "I'll be glad when this is over," he said. "I'm not cut out for this."

Davina unsnapped her seatbelt and joined the other passengers in a synchronous ballet to reclaim property that had been stored away at the start of the flight. She pulled her tote from the overhead compartment and checked once again that the painting was safely stored inside.

As she filed through the narrow aisle and received the obligatory goodbye greeting from the flight crew, she looked at her watch. Only fifteen minutes off schedule but, so far, everything had worked out. She would be back at Justin's house within the hour, and probably arrive when he did. Surely he would find nothing suspicious in that.

Justin pushed the front of his trench coat back and shoved his hands into his suit pockets. He leaned against a column and observed the passengers file into the gate area from the jetway. He was not in a good mood. It had been a long, busy day, and he was tired. He was also mad at Davina. She had become his personal dilemma, an enigma that turned from delight to torment in the span of a day.

He watched the crowd spill through the doorway; the walkie-talkie equipped agents directed the flow with quickly dispensed directions and information. And then, Justin saw her. As always, her striking face caught his eye. And as usual, her full mouth was turned slightly downward in her signature haughty frown. When she looked around, he was disappointed that her hair was severely pulled back in a tight bun. He knew she searched for Natalie.

As the crowd dispersed, she was fully in Justin's view. He allowed himself to stare a moment longer before he slowly strode forward so she could see him, and he could enjoy her discomfort. He wasn't disappointed.

"Justin," she gasped, her eyes wide. "What are you doing here?"

"I could ask the same of you," he replied evenly.

"Well, I . . . I . . ." she stammered between glances about the room before she turned back to Justin. "How long have you been here?"

"Long enough to send Natalie home." He watched her face drop. *Good.*

Davina looked away. "That can only mean I'm riding with you?"

She didn't wait for him or an answer, but walked ahead into the wide aisle of the concourse. Justin easily caught up with her. Leave it to her to show righteous indignation that she was found out.

They walked on toward the terminal until Davina spoke again.

"How did you know I was here? Did Natalie tell you?"

"No, you did." He watched her eyes settle on him a moment before they darted away. "I stopped by your office and saw the flight numbers on your desk. Since your car was still in the parking lot after dark, I became concerned"—he turned to give her a pointed glance—"and I played a hunch that the flight numbers were yours and figured you'd need a ride home. Natalie, by the way, understood completely."

"I'll bet she did," was Davina's stubborn retort.

Justin put his hand on her shoulder and stopped her. "What was so important that you had to leave town so fast? And Miami, no less?" He watched her eyes raise to his, but he refused to hide the anger and doubt he felt so strongly.

Davina's brows slanted in scorn. "What is it you want me to say?"

"Try the truth."

She bit down on the inside of her jaw and continued walking. "I had to check on some things David and I keep in storage in Miami. You weren't in the office when I left."

Out of the corner of his eye, Justin saw her look at him, but he didn't look back. Her lying did little to abate his anger.

"Do you have any other bags to collect?"

"No."

"I'll carry that one for you." He reached across Davina for her tote, but she moved her arm away.

"I'm fine," she said.

"Suit yourself."

They proceeded through the airport in an awkward silence of their own making.

The silence continued all the way to the house. After each bid the other a cursory good night, they parted ways at the stairs to their respective suite.

Justin entered his rooms and slammed the door. He dropped his coat onto the back of a nearby chair and continued into the bedroom. He had given her time to tell him about her father in Miami, the sketch he'd found, even her real purpose for the claims. But, she wouldn't do it—she wasn't going to tell him one thing. He tossed his keys to the dresser and pulled his tie off.

And what about his own stratagem? When would he tell her all he knew, not to mention how he found it out? He shook his head while he removed his shoes. He would miss being with her tonight, but he couldn't go to her, not when he knew she continued to lie. He and Davina made an unlikely pair with their inherent differences, and they'd have to pay the piper soon. As he pulled his shirt from his waistband, he heard a light rap at the door.

"Come in," he called out, and retraced his steps across the carpeted floor to the door. Davina stood there. Justin's eyes locked with hers as she came inside.

Davina had discarded her jacket and bags in her room before she came to Justin. She had been careless to let him discover her plan, but she couldn't allow this coldness between them to build any further. It would destroy the little remaining trust they had. So, she would end it. Davina pushed the door closed and gave the suite a quick glance. She had never been in here before, but the cool colors and styling were right for Justin. She strolled over to him.

"You didn't say much in the car," she said, and stopped in front of him.

"What can I say that hasn't already been said?" He kept a wary eye on her as her hands reached out to his waist, but he kept his own rigidly at his side.

She turned her face up to his. "Nothing, everything . . . I just don't want your anger between us . . . not tonight." Her hands pushed underneath his shirt and massaged the warm flesh there. Justin's eyes narrowed as he tried to figure out this Davina, but his body was quickly succumbing to her lusty distractions. She stretched up against him and reached to kiss his mouth. Without a thought, Justin met her kiss while his hands curved against her hips.

Davina savored the luxury that was his touch. "I'm sorry about the misunderstanding tonight," she whispered between kisses.

"No words."

He picked her up and her legs wrapped around his waist. He wound his hand in her hair as they kissed, and dislodged the pins that held it in the unlikely bun.

They slowly moved in an erotic tangle to the sofa.

CHAPTER THIRTY

The Wagons Are Circled

Justin looked at the painting of his father on the office wall. He sat on the edge of his desk, arms folded, and contemplated the fact that the art continued to be an eloquent statement of Maceo's genius. And the man was still alive.

Connie's theory of an illegal syndicate's attempt to move in since Jacob's death made even more sense now. Somehow, the gallery art was being tapped into, and without his knowledge. The word he had selectively spread last week, that Hardy Enterprises was in dire need of cash and willing to part with some of their valuable art pieces, could bring him closer to the how. This early Maceo painting, often sought after by collectors, had been specifically named. Connie had cautioned him against mentioning his ultimate plan to anyone, including Davina.

Justin let out a loud sigh. He thought about the lustily aggressive Davina who seduced him last night. He had loved it. She was probably smarting from the note he left by her pillow this morning, though, that told her to ride in with Alli.

"Got a minute?"

Justin jerked around and saw Marc's head inside the door. "Sure, come on in," he said, and returned his attention to the painting.

Marc closed the door behind him and joined Justin in his observation. "So, are you really going to part with it?"

Justin raised a brow in his direction. "What makes you ask?" He saw the folded newspaper in Marc's hand.

"This." He handed the paper to Justin, then dropped into the chair.

"Mr. Chavis at the *Business Leader* is at it again, I see." Justin smiled as he scanned the two-column front-page story. He didn't mention to Marc that he had already seen the article. "Sources unnamed. Of course."

"Is it true?" Marc asked. "Your memo said nothing about selling paintings."

"It says here that our cash need has reached a critical point and we're ready to unload some of our prized collection." He looked at Marc. "Now that'll really scare away investors. This reminds me of Dad's predicament about a year ago."

"It was different then. We had a more stable cash picture, and a ready investor to offer us a hand."

"Dennis Knight of Knight Industries offered the hand, right? No hard promises made." It was a statement meant to belittle the deal.

Marc bristled at the suggestion. "We didn't have the option to be selective. You've seen that contract," Marc said. "It was all up front, no hidden agenda."

Justin offered Marc a tight smile. "You're right. Pretty cut and dried."

"You didn't answer me. Are you going to sell this one after all these years?"

"Charlie tells me that with it as the center piece, an auction could easily pull in more than enough cash to stave off the bank until we stop the information hemorrhage here and win back our investors." He handed the paper back to Marc and stood from the desk. "No, never. It would only be a temporary fix, anyway."

Marc looked at the paper. "That means Chavis got screwed with his information source this time."

Justin sat in his chair behind the desk. "True. His source has been impeccable. Until now."

"You don't seem surprised or upset about this," Marc said. "You want to tell me why?" He dropped the paper on the desk.

Justin shook his head. "Not right now. Maybe later. Will you be available?"

"Stephanie wants me to sit in on her meeting. Otherwise, I'll be around."

As Marc stood to leave, Justin stopped him with another comment. "When I was in New York, I usually voted by proxy, so a few of the board members are still unfamiliar to me. Who is the newest sitting member?"

"That would be, uh, Jamal King, from the State House, I believe."

Justin leaned back in his chair. "I had lunch with him not too long ago and he's in his second term. And it's not Helena McDuffie, either." He looked at Marc. "That leaves Andrew Jeter."

"Right, right," Marc said. He shoved his hands into his pockets and jingled the coins there. "It almost slipped my mind. He hasn't been on a full term." Marc chuckled. "He's always pretty vocal about things, like an old-timer."

Justin turned his gaze back to the painting. "He is pretty comfortable making decisions as a neophyte voting member."

"Any reason for asking?"

"None worth commenting on," was Justin's noncommittal answer.

"I'll see you later, after the meeting," Marc said, and left.

Justin thought about Marc's comments a moment more before he reached across the desk and pressed the intercom for Nora.

"Hi, boss. You need me?"

"Nora, pull up the records on the nonfamily board members. In particular, I want nomination information . . . who made the recommendation, references, and the terms of their appointment."

"How soon do you need it?"

"Yesterday."

"I have that much time, huh?" she quipped. "I'll get on it now."

Justin turned again and absorbed the mesmerizing stare from his father's eyes. Did someone make a deal with the devil?

Davina had just straightened her bed when she heard Alli's voice from the door.

"I'm ready to leave when you are, Davina."

"I'm coming," she answered, and gave her appearance one last peek in the mirror. She picked up her purse and joined Alli in the wide hallway. "Thanks for letting me ride in with you."

"No problem," Alli said with a smile as she led Davina down the hall. "I want to let Mom know we're leaving. She's at the end of the wing."

"Does she work at the office every day?" Davina asked.

"She spends time there each week, but not like she did when Daddy was alive. It's been six months since he died, and today she's decided to go through his personal things . . . clothes, stuff like that. She tried to do it before, but couldn't."

Davina understood Mrs. Hardy's reticence in departing with the tangible possessions that defined a loved one.

They reached an ornately carved door at the end of the hall. Alli knocked before she opened the door and called out, "Mom, Davina and I are leaving."

"Come in, dear." Mrs. Hardy's muffled voice floated from the interior room.

Davina followed Alli through to the next room, and they both stopped at the rose-carved entrance. Mrs. Hardy was swathed in a dressing gown and sat in the midst of what could only be described as a chaos of clothing, suitcases, boxes, and such. They cluttered the surface space and a good deal of the floor, too.

Mrs. Hardy looked up at them as she dabbed her eyes with a handkerchief. "I decided to start early."

"Oh, Mom." Alli went to her. "Are you sure you want to do this by yourself?"

"I'll be all right. Here, help me up."

Alli helped her to stand. "Look at you, and you're crying."

"They're not unhappy tears, Alli." She stroked her daughter's hair. "They're from joy and remembrance."

"But, Mom . . ." Alli started.

"Let me get through this, okay? And don't you dare go to that office and tell your brother and sisters that I'm a mess." She smiled. "I'm a happy mess."

Davina had quietly stood near the doorway and watched them, but now spoke. "She'll be okay, Alli. Let her handle it."

The women turned to Davina.

"Thank you, child," Mrs. Hardy said. "I believe you understand."

Davina smiled. She truly did.

Later, in the gallery office, Davina talked with David on the phone and apprised him of what had happened in the aftermath of her trip to Florida.

"I mean, I almost lost it when I saw Justin waiting for me in the airport. I've really come to hate what we're doing. I'll feel better when I tell him everything."

"We're all doing the same thing, Vinny. It's called covering your butt."

"I need to find someone else who knew Dad and Jacob."

"When I return tomorrow, I'll take the pictures and talk with Mr. Carter."

"I'm doing that today," Davina said without hesitation.

"No." David's voice boomed through the phone. "Not when someone out there is after the same information we are. Wait until I get back." At her stubborn silence, he added, "It's dangerous. It s best if we do this together."

"I know," she replied.

"I'll see you tomorrow, then."

Davina lay the phone in the cradle. Time was important, and when he got in tomorrow, she'd be able to tell him what she found out today. She fished in her purse for Otis Carter's number, then quickly punched it into the phone.

Justin studied the paperwork on the board members Nora had pulled together for him when the intercom buzzed.

"What is it, Nora? I wasn't to be disturbed."

"Mrs. Hardy is on line one. She says it's important."

"I'll take it."

Justin picked up the phone even as he continued to read the information in the report. "Hi, Mom. What's up."

Her voice was strained and quietly measured. "Hello, son. I came across some things you should see as soon as possible."

Justin looked up from his reading, instantly wary. "What kind of things?"

"They belonged to your father."

He stood up behind the desk. "Are you okay?" He heard her pause, and knew she wasn't.

"This won't wait, Justin. And I haven't told anyone else."

"I'll be home as soon as I can arrange to leave."

Davina knocked on the door of Otis Carter's high-rise apartment downtown. She heard a voice from the other side, then the door opened.

"Well, Miss Davina, your call was a surprise." He backed away from the door, his cane tapping in rhythm to his steps. He wore black slacks and sweater, and his missing beret revealed a balding golden crown dotted with wisps of gray hair.

"It's good of you to see me at such short notice," she said.

The old man let out a light cackle as he shook her hand. "And you wouldn't take no for an answer.'' He moved from the doorway. ''Well, come on in.''

The room was modest and perfect for the walls filled with all manners of art, a virtual gallery of styles and subjects. She saw one of her nudes near the hallway.

''You have a wonderful collection, sir.'' She turned to view them all.

''I'm proud to add yours.'' He motioned her to the sofa and took his own seat in a huge lounger that dwarfed his small figure. ''Now, the reason for your visit?''

''I'd like you to look at some pictures from Jacob Hardy's records. Maybe you can offer some insight that might help us piece together information about his business relationship with Maceo.''

Davina handed the pictures to him. She watched as he peered and squinted at the snapshots, making assorted snorts and laughs on occasion.

''Have you had much luck talking to anybody?''

''To be honest with you, no.'' She got up from the sofa and moved to his side. ''I recognize some of the people, you and Maceo, of course.'' She pointed to other faces in the pictures. ''Also Lee Randolph, Jacob Hardy, Mr. Bivings, and Mr. Mangley, and that's about it.'' She flipped through the pictures and pointed out one face that showed up on three of the pictures. ''Who is this?''

Otis looked up at Davina. ''Do you know anything about protection rackets?''

Davina stood back on her heels, and considered the question. ''I know they exist, but that's about it. Why?''

''This man here''—he touched the face Davina had pointed out— ''was a poor excuse for a human, but we tolerated him. His name was Perry Knightman, better known as the Night Man to his clients. It's a shame to say that anything illegal you needed done, he could do it.''

Davina stared at the face of the burly man. ''Is he dead?''

''I don't know and don't care, either. In his line of business, he probably is. I know he provided protection back then, among other things, to a lot of businesses. The only thing, his price was high, too high in most cases to pay with money.''

"What do you mean?"

"He preferred to own souls and favors. Of course, he made things happen. He came to know our little group through Lee. They went back a long way."

"Mr. Randolph?" It was hard for Davina to believe that he would have associated with the likes of Perry Knightman. "Mr. Mangley told me that Lee Randolph wouldn't help Maceo out because he was jealous of him."

"A lot of us were, but it was jealousy among friends. But every success has its season. Lee learned that for himself later on. Knightman stayed around because he smelled money in Jacob."

"Do you think Mr. Hardy ultimately used his ties to Knightman to help Maceo disappear?"

Otis nodded his head. "Makes sense, especially if he needed a new identity."

"Why didn't the police figure that out and use Maceo's friends to find him?"

"Oh, they did," Otis smiled. "They were all over Jacob, but they couldn't do anything because whoever helped would never let on to the rest what they did for him, and we liked it that way. Nobody could tell on the other. We knew Jacob and Maceo were more than just good friends, and if Knightman could've helped out, you can believe Jacob went for it. But, he never told any of us anything."

"Why did you say Lee learned a lesson later on?"

Otis looked up from the pictures. "Lee didn't tell you what happened?"

"No. Maybe he didn't have the chance that night we talked."

"It's not a secret anymore. About five years after Maceo disappeared, Lee did hard time for possession of stolen property and art forgery."

The letters sat on the tabletop in the library. There were seven of them, each signed by Maceo James and sent to Jacob Hardy at a post office box. They covered the first few years after Maceo's disappearance, then stopped. No clue in the last letter explained their sudden end. Justin's hands were clasped behind him as he looked out the

library window, and into the solace of the garden. Mrs. Hardy sat
nearby.

"I should have handled your father's things right after he died, and
you wouldn't find yourself in this difficulty," Mrs. Hardy said, her
voice heavy.

"It's not your fault, Mom."

"You will deal with it, won't you?" she asked.

"Yes, but this time on my terms and when I say so. No one else
is to know."

"Of course," she uttered quietly. "Justin?"

He turned from the window, his expression grim as he faced his
mother.

Mrs. Hardy sat forward in her chair. "You love Davina, don't
you?"

"No one else is to know," he repeated as he walked toward her.
"I have to get back to the office." He bent and gave her a peck on
the cheek before he walked from the room.

Davina stood before the painting in Justin's office and, after having
listened to Otis Carter, looked at it with different eyes. Was Jacob's
attachment to this painting about more than the friendship that bound
him and Maceo? She looked at the intricate lines of the frame her
father had built. He had sanded and beveled the wood to perfection,
then lacquered it with faux gold leaf. She reached out and lightly
touched the nicks and imperfections it had suffered over the years.
Surely, it had taken a long time to make such a frame; it was a piece
of art in itself.

The door opened behind her and she turned to see Justin enter his
office.

"What are you doing here?" His voice was light as he tossed a
folder onto his desk before continuing in her direction.

"Remember when you said I could look at the painting whenever
I chose to?" She smiled and turned back to it. "I choose now. Are
you angry?"

Justin placed a kiss near her ear. "No, just wondering if your
explanation is as innocent as it sounds."

Davina spun around and teased, "After last night, I doubt I'll ever be innocent again." When she saw his expression, her own face fell. "Something is bothering you. What's wrong?"

And just as quickly, his expression lifted. "Nothing, except a busy day ahead." He walked to his desk and sat down. "I have a meeting in a while."

Davina followed him to the desk as she tried to fathom his changed mood. She wanted to ask him questions about what she had learned from Mr. Carter, but thought she should tell David first. She also remembered Jacob Hardy's insistence on not parting with the painting. "I hope you plan to keep the painting, like your father did."

Her statement drew Justin's stare. He ignored the warning noise in his ears and told himself her visit was perfectly innocent and what it appeared to be, and not because of the rumor he'd planted. But why, out of the blue, was she concerned about his selling the painting?

His eyes locked with hers. "It stays with the company."

"I'm glad."

Voices from the other side of the door drew their attention. Justin came to the other side of the desk. "That's Douglas here to see me."

"When David gets back tomorrow, I'll be returning to my apartment," she said as they moved to the door.

Justin stopped her at the door. "Listen, don't leave before I see you, okay?"

"But, you'll see me tonight and tomorrow."

He shook his head. "Probably not tonight."

"You're acting very strange." She peered into his eyes.

He responded by sliding his hand into the soft hair at the nape of her head, and tilting her head, placed his lips against hers. And just as quickly, he ended the kiss. "Promise you'll see me before you leave."

Davina laid a finger against her lips, then Justin's, and nodded. "Okay."

He gave her a small smile. "Go on, get out of here."

Justin opened the door and they saw Douglas. He stood next to a flashily dressed man near Nora's office area.

"Davina, it's good to see you." Douglas walked over to them. "I understand your sales are doing well, despite that messy news story."

"Yes, they are," she said, and allowed him to envelop her hand in his.

Justin waved the other man over. "Davina, I'd like you to meet one of our board members, Andrew Jeter."

Davina smiled; actually, she held in a giggle. The slim, middle-aged man had on one of the most flamboyant ties she had every seen. "How do you do?"

"The pleasure is mine," Andrew Jeter said as he stared into her eyes.

Davina was drawn to his distinctively raspy voice and piercing stare, and failed to offer him her hand, caught as she was in a fog of déjà vu. "Do I know you?" she asked. "Have we met before?"

CHAPTER THIRTY-ONE

A Shift in the Fog

Andrew Jeter slowly dropped his hand. "I don't believe so." The gravelly words stretched out into a drawl as he lifted his thick brows to Davina. "It's my loss, though."

"I was so sure of it," Davina said as she continued to study him. When she saw Justin watching with interest, she broke into a smile. "I guess I'm mistaken."

"If you'll wait in my office," Justin said, "I'll be in shortly."

As the men walked away, he took Davina by the arm. "Come over here."

Out of Nora's earshot, he turned to her. "What was that about?"

"I'm not sure," she said. "But, I know him from somewhere."

"Around here?"

Davina waved off his concern. "It's his voice, not his face, that's familiar. It's very distinctive, and now I'll drive myself crazy trying to figure out where I've heard it. Anyway," she whispered, "he dresses like a peacock, and that I would've remembered." As she spoke, Justin let out a sigh.

He glanced down the hall toward his office. "Well, it's time he got a few feathers plucked. See you later."

"Sure." Davina stared after him, still puzzling over his reaction, as he retraced his steps to his office door.

He entered his office and closed the door. "Sorry to keep you waiting, but this won't take long." Both of the men sat in chairs at the front of Justin's desk.

"You said it was important," Andrew sighed as he shifted, then recrossed his leg. "And where is everybody else?"

Justin strode to his desk and opened the folder he had tossed there earlier. "They'll be in for the special meeting tonight." He unbuttoned his coat.

"You didn't mention any meeting tonight," Andrew said. He looked to Douglas, then shot up out of his chair. "What's going on here?"

In an instant, Douglas was up with a hand on Andrew's shoulder. "Just sit down and listen," he said, and pressed the younger man back into the chair.

Andrew reclaimed his seat, but threw a cautious look at Douglas before he turned and met Justin's cold stare.

"We've uncovered a very interesting chain of events we believe are related." Justin saw the recognition of discovery emerge in Andrew's eyes.

The man gripped his chair.

"We'll start with the leaks to the newspaper."

Marc inserted a quarter into the pay phone at the diner near the gallery and dialed the number he had committed to memory.

One ring, two rings. It seemed interminable. *Would someone answer it!* A click, and then a man's voice spoke from the other end.

"Do you want to leave a message?"

"Your man on the inside has been discovered," Marc said without taking a breath. "It's out of my hands."

There was a pause, and then another voice came on, one with a clipped accent. "A slight altering of plans is necessary, then. The merchandise will be moved. Tomorrow. And Marcus, my man, one more thing. Confront the woman and get that last painting." After a moment's pause, he added, "On second thought, I'll join you."

"And what are my choices?" Andrew leaned forward with his hands on his knees. He looked from Justin to the pile of papers on the desk.

For fifteen minutes, Justin had laid out the evidence, and he relaxed. "You can resign from the board with no penalty. I'm sure you'll prepare a resignation worthy of an honorable exit. Or we can turn our evidence over to Legal and you'll be charged with corporate espionage. That way, both the police and the SEC can make even more trouble for you as well as your bosses. Of course, then you'll be ousted by the board and face a stiff penalty."

Andrew swallowed hard and straightened in the chair. "Very well, Justin," he said with face-saving bravado. "I admit to nothing, but it's clear that after your accusations, I can no longer function on the board." He stood up and turned, first to Douglas, then Justin. "You'll have my resignation in the morning." He stalked from the room and pulled the door tightly behind him.

Justin looked in that direction. "Did you hear that crap from him?" He shook his head.

"It could've gone the other way, but you handled it," Douglas said. "When you said you planned to have him out by the end of the day, well . . . I'm impressed."

"All I did was reel him in with the memo."

"I understand why you couldn't share what you were doing with any of us," Douglas said as he leaned back against the chair.

"It was a one-shot chance to trap whoever wanted to undercut our ability to get financial backing." He sorted through the papers on his desk. "Andrew thought everyone had the same information this time, so he slipped tidbits to the press."

"You think Andrew did it to make us vulnerable for a cheap buyout?"

Justin came around the desk and sat next to Douglas. "I checked the records and learned that his appointment to the board came almost immediately after we got the capital last year from Dennis Knight of Knight Industries."

"Jacob initially avoided doing business with them. Coincidence?"

"Well," Justin said, "I could accept the coincidence, until Connie discovered that Andrew is also an officer in a little business entity called Quality Electronics, which, we learned, is a blind subsidiary of Knight Industries. That little fact was buried in corporate paperwork, not meant to be found easily."

"Andrew never disclosed that in his financial statement. He knew the relationship would've been questioned. So, it's not a coincidence."

"Nor is the fact that the person instrumental in changing Dad's mind and arranging the capital from Knight Industries also recommended Andrew's placement on the board."

"That would be Marc." Douglas rubbed his chin in thought. "You think he knew Andrew was on Knight's payroll when he recommended him for the board?"

"Could be," Justin said. "It could all be part of a deal."

"Where's Marc, anyway? Shouldn't he be here?"

"He'll attend the meeting tonight." Justin tented his fingers and turned to Douglas. "We may be facing a bigger problem. After all of Dad's attempts to avoid it, I wonder if we've become infiltrated by a syndicate operation? And how far has the treachery reached?"

"I don't know about this. Are you sure it's the right place?" Natalie peered from the car window into the dark and narrow, deserted street.

"Yes," Davina answered as she parked on the broken asphalt road and cut off her lights. "When I talked with Quilla, she said to make sure I got here in a hurry. She probably doesn't want us to run into Nathan. The man has no sense of humor." She opened her car door and looked back at Natalie, who hadn't budged. "Come on, let's go."

Natalie grumbled as she opened her door and blindly stepped to the ground, which immediately gave way under her foot.

"Davina," she screeched. "Where'd you park? There's a hole here."

"Will you come on," Davina called to her in the dark, and crossed the street to the Randolph house.

They reached the set of stairs that led up to the porch of the dark house. "Watch your step," Davina warned.

"Why? You've already ruined my heels," Natalie complained from close behind.

"Who wears heels anymore, anyway?" Before Davina could rap on the door, the lightbulb on the porch blazed to life as Quilla came through the doorway.

"Davina Spenser?" she asked. Her braids were pulled into a ponytail and revealed a glowing face above her small rounded belly that pushed against the short maternity top.

Davina nodded as she took in Quilla's condition.

"I could hear you inside." She smiled and walked over to unlatch the door. "Lee is waiting."

"I didn't know you were pregnant. Congratulations. David couldn't come this time, and this is my friend, Natalie Goodman."

The women exchanged greetings, then filed into the living room where Lee Randolph sat on the sofa. Davina noticed the blanket wrapped around him and evidence of his stroke from his slanted mouth. Tonight, the room's air was cool and pleasant, the fan unused in the corner.

"Mr. Randolph . . ." Davina reached over and shook the hand that stretched from beneath the coverlet.

"Call me Lee." He spoke slowly, yet clearly. "I prefer that." Quilla motioned to the chairs across from the sofa. Davina and Natalie sat down.

"All right then, Lee. I talked with Otis Carter earlier today."

Lee's brown, creased face broke into a slightly skewed grin. "That scoundrel. I told him you came by and to look you up if he could. Told him you were asking about Jacob and Maceo."

"Thank you for mentioning it. In fact, he saw me at the celebration for my show's opening." She reached in the side pocket of her purse and pulled out the wrapped photos. "He looked at some pictures I had and recognized a man that hung with you and your artist friends, a man named Perry Knightman.''

Both Lee and Quilla reacted to the name by glancing at the other. Quilla pushed to the edge of the sofa. ''Is that why you came by?''

''It's okay.'' Lee reached to touch her hand. ''It's been a long time. That's old history. Let me see the pictures.''

Davina watched Natalie get up and move to study some of the paintings on the wall more closely while Lee looked at the photos, one by one.

''Quilla,'' Natalie called out, ''can you tell me about these paintings?''

''Go on,'' Lee urged her. Quilla left to join Natalie.

''So Otis told you about Knightman, huh?'' At Davina's nod, his attention returned to the pictures. ''We were young and never thought about what was around the corner. You can tell by the way we carried on at Jacob's old place.''

Davina moved to sit next to him and saw the photo. It was the one that Maceo made famous in his oil painting of friends laughing in a checkers game. ''There are two pictures of you guys playing cards and checkers.''

''They were taken at different times.'' He fished the other picture of the men around the table from the stack, then chuckled quietly at the memory. ''We were there all the time. Actually, Maceo wasn't taking our picture. He'd made a frame for that big old painting he did of Jacob.'' He crooked a finger at the beginnings of a frame propped on a table behind the men. ''These are probably shots of his work in progress.'' He chuckled again. ''We just happened to be in the way every time he took the picture.''

She smiled now that she could see what Lee pointed out.

He gathered the other photos and handed them to her. ''Otis is right. That's Knightman in the pictures with us.''

Davina leaned forward and clasped her hands. ''It's important for my research that I understand what went on between Maceo and his circle of friends, and especially his relationship with Jacob.''

''They were friends, but more like mentor and student at first, until Maceo caught the attention of the downtown crowd.''

''Why didn't you help him when he got in trouble?''

Lee turned his head away. "I couldn't. I had troubles of my own. Anyway, by then Knightman was tight with Jacob, more than I was."

"Were you hurt or jealous of that?"

He looked down at his hands. "Knightman could never be a friend. He was a disease, waiting for the moment you were weakest, before he attacked. He was never a friend." He raised sad eyes to Davina. "When Jacob came to me for help with Maceo, I tried to tell him nothing was worth dealing with Knightman, and not to get caught up in that man's fingers . . . like I did."

"But Jacob ignored the warning, and went ahead and got his help for Maceo."

Lee nodded. "Jacob said he didn't care what Knightman's asking price was. He'd figure out a way to pay it."

Davina slumped back onto the sofa as Natalie and Quilla rejoined them.

"He doesn't like to talk about that man much," Quilla said. "And Nathan will be mad if he knows you're here talking to him about this." She gave a cautious look toward the door.

"What is Nathan afraid of?"

Quilla turned to Lee when he shifted on the sofa. "You want me to tell her?" At the older man's slow nod, she crossed her hands over her belly and fixed her gaze on Davina.

"Nathan doesn't want you around because he's afraid someone might discover Lee's past connection to Knightman. He tries to keep that quiet. You see, Lee did a job for Knightman to work off a debt and it cost him jail time. It was a theft and forgery job that went bad when the buyer backed out. Lee was left to take the fall."

"That was in the past, though," Davina said. "Surely Lee has started over?"

Quilla rubbed her belly. "We're having a baby, Davina. Nathan is trying to save and move all of us to a better life. And lately, he's been more worried about our future than ever. He doesn't want the past to rise up and haunt us."

Davina gave Lee a narrow stare. "Is he afraid Knightman may come back and ask a favor of you?"

"Or Nathan," Quilla said quietly. "That's why I'm telling you this, so you'll understand why Nathan doesn't want you around, and why you can't come back."

"I see," Davina said as she looked from Lee to Quilla.

Natalie asked the question that was present in everyone's mind. "I think it's obvious that Knightman helped Maceo disappear, but I wonder what Jacob agreed to that made Knightman help?"

"Maceo's paintings disappeared almost as quickly as he did. Did Jacob or Knightman somehow get them?" Davina asked.

"I don't know," Lee said. "I owed Knightman and I did his bidding. After I got out of prison, I never contacted Jacob or any of the others until Otis found me."

"Do you know where Knightman is now?" Davina held her breath.

"He's been out of sight for years. There's no telling if he's dead or in prison."

Natalie leaned forward. "Knightman is the linchpin to everything. I'll bet he can tell us about the paintings and Jacob and Maceo's arrangement."

"Right," Davina agreed. "Now, all we have to do is find the whereabouts of a bona fide criminal and then get him to open up about his past."

Justin could see night approaching through the window. He sat next to Carolyn at the big, oval table in the main conference room at Hardy Enterprises. Nora claimed her usual place at his immediate right. The rest of the family—Mrs. Hardy, Stephanie, Alli—was also present.

He looked around the table and took in the rigid posture Marc and other board members had assumed, the anxious face of Edward Nelson, and finally the calm nod from Douglas that signaled he should start. The small assembly was informal, and Justin didn't stand. He leaned back and addressed the group.

"Everyone's been apprised of what's going on, although some of you are just now getting word of where we stand in making some monumental business decisions that will affect Hardy's future. We're missing a few board members, but the number present gives us a voting quorum." Justin paused in the pregnant silence that loomed about the room.

"First," he said, and a smile swept across his face, "the bank has given us their vote of confidence by extending the loan we requested." The news was met with a barrage of relieved comments that the bank stalemate was resolved.

"Next," he continued, "Andrew Jeter is tendering his resignation, effective immediately. He's leaving at my request and with the support of the legal staff." Justin looked pointedly at Marc's unflinching stare. "We have reason to believe that Mr. Jeter was the source of the unauthorized leaks that have plagued us since Dad's death. His purpose, while unclear, was not in our best interest and is being investigated for other improprieties."

Marc stood up and braced his hands on the table. "If I may interrupt, Justin, you and I have talked about this, and I admit to my mistake during the nomination process. If the board believes my resignation will heal the wound that's been made, I'm willing to do that for the good of the company." He sat down.

Justin sighed. "I told Marc that wasn't necessary, though we will ensure that steps are in place to protect the character and integrity of the Hardy name Dad fought to keep that way."

"I agree," Stephanie chimed in as nods came from the table.

"Andrew Jeter still didn't admit he did anything," Alli said.

"We don't need his admission to find out who he works for," Justin said. "We've uncovered a paper trail, and the evidence will stand on its own."

"An open investigation won't put this to rest in the minds of the employees and management. It needs to be closed," Marc said from his seat.

Edward frowned at Marc. "I don't agree. No one's asking you to fall on the sword. You let the wrong person in and granted, it was a mistake. We just don't want it to happen again. So we need to find out the root of this." He turned to Justin. "Have we ruled out Davina Spenser and her brother as being involved?"

"Nothing points to their involvement with Jeter." Justin glanced toward his mother. "Which brings us to the other point of this meeting. Information has surfaced concerning the Spenser family's claim about their father."

Marc leaned forward. "What kind of information?"

"Did she find something in our records?" Edward asked.

Justin motioned to his mother. Mrs. Hardy reached into the satchel that sat near her chair and pulled out a small accordion folder wrapped with a satin ribbon. She handed the packet to Justin.

"No. We did." Justin hefted the folder in his hand. "Dad left a series of letters that impacts on this claim Davina Spenser addressed. Tonight, we'll have to vote on whether or not to openly acknowledge what we've discovered. There is something you should know before we get started, something Davina and David Spenser tried hard to keep quiet, and the reason will become obvious. Their father wasn't simply a man who collected Maceo artwork and left it with Dad, and who once knew the elusive Maceo. He is, in fact, the well-known Maceo James."

"I'll be upstairs if you girls need me again." With those words, Mrs. Taylor left Davina and Natalie in the Hardy estate's kitchen, a showcase of stainless steel and ceramics, with platters of food she had put together.

Davina's mouth watered at the sandwiches, salads, cheese, fruit, and bottle of wine that had been set out on the counter. The circular room and its decor, on the other hand, had captured Natalie's undivided attention as she nibbled from a vine of grapes. Their chairs were pulled up to the tiled counter.

"Man, but this place is amazing, Davina. Sort of makes you want to pinch yourself." She gobbled another grape.

"Enjoy," Davina said and bit into a sandwich. "I wonder what was so important that everyone attended a meeting?" She set the pictures on the counter.

"Hard to believe, huh, that nice old man was convicted of forgery." Natalie licked mustard from a finger. "If you ask me, there's too much coincidence going on. Your father, Justin's father, and now Nathan's father all dealt with art and this Knightman character in one way or the other."

"I know," Davina agreed. "Perry Knightman liked favors." She put down the sandwich. "Suppose Nathan has already been approached to do a forgery, like his father was. That would account for Nathan not wanting anyone around. A connection might be made.''

''And''—Natalie looked up from her sandwich—''what if the same thing were happening with Jacob's son, Justin? Suppose he's been approached or pressured into selling forgeries to pay off some debt of his father's?''

''It's like all the offspring of these old friends are being haunted to make good on favors promised by their parents who didn't keep them.''

As the thought took root, Davina wiped her fingers on the napkin, picked up the stack of photos, and flipped through them again.

Natalie abruptly turned to Davina. ''You know, we haven't considered your connection with Knightman. You and David are Maceo's offspring.''

''I know,'' Davina said without looking up from the pictures. ''If Knightman is around, does he know that yet? And, if so, what was the favor and how are we supposed to pay for it?''

''The discussion is over and it's time we vote on the motion.'' Justin now stood. ''I usually don't vote unless there's a tie. This time, though, I'll vote first, and it'll be aye, in favor of the motion.''

Then, his demeanor stoic, Justin's eyes settled on the voting members, one by one, as they pronounced their vote.

CHAPTER THIRTY-TWO

Waking Up Sleeping Dogs

"David, it doesn't mean we have to give up and stop looking for evidence." Davina packed up the remnants of the lunch she and Natalie had shared with him in his office.

Behind the desk in the cramped law office, David ran his hand over his face in frustration. "It's time for us to move on, Vinny. Something did come of it all, though. Your art show, for one, and . . ."

"That wasn't my goal," Davina spouted angrily. "We promised Dad we'd save his name and legacy, and I can't give it up. Look at how much we've learned in just a few days. I mean, we just have to find this Perry Knightman person and he'll confirm our suspicions."

"And how easy do you think that'll be?" David's ire matched hers. "I don't want to give up, either, but it's been months of frustration, we don't know who stole the paintings from you, and now you're a murder suspect. Enough is enough."

"Hey, you two," Natalie interjected from her chair. "Calm down. You're on the same side, remember?"

Davina's arms were defiantly crossed over her chest. "What about the police records on Dad? Are you sure there's no outstanding warrant?"

David came from around the desk and opened his briefcase, which sat near the bookcase. "Like I said, they never got around to indicting Dad. They had enough to question him, but he knew it would lead to his arrest for murder if the guy died, so he fled town. Look at these."

He handed two newspaper articles to Davina and Natalie. "I made copies at the library."

Natalie scanned the print. "This one says the man was found unconscious and was not expected to survive a brutal beating from unknown assailants."

"For a while, there were no new stories on the case after the initial ones," David said. "The other article came later, after Dad had disappeared."

"It's an obituary notice"—Davina read from the article—"for Harvey Snelling, victim of a notorious unsolved beating, allegedly done by rising artist, Maceo James, who has eluded police efforts to question him. Mr. Snelling died of kidney failure, complications from that beating." She looked up at them. "So, that's the name of the man who raped Mom." It was a statement of fact.

"I'll bet the police never heard your mom and dad's story," Natalie said.

"The papers never gave it, and Snelling never told, that's for sure," David said. "The way he attacked Mom, he didn't want anyone to know."

Davina handed the clipping back to David. "Now, we just forget our suspicions of Hardy Enterprises and counterfeit paintings?"

"We don't have hard evidence," he said.

Natalie looked at Davina. "It might be best to come clean and tell Justin what you both suspected early on and own up you have that last painting."

Davina grabbed up her purse from the chair. "Yeah . . . I guess." She walked to David and touched his shoulder. "I need to think. Sorry I snapped at you."

"Forget it. We're both stressed. I just wish we had more to go on."

She had already opened the door and was on her way out. "I'm going back to the gallery for a while to think there."

"Wait up, I'm leaving, too." Natalie called out goodbye to David and scooped up her own purse.

David watched them leave before he returned to his chair. He thought about what Davina had said. Was she right that they were giving in too quickly after the new information from their father's old friends?

A soft knock sounded from his open door. He looked up to see one of the secretaries.

"David, a call came for you while your sister was here."

He motioned to her. "Come on in, Brenda. You could have put it through."

"I was asked to deliver the message only when they left."

Curious, David reached for the folded note she handed him. It was from Justin. He wanted David to call him at the house as soon as possible, and not to mention it to Davina. He looked up at Brenda. "How long ago did he call?"

"No more than thirty minutes," she said, and backed out the door.

David dialed the number jotted on the paper.

"No wonder she stole the paintings. Maceo is her father. And you didn't think that was important enough for me to know?" Nathan shook his head in disbelief as he leaned against the phone booth with Marc.

Marc looked down either end of Edgewood Avenue. No one paid them attention as they stood there; only a few street vendors showed any life at all. "I didn't know, either," he said. "We were both kept in the dark, but now the proverbial shit is about to hit the fan."

"All I want is my money and out of this mess." He spat out the words. "I knew these guys couldn't be trusted. But you . . ." He ground his gaze into Marc. "You were supposed to know what was going on and keep me safe."

Nathan reached for the flat wrapped package that was propped against the booth. "This is the last one, and you can kiss off the one that's missing. Now, I want my money. No shit out of you this time." He handed it to Marc.

"He wants to see you when he makes the payoff. That's how he operates."

"Yeah, yeah. He wants to see me so he can sucker me in to doing something else. That's how he operates. Remember the job he did on my old man? No thank you." He cleared his throat and spit on the sidewalk.

Marc stepped away from the phone booth. "Tell him yourself when you see him at the warehouse tonight." He glanced at his watch. "I've got to go." He lodged the painting under his arm and walked down the street.

Back in the gallery office, Davina tried to win Natalie on the idea that they should persevere with the information they'd uncovered. "The guy that was following me, I did a drawing of him." She scrambled around the desk and dug around the drawer. "I could have sworn I left it in here." Finally, she located it.

"He's cute," Natalie said, eyeing the drawing from her perch on the desk.

"Let's see," Davina thought out loud, "I discover someone following me, there's a murder, and I become a suspect." She turned to Natalie. "It's all connected. Suppose I was meant to find Robert's body in order to be set up?"

"Yeah," Natalie agreed. "If you're being watched, it wouldn't be hard to discover that you stay at the office late."

"And Robert's schedule was always posted in the lab. Even those nuggets passed on to the newspapers helped to defame me with the police."

"That was done by none other that the Queen of Kitty Litter, Linda. You think she could be in cahoots with whoever is doing this?" Natalie asked.

Davina blew off the idea with a wave. "She messes up the theory. I don't think she'd dirty her manicured hands. But, when you add Knightman to the mix . . ."

". . . and don't forget Lee Randolph's forgery conviction."

"Everything started with the paintings I took." She frowned at Natalie. "You know, I started something that I can't quite get a handle on. There's a common denominator I'm missing."

"There are a few: Hardy Enterprises, money, you, and Justin."

"I don't want to believe Justin would let his company become dirty."

"Are you ready to admit out loud that you love him?"

Davina felt her face flush at the comment, and pressed her hand against the single braid at the back of her head. "That's a strong word."

"That's why I used it. You love the man. When his name is mentioned, it's written all over your face."

She looked at her friend and silently moved her hands to her mouth. "God help me, I do love him." She slowly sank onto her chair. "What am I going to do?"

Natalie smiled as she hopped off the desk and patted Davina's shoulder. "My work's done here. I'll see myself out."

Justin allowed Carolyn to pull him into a corner of the salon at the house, away from the others gathered in the library. "All right, what do you want?"

She stared at him. "You love her, don't you?"

"Who?"

"Davina. Who else?"

"What makes you say that?" He brushed at an invisible speck on his lapel.

"After all the objections were brought up, you seemed desperate to right what you considered a wrong. You've gone out of your way to make us see her side in this when you didn't have to. It was a job well done." She stepped back from Justin. "It's not the 'take no prisoners' style that I'm used to seeing you operate with."

He smiled. "Oh, so showing a little kindness is bad form from me?"

"No, but from a man who keeps himself emotionally separate from women in general, and his woman specifically, well, this is an interesting change." She smiled, too. "I like this new, sensitive you, Justin. So, do you love her?"

At that moment, the doorbell rang, and Justin turned to the sound. "That's probably David. Tell Mom he's here and I'll bring him to the library."

Justin took two long strides to the hallway and stopped. "Oh, and Carolyn?" He turned to his sister. "The answer is an unequivocal yes." He gave her raised brows a wide grin before he opened the door on an impatient David.

"Good, you came right over," Justin said.

"You made it sound important," David answered as he stepped into the foyer.

"It is. Come on in. Everyone's waiting in the library."

As they walked through the salon toward the library, David asked, "What didn't you want Davina to know? I hope you don't plan on asking me to do something that's against my sister's best interest."

"Oh, I know you well enough not to even think along that line." He held the library door open. "After you."

David entered and saw Mrs. Hardy sitting with Douglas Bradley on the couch. Carolyn stood at their back. He walked up and extended his hand to each.

"It's good to see you again, David," Mrs. Hardy said. "This must seem so mysterious to you, but Justin insisted we discuss some decisions the company made with you first."

"What decisions?" David asked. He slowly returned his attention to Justin.

"Have a seat," Justin pointed to a set of chairs in front of the sofa where he joined David. Without preamble, he said, "I know what you and Davina have been up to."

David shook his head in confusion. "You're talking riddles."

"Am I?" he asked. "Davina told me your late father's real name. He's the Maceo James we've discussed so much recently, only he's not as late as I was led to believe. We know he's comatose in a Florida hospital."

David's flinch was apparent from his seat. "Vinny didn't tell you that."

"No, she didn't, but I wish she had. It's time you shared the secrets you've kept so long. I'll tell you what I know, and I want you to fill in the blanks. We can work together." He watched David's studied, though hesitant, nod. "I have reason to believe the two of you showed up in Atlanta with the claim charges because you believed your father's paintings were being counterfeited and sold through my gallery. Am I right so far?"

"How did you learn all this?"

"It started with a background check, more or less. Some people down in Miami were impressed with a budding young artist, who was beautiful, to boot. One of her former professors remembers her going—his word—ballistic for no apparent reason when she came across one of Maceo's paintings in a private collection of black artists' works at the home of one of the college's benefactors."

"Is that how your suspicions were first raised?" Douglas asked.

"Pretty much," David said, and shifted uncomfortably in the chair. "She came across the painting by accident. You see, just before the coma, our father could barely breathe or recognize us. He found the breath and was lucid long enough to tell us his secret past and describe some of the paintings he had left with Jacob Hardy. It was a name we didn't recognize. He made Vinny promise to find this Jacob, who would know what to do." He sighed. "We did nothing at first. We were in shock from what he'd said and didn't know what to believe. Later on, while attending that private viewing, Davina saw one of the paintings he'd described."

"I'll bet she was livid," Justin said.

"She had been depressed over . . . some things, and she became alive again when she saw the painting. I was glad. We talked about what Dad had said that horrible night, and we started to believe. She doesn't want to let him down, and her guilt will be heavy if she does. Even now, she prays that he'll hold on until we restore his legacy."

"Is that when you came to Atlanta?" Carolyn suggested.

"I was already here and Vinny joined me. By then, she was sure Hardy was selling off our father's paintings as counterfeits because of financial difficulties."

Justin drew David's attention again. "The next step was to talk with us?"

"She tried. When your lawyers wouldn't let her see or talk with you or the family, and then lied about possessing the paintings, that just ticked her off more."

David stared at Justin, as if to divine if the others knew she was the one who took the paintings from the vault. So, he simply said, "By then, she was desperate for proof."

"They know she took the paintings from the vault, David."

He looked first at Mrs. Hardy, then the others. "Then, I hope you won't judge us too harshly. What she did was out of love for our Dad, not personal greed."

"I suspect she felt there was no other way to get to us." Mrs. Hardy got up and walked to an oak desk near the window. She took a packet from the drawer and returned to the sofa.

"I told them everything, David, because the actions you took, though extreme at times, were understandable given your point of view." Justin nodded to his mother, and she handed the accordion packet to David.

He took it. "What's this?"

"They're letters," Mrs. Hardy said. "From your father to Jacob. I found them yesterday as I went through my husband's things. Seven are from Maceo, signed that way, but the envelopes are printed with James Spenser, and sent to a post office box. It was their way of communicating after that awful tragedy. Three are Jacob's letters returned to him as undeliverable."

David pulled the tie string and released the flap. The letters were in plain white envelopes, nothing to distinguish them, except that they bore the handwriting he remembered as his father's. "You're serious, aren't you?" His voice was couched in amazement. He balanced the bundle in his lap and slowly looked at each of the ten envelopes. "You were right after all, Dad." He said the words to himself.

"Yes, it seems so," Mrs. Hardy said. "The letters start just after Maceo disappeared. He mentions his new life, some of the difficulties and hassles. Jacob received them every few months, at first; and he wrote to Maceo, as well. I never knew of their correspondence."

"For your own protection, Elizabeth," Douglas said.

"The letters stop after a few years," Justin said. "I suspect Maceo was on the move and Dad lost track of him. Dad's last three letters were returned unclaimed."

The room fell into silence as David opened one of the letters.

Justin's deep voice cut into the quiet. "There was a special meeting of the board last night. Partly due to the letters, we agreed to acknowledge Maceo James as a shareholder in Hardy Enterprises. There'll be a new issue of stock."

"It was Justin's decision to do it this way, and quickly," Carolyn added.

Douglas sat forward on the sofa. "The letters are clear. They speak volumes. Whatever the level of business partnership between these men, there was, indeed, obvious honor and respect. I remember when your sister addressed our board meeting. She spoke of the fact that they were honorable men."

David refolded the letter and placed it back in the envelope. "Vinny will be surprised," he said and smiled. "That you actually have letters written by Dad, I mean . . . she'll be amazed."

"When she comes tonight to collect her bags," Justin said. "I'll tell her."

Davina scraped the paint knife across the canvas and tried to keep her thoughts on her work. It was hard. The thoughts she had muddled over with Natalie remained stubbornly planted in her head. Had she put something in motion that night she took the paintings from the gallery? She relived the moment when she believed she had been caught. That had been a close call.

A very close call. Davina sat upright on the stool, her eyes wide as the summoned thought spread through her head like the wings of a bird in flight.

"That's where I heard it," she said out loud. The shock of the memory was as hot as a lightning bolt and she raised her hands to her head. The voice. *It was Andrew Jeter who almost caught me in the gallery with the paintings.*

She absently slid from the stool as she considered going to Justin's office to tell him what she remembered.

Then, a cold thought gripped her. Justin had been eager to learn where she'd heard Andrew Jeter's voice. Why? What if Justin *was* behind her apartment break-in? The inescapable fact remained that no one knew she had taken the paintings. Except Justin. She shook her head to rid it of the distracting idea, but it persisted. Hadn't she decided that he was on her side, that he couldn't possibly be tied to any of the things going on?

Unsteady, she climbed back on the stool, and gazed blindly at the canvas. Her mind's eye became a swirl of names: Nathan, Lee, Otis, Perry Knightman, and now Andrew Jeter. She reached for the nearby phone to call Natalie. As she punched in the numbers, she told herself to stop and think. Justin seemed to be there for her at every turn; but, was that for her benefit or his? *Stop it, Davina.*

At the onset of the voicemail, she hung up and tried David. He was out of the office. All right, she'd march down to Justin's office now for answers. For the second time, she slid from the stool and dropped the paint knife in the cleaner. She grabbed a paper towel and swept through the room, no motion lost as she slipped from the paint smock and tossed it to a chair, pushed against the gray metal doors, and in a half turn was in the gallery. And then came the burn of tears, of frustration. *Good Lord,* she thought, *I won't cry over this.* She sped past Rosa and out the main door as she headed for the ladies' room down the hall.

It was well past four in the evening, and Davina appreciated the vacant serenity the bathroom offered. She waved her hands under the automatic faucet and splashed cool water on her face. Blindly, she reached for a paper towel when her nostrils were assailed by a familiar fragrance.

"Someone bothering you again?"

Davina bit down on her cheek to keep the retort for Linda temporarily in abeyance. She blotted her eyes dry and tried to ignore the remark.

"I'm surprised Justin's not around the corner ready to fight the battle. Unless, of course, he's dumped you already."

Davina, her emotions under control, allowed her disdain for Linda to bubble to the surface. Her voice light, she said, "So this is what you do now? Skulk around in bathrooms." She balled the towel and tossed it into the wastebasket before she turned to Linda at the door. "Congratulations, it suits you perfectly."

Linda touched her upswept hair, and gave a hollow laugh. "I love it when a mouse shows spunk."

Davina gave a wry smile as she casually walked toward Linda. "Listen, I don't like you, I don't even want to be in the same bathroom as you. You showed your real colors when you planted that news story about me. Justin warned me that you had a sick mind."

"Don't tell me," Linda said in mock surprise. "You believe you've won his heart as well as his ear? Justin doesn't have a heart. And he certainly hasn't given you his ear."

"I know more than you think . . ."

Linda cut in. "You know nothing. Justin eats naive little girls like you alive. You're playing in the big league for big stakes, and I'm the wrong woman to cross. Where do you think I got the information to give to the press? Justin, my dear."

Surprise was a mild word for how Davina felt about her comment, but, she kept it inside. "You're a liar," she retorted, her eyes wide. "He was just as shocked as I was, and thinks your attitude is despicable. He didn't give you information."

"And why not? Everything he does, including you, is a means to an end."

Davina straightened her shoulders. "Because I believed him when he said he didn't. Have you ever heard the word trust?" She moved toward the door and reached for the handle. "Now get out of my way. The sight of you makes me ill."

"I'll bet he didn't tell you he's been investigating you."

Davina's hand froze as the words sank in.

CHAPTER THIRTY-THREE

Love Hurts

Surprise streaked across Davina's features. "What are you talking about?"

"So much for trust." Linda curved her fingers and feigned interest in her nails.

Davina's heart squeezed in her chest, but she continued into that dark place Linda had exposed. "If you don't tell me what you're talking about . . ."

"Exactly like I said." Linda's eyes flashed in innocence. "He's had an investigator checking you out from the very beginning." Her brows crinkled as she looked at Davina. "You didn't have a clue, did you? Justin doesn't trust anyone any farther than he can throw them. And, you're no different—a means to an end."

Davina stiffened before she stepped back, not caring that Linda enjoyed the discomfort her words brought. She tamped down the sour bile that threatened to embarrass her further. "Why would you think I'd believe anything you said?"

"Because this was Jacob's company and Justin will never share it," Linda sneered. "That would be failure and he has too much to prove to allow that."

"He doesn't confide in you."

"I knew about the investigations before things got . . . complicated between us. He told me not to mention it to anyone," she added maliciously. "He won't hand over any part of this place—his precious family means too much. In fact, Nora told me he went home for a meeting. He's been in quite a few the last two days."

"What do you get out of telling me this?"

"All I'm doing is warning you that he'll take what he needs to get what he wants, and then he'll grow tired of you."

As though reading the doubt in Davina's eyes, Linda continued on. "How do you think Justin and I met? Jacob wanted my first beauty book for his publishing division, and he introduced me to his tall, handsome son. I was wined and dined and I've been around ever since. Now, he doesn't need me. He needs something from you." She walked to the sink and turned. "You should take a page from the history I've written, sweetheart, and watch out. The writing is on the wall."

Davina's eyes flashed. "A pity you're such a poor writer."

The smug look on Linda's features quickly faded, and helped Davina experience a liberation from the sickness that had built in her stomach.

With a push on the handle, she was out of the door and breathed in a gulp of air. And to think she had once thought highly of that shrew.

Her thoughts were cool and clear, and under control, by the time she returned to the gallery for her purse. She reasoned there would be time enough to burn when she faced Justin at his house, her next destination

With a gloved hand, Detective Jaragoski held the plastic bag up to the evening light outside the home of Barbara Montgomery, the mother of the murdered Hardy employee. Inside the bag was a business-size plain white envelope. "Let's get this back to the evidence room."

"We need to run the warrant by the captain." Detective Lovett opened the driver's side of the unmarked sedan. "You don't think this was a little easy to come by?"

"No. I'm old enough to know you don't look a gift horse in the mouth. Most criminal activity is inherently stupid. That's how cases get solved." Jaragoski slid into the passenger seat and snapped off the rubber gloves. "You aren't becoming suspicious all of a sudden are you?"

The younger man smiled. "I'm a homicide detective. Of course I'm cynical and distrustful." He started the engine and it came alive with first a belch, then a roar. He sped off in the direction of headquarters on North Avenue.

Even though she had a key, Davina rang Justin's doorbell. She remembered her first visit here when she had likened his home to a castle, and he had made her feel like a princess. Her suspicions had broiled into a mass of anger, an anvil that pressed into her heart. The heart had nothing to do with reality, and she stood tall.

After a minute, which seemed an eternity, the door opened.

Justin filled the doorway with his body, his presence. The hurt and betrayal she had tried to ignore returned with a vengeance. He looked every bit as handsome and arrogant as the first time she had laid eyes on him. His coat and tie had been shed and his open shirt revealed a brown throat she knew would be hard and warm and sweet to the lips. She swallowed a tinge of regretful memory.

"Davina, why didn't you use your key?" He greeted her with a wide grin. "I've been waiting for you."

She stepped around him and entered the foyer. Distant, laughing

voices from the direction of the library floated to her and she turned
to the sounds.

"That's Alli," Justin said. "They're all in the library." He slipped
his hands around hers and slowly drew her with him into the salon.
"Come in there with me. I have something I want to tell you."

"So do I." Her voice was dour, and her brows drew together.

For the first time, Justin studied her face. "Are you okay?"

She fought the dynamic vitality he exuded and pulled her hands
from his. As if to destroy the imprint of his touch, she tucked them
into the pockets of her skirt. At that moment, Mrs. Taylor walked by
in the hall, and Davina asked if she would bring down her travel bag
from the guest suite.

After the housekeeper left on the errand, Justin turned to Davina,
his brows quirked in surprise. "You don't have to leave. I was hoping
you'd stay longer."

"We need to talk," she answered, avoiding his eyes. "Somewhere
private."

Justin's earlier exuberance had faded to puzzlement. "All right."
He walked to either end of the large room and pulled closed the sets
of tall double doors. He returned to Davina. "Do you want to sit
down?" He indicated the nearby sofa.

"No, I'm fine."

"Then tell me what's wrong, what's on your mind?"

Davina blurted out in anger. "You're investigating me, aren't you?"

She watched for some sign that he was taken aback by her words,
that he was surprised at the accusation, that he would never do some-
thing like that behind her back. And there was none.

He drew his lips in thoughtfully. "So you know. When did you
find out?"

He was calm and Davina became livid. She answered him in a rush
of words. "You admit it and all you want to know is when I found
out?" Davina stalked away from him. "How dare you investigate my
life like some sovereign prince. Who do you think you are?" She
whirled around and saw he had not moved. "I want to know everything
you learned, and I want all of your reports."

"Whoa. You really are upset." Justin strode over to her. "I had
my reasons for doing it. It wasn't to hurt you." He reached up and

gently brushed back a wisp of hair that had escaped her French braid; his fingers lingered near her ear.

"Yes it was, and it did." Davina steeled herself to his touch, but her eyes blinked of their own accord at the sensation. "You told me yourself one of us would have to lose in our struggle, and you made sure you wouldn't. And if you could get your minions to dig up something, the nastier the better, maybe find out that I really am a golddigger, you could get rid of me. That's why you investigated me." She sucked in a deep breath.

Justin sighed and rubbed a hand across his brow. "You always know the answers, don't you. Do you ever listen to anything besides your own voice?"

"Don't you turn this on me, Justin Hardy. You were wrong."

"And if you'd listen a minute, I can explain why I did it," he reasoned.

Davina crossed her arms in front of her chest and sighed loudly. "There's no good reason for what you did. You invaded what was mine. My life."

"I was concerned when you were attacked. I couldn't understand why a burglar would break in, search your place, and take nothing. And if you remember correctly, you wouldn't tell me a thing, but I figured it had to do with your appearance in my building earlier. I had to find some answers."

"And when Justin doesn't understand something or isn't told what he wants to know, that's a problem. You always figure a way to get what you want."

"You've told me most of what I found out, so why does it matter now?"

"It matters. It matters to me." She gave him a cool stare. "Everything I told you, you already knew. When I opened up to you, told you about my father, I wasn't telling you anything you didn't already know." She stepped closer to Justin. "Every time I opened my heart to tell you more, it was a joke."

"Never that. I understood why you didn't want to tell me everything at one time, Davina. And I waited patiently while I gained your trust."

"How can I believe you? I look back now and it's like, you were pulling my strings. Did you learn how poor we were? What about my alcoholic father? I'll bet that was a laugh after my glowing speech on him at the meeting. I feel violated.''

The bitterness of her tone caused Justin to shake his head as he took a step to her. ''This is all wrong. You couldn't be farther from the truth.'' A rueful smile touched his lips. ''It's ironic that when I finally fall in love, it's with a woman who avoids my trust and continually questions my sincerity.''

Davina's head snaked up. Had he said he loved her? ''You always want control, to have things work your way. What was I thinking attending those parties with you . . . was I your flavor of the moment? I'm sure your family and friends must have thought it a good joke. Squiring around some poor, naive starry-eyed artist.''

She was close enough to touch, and Justin raised his hands to her shoulders. ''You're overreacting, Davina.''

''Don't you dare patronize me.''

''Call it what you want, but it was never like you're describing.''

She shrugged from his hands. ''No? Linda told me how she became involved with you. Funny, but it sounds suspiciously like the way we got together. I'm sure you told her at some point that you loved her, and look where it got her.''

''I've never said it to another woman I was involved with. Only you. Can you say the same?''

Davina looked at him with accusing eyes. ''You knew about Lawrence before he showed up, didn't you?'' When she saw the truth reflected in his eyes, her mouth thinned in renewed anger. She raised her voice. ''What else, Justin?''

He dropped his hands, as if in defeat. ''I know your father isn't dead, and that you made the trip to Florida to see him.''

''You showed up at the airport and let me make a fool of myself?'' She let out a long, audible breath. ''Linda was right after all. You make it your business to know everything. You must be proud at being so clever.''

''Linda told you about the investigator?'' He ground the words out between his teeth. ''She only saw a file on my desk, and she was never privy to anything inside it.'' He reached for her, but she moved away.

"I have to hand it to her. She knows you well, much better than I ever did."

"I've never lied to you about her." Justin followed her across the room. "And I've tried to protect you from her brand of vengeance. She and I were through a long time ago, before I met you."

"Ahh . . . the night we met." Davina stopped her pace and lifted her chin to face him. "I remember now where I heard Andrew Jeter's voice. It was the night I was hiding out in the gallery with the paintings. He called out and almost caught me as I left. As I avoided him and someone else, I bumped into you."

"He wasn't supposed to be there. Someone let him in. Did he see you?"

Davina ignored his look of surprise. "No, but you did," she countered icily. "You are the only person who guessed I had something to do with the paintings."

She watched him as he silently watched her. "I figure you lied about knowing who I was that night. It's no longer strange that my apartment was ransacked the night I had dinner with you. You wanted me to stay longer, but I wouldn't. As a result, I must have surprised the burglar who was sent to recover the paintings. Then, you show up, concerned about my health." She gave Justin a cynical look. "Tell me you wouldn't think the obvious if you were in my shoes."

Justin's eyes narrowed slightly above a thunderous expression. "I'm not telling you anything because you have it all figured out. Heaven forbid that you're wrong about something. No advice or trust is to be taken seriously because your life of hard work and betrayal has taught you that no one, especially a man who shows interest in you, is to be trusted. And you don't make mistakes."

"Not twice, and not when it comes to character. Did your investigator tell you that you were the first person I suspected when it looked like forgeries were being sold through your gallery?" Davina absorbed his wordless stare. "My mistake was believing you weren't the smooth devil I always thought you were, even when the evidence shouted it out."

"Stop it right now." Justin roughly shook her shoulders as though to wake her from some awful nightmare. "After all I've done—putting up with all your secrets and lies, protecting you from the press and the police, not to mention the board, where do you get off lecturing me on trust? Did you ever trust me enough to tell me about your past, the things that hurt, the things that still hurt?''

''You slept with me, all the time lying. What am I supposed to think?''

He frowned. ''Is that what's bothering you? That maybe I slept with you for less than honorable reasons? And what did you do?'' he demanded with cold fury. ''Sleep with me as therapy to help work out the wrinkles you got with Lawrence?''

Davina's head jerked up at his words.

''That should make us about the same,'' he added.

Without thinking, Davina pulled her arm back and struck his face with all her might. The force of the slap turned his head and stung her hand. She knew he could have stopped it, and expected he would, like he had done at the board meeting. This time, he hadn't.

''Do you feel better? Justified?'' His jaw muscle quivered in anger. ''All I do with you is explain every action over and over, and I'm tired. You need an excuse, any excuse, not to believe in me because you don't want to. You'd rather live in the past and wallow in self-pity.''

A hostile glare passed between them, and in that moment, they accepted that this was the end.

Davina spun on her heels and quickly walked to the doors nearest the hallway and opened them. Mrs. Taylor had placed her bag on the floor outside the doors. She stooped to pick it up before turning back to Justin.

''Back at the cabin, we warned each other that the day would come when we'd have to choose between each other and our families. You just forgot to tell me you had already made your choice.'' She placed the house key on the table in the foyer as she disappeared into the hall.

Justin walked as far as the foyer and listened to the front door close. It was like a crush to his heart. Already, he missed her fiercely, and his anger was slowly eroding like a sand castle against the incoming tide. He had wanted to stop her, take her into the security of his arms, and tell her what he had shared with David earlier, but he couldn't. His pride had taken over when she confidently voiced her low opinions of him. She didn't trust him, and wouldn't consider that he had her best interests at heart all along. His eyes became clouded with anger again.

The doors that led to the library now opened. Alli peeked in, then walked across the room to Justin where he leaned against the doorframe.

"I sort of heard some of what was going on. Here are the letters you wanted Davina to have. She'll understand when you tell her the good news." She looked around the room. "Where is she?"

He snatched the folder from Alli's hand and threw it with all his might across the room. It crashed into a jardinière near the window before it tumbled harmlessly to the carpeted floor.

Justin ran his hand across his face. In a belligerent voice, he said, "I have to get out of here for a while." He strode through the foyer like a quick moving storm. The front door's slam announced that he was gone.

The tall lampposts cast long shadows in the dim parking lot when Davina arrived home. She was anxious for the comfort her own apartment would bring and fumbled with her door key. She tried to think about pleasant thoughts, but it didn't work. She continually returned to the ugly scene she'd played out with Justin. *I love him . . . loved him. He said he loved me, but I can't trust that he means it.* The key slid smoothly into the door lock and she turned it. What now? Forget Justin Hardy and get on with life. In the long run, what had happened was for the best.

Davina opened the door and stepped into the dark room, familiarity her guide. A sigh escaped her lips as the door silently closed. She was home again.

Something was not right. Almost as quickly as the thought presented itself, she heard a swish of air from behind before the steely strength of a man's arm snaked about her neck. His other hand slammed onto her mouth, and terror engulfed her; the scream she managed fell ineffectually against his palm.

Writhing and grunting as she strained against the man, she heard a voice from across the room echo through the darkness.

"Is that her?"

Davina's eyes stretched to penetrate the murky shadows and identify the speaker of the clipped words. *A foreign accent?*

"Yes, sir. It's her, all right."

Ears now pricked at her captor's voice, she stopped her struggle. She knew that voice. It belonged to the guard at the Hardy Building.

CHAPTER THIRTY-FOUR

The Whole Truth, and Nothing But . . .

Davina's panic had become as keen as a well-honed razor. These were the same people who had hit her over the head before, and a Hardy security guard was involved. With increased vigor, she struggled against her captor.

"Finally, you're here," the precisely accented voice from the shadows said. "We had begun to worry."

Davina still couldn't make out the face that belonged to the accent, but her eyes followed a bright dot of lightning. It was his cigarette.

"If I allow our friend here to remove his hand," he said, "do you promise not to scream?"

Anything you say, Davina thought, and anger began to replace the panic. She grunted against the hard palm and nodded her head.

"And, as an added incentive . . ." he continued.

Davina heard the loud, sinister click of metal against metal, and knew he had a gun. She gulped, her mouth dry and her eyes stretched from fear. The guard shoved her stubborn legs toward the sofa, and when she was within falling distance of it, pushed her. The travel bag fell from her fingers as she stumbled around the coffee table. She wiped the back of her hand across her mouth and sat on the sofa.

"Who are you, what do you want?" The words rushed out at the same pace that her heart thumped. She didn't let on that she recognized the guard's voice.

"The Maceo painting you took." This came from the man with the cigarette.

Davina peered into the shadows in the direction of his voice. Her eyes were adapting to the dark and she could see a form across the room near the doorway. When she made out no other shapes, she surmised the guard stood somewhere behind her. Her concerns were now divided into two camps: how would she protect the painting and, was Justin a part of this ambush, too?

"Don't you remember?" she asked nervously. "You took them when you ransacked my apartment the last time. I don't have them any more."

A hollow laugh came from his direction. "Don't give me that. Soon you'll have me wondering if you think I'm stupid. And that's not healthy. I know what you took from the gallery, and I want it now."

Davina willed her fragmented courage to present itself and she let out another nervous laugh. "All this trouble for a little painting?"

"It's the centerpiece for a group of paintings worth a fortune. You don't know who or what you're dealing with. I'm here to get it."

"Nothing's worth the trouble you're getting into, what with charges like breaking and entering, and holding a person against their will filed against you."

She heard him whispering. *Is there a third person in here, or is that the guard?* Davina drummed her head for a plan even as she prayed the men would leave and that David and Natalie would keep away a while longer.

As if he were privy to her silent prayer, the man said, "I have to leave soon and don't have time to play games with you. Where is it?"

"I don't have it anymore." She stuttered over the slim excuse.

"Then maybe your friend Natalie, the one who lives at building J in apartment 5, can convince you to find it."

His words hung in the air like black-bellied clouds over a July picnic; the unspeakable was threatening. Davina knew she'd have to cooperate.

"How do I know you won't harm us when I tell you what you want?"

"All I want is the painting. You can't identify us; we're not worried. And in case you try to tell anyone you had visitors, who'll believe you?" He chuckled.

Another laugh came from behind her. It was the guard. So, there were three people in the apartment.

"What's funny about that?" she asked.

"You forget," the accented man in front of her said, "you stole the paintings and have no credibility, especially after the police arrest you for that young man's murder. And they will be doing it, and I'd say within hours."

Davina's brows pulled together. *How do they know that? And what does Robert's murder have to do with the paintings? I must keep them talking.* "I only found Robert's body and soon the police will realize their mistake."

"Unfortunately, not soon enough for you. They've discovered a copy of the letter he gave you."

"What letter?" Davina tried to make sense of his words.

"The letter that said he knew you took the missing paintings, and that if you didn't pay up, he'd go to both the police and Justin Hardy." He chuckled again. "Blackmail. A good motive for murder."

"You did this? Why?" She slid to the edge of the sofa. "Justin won't believe that." Hadn't she given up on Justin because he was as crooked as these men were? Or was he? If the shoe were on the other foot, would he believe the same of her?

"It won't matter what he thinks in the end. We've invested too much in his company to have him close down our operation. Right now, I want the painting."

Davina's eyes flew wide. He said close down their operation, not Justin's operation. Her head swam, partly from the perfidy these men had committed, but mostly from their unwitting acquittal of Justin in their scheme. "Who are you?"

"Someone who has lost patience with your questions. You have exactly—"

Davina had stopped listening. Her mind impetuously played out the scene of what probably happened the night Robert was killed. She scrambled up from the sofa and spun around in the dark to the guard, his black shape a menacing presence. She hurled the accusations at him as they materialized in her head.

"You found me with Robert . . . before I even called you."

"Where is the painting?" The man in the chair interrupted Davina.

"You were supposed to be outside, but you showed up just as I leaned over him, a convenient witness already in the gallery because . . . you killed him."

"Will someone shut her up!" His accent flamed out in anger.

Davina saw the guard advancing on her and backed away. The wall near the hallway held a light switch, and she turned to make a mad dash for it. If she were being set up, she'd be damned if she wouldn't try to see who was behind it.

"What's she doing? Get her. Stop her," the man called out again.

She threw herself against the wall and hit the light switch.

The guard crashed across the coffee table. "Damn you," he shouted.

It was too late. The room was flooded with bright, overhead lighting that spilled like white rain from the ceiling fixture.

Blinking against the sudden glare, Davina fought off the guard now exposed as Mitch Timmins, the giant of a sentry who worked the evening shift at the Hardy building. While Timmins tried to control her struggling body, Davina stared into the frown of the accented man, and was surprised.

He was a black man, elegantly suited, and his almost pretty brown face was capped with low black hair. He sat in the armchair with his legs crossed and a cigarette dangling from jeweled fingers.

Another man behind him, the third man, quickly stole her attention as he stepped out of the light and into the dark kitchen. *Marc?*

Davina shook her head in incredulity and ignored the pain of her arm being twisted behind her back. "Not you, Marc."

He stopped when she used his name, and slowly turned to face her.

The guard spoke up. "Do you want me to cut the lights back off, Mr. Knight?"

Her eyes jerked to the seated man. Knight. Knightman. Any connection?

"At this point, man, whatever for? She knows you and has seen us." He shook his head in defeat. "Marc, where do you get the hired help?"

Davina was filled with contempt when she gave Marc an accusatory look.

"I guess I screwed up your plans? Unless you were going to get rid of me anyway. I'll bet Justin is really proud of your friendship."

"Why didn't you give up the painting?" Marc pleaded. "This didn't have to happen."

Knight stood up from the chair and took a long drag from his cigarette before he dropped it to the carpet and ground it out with his foot. He pointed an angry finger at Davina. "From the first day I heard your name, you've been a pain in the butt."

Davina twisted from the guard's grasp and moved across the room to the men. "Marc, they killed Robert, and he didn't do anything."

"Oh, but he did, Miss Spenser. He did." Knight looked pointedly into Davina's eyes. "He talked to you. You fed his curiosity about Maceo and his paintings. When Marc gave him the paintings to clean, Robert saw they were the ones missing from storage. He checked the records and knew something was wrong. Fortunately, Justin doesn't have the patience for mistakes, so the kid took his concerns to a more understanding Marc."

"You were afraid you'd be found out so you killed him?" She was shocked.

"And who better to blame than the woman he's blackmailing," Knight said. "You see, we didn't know what he'd told you, so you had to be neutralized as well."

"You've planned everything down to the letter."

"There's still the matter of the third painting. Where is it?"

Davina's frustration at these successive revelations had reached a boiling point, and for the second time in less than an hour, she drew her hand back and slapped a man for all she was worth. "You go straight to hell," she screamed.

Knight's grimace was terrible, and he raised his hand and returned the slap with a man's force. Davina reeled from the blow and dropped to the floor.

"You've gone too far," she heard Marc say. "That wasn't necessary."

Dazed, Davina pushed herself up on one hand while she touched her stinging face with the other. Marc's hands reached under her arms and pulled her to her feet. She fell against him and clutched his lapel for support as she found her bearings. Then, she shrugged him off and stood defiantly before the men as her jaw throbbed with pain. "You'll never get away with this."

Knight signaled to Mitch. "You know where the friend lives. Go get her."

"No, no," she answered in painful defeat. "Don't do that." She pointed to the travel bag near the sofa. "It's in there."

"I'm sorry about all this," Marc said, and pushed his hands into his pockets. "And, for what it's worth, I didn't know they would kill Robert."

"You murdered him for nothing because he didn't tell me anything."

Marc shook his head. "You've ruined everything. Justin would have eventually become bored around here and left to go back to New York . . . that was Linda's job. But you show up with all your questions, and you catch his eye, and he not only becomes interested in you, but the business, too."

As Mitch searched the bag, Knight gave Davina an unctuous smile. "I can see what distracted Justin. You are a looker. Too bad I can't enjoy you this time."

While Davina frowned at the crude words, Mitch presented the painting.

Knight took the wrapped package from Mitch's hand and tore back a corner for confirmation. He tapped the package and smiled at Marc. "We've got it."

"What do we do with her now?" Mitch asked. "She can identify us."

"We'll take her with us. Let Mr. Knightman decide," Marc quickly suggested.

Davina's heightened fear had reached another level. So, Knightman was in charge, and she'd meet him after all. Not quite the way she'd expected.

"Bind and gag her," Knight said. "We're overdue at the warehouse."

Justin maneuvered the car through the iron gates. The drive to clear his head had not helped. What he needed was to see Davina, to have her take back the painful words she had hurled his way earlier. He noticed the full house lights on the main floor were bright against the surrounding darkness, and then he saw the sedan with a city license parked with the family cars. He immediately knew it belonged to the detectives handling the homicide case. Why were they here?

He parked the car, and halfway down the walk, the front door opened and his mother preceded the two detectives outside to meet him.

"Justin," she called out. "The police are trying to locate Davina."

He stopped when he met up with them on the walk. "Why do you want her?"

"We've uncovered new evidence, enough to bring her in again for questioning," Detective Lovett said. "We went by her apartment, and no one answered. We understand she's been staying here for the past few days."

"Yes." Justin's brows narrowed. "What kind of new evidence?"

Detective Jaragoski fished a card from his pocket and sighed. "So this is how we'll play it, huh?" He handed the card to Justin.

"If you hear from her or if you have information, call us at that number," the younger detective said. When he didn't get a response, he said, "We'll be in touch."

"Sure." Justin looked at the card before he put it in his pocket. He and Mrs. Hardy watched until the detectives left in their car.

"Is Davina in trouble? If so, we have to help."

"I know," he said. "And, I'll find her. I want you to call David, tell him what happened, and have him meet me at her apartment." He rushed off to his car.

* * *

Justin paced across the small portico in front of Davina's apartment, his anger at her long forgotten. Worry had etched harsh lines across his forehead when, upon arriving, he didn't see her car. He had even walked to Natalie's building, in case she was there, but Natalie wasn't home. Just as his control had been stretched to its limits, David drove up.

"I got here as fast as I could." Wearing the same suit as earlier in the day, David bounded up the steps to join Justin while he fished for her key on his chain.

"Her car's not here, and when she left my house, she was madder than hell."

David gave Justin a reproachful look before he inserted the key into the lock. "We can wait inside. I called Natalie and she's checking a few places before she meets us here. Is there any chance she knows what the police are about to do?" He pushed the door open and clicked on the light.

While David jogged to the back of the apartment, Justin turned into the living room and looked around. "No," he called out to David. "They came here first."

"You were supposed to keep her at your house until I returned this evening," David called back. "So what made her mad? Didn't you tell her about the letters and the board's vote?"

"I never got the chance," he responded absently as he sniffed the air. Cigarette smoke. She wasn't a smoker and neither was David or Natalie. His brows pulled together as he perused the room, his suspicions now heightened.

Then he saw it, the innocuous cigarette butt crushed into the carpet. He dropped to one knee and looked at it closely.

David's footsteps returned to the living room. "There's nothing in the back. Did you find something up here?" he asked Justin as he joined him.

Justin pointed at the floor.

"A cigarette butt." David looked up and saw the worry on Justin's face, and his own became stricken with the same. "You think something's happened to her."

Justin took a deep breath and stood up. "I don't know. Let's look around."

At that moment, Natalie came through the door. "Did you get any word on Davina yet?" She looked expectantly from David to Justin as she closed the door.

David explained. "We think someone was here before we arrived."

Justin walked to the sofa where he saw a glimpse of her travel bag behind the coffee table. He picked it up carefully. "This is the bag she left the house with." Clothes protruded rudely from an unzipped side.

"Let me see that," Natalie said. Coming closer, she took the bag from his hand.

David called from across the room. "Justin, look at this."

He joined David near the kitchen and saw the small gold pin in his palm.

"What do you make of it?" David asked. "It was on the floor here."

It was a tiepin. Justin turned it over and saw the writing on the front. As he recognized the small script, a shiver crawled through him, and he was filled with foreboding.

"David." Natalie said his name slowly. "Did Davina say anything to you about the last painting?"

"What last painting?" Justin asked, looking up from the pin.

David and Natalie exchanged a knowing glance.

"The night her apartment was ransacked," David began, "only two of the paintings were taken. They missed the third one and Vinny hid it away . . . in Florida. She brought it back to Atlanta the other day."

"She took it back to your house in this bag," Natalie added. "Only, it's not here. And if she was going to do anything with it, she would've told one of us."

Exasperation swept across Justin's face. "You're telling me she still had one of the original paintings? Didn't you realize that whoever wanted those paintings would try again?"

"There was no arguing with Vinny," David said. "Anyway, she brought it back to Atlanta to return to you."

Justin looked at the pin again "All of this gets stranger and stranger."

"You know something about it?" David asked.

"It's a Hardy service pin My father received one. And Marc has the other."

CHAPTER THIRTY-FIVE

Into the Pirate's Lair

David looked from the pin to Justin. "You think Marc Randall was here?"

"That's his tie pin," Justin said and paced across the floor. "From the way things look, Davina and the painting left with whomever was here."

"She didn't take her purse." Natalie's words turned both men's heads. They watched while she pulled Davina's shoulder purse from the unzipped side pocket of the bag. "Look. Her money, license, everything is here." Natalie was close to tears. "She's in trouble."

Justin watched as David made a path to Natalie and comforted her with a tight hug. He turned away and walked to the window as he silently berated himself for letting her leave his house for the sake of his pride. If only he had it to do over again. He turned back to them as they pulled apart.

"Why would Marc come here at all?" Justin spoke his thoughts aloud.

"We can't just stand around." David dropped the pin onto the coffee table and pressed his fingertips into his temples. "Where would they go?"

"We may have luck on our side," Justin said, his voice terse. "The investigator I hired is on his way. I called him before you got here."

"An investigator?" Natalie asked. "You mean, like a PI?"

Justin peered through the blinds and into the parking lot before answering. "Exactly like that. I was worried about her, so I decided to see to her safety whether she wanted me to or not."

"What did you do?" David asked.

Justin looked pointedly at David. "I've had her tailed since the break-in."

"*You* had her followed?" Natalie sputtered in surprise and stared at Justin. "Oh, my God. Davina saw the tail, but figured he was the guy who broke into the apartment." She laid a hand across her chest. "And he worked for you?"

David shouted his frustrations at Natalie. "You mean to tell us she knew she was being followed and you two didn't say anything?"

"Both of you would've worried, and she wanted to handle it herself," Natalie shouted back. Then, her voice calmer, she added, "She has the right to master her own fate, even if it means keeping something from the two men she loves most."

Justin pinched the bridge of his nose as he listened to Natalie's words. Did Davina love him? He remembered her anger at his attempt to wrest away the very control she so much wanted. He'd be damned if he ever made that mistake again.

"David," he said. "You asked me why she was so mad when she left the house. She found out about Connie Preston—he's the PI in charge of the investigation I had going on her past. Linda learned of it purely by accident and, out of vindictiveness, told her today."

"She found out from Linda?" Natalie asked. "Oh, Justin, that hurt her."

"I know. Anyway, I tried to explain to her why I did it, but she wouldn't listen." A deep frown grew on his face. "I shouldn't have let her leave. I should have stopped her."

David had been silent up until now. "So, you used an investigator?"

Justin nodded. "When neither of you played square with me, I got answers my own way. As I got to know both of you better, I hoped Davina would share your past with me. So, I kept quiet about what I was doing." He let out a sigh. "I have no excuse for my silence;

and in light of what Natalie said, Davina has every reason to be angry.''

David folded his arms across his chest. "At least there's a payoff to what you did. This investigator of yours could be our only hope if Vinny's in trouble.''

Justin saw the flash of lights through the blinds. "That may be Connie now.'' He briskly moved across the room and through the front door.

Relieved when he saw Connie's bald pate stick out of the Ford Explorer's window, Justin hailed him from the portico, then advanced on the truck. "She's gone, but she was definitely here earlier, and with at least two other people.''

David had come up behind Justin. "Did you follow her this evening? Do you know where she is now?''

"Raphael is the man on the detail,'' Connie exclaimed, and threw the gear in park. "He saw her go into the apartment, but when her car left the complex, there was a man at the wheel. That's when he suspected something was up. He's following her car now and will check back with me when he learns the destination. Come on, get in.''

Justin was already at the passenger door and climbed onto the front seat. David and Natalie were doing the same at each of the back doors.

"Natalie,'' David said, shaking his head. "You're not coming with us.''

"Yes, I am.'' Her tone was intractable. "I won't sit here and worry.''

"Leave her alone,'' Justin said from the front seat. "We don't have time to negotiate a truce.'' He glanced over at Connie. "All right, let's move.''

Connie maneuvered the truck from the parking space. "Raphael last saw the car heading south on I-85, back toward downtown.''

"Then step on it,'' Justin said, his voice taut with apprehension.

Davina tried desperately to change positions in the closed space of the car trunk, to no avail. To keep her folded legs from numbing, she kicked the trunk walls. Her hands were bound together behind her with strips of gray, nylon tape. Tape also covered her lower face. They had added insult to injury by rolling her in a blanket and depositing her on top of a melange of hard, unyielding objects.

To control her panic in the suffocatingly dark tomb, she took comfort in memories of the moments she had spent in Justin's strong arms and wondered if she'd experience that exquisite pleasure again. There was so much to make up for, and she wanted the chance to show him she had no doubts about him or his intentions.

How long had they been driving now? Twenty, thirty minutes? Longer? She couldn't tell. The hypnotic, rolling motion of the car had become a cautiously bumpy one. The terrain had changed.

The car stopped with a jerk. Davina held her breath and waited for it to move again, but it didn't. When the soft one-two thud of car doors opening and closing reached her ears, she knew. They had reached their destination and her destiny.

The cell phone's ring blared above the loud conversation of the Explorer's occupants, and it startled them into an uneasy quiet.

Connie looked at the caller ID box. "It's Raphael. I'll put it on the speaker."

He pressed a button on the center console and spoke to the microphone above the mirror. "Yeah, Raphael," Connie said. "I got a load of anxious people with me. Talk to me and tell me what you know."

"Plenty," Raphael replied. "They're at the old warehouse downtown near the viaduct. Looks like a meeting of some kind. Two cars are already here and our marks just drove up in two cars; one belongs to our bird. She is definitely with them. She's bundled in a blanket and was carried into the building over one of the mark's shoulders."

Both Justin and David let loose with expletives.

"Could you tell if she was okay otherwise?" Justin asked.

"She's alive, if that's what you mean, and strong enough to put up a fight while she was taken inside."

"Keep your post at a safe distance, Rafe," Connie advised. "We should be there in fifteen to twenty minutes. Don't try to do anything by yourself," he warned.

Justin cut in. "We'll alert the police and have them meet us there."

"Will do," Raphael answered. "I'll call if the situation changes."

While Connie disconnected, Justin fished the detective's card from his pocket. He pressed the numbers on the phone console. Within two rings, the homicide office answered, but neither detective was in. However, the dispatcher promised to find them and relay the message.

Justin ended the connection, then punched in another set of numbers.

"Who are you calling now?" David asked.

"Playing a hunch," he said, and handed the phone to Natalie. "Ask for Marc." He watched Natalie as she waited for someone to answer the rings.

"Is Marc in?" she asked, then paused for the answer. "No, but thank you," she responded before she handed the phone back to Justin. "He wasn't in, but he will be later on."

"He's with Davina at the warehouse," Justin said matter-of-factly.

"It was Linda who answered the phone," Natalie said. "I know her voice."

He wasn't surprised. "It makes sense. And, it fits."

David leaned forward to Justin. "I'm guessing you'll explain all this later."

"A lot is falling in place," he said, and glanced at Connie. "You told me the answer to my problems was in my own backyard." Eyes steely, he stared ahead. "We can't go any faster?"

Connie smiled and increased his speed. "We're down to a ten minute ETA."

Justin rested his arm along the window. Linda and Marc's manipulation had always been evident, but he had ignored it, thinking it was harmless ambition. He wondered if they did it for the money or control of the company? He darted another of many looks at his watch. If anything happened to Davina because of his blindness . . . He sat stonefaced in the truck, everyone silent now, as Connie raced along the expressway to the downtown warehouse.

Mitch Timmins gladly rid himself of the twisting bundle across his shoulder. He dumped the load unceremoniously into a heap onto the floor of the warehouse, like the unwanted baggage it was.

Davina lay there, her strength momentarily spent, and waited for the sting of renewed blood flow to pass. The blanket no longer covered her face and her hair had come undone from the braid. The men walked past her crumpled figure and stood together some fifteen feet away, their backs turned to her. With their attention otherwise taken, she grunted for strength and managed to roll over onto her back and view her surroundings.

The place was well lit and cavernous. At least two or three stories high, it seemed the length of half a football field. And it resembled a pirate's hideout. The floor was poured cement, but the walls in her line of vision were covered with paintings, murals, and tapestries of all sizes. Stacked shelves jutted out from the walls, and on their surfaces rested sculptures, vases, and various art objects. This was where they stored the stolen and forged art.

Davina's eyes strained to take in as much of the treasure trove as she could, when she heard the boisterous shout of a man's voice followed by heavy steps coming from the other end of the building.

"What did you bring her here for?" The big voice boomed.

He was talking about her. She craned her neck to see his face, but the men stood in her way. She looked toward the door they had come through and saw Mitch Timmins standing guard.

"We had no choice, Dad."

Dad? It was Knight's accented voice. She turned her head, her ears keened to what was said next.

"We ran into a problem at her apartment." Marc's tone was cautious. "I thought maybe you'd want to decide what to do, Mr. Knightman."

Davina grunted at the revelation. Knightman . . . Knight . . . father and son.

"She saw us and put things together," Knight said. "We have to get rid of her, but I don't think Marc here has the stomach."

An alarm sounded uneasily in Davina's head and she watched as the men turned to her. Davina swallowed hard and tested her tight bindings. And then, the men parted and he was at her side, bent on one knee. Perry Knightman.

Davina's heart thumped madly, but she didn't avoid his stare. She looked defiantly into the almost lineless brown face and strong features of a man who was surely near seventy, yet he was infused with energy.

His eyes were like black onyx, strangely flat, and gave no clue into his soul. She saw his hand come up. Expecting another blow, she flinched; but he reached for a corner of the tape on her mouth, and in one great motion, ripped it away.

Davina let out a loud gasp, then a groan, the pain a horrible creature that skittered across her face. She took careful, deep breaths and stared at him—anger, confusion, and a healthy dollop of fear all poured from her eyes.

"You got the painting?" Knightman asked of no one in particular.

"Yes, sir," Marc said. "It's out in the car."

"So," Knightman said to Davina, "you're one of Maceo's pups, huh? The meddling one, I believe." He slid a hand behind her neck and roughly pulled her to a sitting position.

She managed to swing her legs under her hips in order to rest on her knees. The blanket had dropped away and revealed her tired, disheveled state; but her face was full of strength in spite of the icy fear that totally encased her. She leveled a stare at him and gave him her best voice. "And you're Perry Knightman. I've heard about you, too." She nodded toward Knight. "He's your son? I didn't know that."

"Dennis Knight. That's all you need to know," his son said.

"Shut up," Knightman's voice was angry, but his eyes never left Davina. "I've worked hard so no one hears about me. It pains me to learn you have."

"What are you going to do to me?" she asked.

More footsteps sounded across the cement and all eyes momentarily turned in that direction. Davina's eyes squinted in confusion. It was Nathan Randolph.

"How long do I have to wait in the office before you pay me? I need to leave." He stopped in his tracks when he saw Davina kneeling on the floor. "What is she doing here?"

Davina slowly shook her head at him. "You're mixed up in this, too?"

Knightman got to his feet and motioned to Nathan. "I told you to wait in the office. I'll finish with you in a minute."

"That's Davina Spenser." Nathan pushed his way through the men and knelt by her side. "What are you doing here . . . and tied up?" He looked around at Marc. "What's going on here, man?"

"They killed Robert at the gallery and they want to kill me," she said coldly.

"What's she talking about?" He stood and faced the men. "Did y'all forget who the lady is?" His questions went unanswered and he glanced from one man to the other.

"Nathan," Knightman said, "for all your talent with a paintbrush, you have no common sense. She knows what we've been doing. And since she's seen all of you, get rid of her. If you want to get paid, come along Nathan." He stalked away from the group. "Where's my driver? I have a plane to catch very soon."

Davina could only gasp at his cavalier decision, and knew she had to buy time to figure a way out.

"Don't you want to know how I found out about you?" she called out to him.

The words stopped Knightman and he turned back to her. "That's right. I would like to know."

"From your friends, the artist circle from the old days."

He twisted his lips in a sneer. "Those old men? They know nothing about me. You know nothing." He started to turn.

"I know you elicited promises from all of them." She watched as he once again turned to her. "In fact, you bought friendship with illegal activities on a regular basis. You did it with Nathan's father, and Nathan, too."

"Yeah," Nathan agreed. "But, no more, Mr. Knightman. Let her go."

"I've searched for answers a long time," Davina said. "I knew when I found you I'd learn what kind of business relationship Maceo and Jacob Hardy had. I know now."

Dennis Knight strutted forward. "And what do you think you know?"

"Your father helped mine escape his troubles, but he didn't do it without a steep price. Then it occurred to me. What does an illegitimate businessman want most?" She looked at Knightman. "Legitimacy. You wanted their legitimate business to front your illegal one, didn't you? That had to be why my father wouldn't accept your offer for

help. Later on, a desperate Jacob agreed to a deal with you for part
of the business if you'd help his friend and partner get away from the
police.''

"You're pretty smart.'' Knightman strode back to her. "True, I
needed a legitimate front in those days, and Jacob's was ready made.
But he and Maceo were already partners and Maceo didn't like my
style.'' He gave a cruel laugh as he remembered the times. "When
things got hot for Maceo, they had no choice, and Jacob agreed to let
me come in on his share, but only if I'd help Maceo get away.''

Davina had to keep him talking and allow the conceit of his power
to come forward, so she did what she did best—she continued to
theorize.

"He reneged on the deal, but he had a good reason, didn't he?''
When it seemed Knightman would again walk away without answer-
ing, she baited him. "You screwed up. You messed up your own
sweet deal.''

"He didn't mess it up,'' Knight said. "He just had the job done
right.''

Perry Knightman let out a hollow laugh. "Jacob found out the truth
about that beating. Maceo beat that white boy that hurt his woman,
but Maceo was soft, and didn't have it in him to do it right. So, I
made sure my man was there to finish the job he only started. That
was my insurance that Maceo would need my help later on down the
road.''

Davina was dumbfounded at his pompous admission, and struggled
to stand on her feet. She had to keep him talking. "You let my father
think he was responsible for the man's death. That guilt destroyed
him.''

"Jacob was mad at what I'd done, and called our deal off. He said
he would tell Maceo the truth, but Maceo had been long gone. Jacob
didn't tell the police or anyone else because he knew I was still
powerful enough to cause trouble for him, his family, his business.
So, he kept it with him to the grave. After that, every time I tried to
make a move into his business, he'd fight me off.''

"We warned Jacob he'd be sorry for welching on the deal,'' Knight
shouted angrily in defense of his father.

"And I always make good on my promises,'' Knightman said. He walked to his son's side and put an arm around his shoulder. "It feels good to tell this to Maceo's pup. Too bad I can't tell it personally to Jacob's. I had my son here raised in Europe using a shortened version of my name. And I helped him quietly build a legitimate empire there. Sort of my own private shadow corporation." He patted his son's shoulder. "We were on the verge of taking over Hardy Enterprises, loan by loan, asset by asset, with Marc's recent help, of course, and then you came along . . . a wrench in the works." He dropped his arm. "But not for long."

"There's still the matter of the third painting, Dad. Now that we have it, we still need it worked for the buyer." He looked at Nathan. "You're still our man."

"I'm out of this." Nathan looked at Knightman. "We agreed I'd be paid for the jobs I've already delivered." He looked at Marc. "Didn't you tell them?"

Knight's sonorous voice was insidious. "Plans change."

Nathan held up his hands. "I want my money, and then I'm leaving."

"Not so fast," Knight said. "How do we know you can be trusted, now that you know about her?"

"Marc," Nathan pleaded as he backed away. He looked at the other men. "You're still talking about murder here."

Knightman looked at the man he had complimented only moments earlier, and with a sneer said, "What do you suggest we do? She'll go to the police. Even Marc knows that. She signed her own death warrant when she learned our details."

"Timmins should have killed her the night he took the paintings," Knight taunted.

"You'll never get away with this," Davina said. "You'll be found out. Justin already suspects something now. It'll only be a matter of time before he breaks your scam wide open."

"Then maybe we ought to go ahead and get it over with, right?" Knight produced the gun Davina remembered from her apartment.

"No," Marc argued, shaking his head. "You have to find another way. You can't just kill her."

"And why not?" Knight asked. "She'll disappear, car and all, never to return. The police will figure she ran away to avoid murder charges, just like her daddy did. That's a nice touch, don't you think?" He motioned to Timmins at the door.

Davina watched Nathan do a circular pace nearby, and Marc avoided her stare. They wouldn't—no, couldn't—help. And with that inevitable observation, she could no longer hold back the tears of frustration and fear that had built ever since she had encountered Linda at the office. It seemed so long ago, now. She closed her eyes and the tears flowed freely—through their purity, she found a cleansing of her heart. She knew her father understood, and somehow Justin and David would bring all she had discovered to light.

Davina opened her eyes to Timmins standing at close range, a gun pointed at her chest. When she realized his intent, she slowly backed away, her eyes glued to the gun. "For God's sake, don't do this." She saw out of the corner of her eye that Marc had turned his back on the scene, but Nathan hadn't.

Out of nowhere, Nathan launched his tall lanky frame into Mitch's broad, muscular one. It was no contest, but it was enough to throw the guard off balance.

"Run Davina," she heard Nathan shout, but she didn't have to be told that. She looked back to Nathan as she sped to the unguarded door, and what she saw stopped her in her tracks.

Mitch brought the gun down on Nathan's skull with a mighty force, and the man crumpled to the floor.

"What are you doing to him?" Davina screamed at Timmins.

Knight had caught her, and pulled her by the arm. "Dump him in the box, and get rid of her, too," he ordered.

"No, no!" Davina screamed with all her might as tears coursed down her face, and she crashed into Knight. Both of them went tumbling to the cement, but Knight's hands weren't tied and he quickly regained his balance and grabbed the screaming and kicking Davina around the middle.

At that moment, a black-suited man, heretofore unseen, ran into the warehouse, a gun in his hand. "I think we're going to have company shortly, sir."

Knightman had watched the scenes unfold dispassionately next to Marc, but now stood erect and ready to act. "Marc, give my guard that last painting." Then, to the man who had rushed in, he barked an order "Meet me at the car."

"You'll never get away with this!" Davina continued to scream. "Justin won't stop until he learns the truth. He'll work with my brother and they'll find all of you."

Knightman pulled a handkerchief from his pocket to wipe his forehead. He motioned to Nathan's slumped body. "Get them both out of here, quickly, and will someone shut up her screaming."

Barely waiting for the Explorer to stop behind Raphael's pickup, Justin ordered Connie and Natalie to wait for the police's arrival, when they all heard the screams. The faint, high-pitched screams rent the night air and sent Justin, David, and Raphael racing down the overweeded path along the side of the rundown warehouse. Justin was in the lead, the .38 revolver he had taken from Connie extended in front of him.

Raphael motioned to Justin that he would check the other side of the building and retraced his steps until he was out of sight. Justin and David sidled along the edge of the building and prepared to round the corner. The steel doors at the back wall of the warehouse pushed open and Marc walked out. He was angrily gesturing to someone else at his side. David came around Justin, and led the assault.

Marc and the other man cleared the warehouse door and moved purposefully to the vehicles parked a few yards away. David tapped on Marc's shoulder, and with a neck hold, wrestled him to the ground. At the same time, Justin used the gun and brought it down hard across the other man's neck.

They quickly dragged the two men back to the shadowed side of the building. Justin pocketed the extra gun and moved over to David. Marc, supine on the ground, had David's knee in his chest.

"Where's Davina," David started in. "And if I don't hear the right answer, you'll be eating your teeth in ten seconds."

Marc held up his hands in a defensive gesture. "I swear this wasn't supposed to happen. I swear."

"Where is she, dammit?" Justin demanded.

"In the warehouse." His eyes darted between the men. "Hurry. I think Dennis Knight's going to kill her."

Justin sprang from the ground as fear, stark and vivid, shattered through his body. He heard the crunch of David's fist against flesh and knew he had kept his word. Justin raced back to the steel door Marc had left partly opened and, flattened against the wall, peered inside before quickly pulling his head out. The inside of the building was the antithesis of the outside facade, but the booty inside seemed worthy of that deception. In the distance, he heard sirens, and knew the detectives had finally arrived with help.

David came up behind him. "Do you see her?" he asked.

"No, I don't see or hear anything. Let's go inside."

They carefully moved into the cavernous room, their heads twisting up and down, left and right, to take in the spectacle of the goods stored in the place.

"Look at this stuff, Justin."

"They pirated their stolen goods here."

They stayed near the walls and quietly loped to the other end where Justin pointed to a door. The door was opening and a voice spoke from the opposite side. "Where in the hell is Marc with the painting?"

It was an accented voice Justin immediately recognized as Dennis Knight's.

Two men stepped out into the open, and Justin could now see the second man, Mitch Timmins.

The men had just cleared the door when Justin pointed the gun in their direction. "A strange place to find you, Mr. Knight. And with my security guard." He motioned to the guard. "Stand over here where I can see you, hands out.

Knight looked at the gun, then Justin. He held his hands out in supplication, and in a sarcastic voice, said, "What's this about?"

"You know damn well what it's about," David said as he stepped up in line with Justin. "Where's my sister? What did you do with her?"

"I haven't an idea of who you're talking about." He looked to the stolid Timmins who stood nearby, his hands out to his sides.

"Cut the bull." Justin's voice thundered like a great fallen oak. "We know she's here. Marc and one of your goons are lying outside the door.'' He raised the gun level with Knight's head and stepped toward him. "Where is she?" He reached into his pocket and tossed the gun he'd relieved from the man outside to David. "Keep it on Timmins."

"I don't know who you're talking about," Knight replied, his clipped words tinged with caution as he took a step backward for each of Justin's forward ones. His hands were now raised. "Of course, shooting me won't get you a better answer."

"But it'll give me pleasure." He cocked the lever and the gun barrel twisted ominously. "Now, what have you done with her?"

"Mr. Hardy." A loud voice accompanied by running feet came from somewhere behind Justin. "Lower the gun—now. Connie filled us in on what's happened. We'll handle it from here." It was Detective Lovett.

"They've got Vinny here, somewhere," David said, "and they're not talking."

"We're wasting time, then. Let's start a search. But first, lower the guns."

Justin slowly released his finger from the trigger and lowered the gun. David followed suit.

"All right, let's spread out," Detective Jaragoski ordered the flank of officers who had filed into the warehouse. "We're looking for a young woman."

Justin and David advanced on Detective Lovett and the officer who read the two men their rights.

"I haven't done anything," Knight said with a laugh. "This is preposterous."

Timmins chimed in with, "I'm not saying anything until I see my lawyer."

"You've been caught in a warehouse full of stolen property," David said. "Kidnapping charges are worse, but not as bad as the charge if you've hurt her."

Dennis Knight smirked at David's words and straightened the cuff of his shirt. "I'll be home for breakfast and you still won't have anyone to connect me with anything illegal."

Justin's reaction was instantaneous as he reared his fist back and brought it to bear against Knight's jaw. "If you've hurt her, I'll kill you.'' He watched Knight stumble backward and into the warehouse office.

''Hey, hey.'' Detective Lovett jumped in front of Justin and barked an order to the officer nearby. ''Cuff those guys and get them out of here.'' He turned back to Justin and David. ''Why don't you two cool off. By the way, do you have a license for that piece?''

Justin put the gun in his pocket. ''Yes, but you may want to check out the other one.'' He nodded to David, who handed the gun he held to the detective.

''I'll see if they've come up with anything in the warehouse on Miss Spenser. When I get back, we'll talk.'' He left the office and closed the door behind him.

Justin's heart was squeezed tight; he could barely draw a breath without feeling Davina in his heart. He was supposed to protect her and he'd let her down. He had to think, and looked around the room he and David found themselves in. It was a large office, lavishly furnished for a warehouse locale, with lots of floor space.

''Justin, look at this.'' David was inspecting three easels set up in the middle of the floor. Two held the Maceo paintings that were taken from Davina's apartment and the third was empty. David glanced at Justin.

''Let's search the place,'' Justin said. Both men rambled through the bathroom and closets in search of a spot that might have been used to hide her.

David circled the office. ''This is the only room in this place?'' He looked up when one of the officers came through the door.

''Your friends are looking for you,'' the officer said. ''I told them they could come in here.''

''She has to be in this warehouse,'' Justin said. ''We heard the screams, and Marc said they had her in here. We've overlooked something, that's all.'' He looked at the officer. ''We need to talk to Marc Randall.''

The officer shook his head. ''Both men outside were taken downtown with the others.'' He left as Natalie's voice filtered in.

''David, Justin?'' she called.

''In here,'' David answered.

She ran through the doorway and Connie followed. "The police said you haven't found her yet."

"We're checking this room out," David said. "You and Connie can help."

"Dennis Knight and the guard came out of here." As Justin walked across the middle of the floor, his footstep produced a squeak. He stopped and realized he hadn't noticed it before. This room had a wood floor. It wasn't cement.

"There's a floor below us." When Justin saw the question on their faces, he stomped the floor. "It's wood. The rest of the place is cement." He spun around and looked at the walls. "There has to be a secret door here somewhere."

"Let's find it then," Connie said gruffly, and began his own inspection.

"There's a full length mirror behind the desk," Natalie mused out loud. "Why is it in such a tight space?"

The men stopped to look at the cheap, wood framed mirror among the other excessive furnishings in the room. Nailed to the paneled wall, it rested about six inches from the floor.

In a lightning fast motion, Justin was in front of it. "Natalie's right. Why would a mirror be put there?" Connie and David joined him, and they touched, pressed, and pulled on the mirror.

And then, like magic, one side of the sixty inch mirror swung out from a hidden wall hinge, and a musty odor, combined with a mixture of dust that jettisoned like spores, flew from the space. They saw the mirror was actually a two-way glass. Speechless, they crowded to the opening and looked down into a chasm of darkness that waited below a set of dusty, rickety looking stairs—an ominous passageway in every sense.

"Well, I'll be damned," Connie finally said.

Justin stuck his head into the dark shaft. "Davina!" He called her name twice, but there was no sound except their own hushed breathing. "I'm going down," he said, and stepped through the opening. "Get some flashlights in here."

Natalie ran out to get the detectives while David, and then Connie, followed Justin into the black hole.

CHAPTER THIRTY-SIX

All's Well That Ends Well

Justin swung out at the hanging cobwebs and carefully made his way into the dark on the surprisingly sturdy freestanding stairs. What was this place? He peered into the murkiness and saw nothing, heard nothing, but smelled the moist earth. If she was down here, she was terrified.

"What do you make of this?" David asked from somewhere above Justin.

"We need light," Justin anxiously shouted.

"Natalie went for them," Connie called down. "Hold on."

He stepped onto a soft soil surface and knew he had reached the bottom. David was right behind him. The smell of earth was redolent in the dank space, almost oppressive. The air was moist and cool.

"Davina, are you here?" Justin called out in all directions, but the dirt packed walls absorbed the volume. David joined him in calling her name again and again.

The men paused and strained to hear some sign of life in the place. They both jerked toward something that seemed to come from behind the stairs.

"Hey, I've got some light." It was Detective Lovett's voice as he came down the stairs with twin blazes of brilliance pouring into the obscure darkness.

"Did you hear that?" Justin's voice was hopeful. He caught one of the flashlights tossed his way and pointed it in the direction of the sound. "Over there, behind the stairs."

"I heard it, too," Connie agreed.

The flashlight beams joined forces and illuminated a cone-shaped swatch of murkiness across the earthen floor. They played across craggy walls of packed red clay; various sized empty wire containers and cages were stacked in the long room.

"It looks like some kind of a storage cellar," Connie observed.

Justin called Davina's name again.

David was already on the other side of the stairway. "Over here. It's coming from down here."

Justin joined him and stooped to the soft earth where he pointed.

"Down here, listen," David said.

He could hear it. The scrapes and bumps were erratic and faint, but unmistakable.

"She may be down here. Give us a hand," Justin shouted to the men.

They used the bottoms of the flashlights and dug into the rusty, moist clay in search of a possible false floor. The muffled noises that came from underneath the soil became stronger, more vigorous as the men pushed away the loose dirt.

"I found a latch," Justin roared, and hit at the metal with the butt of the light.

Upon the discovery, the men furiously cleared another two inches of soil away from what appeared to be a wide metal plate. "The latch is open, lift it up," he ordered.

Connie held the lights and the other men lifted the metal plate high, before thrusting it backward into the dirt wall. A cloud of earth and dust dropped into the gaping, rectangular hole revealed underneath.

Connie flashed the lights into the shadowy void.

Davina sat in the corner of a rectangular box. Her hands were tied behind her back and she pressed into the metal enforced walls of the four-foot-high prison. Next to her lay another body, sprawled along the eight-foot-long dirt floor. She blinked into the light when she looked up, a handkerchief tied across her mouth, and dirt stuck to her face. She grunted a sound before her head lolled forward.

"Davina." Justin choked her name and jumped into the box.

"Mother of God, it's her!" David shouted.

In one swift motion, Justin pulled the handkerchief from her mouth before he scooped her into his arms. "Hold on, honey, we're getting you out of here."

His reward was her head against his chest, and her labored, whispered words, "I knew you'd come."

The men helped Justin from the box. "She needs oxygen," he ordered.

"We can get a tank from the ambulance outside," David said as he followed Justin. "Get her to the office."

Justin maneuvered his way to the stairs in a purposeful stride. "I'm not stopping until I get her out of this building," he answered in a tone that forbade questions.

"I'll check the other body in here," Detective Lovett said. "All right, somebody get the paramedics down here, now," he shouted. "And we need more light."

The October night had turned crisp, and the score of police cars that parked haphazardly around the old warehouse gave the area the appearance of an impromptu fall festival, complete with bright lights, noise, and people.

Natalie and David sat turned in the Explorer's front seat while Davina sat in the back seat within the circle of Justin's warm arms. He had not left her side since he'd carried her from the cellar prison. He had also been a great comfort when she recounted her story of the evening to the detectives.

Detective Jaragoski shifted his weight against the truck's open door. "You've had a rough night, Miss Spenser, but this should be enough to start our investigation in a new direction. A crime scene team is already at your apartment gathering prints and evidence."

"Is there any word from the hospital on Nathan's condition?" She spoke in a low tone, her throat hoarse from her screams.

"Not yet," David said. "Before they left, he was alive but unconscious."

Davina rubbed her hand across Justin's. "He saved my life."

"You can testify on his behalf," Justin suggested. "Maybe that'll help him receive leniency on this first offense."

She tilted her head so she could look into his eyes. "It's still hard to believe Marc and your business partners did all this."

"Jeter and Timmins saw you that night in the gallery," Justin explained. "Jeter recognized you before the board meeting started, and left. I don't think he told Marc immediately who you were, but he reported back to Dennis Knight. They figured you were the only person who could have had the paintings."

"Linda Daniels and Andrew Jeter are being picked up for questioning as accessories to kidnapping, theft, and murder." Detective Jaragoski snorted as he said, "I have a feeling they'll all be trying to sing first when they learn you and the young man are alive."

"It's a shame Perry Knightman got away, though." Detective Lovett walked up to the truck with a package in his hand.

"His son's arrest will be a huge blow to his operation," Jaragoski added.

"I thought Connie said Raphael followed him," David said.

"He lost them on the expressway." Detective Lovett offered the explanation.

Justin looked around. "Where are Connie and Raphael?"

Detective Lovett called to Connie who stood with a group nearby, and turned back to Justin. "Some of the work in the warehouse is from your gallery, but we have to temporarily hold it as evidence." He handed her a wrapped package, which Davina recognized as the painting taken from her apartment tonight. "This was in the trunk they put you in, Miss Spenser. I'm afraid it's been damaged."

She took the torn package and removed the small framed canvas. "The frame is cracked. I must have kicked it when I was in the trunk."

"I thought you might want to see it before I take it in with the other property as evidence. I'll be back for it shortly." He left to join the other detective.

Davina looked at David. "Perry Knightman destroyed our family. Dad would never have run if that man had been able to walk away from the beating."

"I've been talking with Justin and Detective Lovett," David replied. "They believe we have enough evidence to clear Dad's name."

"Evidence?" Davina asked. "Knightman's gone."

"Remember when I wanted to talk with you at the house this

afternoon?'' When Davina nodded to Justin's question, he said,   I
still have to, but not here.''

"That's a beautiful frame. Can it be repaired?'' Natalie asked.

Davina ran her fingers along the break formations. "Look at the
clean fractures.'' She showed it to the others. "It's as if he made it
to breakaway.''

"Let me see that.'' David turned the frame in his hands and looked
at Justin.

"I'm going to try something.'' He applied pressure to the frame
and another clean fracture appeared. "You're right. This frame is
pieced together with six sections of wood.'' He pulled an L-shaped
piece away from the nailed canvas and found that the break revealed
a hollow opening drilled through the length of the wood piece.

"What do you make of that?'' Justin observed.

"It's another one of Dad's eccentricities we'll never understand,''
Davina surmised. "Charlie can put this back together.''

Connie walked up to the truck. "Justin, you were looking for me?''

"My man,'' Justin greeted him with a grin before he turned to
Davina. "I want you to meet someone,'' he said to her.

Connie stuck his head into the open truck. His bald pate glowed
from the direct light of the overhead lamp.

Justin slapped him across the shoulder. "This is Connie Preston,
a former Atlanta police detective, a good friend, and an important part
of how we were able to find you tonight. He's the investigator we
talked about this afternoon.''

Davina looked into a pair of compassionate eyes set within a face
as dark as ebony wood and spoke without rancor. "I owe you a world
of thanks, Mr. Preston.''

He flashed a smile. "Please, call me Connie. But I didn't do the
important work. That honor belongs to Raphael DeSantis. He'll be
glad to know that you're fine.'' He stepped out of the way and allowed
another man to fill the open doorway and look into the truck.

The man's satin black hair absorbed the light, and it gleamed like
a raven's back. He lifted his head and smiled at Davina.

She gasped and leaned back into Justin's shoulder, speechless.

"Davina,'' Justin quickly explained, "this is the man Connie and

I had protecting you after your apartment burglary. He watched your apartment tonight and followed the car that kidnapped you.''

Natalie started to giggle at her friend's continued astonishment. ''Davina, he was working for Justin all the time, when we thought—''

''I know what we thought,'' she said and pushed forward on the seat. She quirked her brows at Raphael. ''Didn't you know I saw you? You scared me that last time, yet you didn't tell me who you were.''

Raphael's smile dropped from his face, and he fumbled with a reply. ''That was my job. I was under orders to—''

''Davina, you should be angry with me, not Raphael,'' Justin interrupted.

She glanced at Justin and broke into a smile. ''Angry?'' She reached out to Raphael, and drew him into a hug. ''No, no. I am so glad you didn't do anything so foolish as to tell me who you were because I would've made sure you were taken off my case. Because you did your job, I'm here tonight.'' She released him, glad to see his smile again. ''Thank you.''

She looked at Justin. ''We do have a lot to talk about, don't we?''

''We're ready to take your statements now.'' Detective Lovett had come back to the car for David and Natalie. He pointed to his car parked across the street. ''I'll be over there,'' he said, and left with Connie and Raphael.

Natalie reached across the seat and touched Davina's arm. ''You're okay? You don't need another whiff of oxygen, do you?''

''I'm fine,'' she whispered hoarsely. She could have added that even in her tired condition, she couldn't be happier.

''Come on, David,'' Natalie said. ''Let's give our statements so we can go.''

Davina exchanged a nod and look with her brother that said, ''I'm all right.''

''Sure,'' David said. ''We'll be back.'' He followed Natalie out of the truck and they both walked off in the direction of the detectives.

Justin reached over and closed the truck door. Finally, they were alone. He turned back to Davina and she was sitting there, watching him in the dim light created by the surrounding vehicles. They didn't touch now, but his arm rested along the back of the seat.

''I said things at the house today that I didn't mean,'' Justin began.

"I should have trusted you and you wouldn't have been in danger. It was arrogant of me to think I knew all the answers when in fact I missed what was most important to you, your need for freedom and independence." His eyes settled on hers. "One thing I did say that I meant. I love you, Davina." His fingers moved to her neck and lightly stroked her hair. "I started on that journey the day we bumped into each other."

"When they put me in that hole, my only thought was that I'd never see you again." Her voice trembled and she looked away. "I prayed to God to give me one more chance to make things right with you."

"Davina . . ."

"No, let me finish. You showed me that you deserved my trust. I should have respected the fact that I can't do it all myself, and that relying on someone doesn't mean giving up my independence." She looked at him. "And that secrets have a way of coming out. I'm sorry that I accused you of those awful things. All you tried to do was help me and I reacted—"

"With good cause."

"I reacted because you made me look inside myself and face emotions that would sear me to you forever, and I was scared."

"Scared that history might repeat itself?"

She nodded, enjoying the stroke of his familiar fingers against her neck. "I was afraid because I knew, without a doubt, that I loved you, Justin."

He shifted in the seat and pulled her to his chest as he breathed her name into her hair. "I've never been a man who frightens easily, but I was so afraid I'd lost you tonight."

Davina drew her arms around Justin's neck. "I want you in my life, and I don't want to lose you, either." She dropped her hands to his chest, and stared deep into his eyes. "So, I'm ending this claim business, and that includes the paintings. Even though Knightman said our fathers were partners, you are right. There's no evidence that it's true. It's all hearsay, and David and I want it finished. I was going to tell you this before everything happened."

Justin smiled and studied her too serious face. "A lot has happened that you don't know about. First, the board had a special meeting last night. We agreed that there was compelling evidence to support your partnership claim."

"What compelling evidence?"

"My mother went through Dad's things, and she found a packet of letters he had hidden away, correspondence he and Maceo shared after the disappearance."

"Letters?" Davina's look was incredulous.

Justin nodded. "You could tell from their letters they were good friends, and they wrote about a business arrangement that could be interpreted as a partnership. After a while, Maceo abruptly stopped writing his letters, and my dad's letters stared to return undelivered, including the letter that explained Knightman's double cross. So, he stopped writing. Mom wanted you to have them."

"Does David know?"

Justin nodded. "Last night, I urged the board to vote and accept Maceo James as Dad's original partner. They did."

She raised her head. "You're willing to do that, for me?"

"You were going to do the same for me." He smoothed her hair and pulled her back to his chest. "David knows about the letters and the vote because I had him come to the house this afternoon. We'd planned to tell you when you came home later."

She raised up off him. "Do you think all this was fated? How would we have found each other otherwise?"

"You're beautiful." His eyes caught and held hers in the faint light. They both read a promise that heretofore didn't seem possible. "I think I would have found a way to you, no matter what, because there's an allure about you. Maybe it's your innocence, and your honesty, but it's all the more fascinating because you aren't aware of it." He bent his head and brought her lips to his. Their mouths met with an angel's touch, intensified by the words they had exchanged.

Justin raised his head. "I know you're tired and exhausted. I should be getting you home."

"Not yet. Kiss me again."

He smiled, and readily reclaimed her lips. "Connie will take us back to your apartment where I left my car"—he spoke the words against her lips—"and I'm going to personally see to it that you get showered and get some rest before anyone bothers you, and that includes my family.''

"I like that idea," Davina said, as they came apart. "But I should include some time with David and Natalie. Maybe they'll come to the apartment and talk.''

Justin laughed as he pulled her back into his arms. "I wouldn't worry about them. I think they can figure a way to fill the time without you.''

"What do you mean?''

"You haven't noticed?''

"Noticed what?'' Davina slowly raised her eyes to Justin's as bits and pieces of scenes crossed her mind, then they stretched wide. "You mean they . . .''

Justin nodded his head as a big grin split his face.

Davina looked in the direction they had walked. "My best friend and my brother? Oh, my goodness.'' She reached up and threw her arms around Justin's neck. "So, will you stay?''

Justin nuzzled her neck with kisses. "You won't get rid of me, though after personally seeing to your shower, I don't know how much rest you'll get.''

Davina laughed out loud for the first time that day. She vowed it would be the start of a lot more, and squeezed him tighter. "Promises, promises.''

Justin lay propped on his elbow in Davina's bed and watched as she slept. The bedside clock showed it was close to two o'clock in the morning. He had talked with his family and Douglas, and all were elated that Davina was okay. But sleep eluded him.

He studied Davina's sleeping profile. He wanted nothing more than to make love to her, but had resisted because he knew the extent of the trauma she had suffered tonight, and rest was the best medicine right now. He had held her close to his side until her breathing had become deep and even in sleep. Her thick hair fanned out against the pillow, and one of her hands lay above the covers. She wore no jewelry on her left hand, and he wondered about her ring size. He imagined their children, probably little troublemakers like their mother. He smiled as he allowed his thoughts to roam over the idea.

Davina wriggled from her back to her side and faced him. He watched her slowly open, then rub her eyes.

"Is it morning already?" she asked.

"No," he said, reaching for her hand. "You've only been asleep a few hours."

"I feel better." She scooted over and allowed him to gather her snugly against his bare chest. "Is it all really over now?"

"Except for the vote to keep me on as president."

"Is that what you're thinking about now, why you're not sleep?"

Justin clicked on the bedside lamp, and then picked up the stack of photos she had told him about that lay there. "I was looking through these old photos and started to think about our fathers, about us."

She sat up in the bed and they browsed through the pictures together. Davina pointed out facts she had learned and the men she now recognized.

"This shot is the same as the Maceo painting of the friends playing checkers," Justin commented.

"There's a funny story behind it. Lee Randolph told me that the photo is not about the friends, but the frame my dad was making for your father's portrait." She held the two pictures up for him. "The friends just happened to be there playing checkers and cards all the time. The frame, built in stages, is behind them."

They were both silent for a moment as they studied the photos, then turned to each other. But, Davina's words got out first. "That's really uncanny."

"Do you see it, too?" Justin asked.

"That has to be why your father was so concerned about keeping the painting intact and with the company. Come on," she said, scrambling from the bed. "We have to go to your office."

"Now?" Justin asked, as he threw the covers aside.

"Of course, now," she said. "You can drive."

CHAPTER THIRTY-SEVEN

A Picture Perfect Legacy

"Be careful." Davina jockeyed back and forth across the carpet of Justin's office as she directed him and the huge painting he struggled with.

"All right, it's down," he said. "Now what?"

"We have to crack the frame with the hammer." She ignored Justin's raised brows and heavy breathing. "That's the only way to discover the fractures Dad built into it." She held the two photographs up. "See, if we hit it along here, that should be the perfect spot."

"Davina, I hope you're right. If not, I'll let you explain this one to Charlie."

He lowered the heavy painting flat onto the carpet, and on one knee, gingerly tapped the carved gold wood with the metal hammer. A glance from Davina, who knelt alongside him, told him he'd have to do better. He hit it harder, then harder still, until finally the wood cracked. He hit it again at a lower spot, and another split appeared.

Davina slid her finger along the fissure in the wood piece and pulled. Like a piece of a puzzle, the foot-long piece broke away cleanly from the rest of the frame and canvas. She looked down the end of the piece and saw the hollow center.

"Look, he did it with this frame, too, Justin."

Spurred by the discovery, Justin pulled another piece away from the top. It, too, had a hollow center, but there was nothing else unusual about the discovery.

"Let's try the other side," Justin suggested.

Davina was becoming disheartened. "Maybe I'm wrong, but I keep thinking our parents were leading us here."

He was already hammering at the other side of the frame. Because he knew the pressure points, it took only a couple of blows to crack it. On his knees, Justin pulled a piece of the wood away from the canvas and looked for a hollowed space.

He let out an excited shout. "There's something in this one."

Davina dropped to her knees beside him. "What is it?"

"Let me get it out." He tapped the piece of wood to dislodge the cylindrical item wedged in the hole. It was a slow process, but finally, and with the help of a hair pin, the white protrusion at the end was grasped within Justin's eager fingers.

"It's a rolled up sheet of paper in a clear sleeve," Davina observed from her perch at Justin's elbow.

He lay the piece of frame aside. "I don't know what this is, but remember, Hardy Enterprises is part of your company now, no matter what, okay?"

"I love you, Justin."

He turned and quickly covered her mouth with a hungry kiss before he unfurled the sheet of paper. He held it open so they could both read it together.

The handwritten paper was titled *partnership agreement,* and below that the names, Jacob P. Hardy and Maceo S. James, were boldly entered. At the bottom of the page, below the text of their agreement, was the date, September 16, 1959, and both men's signatures.

"It's their agreement, Davina. There's actually a written account of their partnership," he said, surprise flowing through his voice. "And it's been here the whole time." He looked at her. "You were right all along."

"I can't believe it." She stared at the document, then threw her arms around Justin's neck. "I still can't believe it."

He squeezed her tight. "You realize this paper is only icing on the cake. The board already voted to acknowledge his ownership."

"I know, Justin, but this way, we know for sure what our parents wanted to happen. What you've offered to do will never become a cloud over our heads or a subject of contention later on." They came apart and she looked at him, still in the circle of his arms.

"My father wanted so much to give his children, his grandchildren, a legacy, and in a way, this is vindication for him. His ramblings weren't those of a sad and sick old man. He knew what he was talking about, and that means a lot to me."

She rested on her heels and studied the agreement again before slowly raising her eyes to Justin's. "It also means something else. All of my father's paintings that David and I kept, the ones he painted as Maceo before he disappeared, and the ones he created later as James Spenser, they now belong to Hardy Enterprises."

Justin leaned back and stared at Davina, complete surprise on his face. He gripped her shoulders. "You never told me you had any Maceo paintings in your possession." He swallowed hard. "Originals?"

Her smile was an amused one, and she nodded. "They're all in Florida, lots of them, in storage since we came to Atlanta."

Justin was off the floor in one fluid movement and walked over to the bar. "This calls for a drink. Davina, do you realize the value of that kind of a collection? Boy, are you going to have a field day with Edward when he eats his words about you being the golddigger." He pulled a bottle of wine from the rack underneath and popped the cork. "I have a feeling our friendly newspaperman, Patrick Chavis, will sell his soul to get an interview with you now." He laughed deeply, happily.

Davina watched him and her heart swelled with pride. She stretched out on the floor, resting against her bent arm, and observed his graceful stride as he returned with two glasses of wine.

"Promise me no more news. I don't believe I can take any more revelations." He handed her one of the fluted glasses.

"I promise," she said, and set the glass nearby on the floor. "Of course, there's a chance you'll become bored with me now that you know everything."

Justin had scooped two pillows from the sofa and dropped them near Davina before joining her there. "Not a chance," he said.

She sipped from the glass again. "Will you come and visit my father at the hospital in Florida? David and I don't have any other family that we know of."

"I was hoping you'd ask. I'd be honored to see him. In fact, maybe we can get Connie to help us look into your family tree now that we know a few more details. What do you say to that?''

"I've kept away from the sadness of no family for so long, Justin. It's one of the things I love about you. Your family.''

He laughed out loud and then pushed up onto his elbow. "Do you find them . . . interfering?''

"No, they're great, and protective of you. Your mother is wonderful.''

"What about kids? Do you like them, and want your own some day?''

"I love kids, and I think your sister's two are darlings.'' She tilted her head and watched Justin play with her hand. "As for my own, with the right man, I want to have lots of them.'' She watched Justin raise his eyes to hers. "Is something wrong?''

"Come with me to New York this weekend.''

"I don't know. We're in the middle of the show, and we've got all this police business to deal with, but why New York?''

"I was thinking about some things, while you were asleep earlier.'' He searched for the right words. "I might want to buy my own house, here in Atlanta, now that I'm going to be in town a lot longer than I'd originally planned. Maybe you could see my apartment in New York and help me decide if I should sell it or not.''

"You want me to help you make that decision?''

"Yes.'' His fingers had left her hand and were now stroking her arm. "We could also do some shopping, see a play, visit jewelers. I figured you have a good eye for style, and since family would be visiting the house, kids would be running around, too, even your own kids some day—''

"Justin,'' Davina's breath had caught in her throat. "What exactly are you saying?''

"You once suggested that I didn't believe in marriage.''

"The night we had dinner at Benny's.''

He nodded. "I told you that I did believe in it, and that's why I wasn't.''

"I remember.''

"Well, I believe in it, and I want to believe in it with you at my side.'' He raised up on his arm and faced Davina, his gaze as soft as a caress. "I'm the right man for you and your children. Will you marry me and stay with me forever, Davina?"

Her heart sang. "I think I've always known you were the right man," she whispered. "But, do *you* enjoy children?"

"Love them," he said, puzzling at her question.

"And, about my family. Natalie is already in your corner, but can you learn to get along with David?"

"He'll become the younger brother I never had."

"Then"—she reached out and took his hand—"will you marry *me*, Justin, and stay with me forever."

His smile was broad, and together they answered, yes.

He drew her to him and swept her onto her back against the cushions. The weight of his body was an erotic intoxicant and she enjoyed how his eyes possessed her. He moved his mouth over hers, devouring the softness, before his lips heated her neck and shoulders.

"Remember when I told you I'd make love to you in here one day?" He nibbled at her ear.

Her heart raced as she murmured a response.

"This is the day," he replied, and proceeded to make good on the promise.

The partnership agreement that lay carelessly on the floor near the broken frame and Jacob's stern countenance were, for the moment, forgotten while they lost themselves to the pleasures found in a perfect union, a perfect legacy.

About the Author

Shirley Harrison has enjoyed writing all of her life, and is employed in the tax accounting field. She lives in the metro Atlanta area with her husband and two sons where she is an accomplished artist, a gardener, and an avid reader. This is her first novel. You can write to her at P.O. Box 373411, Decatur, GA 30037-3411 or Email: sdh108@aol.com

COMING IN MARCH . . .

OPPOSITES ATTRACT　　　　　(1-58314-004-2, $4.99/$6.50)
by Shirley Hailstock
Nefertiti Kincaid had worked hard to reach the top at her company. But
a corporate merger may change all that. Averal Ballantine is the savvy
consultant hired to ensure a smooth transition. Feeling as though he is
part of the threat to her career, she hates him sight unseen. Averal will
convince her he's not out to hurt her, but has *all* her best interests in mind.

STILL IN LOVE　　　　　(1-58314-005-0, $4.99/$6.50)
by Francine Craft
High school sweethearts Raine Gibson and Jordan Clymer pledged to love
each other forever. But for fear he would be a burden to Raine, Jordan
walked out of her life when he learned he had a debilitating medical
condition. Years later, Jordan returns for a second chance. In the midst
of rekindled passion, they must forge a new trust.

PARADISE　　　　　(1-58314-006-9, $4.99/$6.50)
by Courtni Wright
History teacher Ashley Stephens ventures to Cairo, following her love for
archaeology, hoping to escape her boring, uneventful life and enter an
adventure. With her mysterious guide, Kasim Sadam, she is sure to get
her money's worth . . . and a little something extra.

FOREVER ALWAYS　　　　　(1-58314-007-7, $4.99/$6.50)
by Jacquelin Thomas
Carrie McNichols is leaving her past to be the best mom to her son. A
lucrative job in L.A. offers her the chance to start over, but she runs into
someone from the past. FBI agent Ray Ransom is her new neighbor and
her old lover. He can't believe fate has given him a second chance. Now
he will do all in his power to protect their love . . . and her life.

Available wherever paperbacks are sold, or order direct from the Pub-
lisher. Send cover price plus 50¢ per copy for mailing and handling to
BET Books, Arabesque Consumer Orders, or call (toll free) 888-345-
BOOK, to place your order using Mastercard or Visa. Residents of New
York, Washington, D.C. and Tennessee must include sales tax. DO
NOT SEND CASH.

WARMHEARTED AFRICAN-AMERICAN ROMANCES
BY *FRANCIS RAY*

FOREVER YOURS   (0-7860-0483-5, $4.99/$6.50)
Victoria Chandler must find a husband or her grandparents will call in loans
that support her chain of lingerie boutiques. She fixes a mock marriage to
ranch owner Kane Taggert. The marriage will only last one year, and her
business will be secure. The only problem is that Kane has other plans for
Victoria. He'll cast a spell that will make her his forever.

HEART OF THE FALCON   (0-7860-0483-5, $4.99/$6.50)
A passionate night with millionaire Daniel Falcon, leaves Madelyn Taggert
enamored . . . and heartbroken. She never accepted that the long-time family
friend would fulfill her dreams, only to see him walk away without regrets.
After his parent's bitter marriage, the last thing Daniel expected was to be
consumed by the need to have her for a lifetime.

INCOGNITO   (0-7860-0364-2, $4.99/$6.50)
Owner of an advertising firm, Erin Cortland witnessed an awful crime and
lived to tell about it. Frightened, she runs into the arms of Jake Hunter, the
man sent to protect her. He doesn't want the job. He left the police force after
a similar assignment ended in tragedy. But when he learns not only one man
is after her and that he is falling in love, he will risk anything to protect her.

ONLY HERS   (07860-0255-7, $4.99/$6.50)
St. Louis R.N. Shannon Johnson recently inherited a parcel of Texas land.
She sought it as refuge until landowner Matt Taggart challenged her to prove
she's got what it takes to work a sprawling ranch. She, on the other hand,
soon challenges him to dare to love again.

SILKEN BETRAYAL   (0-7860-0426-6, $4.99/$6.50)
The only man executive secretary Lauren Bennett needed was her five-year-old
son Joshua. Her only intent was to keep Joshua away from powerful in-laws.
Then Jordan Hamilton entered her life. He sought her because of a personal
vendetta against her father-in-law. When Jordan develops strong feelings for
Lauren and Joshua, he must choose revenge or love.

UNDENIABLE   (07860-0125-9, $4.99/$6.50)
Wealthy Texas heiress Rachel Malone defied her powerful father and eloped
with Logan Williams. But a trump-up assault charge set the whole town and
Rachel against him and he fled Stanton with a heart full of pain. Eight years
later, he's back and he wants revenge . . . and Rachel.

*Available wherever paperbacks are sold, or order direct from the
Publisher. Send cover price plus 50¢ per copy for mailing and
handling to Kensington Publishing Corp., Consumer Orders,
or call (toll free) 888-345-BOOK, to place your order using
Mastercard or Visa. Residents of New York and Tennessee
must include sales tax. DO NOT SEND CASH.*

LOOK FOR THESE ARABESQUE ROMANCES

SPICE UP YOUR LIFE
WITH ARABESQUE ROMANCES